THE
MIRK
AND
MIDNIGHT HOUR

THE
MIRK
AND
MIDNIGHT
HOUR

JANE NICKERSON

ALFRED A. KNOPF
NEW YORK

THIS IS A BORZOI BOOK PUBLISHED BY ALFRED A. KNOPF

All rights reserved. Published in the United States by Alfred A. Knopf, an imprint of Random House Children's Books, a division of Random House LLC, New York, a Penguin Random House Company.

Knopf, Borzoi Books, and the colophon are registered trademarks of Random House LLC.

Visit us on the Web! randomhouse.com/teens

Educators and librarians, for a variety of teaching tools, visit us at RHTeachersLibrarians.com

Library of Congress Cataloging-in-Publication Data
Nickerson, Jane.
The mirk and midnight hour / Jane Nickerson. — 1st ed.
p. cm.
Summary: Seventeen-year-old Violet Dancey is spending the Civil War with a new stepmother and stepsister and her young cousin when she comes upon a wounded Yankee soldier, Thomas, who is being kept alive by mysterious voodoo practitioners.
ISBN 978-0-385-75286-2 (trade) — ISBN 978-0-385-75287-9 (lib. bdg.) — ISBN 978-0-385-75289-3 (e-book)
1. United States—History—Civil War, 1861–1865—Juvenile fiction. [1. United States—History—Civil War, 1861–1865—Fiction. 2. Family life—Mississippi—Fiction. 3. Vodou—Fiction. 4. African Americans—Fiction. 5. Soldiers—Fiction. 6. Slavery—Fiction. 7. Mississippi—History—Civil War, 1861–1865—Fiction.] I. Title.
PZ7.N55812Mir 2014
[Fic]—dc23   2012050893

The text of this book is set in 13.15-point LTC Metropolitan.

Printed in the United States of America
March 2014
10 9 8 7 6 5 4 3 2 1

First Edition

Random House Children's Books supports the
First Amendment and celebrates the right to read.

To Carol Trost, my mother,
who has always thought I could do
anything in the world

—J.N.

CONTENTS

And pleasant is the fairyland,
But, an eerie tale to tell . . .
Just at the mirk and midnight hour
The fairy folk will ride.

FROM *The Ballad of Tam Lin*

HE WAS ALREADY DEAD. Maybe. He had been grievously wounded—he had expected to die anyway—but they did something to him that sucked out the rest of his feeble life and will, except for the tiny spark of soul that hunkered mutely deep inside. That's why he thought of them as vampires.

They half carried, half dragged him to the fire and bade him kneel. The drumming began and his heart thumped with the drums and he was in the flames and in the beating. A blade flashed before his eyes. Silver. Beautiful. Someone called out a question, and the answer—"Raphtah"—swallowed him. He knew nothing more. He was already dead.

CHAPTER 1

TOO MANY BODIES

"There are too many bodies," I said under my breath.

"Of course there are," Laney called from the other side of the wall. (She was keeping baby Cubby away from unpleasant sights. In case he remembered.) "And this is a drop in the bucket compared to how many busted-up soldiers there are. Y'all are going to wipe each other out before you're through. Why'd you need to come look at them again anyway?"

I ignored the question. "What I mean is, the count's wrong. Last night, when they first laid them all out and pinned their toes, there were only eighteen. Now there's nineteen." I shuddered as I brushed away a fly that tickled my forehead. *Don't think about where it might have been.* These men lying in the grim, gore-puddled courthouse yard, who had been carried out feetfirst from the makeshift hospital inside, were dead less than twenty-four hours, yet the buzzing already sounded loud and angry within the blankets.

"Probably you counted wrong. You couldn't see so good in the dark. Or someone else died later and they brought him out.

Whatever. It doesn't matter." Cubby whimpered and Laney sighed. "Come on. I've got to get home and feed this child."

It had been a long day for her. Bouncing and jiggling a fat baby was more exhausting than one would think. But I couldn't hurry away. A heavy sorrow weighted my legs as I paced slowly down the row of blanket-wrapped bodies laid side by side, waiting for the wagon to take them for burial. Each was somebody's tragedy.

"I counted right," I said. "I had a lantern and was careful. I copied down the dead men's names from their tags so I could say a prayer for each and in case no one else recorded them. And no one else was fixing to die soon. Dr. Hale assured me. That's why I thought I could leave after the other nurses came in from Mobile."

The yard hadn't always been grim. In former times, before the yellow hospital flag flew from the courthouse rooftop, deep pots of geraniums and marigolds had lined the walls. The containers were still there, most with shriveled, blackened plants drooping inside. Someone had tossed an amputated arm into an empty flowerpot. A freckled hand reached from it, looking so natural it was as if some farm boy crouched inside, about to clamber out. Once, I would have felt extremely queasy at the sight. However, the past intense days of nursing the wounded from the big battle near Shiloh Church, in Tennessee, had altered my sensibilities. I had knelt in enough pools of blood and bathed enough ragged red flesh to be only slightly queasy now.

I halted. "It's this one that's extra. No name." I squatted and started to pull back the covering.

Laney peeked around the corner and squealed. "Violet Aurelia Dancey! Stop that right now, you hear? You crazy?"

"I don't *want* to look. I just need to see if his name's inside so I can add it to the list. We'd never have known what happened to Rush if someone hadn't written him down." It had been two months since the arrival of our family's black-edged letter announcing the death of my twin brother. I hunched my shoulder to wipe my eyes against my sleeve.

Inside, no tag was attached to a shirt because this young man was naked. I quickly averted my gaze to meet his shocked, dead eyes, which no one had closed, staring up through a swarm of stubborn, engorged insects. The face was wide, flat, and waxy white, the hair a carroty orange. Somehow his homeliness made it worse. So ordinary—he could have been anybody. I gave a gasp and pulled the blanket over him again.

"See?" Laney said. "I told you not to look. And don't you go asking about this. We've got to get home."

"No," I said slowly. "I won't ask."

The death wagon rumbled up for its load, and Laney took up one split-oak market basket and handed me the other. I was trembling; I dropped it twice before grasping it firmly.

Rain had poured down earlier in the week, leaving the roads hopelessly sloppy. I followed dumbly, mulling over what I had just seen. As we squelched along, skirting mud puddles, I had to curl my toes to keep my boots from rattling around my ankles. They were too-big boys' boots—all I could find to buy when my old shoes were so worn out I was nearly walking barefoot.

The town of Chicataw was cradled in a hollow of meadow and field, ringed by sheltering, wooded hills. Our three-mile walk home led past long, dim stretches of woods and pecan groves, as well as cotton fields, where slow-moving workers were breaking the earth with hoes and picks. It was later in the day than I had thought. Long-fingered shadows reached across the road, and the trees loomed black as we passed through a grove.

"Miss Vi, you've got to stop poking round dead people," Laney said, breaking through my thoughts. "Look at you. White as a winding sheet."

I glanced around quickly and whispered, "It was—that body. His throat was cut ear to ear. Like another mouth in his neck." The words felt thick and sluggish as they rose from my throat. "That didn't happen in battle. Somebody murder-killed him, not battle-killed him."

"Stop that right now. You don't know anything. It could've happened in the fight."

"There was a red flannel bag tied to his neck."

Laney stopped in her tracks. "You're joking."

I shook my head slow and low.

"Conjuring," Laney breathed. "Somebody around here's doing hoodoo and they must've stuck that body with the others to get rid of it."

"Why not just dump it in the river?"

"Might be they think it's fitting to show respect for the corpse by returning it to its own folks after they use it for what they want."

Coldness slithered through my veins. "We should probably report it to the marshal before the body's buried."

"Uh-uh." Laney shook her head emphatically. "You tell and you bring those conjure folks down on us. You're not about to do something so plumb foolish. No, ma'am. There's some other reason for that body anyway—you saw wrong or something."

"I didn't see wrong."

As we passed Miss Ruby Jewel's log house, I had the creepy sensation she was watching through the gap in her curtains. Both Laney and I were careful not to speak for a moment, and Laney covered Cubby's mouth. The old woman had ears like a bat and eyes like a hawk and a wormy way of extracting information from passersby. We remained tense until we were past her property, expecting any moment to hear the voice of poor old Jubal, Miss Ruby Jewel's manservant, asking us politely and apologetically to please, miss, come see his mistress. We reached the next patch of woods, safe at least from that danger. Laney took her hand off Cubby's mouth. He gave a shrill squeal.

"Will you look at that wisteria?" Laney said, pointing. "Isn't anything prettier. Ponder that sight instead of the other."

Cascades of lavender dripped from live oaks. The woods were full of blossoms, mingling with the first flush of vivid spring green. Their scent, thick as honey, was cloying, but healing after the odor of death. We were in the middle of the short but intensely beautiful Southern spring, when you rolled up your sleeves during the day but still cuddled beneath bedcovers at night.

"Didn't it surprise you when winter ended this time around?" I asked. "Honestly, I thought it would never—"

Laney clutched my arm with particularly sharp fingers. "Hush."

We had just rounded a bend in the road, and three murky, otherworldly figures slid into view several yards ahead. Two men and one woman, extremely tall and slender, gliding along with a silky grace, slick as oil.

"The VanZeldts," I whispered, and the hairs on my arms prickled. They were easily recognizable in spite of the dusk, even though I'd only seen them once or twice since their master, a Dr. VanZeldt, bought an isolated mansion several miles to the south. They were Africans who came right off the boat from that mysterious continent, in spite of the fact that the importation of slaves had been illegal for more than fifty years.

The way everyone spoke of them as "the VanZeldts" made it seem as if it were the name of an alien species and not the surname of their master. Whenever they came onto a scene, all eyes would be drawn to them and all conversation would stop. The VanZeldts spoke in a soft, melodious foreign tongue and wore bright beads and odd clothing—almost like ours, but not quite. Something in the fabric shimmered as they moved. They peered down upon us regular mortals from their towering heights with a proud, disdainful air, as if they too thought us all a different species from themselves—a vastly inferior one.

Laney waited to speak until the figures had turned off onto a more direct path to the river.

"Their boat must be tied down there." Her voice was still low. "They were the ones who killed your body, I bet you anything. They got hold of a wandering soldier and did some conjuring with him. I've seen the mojo bags tucked under their shirts when they come into town. Full of who knows what nasty things. I'm just glad your daddy sold the store so he doesn't have to deal with that downriver trash anymore."

"Let's not talk about it," I said. "May I tote Cubby now?" I reached for the baby and buried my face in his fat little neck. So warm. So healthy. So alive. I didn't want to talk about hoodoo because somehow that kind of magic seemed more real than good old-fashioned unlikely witches and spells. Especially right after what I'd seen. I didn't want to talk about my father selling the store because that reminded me he was leaving for the war, and even though we had never been close, I could hardly bear to lose someone else. I didn't want to talk about anything at all because I was sick of everything.

A wide brown puddle welled in front of us. I lifted my hem and sloshed through it.

"What you doing, girl?" Laney cried, and scurried around to meet me on the other side. She snatched away Cubby. "If you get mud on my child, I won't let you have any of that peach pie I'm fixing to make for tonight."

"Sorry. I forgot I was holding him."

"Forgot?" She gave me a little shove. "Forgot you were toting my precious baby boy? You're seventeen, same as me—a grown-up young lady. You usually have more sense."

"Sorry," I said again.

Laney couldn't drop the subject. "Since you've been doing your own laundry, I would've thought you'd be more careful about your clothes."

"You'd think."

She scanned the muddy hem of my skirt, shook her head, and twitched at my shirtwaist. "And look at you, grown so bony and baggy. You need to take the sides in. You're way less fleshy now than me."

"I'm growing thin hating the Yankees."

That really was the reason. Not the fact that we limited ourselves to two small meals these days. When I thought of the Federals, my appetite fled. I resented the space they took up in my brain but couldn't drive them from it. We had done them no harm, and yet they had swarmed down to invade our homes and murder our brothers and fathers. Working among the wounded only made me more aware of what they were doing to us. Hacking and blasting away at our menfolk like wild beasts. That was probably why I had stomped through the puddle—because there was nothing that I, a girl, could do about them.

My boots were now weighed down with clinging clay, but we were nearly home, so I kept clomping along without knocking it loose.

First we passed arbors tangled with the still-leafless grapevine that gave our place its name, Scuppernong Farm, and then the field where Michael plowed with Gus-the-mule. Cubby laughed when Laney helped him wave to his daddy. His daddy waved back, smiling wide. Michael was a short man, with a narrow face and thin shoulders. From a distance he looked like a young boy, yet he now did the chores of two men on our farm. All previous springs Rush had labored alongside Michael, while our father concentrated on running the store.

"Go look in the barn right quick, Miss Violet!" Michael hollered. "We got a present from heaven delivered straight to the back pasture with the cows. I cleaned her up—appeared like she been wandering awhile."

I shot a glance at Laney and she shot a glance at me and we quickened our steps.

The fields of our property didn't spread far. Ours was not a plantation; it was just a small family farm, with a big patch for cotton, another where corn was always planted, and another of beans, sweet potatoes, greens, and melons. We had Lily and June, our two brown cows, lots of mostly unnamed chickens and geese, and several bee gums down near the forest.

A surge of love for our place welled up inside me as it came into view. Home. We were home. Safe. Laney's family and Pa and I were isolated here, but we were sufficient unto ourselves within those walls. There our house waited, open-armed, surrounded by a straggling rail fence smothered in honeysuckle. It was a rambling, low-ceilinged, two-story white frame farmhouse, with a bright blue front door. There were outbuildings in the back and a shaggy lawn, overgrown with wildflowers, sloping down to the silver-glittering river. A half circle of piney woods protected our place, with dogwood trees glowing like stars among the dark evergreens.

We headed straight to the barn. The sweet scent of hay battled with the foul odor of manure since Michael hadn't the time to shovel muck as often as needed. He had already brought the cows in from pasture and they were in their stalls. Toby, my father's horse, was gone for the day with my father, but an unfamiliar horse stood in the stall next to Toby's. A velvety gray mare with beautiful lines and a white star on her forehead. She glanced idly back at us as she munched hay.

"Where—?"

Laney shrugged. "Michael said she was in the back pasture. Look. There's the saddle hung up. A fancy one. And there's the bags and blanket roll. Ooh, looky here." She pointed to the letters US stamped into the leather of the saddlebags. "I guess one Yankee soldier's lost his horse."

"If she's a Federal horse, then she's contraband. I bet Pa will say we can keep her. Heaven knows, the Yankees stole Rush's Lady." I didn't mention the fact that the owner might no longer be living anyway. I stroked the mare's shoulder and knelt beside the bags, pulling at the buckles. "Do you think Michael's looked through these?"

"Nah. He'd be in too big a hurry to get the plowing done." Cubby gave a short, impatient whine and Laney patted his bottom. "I'm fixing to go on in."

"Don't you want to see who these belong to? They look elegant for saddlebags. Maybe they belong to General Ulysses S. Grant."

"Ha."

"Or maybe—"

"We're going in, Violet." The gate into the kitchen yard squealed loudly when she opened it.

Laney had never been fanciful; instead, it was she who had always figured out clever ways for us to realistically carry out our schemes. As a child, I had been the imaginative one; nowadays my feet were usually much more firmly planted on the ground. They had to be.

Inside the bags was the usual soldier's gear—extra clothing, a toothbrush, a pocketknife, a ground cloth and twine, a small Testament, a housewife, and a packet of folded letters bound with string. Usual, except that everything was especially refined. The shirt was of soft, almost silky linen instead of homespun, the toothbrush was ivory, and the housewife's needles and thimble were silver. A niggle of discomfort squirmed through me as I handled this soldier's personal items. I suppressed it; he was the enemy. If the saddlebags had been marked CSA, we would have turned everything straight over to the Confederate regiment camping on the grounds of my old school. As the intruder, this person deserved no such consideration.

Some hard objects lay within the folds of the shirt.

First I unwrapped a photograph in a sapphire velvet case. A young lady gazed inquiringly out. She was pretty, with elaborately arranged fair hair and pearl earbobs dangling. A Northern girl close to my own age. Next I withdrew two intricately carved wooden figures, rubbed smooth and polished. Both were slender and elongated and whimsical. The male had a curling beard and wore a sort of tunic; the woman, a narrow, graceful robe. Fantastical characters, perhaps, from some tale. The wood was nearly black. Something about them reached out, clutched at me; it was hard to stop looking at them.

The mare let out a soft nicker, breaking the spell. I stood, stroking her neck and gazing into luminous brown eyes. "What happened to your master?" I whispered. I almost expected her to open her mouth and answer. I gave her a quick pat and then repacked the bags, leaving out only the figures and the letters. Those I slipped into my deep pocket. Of course I had no business reading this soldier's correspondence, but I was curious. If I could even learn the man's name . . .

CHAPTER 2

A LETTER
FROM THE NORTH

Three big geese rushed at me, necks stretched, wings flapping, beaks hissing, as soon as I opened the back gate. Hardly noticing them, I snatched up a handy broom to sweep them aside, left my muddy boots on the porch, and entered the kitchen.

Laney was still feeding Cubby. "You find anything good?"

"A nice shirt that's too small for Pa. It might would fit Michael." I didn't look at her as I washed up at the tin pail on the washstand. Someday I would show her the figures, but not until I had held them to myself for a while. It was my habit with things I needed to think about.

"Now," Laney said, buttoning her blouse and handing me the baby, "you know the routine, girl."

The routine was that I put Cubby to sleep while Laney prepared supper. After my mother died, when I was ten, and Aunt Permilla a few years later, I had tried to help Laney with the cooking, until she kindly but firmly told me to leave it to her. Cooking should be simple—you followed the receipt and were rewarded with successful results. Evidently, though, there was a knack to it I didn't have. Instead of baking teeth-breaking biscuits, I now concentrated on other chores—housework, sewing, and farmwork. It was labor that needed to be done, and I did it adequately. There were too few to do it now.

Laney removed her wedding ring, formed from a bone button Michael had hollowed out and polished smooth. She plunged her hands into biscuit dough in the big yellowware bowl while I dropped into the rocker and rhythmically patted the baby's back until he laid his head against my shoulder.

Our kitchen was just as a kitchen should be shortly before suppertime, smelling of savory cooking and burning logs in the fireplace. The walls were a rich, darkened pine, with hardened sap dripping from knotholes. The ceiling was crossed with white-washed rafters, from which hung sides of bacon, hams, and various black iron cooking utensils, the uses of which I did not know, since I never intended to use them, but probably Laney did. The floor was sanded white, the calico curtains and tablecloth were all Turkey red, and the braided rag rug in the center of the room made a bright splash. The final touch of coziness came from Goblin, who snoozed contentedly upon the rug. She was a hard, bony, narrow-faced black cat with a tail like a snake, but when she was indoors, she had the cuddly soul of a fat, fluffy feline. Outdoors was another story. Outdoors she was a panther.

The rocker creaked softly as I crooned the lullaby Aunt Permilla had sung to us children long ago. As I did so, I could almost hear Aunt Permilla's deep, throaty voice joining in. She had been our slave, blood kin only to Laney, but I thought of her as my mother as well. And now, as I sang to her grandchild, the love had come full circle. The tension and troubles of the day seeped from me like water.

> *"Mammy went away——she tell me to stay,*
> *And take good care of the baby.*
> *She tell me to stay and sing this a-way.*
> *Oh, go to sleepy, li'l baby.*
> *We'll stop up the cracks and sew up the seams,*
> *The boogerman never shall catch you.*
> *Oh, go to sleep and dream sweet dreams,*
> *The boogerman never shall catch you.*
> *The river run wide, the river run deep,*
> *Oh, bye-o, sweet li'l baby.*
> *That boat rock slow, she'll rock you to sleep,*
> *Oh, bye-o, sweet li'l baby."*

Obediently Cubby slumbered, soft and limp and heavy. I laid him in the cradle near the hearth.

Laney was dipping chicken parts in cornmeal and dropping them, sizzling, into the frying pan on the rack. As I watched my friend, who was laboring in bondage, for the millionth time I wondered what her thoughts were about the war. And for the millionth time I couldn't ask, although for the past year that subject had loomed unvoiced between us. I had seen the flash of hatred in the lowered eyes of some Negroes when they dealt with white people, or the patient, ironic twist to the smiles of others. But I'd never seen a sign, however subtle, however I looked for it, that Laney resented me. The more I worried, the more I couldn't ask, for fear of what I might hear. For fear that nothing would be the same between us if she uttered her feelings. Or if I could tell she lied.

She and Michael knew all the ins and outs of current events. They weren't kept ignorant, as the servants were on large plantations, secluded from the world. What would my own feelings be if our positions were reversed? If I were the slave and Laney the mistress?

Full of hope. I would be hopeful about the war no matter how friendly I was with my master's family. I would watch and wait and plan for freedom.

Michael burst in. He washed his hands and, as he dried them, stepped behind Laney and breathed into her neck, "You sure looking good, little wife."

Laney glanced over her shoulder, saying, "And don't I know it," before swooshing under his arm to check the pie in the brick oven. She was a pretty girl, soft and curvaceous, with big, expressive eyes, a shapely mouth, and dark brown skin. She always wore a snowy white head wrap and bright gingham dresses. Michael could never get enough of her.

As Laney straightened, he kissed the back of her neck.

I felt invisible, which caused me to quickly lean over Cubby's cradle and set it rocking frantically. I liked to think that the five of us—Pa, Michael, Laney, Cubby, and me—were a family, but at moments like this a gap widened between us. They made up their own little world. Perfect without me clinging to the edge. If the Union won, Michael, Laney, and Cubby might leave Scuppernong.

In the old days, it was Laney, Rush, and me who were the

threesome. Since my mother had been an invalid, dying slowly, dreadfully, of consumption all the years after we were born, Aunt Permilla had given suck to us all. After we grew from babyhood, we frolicked about the countryside together, wild and free, ignored by the adults and taking care of each other. The fun ended when Aunt Permilla started making Laney work in the house and my father made Rush labor in the fields after his hours at school. I was sent away to Wyndriven Female Academy. My father respected the Stones, who were the proprietors of the academy, and wanted to support their efforts.

When my father prospered enough, he bought Michael. Michael courted Laney and the wedge was formed. They had been married on our porch by a black preacher, with the bride all in white beneath a veil sewn from a net curtain and with me playing my harp. Then Rush went off to war, Laney became a mother, and the wedge widened. But at least my friend—sister—was still here on the farm.

She might not be if the Union won.

For a moment I stared at the flames snapping on the hearth, at the curls of blue-gold licking and the lines of orange writhing among the coals, devouring. Fire was like so many things—a burst of something beautiful and then all was gone.

I stood abruptly and left the kitchen as Laney turned to twine her arms around her husband's neck.

Up in my sloping-ceilinged bedroom in the eaves, I pulled everything out of my pocket. The wooden figures lay in my lap, each detail adding to their whimsy. With one finger I traced the carved woman's intricate curls. The creator of these had an interesting mind; Yankee or not, I would like to meet him.

Now I slipped one letter from the packet and unfolded it. The handwriting was round and childish.

August 10, 1861

My dear darling Thomas,

I have just received your letter of the tenth of July and do not blame you for think-ing you were forsaken after you had written two letters and received none from me. Let me clear myself. I have been dreadfully ill! You cannot imagine how I have suffered! Why, I have had three doctors (enough to kill any common person)! I lived on lemons and ice, and they shingled my hair, which is such a shame when it was so long and so becoming braided and tucked up. You must remember me as I appeared in the picture you carry.

You would not believe how warlike we have become here! The military look is all the fashion with the ladies. I have a new black velvet Zouave jacket with the prettiest gold trimming. And the men in uniform on the streets are as thick as the flies in the dining room of my old school. You remember me telling you how uncomfortable it made me to eat with so many of them buzzing around?

In the newspaper was a photograph of army tents spread out in a field. They looked so pretty! I intend to write a composition about it. "Dotted like daisies on sunny grass." Then something about their inhabitants awaiting fate. The contrast, you know.

I met a young Englishman at a reception the other night. He was polite, smooth, and innocent-seeming. Too innocent-seeming. (I am convinced he is a spy!) So you see, we do get some excitement even around here, far from the front lines!

We had a sewing circle the other day, made shirts, and also rolled bandages. Delia Edmonds was there. I know you always admired her, and we've been friends forever, but she is one of those friends I don't actually like. Or don't gentlemen know about such things? She acts so high and mighty about coming from one of the first families of Bethel—most annoying.

How is sweet Star? Is she keeping you company since I cannot? I hope when you ride her, you remember our adventures together. Kiss her long, bony head for me—how I miss you both!

I hope this letter finds you well. Teach those Seceshes a thing or two!

Much love,
Addie

The Yankee girl's life seemed to have been made more entertaining by the war.

I considered the rest of the letters lying on the bed and fought temptation. It simply wasn't honorable to read another's mail. Examining one was excusable—after all, I had to discover the name of the owner of these possessions—but two . . . Unless . . .

No, no more, Violet.

I replaced the letter and looped the string back around the packet. After I wrapped the figures in a scarf, I tried to think where to place these objects for safekeeping. It was silly to imagine I had to hide them from Laney, but we lived so close that sometimes secrets from each other were amusing; certainly Laney kept things from me as well. I grinned when I remembered my old hidey-hole beneath a loose floorboard in the corner of my room. When I was little, that was where I had kept items that were no one else's business.

I pried up the board with my buttonhook. I hadn't looked there in years. In the cavity still lay a cigar box full of my little-girl trea-sures, as well as a very old book with a mottled cover. Mostly it told how to care for beehives and collect honey, but also there was one important section about talking to bees. I picked it up and blew the dust from it before I tucked the Yankee's things away beside it.

As I lay in bed a few minutes later, I thought of the Northern girl who had written the letter. Such a spritely note with so many excla-mation marks. Obviously Addie was a stimulating young lady. No wonder she had interesting Thomas-the-soldier-and-wood-carver for a beau.

I hoped he still lived.

CHAPTER 3

A SECRET
BETWEEN TWINS

Late that day a rising wind keened a high, wild note in the piney woods outside and rattled the uncurtained windows of the dining room. The panes reflected the lamp I'd lit already due to scowling clouds.

"We're the only folks I know who've *gained* a horse because of the Yankees," my father said over supper. "She can be yours. She'll be a good mount for you when Michael doesn't need her for labor. What will you name her?"

"Star. Her name is Star." Just because my father proclaimed she was mine didn't make it so. Possibly I could forget she actually belonged to a Union soldier, but I doubted it.

"Someone in town told of a mother harnessing her young'uns to a plow, having no horse or mule," my father said, looking grave and shaking his head. "What have we come to, a year into the conflict, with so few menfolk around to do the work? Just last week a bushwhacker gang attacked Joe Jepson's farm, out past Holly Springs.

Shot his fifteen-year-old son and like to wiped the place clean of everything they could steal."

My father was always looking grave and shaking his head these days.

"The government should send troops after them," I said.

"They have too many other problems to deal with. A war, for instance. Deserter outlaws are not the most pressing issue. We need to get that old rifle in the barn repaired, and I aim to leave my pistol with Michael when I go."

"Why can't you leave it with me?"

"Because, Violet, you happen to be a young lady, and young ladies rely on men to protect them."

It was useless to argue. I set down the fork beside my untouched plate. "Pa, can't we talk about something besides war? When Rush was here, we used to chat about books and history and ideas. Can't we do that again?"

A shadow passed over his face. It was because I had mentioned my twin. My brother had been the mediator between my father and me. Without him, we were at a loss with each other.

My father stroked his short beard. Everyone said I looked like a female version of him, with the same honey-colored hair, the same pale, pointed face and gray-blue eyes. Nondescript. I had always wished that, like Rush, I resembled my striking, dark-haired mother instead. "As a matter of fact, some other subjects do need to be discussed. I have two pieces of news." He shifted in his seat. "I know the past year has been lonely for you, Violet, but your quiet life is fixing to change."

There was an ominous pause as I squared my shoulders, tensed to hear what unpleasant thing he was about to spring on me.

"First of all," he said, drawing an envelope from his pocket, "I've had a letter from your mama's aunt Lovina on Panola Plantation, out Richmond way. You know she's had charge of your cousin Seeley since his parents died last year. Even with the help of his nurse, Aunt Lovina says she's gotten too frail to care for a lively boy. She's also worried about the approaching battlefront, so she announces that your cousin Seeley is coming here to stay. No asking involved."

"Surely you're mistaken. Whatever are we to do with a child during times like these?"

"I promise, I'm not mistaken."

"How old is he? Isn't he still in skirts?"

"Not that little. He was born that summer when they sent us your cousin Dorian to get him out of the way for a few months. Let's see, that would make Seeley almost nine. As I said, things are about to liven up around here. He's traveling with a group who's coming through in the next few weeks, taking their household yonder to Texas."

"Where will we put him?"

"We have extra bedrooms."

I twisted my hands in my lap. *I won't put him in Rush's room. I shan't let a wild little boy destroy all I have left of my brother.*

"She also tells me Dorian has lately been running the blockade off the North Carolina coast." My father gave a dry chuckle. "Not surprising. It's exactly the sort of thing I would've expected from that boy."

During the one long-ago visit we'd had from my older cousin, I had liked him very well, even though he had seemed to be forever laughing at everyone and taking all the world lightly. Or maybe that was precisely why he had held a fascination for me. Rush had been a quiet, solemn boy, so Dorian had provided an amusing addition to our household. "Well, then," I said slowly, "we need to make ready for Seeley whether we want him here or not. And what's your other news?"

My father reached over to take my hand. This did not bode well. He never touched me.

"Oh," he said, "you're going to be surprised, but pleased, about this." He paused again for effect, then announced, "I have asked the widow Sluder to marry me."

I gaped. My mouth went cotton-dry and my head reeled as if I'd been kicked by the hind legs of Gus-the-mule.

"The wedding will take place in a few weeks," he continued. "Just before I leave."

"Why?" I said when I could speak. There had been no warning. Not a clue. "Why now, when you're going away?" My voice was unnaturally high.

"That's precisely the reason. So you won't be left alone."

"I have Michael and Laney."

"You need family. With this marriage you'll not only have a mother, you'll have a sister."

I slid my hand from his. "I don't want a mother or sister."

"I'm telling you this for your information, not approval." His tone turned cold. "But I did think you'd be delighted. You and Anna Bess Sluder were great friends at school."

"Sunny."

"Pardon me?"

"Sunny Sluder. Because supposedly she's so bright and breezy. No one calls her Anna Bess. Not even the teachers."

"Her mama refers to her as Anna Bess and so shall I. Sunny, indeed."

How could I explain that I had followed Sunny around at school simply because somehow that was my assigned social position and that she allowed it because she needed stodgy, plainer companions to act as foils for her beauty? "It only seemed as if we liked each other. She was—she was one of those friends one doesn't really like."

"I don't understand." Colder still.

Of course he wouldn't. "She always calls me Violet."

"That's your name."

"It's the way she says it: Vi-let. Making it sound ugly. And everyone fusses over her constantly, even though she says such terrible things about people behind their backs, smiling all the while. I often wonder what she's saying about me when I'm not around." It was against my nature to talk so to my father, but my desperation was rising. My stomach twisted inside, which was the effect Sunny Sluder always had on me.

He stared for a moment as if he didn't know what to say, then turned awkwardly playful and patted my shoulder. "Silly goose. You and your fancies. I thought you would outgrow them. Well, it might take some getting used to, but you'll thank me eventually. Elsa Sluder is gentle, ladylike, and agreeable. You'll learn to love her. And you and Anna Bess will amuse each other—late-night giggling over beaus and fashions. That sort of thing."

"How will we support these people?" This was the only valid

argument I could come up with off the top of my head. "We'll have three extra mouths to feed. More if they bring servants. Sunny eats like a horse."

"That slender girl? When I've been around at mealtimes, she's picked at her food more like a bird."

Now that I'd begun whining about Sunny, I couldn't stop. "Oh, Pa," I said impatiently, "that's part of her façade. In public she starves herself; in private she gobbles everything she can lay her hands on. And her tiny waist is one of the most annoying things about her. I can tell she's thinking about it every single minute of her life. She's thinking, *My waist is so much smaller than hers, and hers, and hers.*"

He looked partly mystified, partly horrified at this unwanted glimpse into the workings of young female society. His mouth grew thin. "She's a delightful little lady, and you would do well to copy her manners."

So my father was about to trade me in for another daughter. One of finer quality. Pretty, petted, spoiled, *stupid* Sunny Sluder, who always got anything she wanted—and anything anyone else wanted, for that matter—was to be my stepsister. No one had ever spoiled me. I should have liked at least a little spoiling in my life. And my waist was nearly as small as hers now—the problem was that my bosom had also shrunk away to nothing, along with every other curve, and bony chests were *not* the fashion.

"As for supporting everyone," he continued, "we have the money from the sale of the store, and there'll be my army pay. Mrs. Sluder is used to the best of everything since she's lived with her wealthy brother for so long, but she assures me she will find our simple life-style refreshing."

"Of course she will," I said, very low. "She'll be the mistress instead of the poor relation."

My father's face reddened. He stood and shoved his chair in so hard the dishes shook on the table. "The wedding is to be April twenty-fifth." He strode from the room.

Unconsciously I had been rubbing the fabric of my dyed muslin skirt between my fingers, and the stain had come off on my skin. I stared at my darkened hands, mesmerized. After the battle of Fort Donelson, where my brother and so many others from our town had perished, mourning clothes had been needed quickly. All of Chicataw had reeked of the dye pots in the yards as women stirred their garments. I had dyed my own dresses and underwear.

Slowly I rose and wrapped my untouched slice of peach pie in a napkin. After fastening on my cloak in the hall, I carried the pie with me as I stepped outside into wild weather. The sun, peeking now and then from glowering clouds, was sinking low in the west.

Cold wind nearly buffeted me off my feet. My cloak sailed out behind as I descended the porch steps, black skirt flapping about my legs like great crows' wings. The sunny, gentle spring of earlier had vanished. Now it was tornado weather. Wind-ripped petals pelted from dogwood trees, and one of the rockers on the porch bang-bang-banged against the wall, making a jarring musical counterpoint to the roaring drone of wind.

Across the lawn and toward the woods I stalked, onto a little slope that led down to the bee gums. The gums were chunks of tree trunks cut from the forest that housed swarms of insects. Several bees buzzed nervously around the logs, as disturbed by the coming storm as I was by my father's news.

I placed the piece of pie on the ground beside the gums as a gift to the bees. I was about to lower myself to the grass when movement deep within the trees caught my eye. A lithe, lean figure sprinted along parallel to the edge of the forest—a man, although his move-ments were so effortless he made me think of a loping panther. As he drew closer, he seemed to notice me and drew up short, con-fronting me straight on.

He was magnificent. It was the younger VanZeldt, shirtless. Dim, mottled leaf light rippled across the muscles that swelled his chest. In his hand was a rifle; he must have stayed behind the others to hunt. We stared at one another. His eyes shone bright and his gaze was penetrating. Neither of us smiled; neither of us nodded. My pulse throbbed madly in my neck.

He was the first to break away, turning and melting into the woods.

For a moment I stood frozen, wind whipping my hair and clothes, and watched where the trees had swallowed him whole. That a Van-Zeldt was here on our property, so close to our house . . .

The insects' frantic droning grew louder. I shook myself. *Forget the man.*

I murmured softly:

"Tell the bees of births and deaths
Tell them all that's true,
And when in need do summon them,
They'll surely come to you."

It was a bit childish—the rhyme and all—but we had been chil-dren when we first used it, and it still worked. We had probably been about nine years old when Rush found me crying my eyes out beneath the old magnolia tree. Pa had harshly reprimanded me for being noisy around Mama. Rush hadn't mentioned my tears or the scolding. He had merely said, "Want to try something amazing? I read about it in an old book I found in the bookcase. It tells all about bees. It's a secret, though. Just for us twins. Don't even tell Laney." Then he put his arm across my shoulders in the casual, protective way he had and led me to the gums. He told me about the waxen city of the bees inside the hives, complete with a royal court, just like in a fairy tale. He taught me the rhyme and showed me how to talk to the bees and, in times of necessity, how to call them.

Strips of black cloth, pinned to the gums, now flapped in the gusts. When the news about Rush reached us, I had gone immediately to Laney, while Pa locked himself in his room. Laney had put her apron over both our heads as we sobbed together. From there I ran to the hives to tell the bees and to attach the streamers. *Our Rush is gone.* The insects swarmed up and mourned with me.

My brother had already been dead for two weeks when we received the news. That was part of the agony—that we'd been going about our daily business, not knowing his body lay buried in a common trench. Why hadn't I sensed it the instant his life was cut short? If only the awareness had struck me at that moment, a piece of me would have been with Rush. He would not have died so alone amid the noise and terror and horror. But I didn't know.

Beside the bee gums I now dropped down on my back in the spiky grass of the hollow, protected from high winds. Preserved warmth from the earlier bright sun still spread upward from the ground. This gift of mine and Rush's was uncanny; it frightened me a little. "My lady queen and noble bees, I summon thee," I whispered. My fingers spread and I sensed the life and deepness and richness of the earth with my open hands, with all my body, head to toe. I willed myself to lie perfectly still. Still as a stone buried in a mountain. Even my hair I willed not to ruffle in the gusts. Images of flowers grew detailed in my mind, each intricate petal of clover and redbud and wisteria. Scents enveloped me. There was the perfume of honeysuckle and blossoms in distant gardens.

The hum of the bees drowned out the mourning wind. Closer, closer.

And then it began to happen.

First one bee lit on my hand, its delicate wings whirring and brushing frantically, then another on my cheek, then more on my hair, arms, and clothing. Hundreds of sun-yellow-and-black-velvet bodies caressed and soothed. In my mind I related the havoc my father was bringing upon us, all my worries. Gradually every aching hollow within me filled with honey-gold light. With their wings they carried my essence far, far away to some elusive, glorious place, a place I was always homesick for but never could quite recall. Perhaps it was where Rush lived now.

It didn't last long; eventually the bees floated off. But that they still came at my summons delighted and relieved me in an indescribable way.

I rose and went to the house, moving in a daze of wonder.

Once I was up in my little bedroom, the torrent let loose from the sky and beat passionately against the roof. I lay on my narrow bed and sank down, down into the comforter filled with pulled wool.

A knock sounded and Laney entered. "You didn't come down for your nightly honey milk, so I brought it up. There's even a heap of thick cream on top."

I sat up and took the milk, warmed as much by her consideration as by the cup. "Thank you."

"Mr. Dancey told us what's going on, and I'm sorry," Laney said, lowering herself to the bed beside me. She gave a rueful grin and nudged me with her elbow. "Of course, I'm the one you should feel sorry for if I'm expected to tend to that boy and wait on the women too."

I pulled myself together enough to reassure her. "Don't you worry about that. I'll be in charge of Cousin Seeley, and there's no way we'll let you turn into those *Sluders'* handmaiden. They'll have to shift their own weight."

Laney gave a low chuckle. "The way you said Sluders made it sound like you were calling them a dirty name."

My lips curved into a reluctant smile. "What will I do with a little boy, though? I'll have no idea how to handle him."

"Do the things we used to do with Rush. Let him run wild in the woods. Any child would love that. If we help each other," Laney said, rising, "it won't be nearly as bad as we fear."

After she left, I began sipping the sweet, pale gold honey milk.

Eventually I rose and lit a candle. From under my pillow I drew a fat volume covered with crimson cloth—my journal. To it I took every extra agonizing or extra beautiful thought or occurrence, writing them out until the intensity ebbed. If any of my descendants were to read it, they would think me a creature of great extremes of emotion, because that was when I wrote.

I dipped my pen in the inkstand on my rickety bedside table and wrote and wrote and wrote. After I had exhausted myself, I pried up the loose floorboard and stashed my journal with the soldier's items; if the Sluders really were coming to live here, I must be extra careful with my privacy.

I closed my eyes and tried to forget about my father's news. I tried to forget about the expression in the VanZeldt's eyes as he had looked at me, and the fact that he must be out there somewhere still, half naked and dripping wet.

CHAPTER 4

A WEDDING IN APRIL

Maybe I can't go to the wedding tomorrow because I have diphtheria.

Scratchy throat, aching head, sneezing constantly—could be, but probably no such luck. It was most likely just a nasty, oozing, forever-lasting cold.

I was sitting on Rush's bed, rubbing my forehead, when Sunny poked her nose in the doorway.

"Oh. This is where you got to," she said in her sweet, tinkling voice, which immediately brought on my stomach-clenching reaction. "We wondered."

Years ago, back when we were small together at Miss Reed's little school, Johnny Croft had described Sunny's nose as being arrowhead-shaped. He had been an observant child. It still stabbed out sharp as ever.

She flicked her eyes over Rush's playthings spread out on the bed, waiting to be packed away—the lead horses and soldiers that had carried out so many adventures for Laney and Rush and me. She made a face and said, "Is that all you're going to do this afternoon?

I'd help, of course, except I won't handle dead people's things. Why on earth did your brother still have toys around? Wasn't he our age?"

Of course she knew he was my twin. I didn't try to explain that Rush was loyal to his old friends and would never have gotten rid of these belongings. "He left them under his bed," was all I said.

She raised her eyebrows and withdrew. I sneezed and finished packing up.

Rush's bedroom felt bare and empty of his possessions, but the bed was comfortable, everything was clean, and it was good enough for an eight-year-old boy. Except . . . I snatched off the bright, beautiful Eye of Heaven quilt. It was what Rush always used to wrap himself in when he came down to breakfast, even when it was ninety degrees out. I draped it tightly around me and sank to the floor. Dust motes floated about in the light streaming from the windows. I exhaled a long breath to send the close ones frantically dancing, and closed my eyes.

Rush, Laney, and I have done a terrible thing. We found a great horned owl caught in a trap. He was such a glorious creature, we couldn't bear to turn him loose just yet. Rush declared his name to be Judge Solomon. We fed him bits of chicken, and Rush tied the owl's leg to the end of a rope attached to a pole in the barn. During the night, Solomon struggled so to escape that in the morning we found him hanging, strangled by the rope.

The burden of our grief and guilt is immense. We paint a crate with the most beautiful designs we can conceive. It is autumn and we line Solomon's coffin with crimson sweet gum leaves. Each of us, in penance, lays a precious possession beside him. Laney gives a stone, naturally heart-shaped and polished smooth by the river, I provide a single, cherished Venetian bead, and Rush sets in one of his beloved lead soldiers. We strew more leaves on and around Solomon so that only his noble face shows. We find a lovely, sunny spot in a meadow and dig a deep hole. Before lowering the coffin, we hold a moving funeral.

"What have y'all got there?"

It is Sunny Sluder. Her mother has come to pay her respects to my mother, although they are not friends. It is only because it is rumored that Mama has not long for this world that people come calling.

We do not answer Sunny, only stare at her solemnly. She peers into the open crate—

And giggles.

A burst of shrill laughter from downstairs jerked me back to the present.

"Oh, Rush, how could you have left me alone with these Sluders?" I whispered.

During the last couple weeks, they had popped in constantly. The first time was to "welcome" me into the family. After that it was to move in their possessions, mostly tasteless gewgaws, billowing mounds of clothing, and lots of canvases—some blank but some splashed with garish, clashing colors, which Miss Elsa called her "art." According to her, she was a slave to it.

I couldn't understand why my father wanted to marry her, although she was handsome enough for an older woman. She resembled Sunny—in a faded, softened, slightly shriveled way. She had the same sleek chestnut hair (although Sunny kept hers in ringlets, partly her own and partly pinned-in false tresses), the same arched eyebrows and jewel-green, slanted eyes, the same full, pouty lips, the same long neck and fashionable figure—tiny waist with swelling bosom and hips. However, where the daughter's eyes snapped and sparkled, the mother's dreamed. Where Sunny had a high color and moved with an exhausting vivaciousness, Miss Elsa was pale and drifted about with chilly grace. While the impression Sunny gave was of being sharp, snippy, and pretty, there was a remoteness about Miss Elsa. A sweetness as well, so perhaps that had been the attraction for my father.

"Vi-let!" Sunny hollered. "Come see these!"

Reluctantly I went down to the sitting room, where Miss Elsa drooped languidly on the sofa. Standing before her, Sunny dangled a pair of brilliantly striped cambric pantalets between her fingers and made them do a ridiculous dance ending with a kick. "Aren't they delicious? They were in the attic among the old things Papa William said we might make over for the wedding."

"Those belonged to my mother," I said. "They were in style when Pa was courting her."

"Obviously," Sunny said. "So countrified and old-fashioned. Like you, young lady, calling your father Pa."

"True," Miss Elsa said. "Just as my mother would have done. I had meant to speak to you about it, my dear. Mr. Dancey has asked me to help him if he slips and uses rustic language, and he wants me to give you little hints now and then. . . ." Her soft voice trailed off, as it so often did.

I bit my lip. What was so bad about being countrified when we lived out in the country? And sometimes it was nice to be old-fashioned.

I wanted to be happy for my father, but how could I be? I had muddled over this thing—this awful marriage—ever since he had told me his plans. I fretted over it as I untangled snarls from my fine, flyaway hair. I had wept about it as I lay curled up in bed. I had brooded over it as I made candles and milked cows and swept floors. It was no use; Pa was going to do this, and nothing I could do would stop it.

"Fine day for a wedding," Michael said as he helped me into the buggy the next morning. I could only nod miserably.

The weather mocked my mood. It was church-bell-ringing, bird-singing, blossomy April. Inside the chapel, the ladies had twined the columns with vines and festooned the pews with ivory ribbons and lilies.

Most of white Chicataw waited downstairs, while Laney, Michael, and other colored folks sat up in the balcony. It was the way we did things. I avoided Laney's eyes.

That morning, in front of my greenish looking glass, I had thought I appeared all right, wearing a black silk that had once belonged to my mother. My hair was in ringlets twisted from rag curlers, which, combined with my cold and my dread of the wedding, had prevented sleep all night. All the curl would fall out shortly, but I had to try. Now, with Sunny perched in the pew beside me, I felt dowdy.

Sunny glowed in a frock of golden paisley-printed voile with coral silk fringe. She had pilfered it from my mother's trunks and raised the waist to modernize it. I had loved that dress. My soon-to-be stepsister also wore white lace gloves, a pierced ivory fan tied by ribbons to her wrist, and dainty high-heeled slippers (although her feet were too large to be truly considered dainty). With so many of the guests in mourning, Sunny shone like a parrot among crows. Her satisfied expression showed she was happily aware of it.

My own face hurt from the effort of smiling.

The Reverend Mr. Stone, our minister, stood waiting to perform the ceremony. The Stones were the proprietors of the school I had attended from the time I was twelve until this past December. When it was announced that the academy would be closed for the duration of the war, so we might be with our families, most pupils had wept openly. Tiny Mrs. Stone, with her dashing clothes, ready smile, and kind ways, was adored by all the girls. She now slipped in to sit on my other side, her arms full of her latest darling redheaded baby swathed in a fluffy shawl. "Are you all right?" she whispered. I nodded. She reached down and squeezed my cold hand with her warm, reassuring one.

The organ commenced playing and my father and Miss Elsa moved up the aisle on a carpet of flower petals. Pa appeared distinguished in his new gray army uniform. Wraithlike Miss Elsa carried a bouquet of lilies and wore silver satin trimmed with a froth of misty lace.

I clutched a crumpled handkerchief and felt as alert as a soggy dishrag. Throughout the ceremony an irritation scratched at the back of my throat. It took all my concentration to keep from coughing, never to stop.

The groom slipped the pearl ring that had belonged to my grandmother onto the bride's finger. He had assured me the ring would be mine someday, but this showed the worth of his promise.

Thankfully I got through the vows without making a coughing spectacle of myself. The moment my father and Miss Elsa headed down the aisle and out the archway, I scuttled to exit the back door.

I was bent over, hacking away, eyes streaming, when a deep voice from behind said, "May I fetch you some lemonade right quick? It might would help."

Without knowing who had made the offer, I could only nod blindly, intrigued by his beautiful voice. Cough smothered, eyes wiped, cheeks pinched for a little color, I waited to see who would step back around the corner of the building.

A shadow preceded my benefactor.

It was Pratt Wilcox.

He came striding over holding a cup and something wrapped in a napkin. Naturally. Pratt Wilcox, whose unfortunately repellent self I hadn't laid eyes on for at least five years. Something about him had always seemed slimy, and it wasn't just the fact that his hair hung lank and greasy. It might have been his lips, which reminded me of sliced liver, or the way he stood a little too close. . . .

Oh, well. He'd been nice to offer the lemonade. "Thank you," I said, and took a long, welcome swallow.

"You've got a cold," he remarked astutely.

"Yes. It's the kind that lasts forever."

"The kind where you feel as if your head will cave in when you blow your nose."

That actually was rather funny and I laughed. "Exactly." My gaze fell on the three stars adorning the collar of his uniform. "Why, Pratt Wilcox, you're a colonel."

"So you do remember my name. Didn't know if you would since I've been gone so long. Went into business with my uncle in Memphis, and then the war, of course. And I am indeed a colonel, in command of the Fifty-Sixth Mississippi."

"Impressive," I said. "You've certainly risen quickly."

He colored modestly, moved a little closer, and cleared his throat. "Well, you see, my main accomplishment was not dying at Fort Donelson. I was one of the few in the regiment to make it out, so the powers that be rewarded me with stars." He shifted his booted feet uncomfortably. "Oh. I forgot about your brother being there. Sorry. A capital fellow."

"Yes," I said. "He was."

We were silent for a moment, and I thought what a pathetic pair we were, having absolutely nothing to say. Poor Pratt. It wasn't his fault (probably) that he put girls off. I would be kind. I gave him what I hoped was a kindly smile.

"Would you," Pratt said, unfolding the napkin to display a dark, fruity slab, "care for this? You know young ladies are supposed to place a piece of wedding cake beneath their pillows to dream of their future husbands."

I didn't want it, but to help him out I said, "Yes, thank you." Mischief sparked in his washed-out hazel eyes.

"What will you give for it?" he demanded, holding the cake above my head.

I stared. "I beg your pardon? My gratitude, of course."

"What if that's not enough?" He edged closer still. "You ladies always want to support the soldiers—wouldn't you like to kiss a colonel?"

I stepped backward and would have fallen if he hadn't grabbed hold of me with one damp hand. He smirked unabashedly. "You're a pretty girl; sometimes don't you want to be a naughty girl as well?"

At times I labored under the misconception that unattractive people would automatically be nice, humble people. Pratt's face loomed closer to mine. I jerked out of his grasp and ducked under his arm. My hair snagged on one of his brass buttons. "Mr. Wilcox—"

"*Colonel* Wilcox."

"I can't imagine what I said or did to make you think—anything." I painfully yanked my hair loose, scurried toward the corner of the church, and flung over my shoulder, "And I don't even want any of that stupid cake."

He sputtered, then came back with, "And you're not all that pretty."

I stepped out with Pratt following just behind, painfully aware that both of us were red of face and that my hair was disheveled. Sunny was holding court among a cluster of young people in either gray uniforms or outspread hoopskirts on the side lawn. They all looked up. Sunny's bright, curious eyes took in our appearance. She gave a meaningful smile. *Oh no. Oh no.*

And there sat Ben Phillips, who had paid so much attention to me last year until I began to really like him and then had instantaneously transferred his attentions to Mary Clare. I had thought all was flourishing between us till the day I showed up at church and she was sitting with him in my place. Now whenever I saw Ben, I felt acute embarrassment, even though I hadn't done anything wrong. At least not that I knew.

I hastened over to Nannie Kate Smith, who, as usual, was standing on the fringes, bless her poor heart.

"Will you come with me to get a plate?" I asked urgently.

She nodded, visibly relieved to have someone to talk to.

As we made our way toward the refreshments, I fumbled to

retwirl my now-limp ringlets. I thought glumly that Nannie Kate and I made a fine, dowdy pair. Her thin greenish-yellow locks were plastered to her head with sweat, and her sallow complexion was extra sallow today due to the unpleasant shade of pea green she wore.

The bridal couple was seated beneath a latticework arch at a small private table. I watched how Miss Elsa and my father responded to each other. When she was with him, she laughed occasionally and looked more animated. My father beamed down at his wife. He was truly smitten and had not told the complete truth when he claimed he was remarrying for my sake. I *was* happy for him.

Everyone else was to dine standing or sitting in the grass. The church grounds were full of chattering, eating people. From somewhere the church ladies had procured a feast nearly fit for a wedding in the grand old Southern style. There was duck with a sauce of stewed peaches, beaten biscuits, and terrapin stew. The plummy wedding cake was dusted with sparkling white sugar.

Nannie Kate and I took our filled plates and huddled near the throng of young folks. Sunny was in her element. I couldn't help watching in fascination.

She stole a lieutenant's hat. "There," she said, setting it on her head at a coquettish angle. "Wouldn't I make a fine soldier?"

"A devilishly stunning rebel!" exclaimed the lieutenant. "The Yanks wouldn't stand a chance."

"Oh," Sunny said, fluttering her fan, "you're exaggerating." A moment later, she announced "I'm bored" in a challenging tone. Immediately young men vied with each other to increase their level of charm and rescue her from such a wretched state.

Nannie Kate whispered from behind her hand, "Look how she touches the men. She's constantly fixing their hair and *patting* them. Nauseating. Oops!" Her fingers flew over her mouth. "She's your sister now, isn't she?"

"Yes," I said bitterly. "More's the pity." I scorned the piece of me that wished for a few shabby little wiles of my own.

"She paints her face, doesn't she?"

I nodded.

"I knew those rosy cheeks couldn't be natural. Not with the rest of her complexion so white." Nannie Kate sniffed. "Does she use arsenic to make it that pale?"

When I said I didn't know, Nannie Kate sniffed again.

"Of course she does. And burned hairpins to darken her lashes, and belladonna to brighten her eyes. I bet she uses all the tricks."

Amazing. I had never even heard of any such tricks.

"Painted up like an actress." Nannie Kate shook her head in disdain. "I daresay we could all look just as good if we weren't ladies." She smoothed out her skirts virtuously.

As folks gathered around the newlyweds' table to offer toasts, Miss Elsa stood. "Before we start . . ." She scanned the crowd. "Where is she? Where is my new daughter?"

Reluctantly I stepped out so she could see me.

"Did you bring it?" she asked.

I nodded. Michael dashed up, carrying my dulcimer wrapped in a shawl. Miss Elsa had wanted harp music at the wedding, but my father didn't want to risk damaging my big harp by transporting it. It was he who had suggested I play my mother's small cherrywood dulcimer, which she had brought to Mississippi from her Virginia home, along with the harp. Miss Elsa and Sunny had feared it would be too rustic and the guests would scorn it, but my father had insisted.

A chair was brought for me. I seated myself and dropped the shawl from the teardrop-shaped instrument. I hesitated for a moment, as I always did after picking it up, running my fingers up the slender neck. Each time I played the instruments she had once used, I felt a connection with the mother I had never known well. I began to strum the four strings, two for melody and two for drone. In only a second I forgot where I was as I played and sang "Believe Me If All Those Endearing Young Charms."

When I finished, my father sucked in his cheeks and looked downward. Miss Elsa, tears streaming down her cheeks, clapped and begged in a tremulous voice, "Will you play 'I Have Loved Thee, Dearly Loved Thee'?"

I did as she asked. Rather than their scorn, I could feel the audience's spirits collectively caught up in the sweet music. They burst into applause and there was a flurry of requests.

I played a few more melodies. My stepmother hugged me when I finished.

Deacon Johnson invited us to raise our glasses in a toast to the happy newlyweds. "And may the joys of their 'blessed union' not make us any more tolerant of that other 'union' that is causing such misery throughout our homeland," he concluded.

On the way home, Sunny turned to me with a knowing smirk. "You slyboots! You're setting up a flirtation with Pratt Wilcox!"

"I'm not!" I cried. "I wouldn't!"

She laughed through her nose. "Don't be coy. I declare, you two go very well together. You're both scholarly and—oh, I don't know. You just seem to belong with each other. He's leaving the same time as dear Papa William. One looks at a boy so differently when one thinks he may be killed tomorrow, fighting to preserve us." She gave a sentimental sigh. "You know, of course, that you don't have to actually *like* a beau to encourage him. No matter what, it's good practice."

Desperately I said, "Oh, look what we gathered up," and uncovered a basket of leftovers from beneath the seat.

Sunny snatched a biscuit, split it, and stuffed the top half in her mouth. "Here"—she thrust a napkin-wrapped piece of wedding cake into my lap—"put that under your pillow so you can dream about your true love. I won't need it. My head is *that* full of dreams already."

I had thought I would never tell another soul about my encounter with Pratt, but before I went to bed, I found myself relating it to Laney.

She laughed and laughed, and her laughter took the sting out of the incident.

"The thing that annoys me about Sunny—" I started to say.

"Only one thing?"

I grinned. "Well, the thing that comes to mind right now is that she says Pratt would be a good match for me. Surely, surely I can find someone better than him, can't I?"

Laney was trapped in the kitchen rocking chair beneath her sleeping baby. She beckoned me closer with her fingers. I squatted down and she put one arm around my shoulders and squeezed. "Of course you will."

"If not, I vow here and now to remain an old maid forever."

"You won't be an old maid. You'll meet someone. Your father waited a long time after your mama, but he seems happy with his choice."

"I wonder if he thought about my mother at all today. I doubt it." I pondered a minute. "Laney, how did you know Michael was the husband you wanted?"

She shrugged. "Instead of liking him less and less the more he was around, I liked him more and more. And that's still how it is, even though sometimes I want to hit him over the head with the skillet."

I was taken aback. "I've never seen you get mad at Michael."

"That's because I won't be a whiny baby about my man. But when he won't tend Cubby for five little seconds while I'm doing something I need to do—whooee!—bring on that skillet."

We sat together comfortably in silence as Laney rocked Cubby and I looked into the fire.

"You know," Laney said suddenly, "your features are actually nice as Miss Sunny's. Fact is, though, she flounces around silently telling everybody, 'Look at me! Aren't I gorgeous?' and folks believe her."

"I don't know how to announce such things silently, and if I did, no one would hear."

"It's the way she totes herself so wiggly and prissy, and how she looks at men, inviting them. Try it sometime."

"Like this?" I said, and sashayed across the room, wiggling energetically.

" 'Fraid not, sugar," Laney said. "Menfolks don't want a girl jig-gling like a catawba worm on a fishhook."

"Don't men like that sort of thing?"

"Well," she said doubtfully, "maybe *white* men . . ."

We both laughed again and I helped her stand up with Cubby.

Afterward, in the comparative safety of my bedroom (it was only comparative now because I could hear Sunny moving around on the other side of the wall), I debated using the cake-under-the-pillow trick. Such danger. What if I discovered my One True Love really *was* Pratt? Or the Chicataw coal deliveryman? I placed the slice firmly on the bedside table. Then, in case that was still too close and some night vision might manage to make the leap from there into my head, I moved it to the table in the hall.

CHAPTER 5

RELATIONSHIPS

My father's knapsack lay at the bottom of the stairs, bathed in golden light streaming from the hall's amber glass sidelights. He had returned from his honeymoon the day before and was leaving for his regiment shortly. He had barely mumbled two words to me, which was worse than it had ever been before.

Through the dining room doorway I could glimpse Miss Elsa draped over him as he sat at his breakfast. She was probably salting his eggs with tears.

"Vi-let!" Sunny called from the parlor, where she lounged gracefully in her wrapper on the scratchy horsehair sofa. Her rumpled, uncombed hair only made her more picturesque. "Will you tell that girl to bring my breakfast in here?"

I stepped into the room. "Why?"

"Obviously I'm not about to eat in the dining room with the lovebirds."

"Go get what you want from the kitchen yourself, then."

She stretched like a languid lioness. "That's not something a lady should do. Anyway, that girl doesn't know her place. She's so bone lazy I have to remind her to do everything for me and Mama. Had to slap her the other day."

I stiffened. "You hit Laney?"

Sunny gave a delicate yawn. "She had the impertinence to say she needed to finish feeding that baby before she tightened my corset."

"Don't you ever, *ever* touch Laney or Michael. Never! You hear?" I was shaking.

"Gracious, child, of course I hear you, all shrill and screechy as a jaybird. You needn't worry—I doubt I'll have to discipline her again, now she knows she can't get away with insolence around me. Don't feel bad; you just don't know how to handle Negroes."

I made myself take several deep breaths. "Laney and Michael are considered family. That's how they should be treated."

Sunny rolled her eyes. "Y'all have always been outlandish here at Scuppernong. As if the rest of the world doesn't matter. Remember how you and Rush used to go to Miss Reed's school barefoot? Even through the mud."

I laughed a little in spite of the anger that still smoldered in my breast. "No one at home knew about that. Our shoes raised blisters, so we usually took them off and stuck them in the bushes on the way."

"It didn't matter to you how often Miss Reed told you that shoes must be worn." A pucker appeared between Sunny's brows. "Rush always stood a little in front of you when she scolded. He made me wish I had a brother." The wrinkle smoothed out. "I was sure a silly little goose."

It was time to return to the subject. "About the corset—I told you before that Laney hasn't time to be your lady's maid."

"Well, sorry, but she's going to have to do it since selfish Uncle Frank wouldn't let us bring Carlotta. I can't fasten my own stays, after all."

"You've been making Laney do that all this week? Never again. Next time call me, or learn to do it yourself, as I do mine."

"I don't mean to be ugly, honey, but no wonder your waist got the size it did during your awkward stage. A girl can't cinch in her own laces worth a hill of beans. Surely you know that."

I opened my mouth to retort and then closed it. The fact was, I didn't know that. Aunt Permilla knew nothing of such things, so no one had told me when to start wearing stays. When I began attending the academy and saw that everyone else wore them, I had scuttled to the dry goods store and made the purchase myself, scarlet-faced lest anyone should see me. I had always pulled the laces the best I could on my own.

Without another word I turned on my heels and went off to the kitchen to find Laney.

"Don't forget!" Sunny hollered after me. "Tell her I want my breakfast!"

Laney was not inside. I found her hauling a too-heavy basket heaped with wet clothes out to the line behind the barn. I grabbed up one of the handles. "Laney, why didn't you tell me Sunny slapped you?"

She hung two aprons before answering. "Same reason I would never tell my husband—what good would it do? Michael'd get all heated up and I'd have to stop him from making trouble. Then you'd start a catfight with Miss Sunny, and after all that, everything would be the same, except more miserable."

"You should've slapped her back."

Laney gave me a look and I lowered my eyes. I knew it was a stupid thing to say even as I said it.

"Well," I said, "I informed her she better never touch you again."

"Huh. I bet she's so scared her big feet are shaking in her big shoes."

I shook out a head wrap so sharp it made a loud crack. Through clenched teeth I said, "She will not touch you again." Then I laughed weakly. "Maybe we should go ask your aunt Anarchy for some herb to protect us from my evil stepsister. It would be nice if it involved something fun, like rubbing poison ivy between her sheets."

Laney laughed. "Ooh, girl, you're mean. Or what about some of those other things Aunty says conjure men can do?"

"Like what?"

Laney removed the pegs she was holding in her mouth. "There's a powder you can blow in folks' eyes so they'll only see what you want them to see. And ways to make folks forget things you don't want them to remember."

"Such a shame we're not mean. We could never really do any of that, could we?"

"No. And I don't see how those things would help, and Aunty wouldn't tell us how to do them anyhow. She would never mess with dark stuff. Fun to think about, though."

"I guess we could always consult the VanZeldts," I said, very low.

"Well, stop tightening Sunny's corset. I'll do that from now on.

And if she raises a finger against you, you tell me. I'll take care of her somehow."

Laney snorted. She would never let me know if anything else happened. And there wasn't much I could do if she did.

My father sought me out soon after, as I packed his lunch in the kitchen. He said nothing for a moment, just rolled the brim of his hat between his hands.

"Here's your dinner," I said, handing him the packet.

"Thank you."

I waited, refusing to say anything else until he did.

"Violet, I've never been good at expressing myself," he said slowly, "but before I go, I want you to know that you and your mama will never be replaced by Anna Bess and Elsa, however much I do care for them. The circle's simply expanded. I rushed all this—the marriage and all—because I couldn't leave you alone with the dangers of war so near. I trust Michael and Laney, but   ."

Now I would help. "I understand. They might leave."

"I—um . . . yes."

I smiled. "Thank you for telling me this, Pa. It helps to hear it." And it did.

CHAPTER 6

FINAL DEPARTURES

Michael drove the ladies to town in the buggy, while my father rode ahead on Toby.

Spring was over. The glowing foliage had faded and deepened to a dark green. Mugginess weighed on us, along with a sense of oppression. Miss Elsa drearily fluttered her fan to move the sluggish air.

When we reached town, my father went on to join his regiment at the Wyndriven campsite. He gave us only a hasty backward glance since he had already said his goodbyes at the farm. We would see him once more when the soldiers rode through town on their way north.

I left Sunny and Miss Elsa to run into Maloney's Mercantile for a paper of pins. The block-lettered name on the sign still gave me pause. Until five months ago it had read DANCEY'S. I was always curious (and, for some reason, apprehensive) to see what new changes Mr. Maloney might make. Even when my father kept it, the store had been dark and dingy. Now it seemed darker and dingier because the shelves were nearly bare. The floor was crowded with barrels and crates, most of them empty. The coffins that used to be displayed in the back were all long gone, as were all the guns and ammunition. There were still some bolts of cloth, cooking utensils, soaps, patent medicines, and tobacco, but prices were ridiculously dear.

Only one other customer was in the store. The young VanZeldt woman stood at the counter with items laid out in front of her—a jug of molasses, an iron pot, a lantern, a long bone-handled knife. Her flowing skirt of some slightly glistening fabric was tied with a wide brown sash and was short enough to show slender, dusty bare feet and ankles. Her hair was elaborately braided and twisted, inter-twined with a green ribbon.

It seemed all wrong to see her like this. She should be blending into the trees in the wildwood. Not here. Not shopping at Malo-ney's Mercantile, arguing with Mr. Maloney. I tried not to listen to the dispute in case it would embarrass me. The woman reached beneath the low neckline of her thin white blouse to pull out a leather pouch that hung there—along with one of red flannel. I turned quickly away to stare instead at the scythes hanging on the wall behind the storekeeper like so many gleaming new moons.

However, I accidentally let Mr. Maloney catch my eye and was involuntarily drawn into the problem. He viewed me with relief. "Girl dear, it's glad I am to see you!" he said in a voice that sounded unusually loud and blustering even for a loud and blustering Irish-man. "Come right on up to the front of the line. This person can wait, to be sure. She'll never figure out her money anyway. Now, what can I do for you?"

I opened my mouth to request the pins, then closed it again. Yes, the woman was a VanZeldt and a servant, but this was too rude. I had to lean my head back to look up into her face, she was that tall. "Do you need help?"

Her great brown eyes widened so that the whites showed around the irises. I had never been this close to a VanZeldt before. She was younger than I had thought—maybe in her late teens or early twenties, but it was hard to tell. Her face was narrow, her cheekbones high and sculptured, her nose long and thin. And she was so beautiful that I couldn't help staring at her in awe.

She raised one hand to tuck the dangling ribbon back in her hair. There was a grace about her gesture that I had noticed in all the VanZeldts when I had seen them from a distance. The grace that gave their slightest movement a liquid smoothness. However, the ribbon wouldn't stay tucked in, and as she tried to fix it and it kept coming out, her dignity raveled. Standing so close, I saw her hand begin to shake. This simple thing—a trip to Maloney's Mercantile—must be frightening for her. To this girl, we were the strange ones.

Automatically I reached out to help. "Here," I said. "Let me tuck it in." I pushed the end of the ribbon deeper beneath a braid.

She gave me a shy almost smile. "I thank you."

"Now," I said, "what is the matter here?"

"I have money," she said in careful English. Her voice was unusually deep and lyrical. "I have money, but this man—I am afraid he will take too much."

"The nerve of her!" Mr. Maloney said. " 'Tis change in Confederate dollars you'll be getting, but 'tis the correct change. No one can be saying Rory Maloney is not an honest businessman."

"Of course you are," I said quickly. "How much does all this add up to?"

"Twelve dollars gold, twenty in paper." He eyed me defensively. "And hardly making a profit I am, neither."

"Will you let me see your coins?" I asked the girl.

She nodded slowly and reached up to lift the pouch from around her neck. Several silver bangles clicked together.

I drew out a single twenty-dollar gold piece and placed it on the counter. Mr. Maloney counted out the change in currency. He did this awkwardly since he was holding something in his left hand. He suspiciously eyed the girl all the while, and I now felt included in the suspicion.

"There," he said. "Barely making a profit I am."

"Times are trying for everyone." I smiled brightly.

The hard lines of his mouth softened. "Well then, now that's done, will you be telling me what you need, dear girl?"

I made my request. While he was fetching the pins, I helped the VanZeldt girl pack her purchases in her basket. After she had slipped out the door, Mr. Maloney said, "For all their fancy gold, I wouldn't be after having them VanZeldts coming in here. They're ill to deal with. Makes the hair stand up on me arms. I'd as lief they took their business downriver. When they come in, I hold to my bit of cold iron to ward off all unnatural beings." He opened his left hand to reveal a piece of horseshoe. "And him they call Dr. Van-Zeldt ain't even a proper doctor."

"I've never seen him before. What kind of improper doctor is he?"

"If ever he learned real medicine, he's forgotten it. He came in here himself once—a little, puny fellow—and he told me he lived in the back hills of Africa among the natives for years to learn their outlandish methods. Said how grateful he was *they* were willing to accept *him*. When the Morgans' little girl took the typhus, they ran for VanZeldt on account of they couldn't find Dr. Hale. VanZeldt mixed up a foul-smelling brew he said was made from some kind of crushed beetles."

"Did she take it?"

"To be sure, she did, they were that desperate, and she got well, but for the rest of her life she'll know she ate beetles. No one trusts him after that."

I shook my head, hoping it was the right response to his story, paid him, and left the store.

A shadow fell across my path as I was walking briskly past an alley. The VanZeldt girl had been waiting just around the corner.

"Please, miss," she said, "may I speak to you?"

I hesitantly stepped into the gap. "Is there something else you need?"

"It is only that you are the first person in this place to treat me kindly. I want to thank you."

I smiled and nodded, uncomfortable, and would have hurried away but she plucked at my sleeve.

"My name is Amenze. What is your name?"

"Violet Dancey."

"Violet Dancey. I will remember that and I will remember you. Does your man leave today?"

"My man?"

"All the young white men go to die. All the husbands. All the beloveds." A strange note crept into her voice and a strange look into her eyes.

I took an involuntary step backward, farther into the alley. "I don't have a man—a sweetheart. It's my father who's going."

My heart lurched, although outwardly I remained perfectly still, when she suddenly tossed an object from hand to hand and then flung it at my feet. It was an amulet of unpolished amber, golden as hardened honey, strung on a leather thong. She squatted down and studied it as it lay there. I stood unmoving while Amenze somehow communicated with mystic forces. I could not see her eyes well, but they seemed to shift oddly as she stared downward. She gave a nod, scooped up the amulet, and stood. I flinched when she slipped it over my head.

"Your father will return," she said. "And you will have a sweetheart soon. I give you this grigri as a sign of our goodwill one to another. It will help you in the days that come."

"I don't—I don't really believe in that sort of thing," I said.

She gave a faint smile. "The spirits do not need you to believe in order to do their work."

I thanked her awkwardly, turned, and started to leave the alley, tucking the amber beneath the neckline of my dress. I didn't look back but still could feel her eyes following.

"Something else," she said. Her voice, quiet yet clear as crystal, stopped me in my tracks. "There is one who is anxious for you. Because you yet weep. Rush . . ."

I whirled around, my mouth hanging open, and returned to her side. "How—?"

"He is not a loa—an earth-trapped spirit who must do our

bidding. Still, a thread ties him here, spun by your grieving. Come
with me."

Amenze was edging backward, beckoning me to follow. I went
with her behind the building, where no one could see us.

She grabbed my hands and held them tightly. "I will bring him
to you," she whispered eagerly. "Right now I will do this thing. You
may talk to him, hear that he is well. Ask him what you must do."

A fierce longing welled in me. To see Rush once more as I did in
life, to grasp without doubt that he still existed somewhere, to know
his feelings at the moment of his death . . .

Amenze must have read assent in my face. She dropped my hands
and reached into her mojo pouch to bring out a pinch of something powdery. She rubbed it between her fingers, breathed it into
her nostrils, and then blew it away in a little puff. Murmuring low
and sibilant, she raised her long, bony arms to the sky. An ethereal
yellowish-green light suffused the air around us.

I did not speak or move, except to tremble a little.

A sighing sounded that might or might not have been the wind
whooshing around the corner. A beam of light that pierced through
overhead clouds gathered brightness between Amenze's arms.

Her voice deepened in intensity, as if the words were tugged out
of her throat. Her eyes rolled back in her head. She dropped to her
knees. The shapeless glimmer before her gained form, a column
roughly the shape of a man, the height of my brother. In a moment
I would see his face.

I gasped and cried out, "No! No! Stop! Don't do this to him!" I
covered my eyes with my hands.

I had almost done a terrible thing. A Witch of Endor—like terrible thing. Because of King Saul's encounter with the witch and the spirit of Samuel she conjured up, Saul despaired completely, and he and his family all died shortly after. Only bad could come of wrenching Rush from heaven because of my selfishness.

I lowered my hands. Amenze was watching me. She slightly lifted her shoulders. "As you wish." She stood.

"Thank you for trying to help," I babbled. "It's only that it couldn't have been right."

Without another word, she left me alone and shaking.

"Rush," I whispered to the breeze, "I'm so sorry for that. Don't worry about me. We miss you, but we'll be all right. I'll try not to cry about you anymore. Be happy, and when it's the right time and place, I'll see you again." Against my chest the amber amulet glowed with its own warmth.

It took me several minutes to pull myself together before I could move slowly out to the street to face other people.

"Where have you been?" Sunny asked when I found her and her mother waiting in a crowd at the square. Her speech sounded especially shrill after Amenze's melodic tones.

For a second I couldn't speak. I shook my head a little and could feel the amber, still warm. When I finally spoke, my voice was hoarse. "I bought my pins and then—and then I had to help someone."

She seemed to lose interest. "Had Mr. Maloney any new shoes in?"

"No. Not a single pair."

Sunny looked pleased. "I bought the last, you know. For the wedding." She displayed her high-heeled slippers, which she was tapping about in for everyday use.

For the send-off some children were having a warlike parade down the street, complete with wooden swords, rifles, and small flags on poles. Some wore miniature Confederate uniforms. Most of the onlookers smiled upon them fondly, but the sight made me shudder.

The sound of horses' hooves and marching feet reached us. Over the hill they came, long lines of men clad in ghostly gray, some on horseback, some on foot. Sunny, Miss Elsa, and all the others waved handkerchiefs and shouted goodbyes and God bless yous. I shrank back against the brick wall of the building behind me, watching, frozen, as my father and the soldiers moved through town, leaving us behind.

A year ago, when Rush's company left, newly sewn Stars and Bars flags hung from every balcony, along with paper rosettes and streamers. We showered them with flower petals as if it were a celebration. "It'll be over in a month," the boys had bragged, all jaunty and proud. We were free and independent. We hoped for little or no bloodshed, that they'd let us depart from the Union peacefully. We were innocent and stupid then. And sinful to be jolly over such a terrible thing. But we didn't know. No more than Addie, the Northern girl whose letter I had read, had known as she and her friends played at war, with their military fashions and fancies.

The good wishes hung heavy and mournful and echoing in the air. Just as the soldiers were nearly out of sight, they turned in their saddles and gave a resounding rebel yell, sounding like the scream of a banshee. I clapped my hands over my ears.

Sunny burst into sobs. A little crowd gathered to pat her shoulders, offer handkerchiefs, and tell her everything would be all right.

"I try not to be so sensitive," she said in a choking voice, "but I can't be like Vi-let." She turned to me. "How can you be so unfeeling? How can you remain dry-eyed?"

Several pairs of eyes turned my way and I went rigid under their examination. My fears and sorrows were deep, but private; I kept them to myself.

As I silently waited for Sunny to regain her composure, my eyes were drawn to a group standing across the street, remote from the rest of the crowd. Amenze, the young VanZeldt fellow I had seen in our woods, and the older, bearded man loomed like shadows surrounding a slight man with spectacles and a forked silver beard. He wore a neat white suit and straw hat. The "improper" doctor. He appeared squat and gnomelike next to the VanZeldts.

The shadows might well have been members of one family. All had the same loose, elongated limbs and severe, beautiful bone structure. While Amenze glowed in her shimmering garments, the two men wore shapeless shirts and ill-fitting dark trousers. I got the sense that their clothing was no more than a covering for them, that they hardly noticed what they wore. Their expressions, as they looked down their noses upon the world of men, were aloof and contemptuous, although I reminded myself not to judge too quickly; Amenze now appeared every bit as haughty as the others, yet she had tried to help me and had needed my help.

Dr. VanZeldt must have felt my gaze, because he looked up now so that his spectacles glinted straight my way, causing me to blink. He flashed a swift, rather sweet smile and tipped his hat.

I turned away, flustered, barely acknowledging the gesture. "Come on," I said. "There's Michael now."

Sunny squelched through the mud to the buggy, squealing, "Ooh! My shoes! My new shoes!"

CHAPTER 7

EXPANDING THE CIRCLE

"This farm has got to be the lonesomest place in the world," Sunny said as she sulked in one of the shabby, overstuffed sitting room chairs.

I shrugged. "Don't worry. We won't be lonesome once Cousin Seeley arrives. He'll love to have you go on adventures with him all day long."

"Bite your tongue. I hope I never even have to see the child. Where can we keep him? The chicken house? Or better yet—aren't little boys kind of like dogs?—can we tie him to a tree out back?"

"Anna Bess, hush," Miss Elsa said in her sweet, plaintive voice. "You know how wretched I'm feeling." She seemed to be perspiring more than the temperature justified.

A striped sock she was knitting had been lying limp in her lap for the past hour. She dabbed her forehead with a handkerchief.

I stroked Goblin, who was curled, purring, on my lap under the book I was reading, and wondered about my stepmother. She had always appeared pale and fragile, but in the week since my father's departure, she'd begun looking consumptive—thin and almost bluish white, with purple shadows beneath her eyes. She would fall asleep sitting up, in the middle of the day. I had asked her if she was ill, but she had brushed me off. Maybe when I knew her better, I could inquire more persistently. *If I ever know her better.* Conversations with Miss Elsa were fragmented, with a detached quality, as if she weren't quite with us.

"Mama!" Sunny said loudly.

Miss Elsa winced as though her daughter had thrown a fire-cracker at her feet.

"Mama, don't you think we ought to redecorate this room?"

My stepmother fluttered her hands without looking up. "I'm not sure. . . . Perhaps Mr. Dancey . . ."

"You know it's hideous," Sunny said.

"It's not!" I cried.

"Shows your taste, miss," Sunny said tartly. "The carpet's all nubby and homespun and holey, there are cracks in the plaster, and there's not even a lick of wallpaper. And that ghastly bird on the mantel!"

"It's a bittern," I said under my breath.

"It did what?"

"It's a bittern," I said, louder. "My uncle Ed trapped it and had it stuffed."

"Whatever it is, must it lurk up there staring at me?"

Once I would have agreed with Sunny that the bird was ghastly; as a child, I had been frightened of its long, pointed beak and its beady little eyes glaring down from the polished black mantel, but now

I loved it because everything in this shabby room meant home to me. I loved the furniture in the simpler style of the last century and my graceful harp of burnished wood, whose strings tinkled softly, hauntingly when anyone walked near it. The flaws—a cracked pane in the bookcase door, the funny, warped shadow the bittern cast on the wall, the indentations on the floor Rush had caused when he was stomping around inside with homemade stilts—only made everything more endearing.

"Mama!" Sunny said piercingly again. When she saw her mother shudder, she lowered her voice and continued in a wheedling tone, "If you'll just give me the money, I'll take care of everything. Even these days, Memphis is sure to have all we'll need, and Papa William left you plenty of cash—I saw."

"I don't think—" Miss Elsa began, closing her fingers protectively over the purse she kept in her pocket.

"You can't spend Pa's money on wallpaper!" I interrupted hotly. "Not when we need it for food, and heaven knows how long this war will last." The stimulation of speaking my mind to Sunny these days was enjoyable. It felt as if I had loosened the corset laces I had begun cinching more tightly since Sunny's comment about them.

"It'd be fun, Miss Priss!" Sunny retorted. "Don't you know anything about fun? *I've got to have something to do here.* I'm dying of boredom. Can't you see I'm bored as a pancake?"

I laughed out loud. " 'Bored as a pancake'? What is that supposed to mean?"

My stepsister stared, baffled by my amusement.

"Poor Sunny, you have no idea how idiotic that was, do you? The saying is 'flat as a pancake.' Who knows what someone as silly as you could be as bored as?" I laughed again. "I have to admit it was funny, though."

She compressed her lips. "Do you always have to make me feel stupid?" Her voice shook and she turned her back on me. "You're just like my aunt and the teachers at school and—and *everyone* else. Always treating me as if I'm a useless fool."

These last words stopped me short.

Could it be true? Could it be that all the while Sunny had been making me feel despicable and inferior, I had been making *her* feel despicable and inferior? That we were even? This was a new thought.

Sunny still faced away. Now it was her turn to rub her forehead as if it ached.

In a surprising, jerky movement, Miss Elsa kicked out her legs beneath her skirt and put her arms over her head, moaning.

Sunny gave a great sigh. "Oh, for heaven's sake, Mama, go take your medicine."

"Yes," Miss Elsa said, rising. "Yes. I need it, don't I? Excuse me. . . ." She drifted from the room.

"Bless her heart," Sunny said, shaking her head.

"What is her medicine?" I asked.

Sunny was silent for a moment, gnawing at her lip, before replying. "Laudanum, if you must know." She looked down at the carpet and burrowed the toe of her slipper into a hole. "Your father is aware of it and scolded her, so that's why she didn't have any this morning. She's trying to cut back, but it makes her miserable."

"Does she take many doses?"

"Only constantly," Sunny said shortly.

"That much?"

She groaned. "Surely you've noticed she's never really with us. I've always felt a bit like an orphan."

I tried to return to my book but ended up going over the same page three times without really seeing it. How often had I felt unnoticed around my invalid mother? And I had had a homey home, a father, a brother, Laney, and Aunt Permilla as well. I glanced at my stepsister. "Did you always live with your uncle?"

"Yes. Ever since I was a bitty baby. Our aunt kept us cooped up in one little room. She didn't like to be reminded we lived there." Sunny tossed her curls and looked away so I couldn't see her expression.

I sat silently stroking Goblin and thinking. "Sunny, this is your house now too," I said at last. "Let's paint this room. Paint doesn't cost much and we could do it ourselves. What color do you think?"

She turned and looked searchingly into my face. Then she gave a little cry, smiled brilliantly, and threw her arms around me. I braced myself.

"Oh, you darling thing!" she said. "A cheery buttercup yellow, I'm thinking. Sorry I was cross. You know I can't help my temper—it's the Irish coming out."

Later, when Sunny was pacing the floor and making her plans, I took a cup of warm honey milk to Miss Elsa's room. She was huddled on a chair by the window.

"Are you all right, ma'am?" I asked. "I've brought you something to drink."

"Thank you," she said, lowering her hands. She looked appalling. "How considerate, Violet, dear."

I dropped to the floor beside her. "Does your head ache terribly?"
"Not now that I've taken my medicine. Your papa doesn't like me
to use it. I know I'm weak and foolish. I've tried and tried to quit,
and obviously I lack character. I began dosing myself because of my
headaches, but now . . . I seem to need it always. And it helps me be
more creative with my painting. It really does. I'll take less . . . starting tomorrow." She let her gaze drift toward the window. "Perhaps
I'll wander outside since I feel better. Find something to trim my
bonnet . . ."

A while after I rejoined Sunny in the sitting room, Miss Elsa
floated in with a basket of cut blossoms. To our amusement—and
my amazement—she began sewing real flowers to her oldest, shab-
biest bonnet. Sunny and I looked at each other, then ran to fetch
our own.

I hollered to Laney in the kitchen, "Come in here and bring your
bonnet!" Sunny sniffed but said nothing.

Laney entered, mystified. Her eyes widened when she saw what
we were doing. "Y'all are crazy," she said, shaking her finger. However, she pulled a needle from my pincushion and threaded it.

We stitched away, dissolving into giggles as each creation got
more and more flamboyant. Tiger lilies dripped down the sides,
crape myrtle fronds became plumes, and daisies lined the interiors.

Miss Elsa did not work for long. Soon after Laney entered, she
drooped onto the sofa and closed her eyes.

Once I was satisfied that my bonnet was outlandish enough, I put
it on and sat down at my harp. I sang, "Begone, dull care! I prithee
begone from me." Laney warbled along, rich and full-throated.

Sunny hummed, slightly flat. A little smile played about Miss Elsa's lips. "Angelsss." She let out her breath with a sigh. I glanced at my stepmother lying there peacefully. I was beginning to see what had attracted my father to her.

Life at Scuppernong was more interesting with my stepfamily, I had to admit. Miss Elsa was kind and sweet in her own wistful way, and a far cry from a cruel stepmother. And, yes, Sunny was too pretty, too flirtatious, and too vain, and not the most clever girl in the world, but if I could accept her as she was and expect nothing more, I might actually enjoy her company.

CHAPTER 8

EXPANSION

That evening the world was permeated with a weird beauty. Filmy white moths flitted across the front lawn like tiny ghosts, and the sunset behind the black trees was an odd pinky-purple. For some reason I thought of the VanZeldts, with their unearthly looks. Their silhouettes would suit such a setting. I was idly swinging a fussy Cubby in our grapevine swing beneath the live oak while Laney made supper.

When someone caught the ropes from behind, I jerked and nearly fell out of the swing.

"My dear cousin," drawled a voice. "I didn't mean to startle you that much. I only meant to startle you a little."

I jumped down and whipped around. A fashionable young man with a merry, laughing face held the ropes. He wore a long buff-colored duster and subtly striped trousers. He tipped his straw hat with a flourish.

"Cousin . . . Dorian?"

"In the flesh."

"You haven't hardly changed at all since I last saw you."

His eyes were still so blue I couldn't quite get over the shock of them, and he had the same engaging smile and bright hair. My mother had called him "the golden boy."

"Can't say the same for you, Cousin Violet. You were a little girl in pigtails that summer I stayed here, back when Seeley made his debut into the world. Somehow I expected you to remain the same. Instead you have turned into a very pretty young lady. With a baby."

"Oh, this is Cubby. He belongs to Laney, if you remember her."

He laughed. "Well, I didn't really think he was yours."

Of course, now that I looked closer, there were changes. "You've got a mustache," I said, thinking out loud and immediately wishing I had kept my mouth shut. Silly. He was good-looking, and good-looking men made me nervous. "I guess we both grew up."

"I do indeed have a mustache. Thank you for being so perceptive; I'm awfully proud of it. Of course you wouldn't remember, but like many sixteen-year-old boys, I was trying to sprout a beard last time I saw you. To my sorrow, even after weeks of putting all my efforts into it, no one could tell at all."

"Aunt Lovina's letter never mentioned you coming. Are you here—what exactly are you doing here?"

"You might well ask since I'm showing up uninvited but, I hope, not unwelcome."

"Oh no! You're very welcome."

"I'm glad. You see, I was accompanying Seeley and Co., but I rode on ahead to give you fair warning of our arrival. I took the liberty of putting my horse in the barn just now, by the way."

"Good. I hope you gave him oats too. But I thought you'd be

too busy to come. The letter said Cousin Seeley was traveling with another household."

"He is, and the whole Tingle entourage will arrive shortly. I came along with the poor little fellow so he'd have a familiar face here at first."

Something in me that had been holding back warmed to Cousin Dorian. "How nice of you! That should help Cousin Seeley feel at home."

"I'm afraid I can't stay more than a couple weeks, though. Duty calls."

"Yes. Pa told me you were—um—running the blockade."

"Me, as well as a big, fast ship and lots of other, far more daring associates." His eyes scanned the road. "There. That's the first of them."

A carriage lit by lamps, followed by slow-moving outlines, topped the little hill. As I watched, more lanterns came flickering on like fireflies.

Cousin Dorian slipped his hand firmly into the crook of my arm, and I readjusted Cubby. "Let's meet them up at the house. It's been an interesting trip. Did Aunt Lovy write how the Tingles were moving every last person from their plantation to Texas? All hundred of their slaves? Well, with each stretch we traveled, they lost more of their Negroes to the lure of the Yanks. They're left mainly with women and children now. Serves them right for vamoosing from their property."

"You think they're wrong for fleeing before the Federals?" I asked. "Cowardly?"

"Not so much cowardly as stupid. So far the Yanks mainly burn abandoned homes. I would never for a second leave Panola if I didn't know Aunt Lovy and the rest of the caboodle were there. We've got a good overseer, who keeps me informed of what's going on, and the fields are still being cultivated. We'll keep at it till the bitter end. If you'd ever seen Panola, you'd understand how it gets in a person's blood."

In an instant I remembered that the Panola my cousin spoke of had been my mother's childhood home. The few times she had mentioned it, love had misted in her eyes. It was from there she had brought the musical instruments that were first hers and now mine. I'd not thought of it before, but what must it feel like to leave a beloved place knowing you may never return? I felt a rush of compassion. Poor little Cousin Seeley.

"I hope I may see it someday" was all I said.

The carriage stopped in front of the house, and a middle-aged man and a pleasant-faced woman alighted. The woman, seeing me, came forward and held out her hand. "I'm Jacintha Tingle, and this is my husband, Matthew. And you must be Violet."

I dropped a quick curtsy and took her hand. "Yes, ma'am. I'm pleased to make your acquaintance. Won't you both make yourselves at home inside while your people camp on the lawn? I expect y'all would relish a warm meal and soft bed after traveling so far."

"We would indeed," Mrs. Tingle said, beaming from ear to ear. "We're most grateful."

"And we appreciate you bringing Cousin Seeley," I said, glancing around. "Who is—where?"

"Oh," Cousin Dorian said, "he generally hangs back with my body servant. He and King are great cronies. Seeley!" he called. "Come meet your cousin Violet."

A small figure hesitantly broke away from the others and shuffled toward us. He was undersized for his age, with a head that looked too big for his body and a slouch hat pulled low. He reached out a reluctant hand for me to shake. I still couldn't see his face, but his jacket sleeves were slightly too short and his wrists bony. "How do you do, Cousin Violet?" he mumbled.

"Very well, thank you, Cousin Seeley," I answered. "I'm so happy you arrived here all safe and sound. And you know what I think?"

He shook his head slowly. Sullenly. Obviously he didn't consider what I thought of much importance. But then I stopped myself from sizing him up too quickly.

"I think," I continued, "you should call me Violet without the 'cousin' business attached, and I'll call you Seeley. Much more convenient. And by the way, this little baby I'm holding is Cubby. His parents are around here somewhere. In fact, I need to hurry and tell his mama to toss lots more potatoes in the stew to make it stretch for everyone who'll be eating it. As soon as you've washed up and brought in your things, I'll introduce you to the others." I turned back to the Tingles. "Please get yourselves settled and I'll call y'all for supper shortly." I started to usher Seeley indoors.

He hung back. "I'd rather eat out here."

"Seeley!" Dorian said sharply. "You're not a Yankee. Maybe you've forgotten that civilized people dine at tables."

The boy stammered something apologetic, and I found myself immediately on his side and not at all hesitant to go against Dorian.

"No," I said. "He's right. I love twilight too. I guess I'm not civilized either. Let's all sit on the porch. The mosquitoes aren't bad yet, and we'll be more comfortable outside than in the stuffy dining room."

Seeley shot me a swift upward glance. He was not a particularly attractive little boy, but he had beautiful, long-lashed eyes. I smiled at him. "I'll go tell Laney where we'll be."

"What's that?" he asked as I was turning to go. He was pointing to where, barely visible, a shadow darted across the lawn like a thing possessed, pouncing first here, then there.

"That's our mad cat, Goblin," I said. "There's moths out there and she's being the mighty hunter."

"Would she let me hold her, do you think?"

"I'm not sure we can catch her when she's in her wild creature form. Once she comes in for the night, though, just try to keep her off you. Wouldn't you rather hold Cubby? He's a very nice baby and only scratches when he's trying to pull your nose off."

Seeley shook his head, but I was rewarded with a faint smile.

"If we eat on the porch," I said, "we'll lure Goblin with food. She'll be your friend for life if you feed her the rabbit stew we're having tonight. She likes her rabbit neatly chopped up with vegetables. Especially parsley. Isn't she silly for a mighty hunter?"

My young cousin grinned. His teeth were too big for his mouth and pointed chin, but maybe his face would grow around them eventually.

Dorian followed me inside. "Rabbit stew, eh?" he said. "So y'all in Mississippi have been driven to living off the land. Soon you'll be scrounging for catfish whiskers to nibble. Or—don't tell me—are you already?"

I widened my eyes. "Well, we Mississippians don't care for that sort of thing, but if y'all Virginians have a hankering for whiskers, we'll find you a cane pole so you can go fishing tomorrow."

Over Dorian's head I saw Sunny pause at the top of the stairs. She wore the paisley voile she'd worn at the wedding. Since she'd sported blue muslin earlier, she must have thrown on the voile at the first inkling of company. Her hands smoothed down the fabric over the curve of her bosom and then over her hips as she prepared to descend.

Dorian was still laughing about catfish whiskers when she swept up to him.

"And who do we have here?" she asked, inspecting Dorian with her head cocked slightly to one side. The light shining from the doorway sent fiery glints shooting through her chestnut hair. She looked rather bold and very beautiful.

As I introduced my cousin, I caught his glance fix on her low-cut neckline for a second too long before he bowed slightly and took her hand.

"Hopefully you'll stay for a good while, Mr. Rushton," Sunny said, looking up at him through her lashes. "Long enough to appreciate our Mississippi hospitality."

"As Violet said, we needn't bother with titles," he said quickly. "Call me Dorian since we're all family. And I'm sure I will enjoy your . . . hospitality."

I drew in my breath. I wasn't sure, since I was already turning away, but he might have winked at her.

At suppertime the two of them—Sunny and Dorian—sat together on the front porch steps. Sunny's skirts were spread so wide there was little room for anyone else. Since the Tingles and Miss Elsa occupied the rockers, I hunched on the bottom step, trying feebly to join in the conversation, which mostly was about my cousin's blockade-running.

Sunny raised her hem high enough to expose her ankle and shapely calf encased in delicate lace. "So," she said, "you, sir, are one of the valiant gentlemen responsible for bringing Southern ladies their pretty Parisian finery, such as my new stockings. A girl really shouldn't have to give up *everything* for the Cause."

Dorian's eyes twinkled. "How noble of you, Miss Sunny, to remind this gentleman of some of the pleasures of home worth fighting for."

She giggled. "It's a demanding responsibility, but someone must do it."

Miss Elsa, who had been rocking dreamily, only occasionally interjecting into the conversation, roused herself enough to softly say, "Anna Bess," in mild remonstration. She settled back into her seat, her motherly duties done.

Meanwhile, I, bunched below in my stiff black calico, was thoroughly squelched—the effect Sunny always had on me around gentlemen. I fiddled with the amber amulet Amenze had given me, which I wore beneath my bodice nowadays. The feel of it under my fingers was heartening somehow. I made myself stop. It would not do to draw attention to the stone and have to explain it.

Out on the lawn the Tingles' servants had lit cooking fires. Their dark shapes moved back and forth between the gleams and flickers, casting distorted shadows on the woods behind. Low voices and occasional laughter drifted up. Someone had a harmonica, and the mournful, wailing tones trailed off into the night.

Seeley was slouched cross-legged just outside the lantern beams from the porch, facing away. Goblin had engorged herself on the boy's supper before daintily trotting off to take care of whatever business cats take care of at night. My cousin looked small and alone. Poor little boy.

I gave up on being a third wheel and went to join him. He was rubbing his thumb back and forth over something miniature that lay in his hand. It was a tiny horse, molded of lead and brightly painted. When he noticed me standing above him, he hurriedly slipped it into his pocket.

I sank down to the grass. "You might have noticed you can't see the stars very well tonight. It's because of the humidity. When the wind blows it away, they're bright here as anywhere."

He gazed up at the hazy blackness for a moment before saying hesitantly, "I know all the names of the constellations."

"On the next clear night maybe you'll point them out. My brother, Rush, used to do that, but without someone to show me, I can't make out anything." I paused. My breath had caught, as it always did these days, when I said my twin's name. But no more grieving. I had promised. "If you like lead horses and soldiers, Rush had lots of them."

Seeley shrugged.

"They're up in the attic," I said. "I'll bring them down tomorrow. They've been unhappy without a boy around for so long."

He raised his thin shoulders again. "If you like."

"There's boys' books you can have too. And a bandalore. Have you ever seen one of those?"

"No, ma'am."

"Do you know what it is?"

"No, ma'am. Is it like a banjo?"

"It's a spool tied on a string. You hold one end and sort of tug on it and it rolls and unrolls and goes up and down. At least it will if you know how. Rush could do lots of tricks with it, but I never had the knack. I bet you could."

He gave me a quick look. "Why?"

"Why do I think you could? Because you seem to be the sort of boy who can do things. Like my brother. He was my twin, you know. He and I and our friend Laney used to have the best times together. Rush did girl things with us, like dressing chickens in doll clothes, and we did boy things with him, like swinging out on vines over the river."

"Is that person Laney?" He jutted his chin toward Sunny.

"No. That's my stepsister, Sunny. Laney's in the kitchen. She's our servant but also my friend."

"I'm glad that person's not Laney. She has mean eyes."

I laughed. I couldn't help it.

"Can I swim in the river sometime?" he asked while I was still smiling.

"Of course," I said. "This is your home now, and you'll have lots of time to do everything since school won't start up again till fall."

"Panola is my home." A defiant little gleam came into his eyes. "I own it."

"Yes, you do, and you'll go back there someday. But you couldn't stay there by yourself."

"I wasn't by myself."

"True, but Aunt Lovina's too old to continue caring for you."

"I had Mammy. Mammy took good care of me."

"I'm sure she did. But the responsibility was too much, especially with the beastly Yankees so close. Aunt Lovina thought you'd be safer here."

"It wasn't Aunt Lovy. Dorian wanted it. It was Dorian's idea. He said I needed to be sent farther away from the war. Mammy asked to come with me, but Dorian wouldn't let her."

So that was what was wrong. Seeley hadn't wanted to leave Panola and resented Dorian for making him. Hopefully he'd get over his sulks soon. "Well, I'll be here for you." I hesitated. "I've been lonesome since Rush died. I need someone to help me do the things I used to do with him. Hunt for arrowheads and explore the woods and that sort of thing."

"I wish I had a brother."

"You have Dorian. He always lived with you at Panola as an older brother would. I bet he thinks of you that way."

"Maybe. He never took me exploring, though."

"When he came out and stayed here with us one summer, he was a lot of fun. He could think of the most amusing adventures."

"He doesn't ever play with me—we've never had any adventures."

"He's a lot older than you. Probably that's why."

"Maybe." Seeley turned away and gazed off into the darkness.

Try as I might, I couldn't get him talking again. Over on the porch Sunny and Dorian were doing a great deal of bantering and laughing.

It was late and Seeley had to be tired. I stood and reached out a hand. "Come on," I said. "Let's take you up and tuck you in bed. You get to sleep in Rush's old room."

Again he shook his head and remained sitting. "I'll sleep out here."

Dorian evidently had been watching. He strode up behind us and nudged Seeley with his knee. "Stand up, boy."

My little cousin's features were set in stubborn rebellion, so Dorian gripped his shoulders and lifted him to a standing position.

"Go with Violet," Dorian ordered. He glanced at me. "It doesn't do, coz, to mollycoddle him."

Seeley ducked under Dorian's touch, glaring out into the darkness and refusing to look at either of us.

"Go with her," Dorian said, "unless you want *me* to tuck you in bed instead."

I walked off, unable to watch how badly the older cousin handled the younger. Seeley scurried to join me. I put an arm across his back, but he flinched away. "Sorry," he said, very low. "I don't like being touched."

"How about I bring Goblin up to you in bed?" I said, dropping my arm. "You'll like touching her. She's nice to sleep with for all she's so rangy and skinny. Although sometimes she snoozes right on your chest and it's hard to breathe. You don't have to let her, though. You can push her off."

"I'll let her."

After Seeley was tucked away with the cat and his own cup of warm bedtime honey milk, I joined the others, who had retired to the sitting room and were chatting quietly. No one had drawn the curtains and the dark outside turned the windowpanes into squares of opal. Firelight flickered up and down the walls and ceiling, making the bittern seem to stir and threading my harp with strings of flame.

"Why don't you play for us, Violet?" Miss Elsa said suddenly, her cool voice sounding affectionate. Our company's arrival had awakened her. "That piece I heard you working on yesterday."

I looked down at my hands, with calluses on the fingertips from plucking strings. "I didn't know anyone was listening. It's just something I made up as I went along. It doesn't have an end."

"Play it," Miss Elsa said. "I thought it pretty."

Refusing would only draw more attention, so I sat down beside the harp, leaned in, and let my fingers find the strings. My short little piece had a haunting minor key that was so beautiful it made me happy and so mournful it made me sad at the same time. I ended, my hands quieted the strings, and there was a moment's hush before Dorian turned his full, glowing smile my way. "Bravo!" he exclaimed.

I smiled in spite of myself.

Sunny watched me with a narrow-eyed, new appraisal. "Will it be a sonata when it grows up?" she said, her tinkling voice sounding more like breaking glass.

Her tone shocked me.

Dorian darted a look back and forth between Sunny and me, his expression quizzical. "How about some rebel songs now?" he said quickly.

And so I went through "Dixie," "The Bonnie Blue Flag," and "Lorena." As I started the last verse of "Lorena," I glanced up at the photograph of Rush, all straight and proud in his new uniform, on the wall beside me. And in a trice I noted a resemblance to Seeley.

"There is a future! Oh, thank God!
Of life this is so small a part!
'Tis dust to dust beneath the sod,
But there, up there, 'tis heart to heart."

CHAPTER 9

A BIT OF A BULLY

I awoke to sounds—first the *comeback, comeback, comeback* warbling song of the guinea hens down by the edge of the forest, next the crowing of the rooster, then the distant clanging of a wake-up bell on some plantation upriver, and then more bells and a ram horn from other plantations. Gradually the low voices of the Tingles' Negroes rose up from their camp on the lawn.

Pale sunlight sifted through net curtains covering the low, arched windows of my bedroom, casting delicate, lacy patterns on the wall. Smells came too, wafting in through cracks. The Tingle servants were frying sowbelly and hoecakes. From downstairs drifted the tantalizing fragrance of baking gingerbread. That enticed me further awake, but I paused after I dressed, and ducked down low to pull back the curtains and peek outside.

From this viewpoint, myriads of interlaced footprints showed up dark green in silver dew on the grass. People were scurrying about, preparing to move on. Big, hulking King, Dorian's body servant, was plodding back and forth, alternating between hefting fantastic loads and conscientiously picking sowbelly from between his teeth with a long, shiny goose quill. He had a big, bald head and flat face. His eyes were small and dull, but he must perform his tasks well enough or Dorian wouldn't have brought him. Last night King had made himself a pallet behind a partition in the barn, and seemed as if he'd be perfectly comfortable sleeping anywhere.

Michael was helping load wagons, and Laney was distributing gingerbread to the little ones clustered about. I wondered if the two of them had been listening to a great many stories of runaway slaves.

I shook myself. All night long, the crate full of Rush's playthings had called to me from the attic. As eager as I had been to hide everything away from my young cousin, now I was even more eager to shower him with them. To see him smile. I fetched the crate down now and knocked softly on Seeley's door. No response. Inside his room the bedcovers were flung on the floor, with no boy in sight.

A thump sounded from the wardrobe. Mystified, I watched as the door swung open and out onto the floor tumbled my cousin, all tangled up in his nightgown and a blanket, with his hair sticking up as wild as a particularly messy crow's nest. His eyes opened groggily.

"Seeley," I said, "did you sleep in the *wardrobe*?"

"Only after Goblin left," he mumbled. "I didn't make her go in there 'cause I didn't know if she'd want to." He pulled his blanket closer and added shyly, "Little places are my favorite spots to be in."

I smiled. "That's one way we're alike. My bedchamber's the smallest room in the house except for the box room."

"Where's the box room?"

"Right between my room and this one. Full of boxes."

Seeley scampered over to the door and peeked inside. "Could I sleep in there? You don't even have to move the boxes. I really would like it better—you never know who might be hiding in a big room."

When I was little, before I climbed under the covers, I always checked in the wardrobe and beneath the bed for the boogerman. I glanced at Rush's carpet, the fireplace, and the soft bedstead and then back at Seeley's anxious expression. "I guess. If you really want to. I'll clear out the junk today—including the boxes. There's a cot in the attic we can bring down that might fit in there. You can still use Rush's room too for setting up armies and cities and that sort of thing."

"King will bring the bed down. He's strong."

I began removing Rush's toys from the crate. This time no heartache gnawed at my insides as my brother's beloved objects were piled on the bed. They seemed brighter and more inviting, exuding a new energy in response to a boy in the house once again.

Seeley reached in to help. When he came to the wooden box of soldiers and steeds, he held it against him. "I can have these?"

"Yes," I said. "They're yours now."

He dropped to the floor, his scrawny knees poking out from his nightgown, and took out the horses, one by one, to stand them on the crimson carpet. "In the horse world," he announced, "the grass is red and the sky's yellow and the sun is green." He looked up. "Have you ever thought of that kind of place? Where everything's different-colored?"

"Sometimes when I'm sitting in church, I picture a world with colors we don't even have here."

"How can that be?" He wrinkled his forehead. "It hurts my head to think of it." One of the horses kept falling over, so he leaned it against the box. "My animals at home stand better and their paint is brighter. Your brother must have played with these a lot." He added quickly, "But thank you for them. They're perfect because they're here and mine aren't."

"It's too bad you didn't bring yours. You could have had armies and armies of horses."

"Dorian made me leave them behind," he said in a muffled voice. "I didn't know there'd be any here, so I snuck one in my pocket." He trotted over to the wardrobe and drew out the little steed I had glimpsed the night before. He handed it to me. "I need my horses because they help me—they help me think when I hold them."

I studied the tiny figure. "It is nicer than these. Surely Dorian had a good reason not to let you bring them, though. Probably no room in your trunk."

Seeley shook his head, and a closed look came over his face. "No. Mammy packed them in perfectly. He took them out. He had another reason. A mean one."

"You must be mistaken."

"No. He told me. He called me—he called me namby-pamby and said I didn't deserve my little horses until I could ride a real one. He said when I got on Grindill's back and rode for ten minutes, he would let me have them again."

"Is Grindill Dorian's horse?"

Seeley nodded solemnly. "But I'm scared of all real horses and especially that one."

"I don't blame you—I've seen Grindill." During the previous evening's milking, I had glimpsed Dorian's massive roan in the barn. Not only did he seem big as an elephant, he was particularly bad-tempered, trying to reach over the stall partition to nip Star. "Luckily most horses are nice."

"Their teeth are big. And their hooves step on you, and their tails hit you in the eye."

A gentleman simply couldn't survive in our day and age if he was afraid of horses, but Dorian's methods of helping Seeley overcome his fears sounded harsh. He should have known you catch more flies with honey than vinegar. "We have a nice, gentle mare here. Her name is Star and she magically appeared in our pasture, so she's extra special. I'll introduce you later. What about cows? You had them at Panola, didn't you? They weren't scary, were they?"

"I don't know. I've never really been around them. Mammy never let me play near animals. She liked me to keep my clothes clean."

I had noticed that Seeley's open trunk was filled with the wardrobe of a very fine and wealthy young gentleman—linen shirts, brocade vests, every style of jacket, copper-toed boots, straw hats, cloth hats, and caps. All carefully tucked in place by the hand of a loving, overprotective nurse.

"You can't have fun in the country without ever getting dirty," I said.

"Did Rush get dirty?"

"Filthy. Me too, truth be told, but clothes are made to be washed. At least playclothes. There's a creek running through the pasture with the best mud in the world. It feels creamy oozing between your fingers. We used to wallow in it and come up looking like monsters."

Seeley beamed. "Do you think Dorian would mind?"

"I doubt it, since he wallowed with the rest of us all those years ago. . . ."

Laney and Rush and I are playing house beneath the magnolia tree. One low limb is our sofa and another is our table. We have Laney's and my rag babies, both stitched by Aunt Permilla, as well as bits of broken china for dishes. Rush doesn't particularly like doing this with us, but he goes along with it since we need a man about the place.

Dorian has been splashing in the creek by himself. He seeks us out when he grows bored. He's shirtless, his dripping pants held up by braces. Even then, I think him handsome as a fairy-tale prince. "Come help me build a levee, Rush!" he calls.

My brother shakes his head. "I told Laney and Violet I'd play here."

"All right, Rush-olet," Dorian says, sauntering over. "If you want to be a gal-boy . . . I'll give you a dime if you'll put on one of Violet's dresses. Let's see if I can tell y'all apart."

"Rush has dark hair," I say. "He doesn't look like me."

"Don't matter. What do you say, Rush-olet? A whole dime."

Rush grins and agrees good-naturedly. He does it to be nice to Dorian, not for the dime.

He never should have done it. From then on Dorian teased him unmercifully, calling him Rush-olet and making fun of his quiet ways and long eyelashes. That was the summer Rush quit playing house and began pulling out his eyelashes.

For all his amusing ways, Dorian had been a bit of a bully. Maybe I didn't mind that he and Sunny promised to be a couple, at least for the few weeks he was here.

CHAPTER 10

DALLYING

The Tingles left later that morning. Soon after we saw them off, I was caught up with showing Dorian about the farm because Sunny didn't want to get her slippers dirty. It must have been hard for her to choose between her shoes and keeping herself bodily between Dorian and me. I pitied her for the dilemma (not really). Of course she would have come if she'd actually believed I was a threat.

At one point my boys' boots tripped me up. I would have sprawled flat on my face if Dorian hadn't caught my arm and righted me. He eyed my boots with disgust. "Those things are dangerous. A first-rate position the South is in when well-brought-up young ladies are shod like clodhoppers. If I'd known you needed shoes, I would have brought you some that fit. We got a shipment not long ago— elegant Moroccan leather—but it all went to Savannah."

"I really am fine with these," I said lightly, "as long as I never need to run for my life."

"You'd be in trouble then," he said. He was still holding on to my elbow, steering me away from the fields and over toward the river's edge. We scrambled down the bank and lowered ourselves to perch on a protruding root that hung out over the water. The river sparkled in a pattern of blue and green and gray like crumpled foil.

"Here," Dorian said. "I'll help you take off those enormous boots if you want to dangle your toes in the water."

I didn't object. He leaned into me and he smelled of tobacco and expensive soap. He could nearly pull off my boots without unlacing them. There was something pleasant about the attention and about having an attractive gentleman see how small my feet were minus the galumphing shoes. He tickled the soft pad of one foot. I giggled and wriggled almost like Sunny.

Stop it right now, Violet Dancey.

Obviously, flirting with any female came as naturally to Dorian as breathing. He'd been expertly dallying with Sunny only last night, and today he was being frolicsome with me. With his type, I guessed, it was any girl in a storm.

The sunlight made him blink as he gazed out over painfully twinkling water. "You've probably noticed how Seeley avoids me."

I nodded.

He held out his open hands. "When he was smaller, I was his idol. He was the cutest little fellow—used to trot behind me like a puppy dog and mimick everything I did. But since his parents died, I admit I've handled him wrong. He was spoiled and cosseted by his parents and his nurse, and it's been my job to toughen him up. Because—you know who else is there to do it now? Who else to teach him how a gentleman should act? That's part of the reason I had to get him away from Panola—Aunt Lovy and his nurse kept him in cotton wool. True, he's a clumsy kid, and was forever getting scraped up, even with their care, but still, a boy's got to learn."

I licked my lips. "He did mention you were the one who made him come here. I don't know much about little boys, but I remember how my brother was. He was sensitive like Seeley, but he grew up plenty manly without being purposely 'toughened.' I would think that if you ridicule Seeley, he'll just act more awkward and avoid you. Teach him by example and kindness."

"Will you help me?" Dorian seemed genuinely anxious. "I really do want him to like me. I mean, for all intents and purposes, he's my little brother. I thought of his parents as mine too. You know, my own father died young, and my mother remarried and went off to live in France with her new husband when I was a tiny tot. They dumped me at Panola."

"That's . . . sad."

Dorian made a careless gesture. "Really never bothered me. My aunt and uncle acted as if I was theirs. Besides, Panola is paradise."

"What's it like?" I asked eagerly. "I've always wondered. My mother was never well enough to tell stories of her childhood. Or tales about anything at all, actually."

"You want a story, little girl?"

I nodded. "Please."

"Glad to oblige." He settled himself more comfortably and his expression grew thoughtful. "Not once upon a time, but right now, today—which makes it even more magical—there is a palace called Panola, and I was its prince. The gods have blessed it so that it is the most beautiful place on earth. In the universe. There is a dome at the top, three stories up from the front hall, set with stained glass.

And those jewel colors shine down and dance all around so you walk in rainbows. The moldings were carved by a slave carpenter of great talent. Each room has a different theme—birds chiseled into the parlor woodwork, Bible stories in the dining room, and mythical creatures in the study. All so realistic they could come to life and jump out at any second." Dorian's bright eyes may have been gazing out over the water, but that was not what he was seeing.

"And my mother was a princess there," I said. "Scuppernong must have seemed like a mean little backwoods hovel when she came here, and it's only gotten shabbier since."

Dorian acted as if he didn't hear me. "There are gardens at Panola too. The soil is so rich that flowers, tobacco, and all crops can't help but flourish. I always planned that I'd—" He stopped abruptly.

"What did you always plan?"

He shook his head. "Nothing. It doesn't matter." He snapped off an overhanging twig and hurled it out into the water. "Oh, well, let's get back to the subject of Seeley. How do you propose I should handle him, since obviously I've been failing in that area?"

"What you need to do," I said carefully, "is to see the world through his eyes."

He looked charmingly confused. "How do you mean?"

"Be whimsical. Seeley's awfully imaginative."

A blue-winged dragonfly lit on the bank near Dorian's hand. For one lightning-quick second I considered trying to call it to me as I did the bees. I had never tried my gift—my knack or whatever it was—with other creatures. I wondered what Dorian would think of it. Would he find it fascinating? Or alarming?

He flicked the poor creature with his fingers so sharply it fell lifeless into the water. "There!" he said in triumph. "That's hard to do—have you ever managed to flick a dragonfly? They're faster than you'd think."

I would never tell anyone about the bees.

We were silent for a moment while I removed my bonnet and let the sun's warmth bathe my face.

"Aren't you afraid of tanning?" Dorian asked. "I'm bound your stepsister would be."

"Yes, she would. And that's partly why she looks as she does and I look as I do." I closed my eyes. Sparkles dazzled behind my eyelids. "At this moment I don't care. It's worth every freckle to feel the sun this way."

Dorian laughed. "Like a lady snake sunning herself on a rock."

"Exactly."

"You're an unusual girl, Cousin Violet. No wonder you've already won Seeley over. How does someone so beautiful get to be so interesting as well?" He inched closer.

I am not beautiful. Nobody could honestly call me beautiful. He'd made a mistake using that word. There was an awkward pause as I shook my head, my eyes still closed. "Oh, Dorian, Dorian, Dorian," I said finally in a lofty tone.

"What? Why do you 'Oh, Dorian' me?"

My eyes flashed open. "You know perfectly well." I stood. "It's time for lunch."

After we ate, I searched out King to help me fix up the box room for Seeley. By the time we finished, the boy was missing once more. At last I found him outside beneath the bridal wreath bush.

"Would you like to come see a hideout Michael made in the woods?" I asked. "He built it in case the thieving Federals arrive and we need a place to duck into."

Seeley jumped up enthusiastically. We brushed ourselves and each other off and made our way through lush undergrowth. Seeley created a lot of noise as he bounded through the brush.

"Watch out—" I started to say.

He stumbled and barely caught himself by clutching a branch.

"—for the roots," I finished. Dorian was right: Seeley was indeed an ungainly child. His feet seemed to constantly trip each other up. As we went, I showed him how to be mindful of poison ivy, snakes, and other lurking dangers of the wildwood. I would teach him the best I could to take appropriate care, but no mollycoddling. He had to learn to manage himself in the outdoors.

"If Mammy had ever let me go into the forest to practice, I would already be an expert woodsman," my cousin said. "For one thing, I've read all about it."

He snatched up a straight stick, splotchy with lichen, and commenced shooting at nothing, making explosive sounds. "I'm being Heath Blackstock," he confided when he remembered I was there. "He saves people from bushwhackers and outlaws and Indians."

This sounded so familiar. "Rush was usually named Max Kerrigan. Laney and I always had to be the bad men. He used my mother's red satin petticoat for a cape. Very swashbuckling except for the lace ruffle at the bottom. I'll have to see if it's still around—and if you're very good, I'll even take off the lace."

Seeley fired his stick especially loudly at a scolding squirrel.

"I don't know why you boys are all so fond of guns," I said. "Guns and loud, bangy things like firecrackers. Honestly."

Seeley looked earnest. "If I had a rifle, I would only shoot what we need for food. We would have possum and squirrel for supper every night."

"You make my mouth water. In some places where our poor soldiers haven't much to eat, they're devouring rats. They say fat ones taste like squirrel."

"And we would have rats too," he assured me. "Anytime you wanted them. Last year before—last year I asked Father if I might have a gun for Christmas, and he said he had one all picked out. But then afterward—nobody remembered that. Aunt Lovy gave me a hobbyhorse. She thought it would make me like horses better. It didn't," he finished with disgust.

Poor little boy. His parents had both succumbed to diphtheria the previous spring and had died within two weeks of each other.

"Now"—I indicated the little dell, creamy with clover—"can you find the entrance to our hiding place?"

Seeley meticulously inspected tree trunks, as if he expected concealed doors to pop open on springs, and poked beneath brambles and bushes.

"Do you give up?" I asked.

"No," he said—then, "Aha!" The ground beneath him had yielded a bit.

Michael had made a trapdoor and covered it with dirt and a mat of tangled creepers, undetectable unless someone was looking for it and stepped right on top. I showed Seeley the handle. He lifted it with some trouble but, refusing all help, revealed the black, gaping hole beneath.

We descended the ramp, which Michael had made sturdy enough to support our stock. I warned Seeley that there was always an inch of water seeped into the floor below.

An odor of damp earth and fungus hit us. Inside, in the murky light, we could just make out the shelf, which held a stub of candle and my family's few pieces of silver, wrapped in burlap sacking.

"At the first sign of Yankees," I said, "we'll stash anything here they might be interested in. So, would Heath Blackstock approve?"

"It's a good hideout," Seeley said.

On the way back to the house I showed him the big magnolia tree with branches spaced so perfectly it was almost like climbing up stairs. It was the same one Laney and I had often played house beneath. "I still go up there to read sometimes, just so I can suddenly look at myself and think, *What an unlikely place I'm at.* And so no one will ever suspect in a million years where I happen to be."

Seeley scaled the branches. When he came down, I taught him how to suck honeysuckle nectar and fight off the attack geese in the kitchen yard.

It was a splendid afternoon, and at suppertime Seeley seemed more relaxed because of it. He still twitched some, but he spoke more easily, and didn't put on the sulky face he had previously worn with the others. He told about his adventures that day. "Violet likes to read books up high in the magnolia tree," he announced.

Sunny rolled her eyes. "Really, Vi-let?"

I smiled brightly back at her. "I do. When the wind blows, it's like being in a green ocean."

"Whimsical . . . ," Dorian murmured, so softly that only I heard.

"Tomorrow I'm going to stay up there all day," Seeley said. "I'll take one of Rush's books that has pictures of the Huns riding around with heads tied to their saddles."

Sunny made a face. "Horrid child," she said. "Look at how he relishes that sort of nasty thing."

Seeley laughed out loud at being called a horrid child.

"Just be careful when you're climbing, Squid," I said.

"I know, I know," Seeley said. "Why do you call me Squid?"

"Because I like that word and I like you, so the two of you just sort of go together."

"My mother always called me Seal." The smile faded from my little cousin's face.

"Tomorrow," I announced, changing the subject, "I'm going to help at the courthouse hospital."

"Why must you go to that foul place?" Sunny asked. "They've got other folks to nurse those fellows now—all the snotty women from Mobile who think they're so vital to the Cause."

"I want to see the patients once more before they leave."

"Who are these Mobile women?" Miss Elsa asked idly.

"And what makes you think the patients are leaving soon?" Sunny demanded.

I tried to answer them both. "They're volunteers with the Army of Tennessee's hospital division. That's why I haven't gone much lately, since they don't really need me. But Michael told me that this week all the patients are to be moved by rail to Corinth. They think there might be a battle near Okolona soon, and that's too close for comfort."

"Ha," Dorian scoffed. "There'll be no such thing."

"How do you know?" I asked.

"I have my connections. Y'all may rest easy. The boom of cannon shall not rouse us from our beds anytime soon." My cousin had a talent for imparting confidence; somehow we believed him. "By the way," he added, "if any of you like books, I've a new French novel for you. *Les Misérables*. Just finished it. Everyone's wild over it. Not for you, though, Seeley-the-squid. Stick to your innocent schoolboy reading about heads banging along on saddles."

After supper that evening we gathered in the sitting room. Dorian was gentle with Miss Elsa, seating her in the soft lamplight and fetching her needlework. For the masculine attention she rewarded him with smiles. He then set himself to teach Seeley how to use the bandalore, and before long Seeley relaxed further and could even do a few tricks, while Goblin batted at the spool with her black paw.

"You know, of course," Sunny said, tugging at a knot in her embroidery, "the child will drive us all daft with that thing before he's through."

"A boy needs a bandalore," Dorian said comfortably.

"Thank you for helping him," I whispered to my older cousin, so Seeley couldn't hear.

"See? I'm following your advice," Dorian whispered back as he squatted beside my chair.

"And it's working. He's much more at ease with you now."

"Anything to make you look at me approvingly, coz," Dorian said, peeking up mischievously.

I rolled my eyes and looked down at the sock I was knitting

furiously to hide my blushes. As he kept watching me, I felt a silly, nervous grin stretch my lips.

"When you smile so mysteriously," Dorian said, "it makes me wonder what plots you're hatching."

"None at all. I was wondering if this sock needs one more row before I cast off. All very boring." I started on another row. "And you should be kind to people for their own sake, and not for anyone else's approval," I added severely.

"I'll try," Dorian said, "if that will make you approve of me."

I snorted, and Sunny, who had been eyeing us vigilantly, immediately came to stand between us.

"Dorian, would you help me with my necklace?" she asked. "The catch is stuck." She smiled a little secret smile as she held up her curls above her long neck. He stood close behind, working on the clasp.

Once he got it unhooked, Dorian settled himself to entertain, relating slightly scandalous and self-deprecatory stories of his recent dealings with high society in the Confederate capital of Richmond. With his bright hair and bronze skin, he glowed like one of the lamps. Miss Elsa quit feebly jabbing at her canvas and listened, entranced. From time to time she even commented on places she had also visited.

"Have you actually seen President Jefferson Davis?" Sunny asked.

"I have," Dorian said. "And had a lengthy conversation with him. I could tell he was most impressed by me. I was crossing the road and Jeff Davis's coach nearly ran me down. The great man himself poked his head out the window and said, 'Watch yourself, young man. We can't afford to lose Southern blood in such a way.' Our president looked and sounded every bit the gentleman. A momentous meeting. I wouldn't have minded being nearly run over by the president's coach at all except that I got grease on my new sack coat and King had the devil of a time—oh, sorry for cursing, Miss Elsa—getting it out. Now that I think of it, maybe I should have left it stained as a conversation piece. My presidential grease spot."

Miss Elsa and Sunny shook with laughter and lavished him with admiring glances. My stepmother tapped him with her fan and fluttered her eyelashes. For a moment I saw a girlish Elsa, one who had been a sought-after belle. Dorian was certainly very different from the young men we knew around Chicataw, who only seemed to care for fighting, hunting, and chewing tobacco. Dorian was so polished—and he read books!

"Meanwhile," Sunny said, shaking her head, "the North has a rail-splitter for a leader. So hard to understand those people."

It was late when I finally deposited Seeley, Goblin, and Seeley's cup of honey milk in bed. The cows would be anxious. I lit my lantern with an ember from the kitchen fire and headed out into the night.

I jumped a little when Dorian emerged from the darkness and swung into step beside me in my circle of light.

" 'Where are you going, my pretty maid?' " he said, quoting the old nursery rhyme.

Without looking at him, I smiled. " 'I'm going a-milking, sir.' "

" 'May I go with you, my pretty maid?' "

" 'You're kindly welcome, sir,' " I said.

"Do you ever wonder why milkmaids are always so pretty?" Dorian asked.

I unbarred the great barn door. "Obviously it's so men will ask to go with them and rhymes can be written about them."

"Seriously, may I help you with your chores?"

"If you like," I said, but wished he wouldn't. Besides the fact that his flirting made me uncomfortable, I preferred to be alone in the barn for the evening milking. It felt sheltered and intimate, with the soft sounds and warmth of the animals, the glow of the lantern, and the smell of hay. Another person spoiled it.

Inside the doorway the pail hung on a nail just a little too high. As I stretched for it, Dorian stood close and reached over my head to lift it down. "Let me do that."

I turned around to find myself trapped in his arms. "My pretty maid," he said softly, gazing down into my eyes. His were *so* blue. "I wonder . . . shall I make you fall in love with me?"

"What makes you think you could?" I said into his chest, and tried to duck under his elbow.

He lowered his arms and closed them tighter. "Oh, I'm not sure at all; that's what would make it intriguing. When I see you smiling so mysteriously—"

"Yes, you said that before," I cut him off. His tone was too practiced. Too smooth. "To lots of girls, I bet. Does it usually do the trick?" I glanced up to see how annoyed he was by my words.

At first he appeared taken aback, then delighted. He slapped his hand on his thigh and laughed. "You'd be surprised how well it usually works."

"Now," I said, "stop being silly and let me get on with my chores. Sunny's the one to work your charm on."

"Oh, Sunny . . ." He dismissed my beautiful stepsister with the flick of a hand. "Too easy by half." With one finger he brushed back a strand of my hair that had escaped its pins. "Well, then, if you don't want to be kissing cousins, why did you give me that come-to-me look?"

"I—did—not—give you a look!" I shoved against him, not hard, but the post he was standing next to shook and some objects that were stored in the rafters banged down on us and clattered to the floor.

Holding his head where a tin pail had hit, Dorian made a face and reached up to pick away the cobweb that now draped him. "You all right? That was quite the booby trap."

I began laughing so hard I could barely speak. "Sorry. The look on your—what a surprise! It's all junk Pa put up there to fix later on. Naturally he never did anything about it."

Dorian chuckled as he bent to poke through things. "Huh. This is actually a pretty good saddle to be stuck away forgotten. And this old rifle."

"It's broken. And there was something wrong with the saddle too. Lopsided or something. The pail has a leak. Pa can't throw junk away."

Dorian replaced everything. "So—you think I'd better concentrate on Sunny?"

"I do."

He nodded slowly and left me, as I had wished to be, alone with my milking. Now, contrarily, I felt lonely. I leaned my head against Lily's warm brown side and watched the milk spurt foaming into the pail.

Amenze had said I would have a sweetheart soon. Except for Dorian and the patients in the courthouse hospital, there were no young men left for miles around.

CHAPTER 11

COMPLICATIONS

"Please." The young man—the boy—caught at my skirt.

"Here you go." I removed a hunk of bread from my basket and held it out. I did not remember this fellow from the earlier times I had been at the hospital, probably because the patients had been more numerous before.

He ever so slightly shook his head on the pillow. "No, miss, I'm not hungry. I only wanted to talk some. They're cutting off my arm today." Two red spots of fever glowed on his hollow cheeks.

"Oh, dear." I tried to control the dismay in my expression as I settled myself on a barrel beside his cot. "What a shame to have gone so long and have it taken off now."

His mouth twisted. "The rumor is that the Yanks poisoned their musket balls. That's why we seem to be getting better for a while and then our wounds fester. The thing is . . . I know I'll die because everyone who's had limbs removed in this hospital has died."

For a moment I could not speak from the swelling in my throat. "Are you afraid?" I asked finally, softly.

"No. I'll go to a better place and I'm curious to see it. It's only that I wish I could have seen my home and my family one more time."

"Tell me about them. And you." I put my hand over his and clutched tightly.

He was Mr. Isaac Lafarge, of Louisiana, and he was fifteen years old. He was the only son, with five older sisters. He had a coonhound named Badger.

As it so often did when I was distressed, my amulet glowed warm and comforting against my skin. I lifted it from over my head and placed it around Mr. Lafarge's neck. "Wear this until it's all done," I said. "The stone is supposed to bring luck." I got his address and promised to write to his family.

When the men arrived to take him to the surgeon's table, I watched after, wondering if I should make myself go along.

However, there was nothing more I could do for Mr. Lafarge, and there were others who needed care.

During the past weeks, cots had been brought in so the patients were off the floor. Most of the filth had been cleaned up, and an army doctor and surgeon were in attendance, replacing Dr. Hale. Many of those patients I had attended were gone, either to their graves or removed by relatives. Although the men left here were mutilated in every imaginable way, several appeared quite cheerful now, certain they were on the mend. Others . . . Mr. Miller of Georgia, who had a dreadful wound to his shoulder, was wandering in his mind.

Each time I came, my heart was struck anew by the horrors that the Yankees would work upon their fellow men.

However, there was no time to think of such things. I offered water and food, bathed feverish faces and wounds. I listened to talk of "home, sweet home" and wrote letters. So little, yet the poor sufferers were grateful for it.

A commotion sounded at the door. I looked up to see Dr. Abbot trying to shut out someone who was attempting to enter the gallery. "Oh, no you don't," Dr. Abbot's voice boomed. "Today's no different from those other times you came. We don't want medicine such as yours here."

I caught a glimpse of a pink face with pebble-thick spectacles knocked askew as Dr. VanZeldt was shoved outside.

"But you *should* want it." The doctor's raised voice beyond the slammed door sounded deeply distressed. "You simply do not know what I can do to help."

"Begone, sir, or you will be escorted bodily out of town."

This threat was met by silence. Dr. VanZeldt must have given up.

By now Mr. Lafarge's surgery was completed. I was ashamed of my cowardice in leaving him and went to his side as he slept. Gently I bathed his face. He had bitten through his lip; I washed the blood away.

He was so still . . . so . . . *empty.*

Cold.

I reeled, shaky and sick.

Rush. Oh, my Rush.

No. Not Rush. This was Isaac Lafarge. I steadied myself against the edge of the bed and said a quick prayer for Isaac Lafarge. He was the darling of his mother and five sisters, yet I was the only one in the whole world who knew at this moment that he was dead.

He no longer needed my amulet. After steeling myself to remove it from around his neck, I did so. The amber was cold. It had not been lucky for him.

I informed a nurse about his passing.

"Poor little Mr. Lafarge," she said. "He was one of my favorites."

With the back of my hand I swiped at my cheeks. "Mine too," I choked out.

I stumbled outside and leaned against the brick wall. At one end of the yard was a well. I pulled up a bucket and plunged my face into the cold water. I came up gasping and did it again and again. The drenching and the few minutes allowed me to regain self-control.

Soon after I left the courthouse.

"Miss Violet Dancey!"

The voice sounded from behind. I whirled around.

Dr. VanZeldt was scurrying down Main Street, his pale kid leather shoes scuffing up dust. He held out a walking stick before him as if he would attack me with it, but his expression was eager and benign.

I might have run in the opposite direction if I hadn't pitied him for his experience at the hospital.

He reached me, puffing a little, and touched the edge of his hat. Up close, his eyes were distorted by the thick glasses, and his shiny pink skin had an odd, stretched look.

"Yes, sir?" I said.

"Miss Violet Dancey, I want to thank you for your kindness to Amenze. You impress us. Impress us, indeed." He held out his hand as if to shake mine. Instead, he captured my fingers in his damp palm and enclosed them tightly with his other hand. He had a slight accent.

"It was n-nothing," I stammered, trying unsuccessfully to regain my hand. "Just a little confusion about her money. Anybody could have helped."

He seemed not to hear what I said. His brow furrowed and he held up my palm as if to study it. "You have been . . . touching someone who departed this world very recently."

I wrenched my hand from his grasp and wiped it against my skirt. "At the hospital." My breath came out heavy.

"What a pity," Dr. VanZeldt said, and his eyes were full of compassion. "He was very young."

"What . . . How do you know?"

"Ah, some of his energy yet clings to you, and sensing such things is one of my skills. But you sell yourself short when you say anyone would have helped our Amenze. Around here, very few would. My people are the—ahem—proverbial pariahs."

"I'm sorry folks haven't been welcoming. And I'm sorry they won't let you assist with the wounded."

"Yes, you saw." A knowing, bitter look sparked in his magnified eyes. "They do not understand what they are rejecting. They are fools. Nevertheless, that is neither here nor there. What I want you to please know is that we are in your debt. Amenze is most precious. It is our hope that we will all get to know one another better. I have been asked to invite you to dine with us one day at Shadowlawn."

The thought of seeing the VanZeldts doing anything so ordinary as eating made the invitation almost tempting. However, I did not want to know the doctor better. Although he looked well scrubbed in his white suit with his shiny pink skin, a sense of something unclean oozed out of him.

I managed a vague smile. "Maybe someday. Amenze seemed very sweet. I . . . um"—I half turned—"ought to be going."

He tipped his hat again and I hastened down the road, anxious in a way I did not fully understand. I needed to get home.

At Scuppernong, I entered the sitting room to find Seeley sprawled, scrawny and shirtless, on the sofa, very pale, with a bloody bandage wrapped rakishly about his head and a sling around his bony shoulder. Sunny, Miss Elsa, and Laney hovered near.

At the sight I gave a gasp.

"He's fine, Vi-let," Sunny said as I darted to Seeley's side. "No need to look all wild-eyed. This is what happens to boys who climb magnolia trees like monkeys. A branch broke beneath him. Other limbs slowed his fall and he landed on soft grass. That's all."

"I did see stars when my head thudded," Seeley said. "I wondered if people really did."

Miss Elsa stood wringing her hands nearby. "Dorian's King snapped his shoulder back in place. What if the fall . . ."

"You should've heard the pop," Seeley said.

"No. No one should ever have to hear such a thing," Laney said, making a face. "Not if they know what's good for them."

"He was lucky. Devilishly lucky." Dorian's voice startled me. I hadn't noticed him leaning carelessly against the wall behind the door. "And now he's being a trump about it." He gave Seeley a grin.

Later, when I went out to find Goblin for Seeley, King loomed against the sunset as he stirred the blazing rubbish fire with a pole. I shuddered at the sight of the huge limb that had broken beneath my cousin, flames dancing along its length. Goblin's golden eyes glowed nearby, watching.

CHAPTER 12

JUBAL AND MISS RUBY JEWEL

As I stepped softly past Miss Ruby Jewel's little house, Jubal's deep, gravelly voice reached me. "Miss Dancey! My mistress requests a word with you."

Drat! And I had walked so softly. I was returning from the long trip into town to make certain the patients were all transported and was ready to get home to Scuppernong. However, I couldn't ignore the tall, skinny old black man. Jubal stood with his head bowed below a tangled arbor framing the front steps. I made my way up the overgrown path toward the house. Rather than cooling the air with their shade, the thickly interwoven branches of the live oaks held in oppressive heat. I forced my lips into a smile.

No answering smile lightened Jubal's weary eyes or lifted the melancholy droop of his face. With an almost courtly gesture, he held back the encroaching tendrils of a climbing rosebush. A streak of bright blood beaded up where thorns had torn his forehead, but he showed no sign that he noticed. He indicated the gaping mouth of his mistress's parlor. "In here, please, ma'am, Miss Dancey." His tone was gracious.

"You catch that girl, Jubal?" Miss Ruby Jewel screeched from inside.

"He caught me," I said, entering the room, which was close with tobacco smoke, humidity, the stench of the old woman and her many cats, and a crowded jumble of musty, dusty furniture, knickknacks, and odds and ends. Jubal tried to tidy up, but it was more than one tired old man could possibly triumph over. I had forgotten to take a lungful of clean air while I still could. From the smell there might even be a dead kitten among the drifts.

A mottled tom sidled up. Some skin disease left his fur patchy, with splotched bits of flesh between. I twitched my gown away. The beast somehow managed to get under my skirt, and I shuddered as he purred loudly and rubbed against my legs. I shooed him out and gave him a subtle little nudge to send him on his way. Another feline leaped down from the mantel, and in the corner of my eye slinky shadows crept constantly, making the room seethe. All cats in the world were beloved by me except Miss Ruby Jewel's. These made my skin crawl.

Miss Ruby Jewel took a puff of her pipe and said in a voice like twigs scraping against a glass pane, "Make room for yourself on that there settee." Huddled and sunken into a low chair wreathed by bluish smoke, she resembled a bag of bones in her rusty black dress. The old lady's back was humped, her hands twisted with arthritis, and her legs too short to reach the floor. With her miniature stature Miss Ruby Jewel looked like a very ugly doll. The sort of doll to give a little girl nightmares.

Hesitantly I shoved aside clothing and papers to carve out a place to sit.

"Been losing weight, ain't you?" Miss Ruby Jewel commented while my back was turned. "Your hiney don't spread out wide like it used to. You still favor your daddy's cousin Winnie, though. The one who come out here to settle her own place and ended up marrying a Choctaw Indian and living in a tepee behind his saloon."

Why was it that whenever people said I resembled anyone, it was always someone I didn't want to resemble?

I perched gingerly at the edge of the sofa. "How are you, Miss Ruby Jewel?" A stream of perspiration trickled down my back.

"Tolerable," she said. "Just tolerable. Jubal! You, Jubal! Fetch this young lady a cold drink right quick and grab me up some ginger-snaps."

The old man sighed and shook his head. "Now, Miss Ruby Jewel, ma'am, you know Dr. Hale doesn't want you eating sweeties. They make you sick. He says one of these days they'll be the death of you."

"But what a way to go, eh? Hale's an old fusspot. Now, no more impudence, you, Jubal. Take your raggedy black tail out of here and bring back what I done told you. Lots of them. Lots of ginger-snaps."

"Yes'm." Jubal shuffled from the room.

"Now," the old woman said, "I ain't talked to you in a month of Sundays, but I did want to tell you I was right sorry to hear about your brother. He wasn't a bad young'un."

I thanked her and looked down at my hands, wriggled, and removed from beneath me a brass swan. It had been lodged between the sofa cushions, with its beak digging into my less-spread-out posterior. Then, because I didn't want her to say anything more about Rush, I asked, "Ma'am, how long has Mr. Jubal been with you? Years and years, isn't it?"

" 'Mister,' is it?" Her beady black eyes sparkled. "Don't let him hear you call him that. Don't need to give that one no more uppity ideas. Yep, he sure 'nough has been with me nigh sixty years."

"And how did he come to you?"

She gave a screech of laughter so sudden and shrill that I jumped. "You been conjecturing on that forever, ain't you? You been pondering how someone like Ruby Jewel Clewett come to own a fancy-pants Negro like Jubal. Well, I guess 'twon't hurt none to satisfy your curiosity, even though curiosity done killed the cat. Didn't it, my precious?" She nuzzled the neck of the mangy marmalade feline that had leaped momentarily on the arm of her chair. With her head nodding she looked more than ever like a grotesque doll—this time the kind that wags its head on a spring. "It happened like this: back when I was a beautiful young gal—ho-ho, I see your eyes pop. You don't believe I could ever have been pretty, do you?" She cackled again. "Well, you're right. I done told you a story. I always been so homely I'd run a dog off a meat wagon and that's a fact, but Billy Dean liked me well enough when I married him at the ripe old age of thirteen. At the time he was already older than the mountains and had twice as many skunks.

"Anyways, we'd been together a year or two and Billy Dean went to work on one of them riverboats. One day he come home leading a strapping young buck of a Jubal. My old man says, 'You come up in the world, girl. I brung you a Negro of your very own.' He won

him with the cards off some highfalutin Virginian." She reached for
a fuzzy horehound drop that was stuck to the table beside her but
couldn't pull it free. I was wondering if I should offer to pry it loose,
but she shrugged and continued, "Later the gentleman brought a
passel of money and begged my old man to take it instead—way
more'n Jubal was worth—but my old man says, no, he'd always
wanted to own property and Jubal suited him just fine."

"Well, I did wonder. You never had any children, did you?" I said
this last hopefully. The image of young Miss Ruby Jewels popping
up everywhere like toadstools was a terrifying one.

"Shoot, no. Billy Dean stayed gone most of the rest of his years,
and even when he come home, the fat old coot didn't hardly bestir
hisself to put me in the family way. But I never cared none for chillen
underfoot noways. Liked my kitties better. Jubal done always took
care of me. When I needed more money than my old man sent—
never did know what would come or when—I'd hire Jubal out. He
been with me through thick and thin." She paused and puffed again
on her pipe long enough to make me think she'd forgotten I was
there. Then her lips stretched into an evil grin, showing black gums.
"When I was younger, I used to think I'd have my way with Jubal,
and I'll be bound both Billy Dean and yonder old cotton head was
afeared of that too, but I never did, and now it's too late. Or is it?
What you think, sugar? You think we still got what it takes?"

Such a foul old woman. I carefully smoothed out my skirt as if
I hadn't heard. "What did you want to talk to me about, ma'am? I
need to be getting home."

She gave a ghastly, exaggerated pout. "Oh, all right. Be that way.
I won't make you answer that question if you'll answer my others."

Jubal entered, his trembling hands bearing a tray of clinking, chipped glasses, a pitcher of a grayish-looking liquid with slices of shriveled lemon agitating madly in it, and a plate of gingersnaps.

"You be careful, you, Jubal," Miss Ruby Jewel snapped. "That's my good crystal you're fixing to drop, shaking like a dad gum earthquake."

"I'll be careful, ma'am." Slowly Jubal offered me a glass, and because he had poured it with such effort, I would drink it if it killed me.

Miss Ruby Jewel guzzled hers down, dribbling all over the front of her dress. Jubal, who had been standing to the side, unfurled a napkin and patiently dabbed at her chin and the stringy cords of her neck.

The old woman clutched at his wrist. "Take notice, you, girl, how this feller can't hardly keep his hands off my bosom." She cocked an eyebrow at her manservant. "What you think, *Mister* Jubal, sugar? You believe it's too late for a charming little illicit romance between the two of us? Some scrumptious smacking behind closed doors?"

Jubal shook his head, and his lips twitched in an odd way. He said firmly, "Don't you talk that way in front of Miss Violet, ma'am. You know it's not fitting."

I quickly swallowed the rest of my lemonade so Jubal could escape with the dishes. What had his life been like, day in and day out, for sixty years with the old witch? Did he lie awake at night plotting revenge?

Miss Ruby Jewel grinned. "Shoot, be that way, then. I reckon we both just gonna have to keep on pining for what might've been."

To my surprise, the twitching lips slowly turned into a smile, and

Jubal gave a rusty chuckle as he shuffled out the door. "You're a caution, Miss Ruby Jewel. That's what you are. A caution."

The old lady grinned at Jubal's back before her shrewd little eyes burrowed into me. "Now," she said, "what I want to know is who's the young gentleman come recently to your place?"

An easy question, thank goodness. "The very young gentleman is my cousin Seeley Rushton. The older one is my cousin Dorian. He's visited us before, years ago, back when Seeley was born. You hollered at us once for losing our ball in your hydrangeas." Rush and I had been so petrified by Miss Ruby Jewel that we couldn't move, but Dorian had thrown back his head and laughed, made a sweeping bow, and retrieved the ball. I had been awestruck by his courage.

"Yup, I do recall. From up Richmond way, wasn't he?" She tamped out her pipe.

I nodded.

"He's the one had the disappointment—thought he'd be his uncle's heir, and then along come a surprise?"

I stared, mystified for a moment, before realizing her implications. "Oh! You mean Seeley being born. It really didn't alter anything for Dorian. He was only sixteen then, so I don't guess he'd thought much about the future. For one thing, my aunt and uncle weren't that old."

"Oh, they was old enough no one thought they'd have young'uns of their own. I know. My friend Sissy Hinds lives yonder that way and she done told me all about it."

"Not that much changed for Dorian." I resented her making

me speak about my family's private affairs, but I couldn't leave her insinuations unanswered. "My aunt and uncle loved him and raised him as their son since he was a baby. He thinks of himself as Seeley's brother."

"If he really was the older brother, he'd inherit."

"Oh, he's busy making money on his own, and he knows he'll always have a home at Panola. Till the war he managed the place. He's fine."

"I reckon he's been managing things all right." She gave me a sly, sidelong look. "You fixing to set your cap for that fellow? Cousins right often marry each other in these parts, you know."

I drew in my breath. "Certainly not."

Her lips stretched placidly. "He wouldn't care for your type noways, not with that minx of a stepsister prancing round. Thinks all the fellers in hollering distance belong to her. Thinks she's better'n snuff and not half as dusty, don't she?"

Which Sunny did. But still. The people Miss Ruby Jewel was maligning were *my* people. The old woman's mind pounced about like Goblin in the field of moths, and she wore me out with the pouncing. I fingered the reassuring bulge of my amulet and said quietly, "Sunny is a good person and I won't listen to such things about my family." I stood.

She snorted. "My, aren't we hoity-toity? Now, what's that you're hiding under your blouse? What you got round your neck?"

I drew myself up stiffly and managed to squeeze out, "Good day, ma'am," as I started for the door.

"Don't want to show me, eh? Well, be that way, but don't go

running off." She turned cunning. "Stay one more minute and I'll tell what I heard about them VanZeldts from downriver."

I absolutely could not help sinking down to the sofa once again. "What have you heard?"

"Interested now, are you? Well, I'll blab if you show me what you're wearing. Tit for tat. A necklace, isn't it? What kind of necklace?"

I had to break the habit of fiddling with the amulet. Once again I rose.

"No," she said. "No, no, no. Sit down. I'll tell you." She paused, then waggled her eyebrows. "I heard tell they dance around a bonfire at dead of night in the middle of the woods. Outrageous, heathen dancing. With drums." She realized I was unimpressed and added, "Stark naked." A cat jumped on her lap and she stroked its lumpy, crusted tail. "With snakes. Don't you wonder what nasty, carnal things they do with them serpents? And the good doctor prances right along with them." She grinned with malicious glee. "You're picturing it, ain't you?"

I stopped myself short because I had indeed been trying to visualize the dapper little man leaping wildly and nakedly; luckily it was far beyond my imagination. "No," I said, "and I don't want to. But who told you this? Who's been skulking out in the forest at nighttime?"

"Now, that's something," Miss Ruby Jewel said, shaking a crooked finger, "I'll never reveal."

It really was time to leave. I jumped up, planning to race out before she could stop me again. "Thank you so much for the lemonade."

"Stay," she whined. "You just got here."

"I really have to go," I said, but her expression was so unhappy that I grinned and said, "I need to get busy if I'm going to ensnare Dorian."

She hooted. "Be that way, then, but give me some sugar first."

I braced myself and gingerly kissed her age-splotched cheek.

As I came out, Jubal stood up from the cane-bottomed chair on the porch where he had been sitting, clutching a book. I tilted my head sideways to read the title.

"*Robinson Crusoe*," I said. "That's a good one."

"Yes, Miss Violet, it is. Right exciting. I've been reading it to Miss Ruby Jewel in the afternoons before her nap. She says it gives her interesting dreams about cannibals and such."

Miss Ruby Jewel hollered through the open door, "Jubal's my 'man Friday.' "

Jubal's eyes began to twinkle and his lips began the twitching until they slowly stretched into a smile. He bobbed his head. "And I call Miss Ruby Jewel my 'woman Friday.' "

Her cackle sounded delighted.

"Have you shared other books together?" I asked as I stepped down from the porch, with Jubal at my side.

"Yes, indeed. Poor Miss Ruby Jewel doesn't know her alphabet, but she relishes a good story. My former master taught me to read at the same time he was learning. I've probably read my mistress a hundred books through the years, and that's not counting the serial stories from periodicals. We like the lively ones. The ones written for boys."

I smiled as I realized that perhaps Jubal didn't mind working here so very much. Perhaps the two old people were friends in their own way. Folks who had been together for sixty years had to have figured out how to make their relationship work.

I had started on down the path when Jubal cleared his throat, and I realized he was shuffling after me. I waited.

He glanced toward the house. "Just wanted you to know 'twas me who saw the VanZeldts carrying on in the woods." His voice was low, so I had to strain to hear. "I heard Miss Ruby Jewel telling you about it."

"Oh." I nodded. "What on earth took you out there in the dark?"

"The mistress likes her black-and-yellow mushrooms, and so do I. I go out hunting for them with a lantern in the night because these days she doesn't like to be left alone when she's awake. She gets lonesome and I worry about her. There's a nice patch of mushrooms that grows near the clearing where I saw them carrying on. You don't guess they're cannibals, do you?" He made a sort of amiable grimace, so I knew he was making a little joke.

I gave an exaggerated shudder. "I hope not," I said, "for the sake of the county."

"I thought you might not believe Miss Ruby Jewel, seeing how she is sometimes, so I just wanted you to know she told the gospel truth about the VanZeldts."

"Thank you, Jubal," I said. "Coming from you, I know it must be."

He nodded, satisfied, and turned to trudge back up to the house, and to share *Robinson Crusoe* with Miss Ruby Jewel.

◆ ◆ ◆

Back at Scuppernong, Michael met me before I could go inside. "Miss Violet."

I looked up from stroking Goblin. "Yes?"

"I reckoned I'd best ask you before I followed Miss Elsa's orders."

My stepmother so seldom bestirred herself to request anything that I was surprised. I straightened. "What does she want?"

"Poppies. She says I'm to plant rows of them big poppies right quick."

I sighed. "I wish she hadn't asked, but I guess you'll have to do as she says."

Michael nodded. "That medicine ain't a good thing, but I know lots of folks use it."

"Besides, I've heard it's bad if people are cut off too abruptly. There's almost no laudanum left in town now. I will speak to her, though."

We looked at each other in silent, concerned understanding. These new people at Scuppernong certainly complicated life.

That night I knocked on Miss Elsa's bedchamber door.

"Come in," she called.

A candle still burned near the bed. My stepmother lay propped against several pillows, her eyes shining, remote, but without the wistful look they held so often. Instead they were filled with a distant delight. As I neared her, I was met by a slightly sweetish odor from the open bottle on the bedside table.

She smiled faintly and held out her hand. I took it. It was thin and hot and dry.

"Dear Violet," she said. "My new, darling daughter."

"I need—" I said, and then was unsure what to say next. What I needed was for her to be an adult. I hoped for reassurance.

"No one needs anything," Miss Elsa murmured. "All is perfect . . . if I have my pint or more a week. . . ." Her voice trailed off, her gaze shifted, her fingers loosened from mine, and she dropped her hand. She was asleep.

CHAPTER 13

PROTECTION

Plantation bells no longer pealed, and neither did the chimes in church towers. Back in April, General Beauregard had called for all the bells in the South to be melted down and molded into cannon, and we answered his call. Many other changes were occurring at Scuppernong Farm.

In these first sultry, glowing, green and golden summer days, Seeley flourished in his new life, once his shoulder was healed, like a busy, skinny weed. His thin face grew brown from forgetting his hat, his countenance became open and trusting, and his big eyes were now lively. His clothing needed constant cleaning and mending.

I began to lighten my own black garments with white collars, violet ribbons, and plain jewelry so that I looked less like a gawky black crow and more like one who'd found random bits of treasure. I also rarely wore my hoop unless I was going to town. With chores to do and with Seeley's and my frequent adventures, it got too hard to maneuver, so I limited myself to one petticoat.

There was more work, of course, with the others here. I had expected to resent this, but somehow I didn't.

I was out back with Laney one day while she plucked a chicken and Cubby played in the dirt and flying feathers. My hands were deep in soapsuds, rubbing and wringing, rubbing and wringing. I held up Sunny's chemise to see if it was clean. "Why do you suppose I don't mind the extra chores these days?" I asked Laney. "Shouldn't I hate every button I sew back on Seeley's shirts and every second I spend scrubbing Sunny's underclothes? But it doesn't bother me. It really doesn't."

Laney gave a wry smile. "Might be because you've grown fond of those folks."

I pondered as I scooped out soggy feathers from the water. "You're right. I have. I thought I didn't want anyone else, but like Pa told me before he left, the circle has simply expanded. Since when did you become so wise, Laney?"

Cubby dumped dirt on his own head.

"I reckon this child has beat the learning into me," Laney said as she brushed him off. "Maybe it has to happen when you're a mother, or you'd never survive."

I didn't tell Laney, because I felt shy and a little silly about my feelings, but since Seeley had come to Scuppernong, I could understand, at least somewhat, how she felt about her little boy. How she wanted to teach him things and protect him. No wonder Laney's and my relationship had changed after Cubby entered the picture—so often her mind must have been crowded with thoughts of him.

A little over a year into it, the war raged on. We heard stories and read terrible accounts in the papers and in my father's letters, but still the actual fighting stayed away from us. Of course, there were privations. Nearly all the lamp oil was gone, with no more to be had, and our spice jars were empty. Sometimes I opened the lids just to sniff inside. Laney had to be clever about making do with the limited food we could grow or scrounge, and our only new clothing was refurbished from out of my mother's trunks.

I was surprised to discover that I was becoming happy again. It happened in unexpected bursts. It would come when Seeley and I were sitting on the sagging front steps, watching the twilight fade and the lawn flush purplish and the woods turn ghostly and the bright moon rise. It might come as I worked with Laney to create a dessert from substitute ingredients to tempt Miss Elsa's finicky appetite, or as I shook my head over something outrageous Dorian had said. Suddenly I would be smiling without a painful edge. I missed my father and remembered Rush with love, but the hole in my heart was starting to fill in.

Dorian was truly being a kind brother to Seeley, and I congratulated myself that it was partly due to my advice. One scene stands out.

Miss Elsa, Sunny, and I are all on the porch, watching Dorian and Seeley throw an India rubber ball back and forth out on the green sweep of grass. Seeley overthrows and the ball ends up in the woods. He waits stiff and tense for Dorian to yell, and I prepare to jump down and stand beside him, but instead Dorian meets my eyes above Seeley's head and hollers, "Did you see the arm on that boy? Whooee, he nearly tossed it clean to Chicataw!" He plunges into the trees to find the ball and Seeley scampers after. "Listen to them laugh," Miss Elsa says.

With so little, Dorian could make Seeley happy.

When he didn't have other work to do, King had begun teaching Seeley to ride Star. He seemed to have exactly the right temperament for the task. I witnessed the first time as he led Star by the reins, trudging round and round the pasture, with Seeley, rigid and pale, in the saddle. Gradually the boy loosened up. After the twentieth (perhaps) round, King gave Seeley the reins and showed him how to handle them himself.

Seeley grabbed King's arm. "You're not leaving, are you?"

"No, I ain't. I be right here alongside you. You don't need me, though. This here mare ain't going nowhere you don't want her to."

"She's sort of polite, isn't she?" Seeley said. "She would think it was rude to do anything to scare me."

Eventually King slipped farther and farther back until Star was trotting smartly along, far ahead. King stood watching, wiping his brow. "If that don't beat all," he mumbled, low, like thunder in distant hills. "Look at Master Seeley already going lickety-split."

Seeley heard. He looked over his shoulder and laughed. "I am, aren't I?"

I could have hugged King. Once Seeley had a little more practice, I would take pleasure in showing off his riding to Dorian.

It had been more than three weeks since my cousins arrived at Scuppernong Farm, and Dorian made no mention of leaving. He and Sunny wandered about alone, which wasn't proper, but what could I do? Sunny's mother should have been the chaperone, but she either ignored them or watched with fond satisfaction as she lounged and dreamed or painted her bad paintings.

Seeley was never so contented as when tromping in the woods, exploring nature. At first, when some responsibility kept me from joining him, I worried about catamounts, alligators, and other beasties with slavering jaws that were rumored to roam the wilds of Mississippi. My anxiety ceased when I saw a few bees following him. I had asked the bees to watch out for Seeley. They were winged like angels, with drawn blades in their tails. If my young cousin had their protection while in the forest, all would be well.

At suppertime Seeley and I would come home from our explorations bubbling over about this animal we had seen or that trail we had taken. When Sunny said one evening, "Really, Vi-let, you act as if you've fallen madly in love with the outdoors. I'm sure it's all very delightful, but kindly spare the rest of us the romantic details," I cautioned Seeley that we must stop boring everyone. Because of what happened after, it was a good thing we ceased our habit of gushing over our activities.

Sunny and I spent two days painting the sitting room. My stepsister had chosen the color an ocher yellow that brightened the drab walls.

On the first day, Dorian helped us move furniture into the center of the room. After that he lounged on the sofa, smoking a pipe, idly watching us paint, snoozing, and offering casual remarks. Once, when I glanced his way, he smiled blindingly and commented on the grand view he had of our figures as we stretched to reach far corners. I threatened him with the brush.

"Don't you get that thing near my coat!" he cried, scuttling out the door.

On the second day of painting, Dorian sauntered off in the morning to be gone till late, claiming he had some mysterious business to do for the Confederacy. I sent a letter with him to mail to

Aunt Lovina and a request for more salt if it could be had for love or money.

"There," I said to Sunny, "if he's performing a task for us, he won't have to feel guilty about not helping with this work. If it's possible for Dorian to feel guilt. Do you think he really has business to do, or is he gone off to play somewhere?"

Sunny shook her head and gave a trill of laughter. "No telling. Men!"

I was carefully outlining the mantel and she was splashing the second coat on the wall nearby. She gave an exaggerated sigh. "They're so nonsensical," she said.

"Who?"

"Men. Isn't that who we were talking about?"

"Well, yes, they are," I readily agreed. "But what are you thinking of in particular?"

"They want a girl to have a dainty little waist they can span with their hands, but they don't want to know how she does it."

"You mean Dorian?"

"Yes. Who else? When he puts his arm around me, he doesn't like the hard feel of my corset. He calls it my armor."

"He's already put his arm around you?"

"Well, of course."

"Ought you to let him? I mean, you've only known him—"

"How else can I be sure I want to know him better? Wouldn't it be awful if I said yes to a gentleman's proposal, and then when he kissed me for the first time, it was nauseating or I found him completely unpracticed?"

My brows drew together. "I don't have any experience in this, but couldn't you tell that you'd enjoy a gentleman's touch by how much you like his personality? And the anticipation building up would be all the more exciting."

"You innocent baby," Sunny said airily, and her attitude didn't annoy me as much as it would have a few weeks earlier. Now I could tell there was affection mixed with the scorn. "It's like this— you know how gentlemen act when they're attracted to a girl?" She paused and flicked her eyes up and down me as I squatted there, paint-spattered and bewildered. "Or maybe you don't. But anyway, there's a kind of energy pinging between a couple that has nothing to do with how competent as kissers they are. For instance, when Mr. Walton embraced me, I was surprised at how nice it was. I mean, he was at least forty, and one of Uncle Frank's friends, and had bushy muttonchop sideburns, and I was only twelve years old. But then he did give such pretty presents and call me his adorable pet, so maybe that's part of the reason it was nice."

"Sunny, only twelve? He was disgusting! He was—"

"Oh, posh! I assure you he was exceedingly rich and admired and I was mature for my age. The point is that, on the other hand, when a certain fellow, forever nameless, caught me out behind the garden shed, his mouth was slimy and strangling, even though he was young and handsome. I think of him now as the Anteater, for obvious reasons. So that just goes to show you never can tell about the physical thrills with a gentleman until you experience them."

I pondered over the reasons Sunny might think of the man as the Anteater, and was disconcerted. "So how does Dorian kiss?"

Sunny's eyes shone. "Delicious. I melt into him and can't think of another thing except my darling."

This was all very interesting, but also disturbing. "Hadn't you better be careful, Sunny? He's such a flirt."

"I *want* someone experienced. I hate the thought of a boy all clumsy and awkward and *young* slobbering over me." She shuddered.

"Well, you'd better not fall too hard. I can't see him settling down soon."

She glanced at me from beneath lowered lids. "Shows what you know."

"Be careful, Sunny. Dorian seems so easygoing, but I have a feeling he can be heartless."

My stepsister stood back to survey the patch of wall she had just finished. "I like a man with an edge. He needs it in order to be dangerously attractive. Dorian is—well, he's the most exciting person I've ever met. And until now he hadn't come across the right girl. He told me so himself." She continued to stare at the wall for another moment with a look of self-satisfaction, then shook herself and blithely touched the tip of my nose with her paintbrush. "Don't you worry about me, li'l Miss Vi-let. Just because you're an ice maiden doesn't mean everyone has to be."

I rubbed the paint off my nose and worried.

The next day, late in the afternoon, I was hugging a squirming Cubby while Laney fixed supper.

"He won't hardly let me hold him anymore," I was saying. "Always wanting to—" I broke off when men's voices sounded from outside, and then a great banging at the front door shook the whole house.

"Where's Seeley?" I said sharply. "Is he with Michael and King?"

Laney drew in her breath. "I don't know. They're out digging a ditch past the far pasture."

I handed her the baby and entered the front hall just in time to see Dorian disappear up the staircase. Miss Elsa and Sunny clutched at each other in the sitting room doorway, wide-eyed.

A crash sounded, and shards of glass from one of the amber side-lights came flying in, smashed by a bayonet.

I hurriedly opened the front door a crack. It was torn from my hands and pushed wide by the ragtag group on the porch. There were five of them, their gaunt, bewhiskered faces blackened from the smoke of pine knot campfires, their hats pulled low, and their clothing, partial remnants of both armies' uniforms, filthy and shabby. They smelled. Three of them brandished rifles, one clutched a cruel-looking butcher's knife, and one had a sword strapped to his belt. Although he was just as ragged as the others, there was a set to the jaw of the sword-carrying man and a masterful cast to his eyes that showed he was the leader.

In a flash I remembered the horrific stories I had heard about bushwhacker outlaws. Randomly I hoped they would shoot rather than stab us.

"We've come for your valuables, miss," the leader said. "Give 'em here and we won't hurt no one."

"We don't have any valuables." I was amazed that my voice didn't shake. "We're poor farmers."

"O' course. And you don't got no stock and no money hid away no place. Where's your menfolk?"

"Not at home." *Please, please hide well, Dorian, and don't return, King and Michael.* And my Seeley—where was he?

They shoved past me. The knife holder pried open the hall chest with the point of his blade and broke the lid.

"I would have given you the key," I said.

"Takes too long," said the leader over his shoulder, his sword clanking on the steps as he and two of his companions surged up the stairs.

Sunny, Miss Elsa, Laney, and I cowered in the hall, flinching and staring at one another, while the sounds of smashing and clattering and tearing seemed to go on forever. *Not my harp. Not our books.*

"Should I give them the money Mr. Dancey left?" Miss Elsa asked in a low voice.

"Not yet," I whispered back. "It's all we've got. Is it well hidden?"

"Yes. It's in—"

"Don't tell me where."

Then came the pounding of feet as the three who had gone upstairs descended, pushing Dorian in front, with the barrel of one of their guns poking in his back. Dorian flashed a quick, painful grin our way. "Ladies, don't you worry. Ouch! Watch the waistcoat, boys." They pushed him harder and he stumbled, so they grabbed his arms and dragged him out onto the porch and down the steps, banging his shins all the way.

I couldn't think of anything except that I mustn't leave Dorian alone. Perhaps if I stayed at his side, they wouldn't hurt him. I scurried over and stuck as close as I could until one of the bushwhackers took me by my arms and moved me bodily out of the way.

They led my cousin to the great magnolia tree. One of them procured a rope from his scraggy mule, formed a noose on one end, and threw it up around a thick, high limb. They placed the noose around Dorian's neck and pulled him up until he gasped for breath, then lowered him.

"Where's your gold?" the leader demanded.

"Don't—don't have any," Dorian panted. "You already got my ring and cravat pin."

They pulled him up again, all the while scrutinizing us four women. Sunny was sobbing into my shoulder.

Miss Elsa gave a little cry. "Stop. I'll get the money." She scuttled back into the house. The bushwhackers lowered Dorian and waited for her return. At one point one of them said something to my cousin, and Dorian slapped him on the back and laughed. It was brave of Dorian, to act as if they were comrades when they might hang him any second, but somehow terrible to watch. Miss Elsa came scurrying out the door, holding forth her purse in trembling hands. She shoved it at the leader and he counted the contents.

"This is all dang Confederate bills. Where's your gold?" he demanded.

Miss Elsa shook her head. "We don't have any."

"Ha!" the man cried, and once again they heaved Dorian up.

Something had to be done. They would kill Dorian, or we would lose every last penny we had—or both. I strode deliberately up to the tree, looked at my cousin struggling for breath on the end of the rope, and said calmly, "Dorian, supper's ready." I turned to the bushwhackers. "Would y'all care for some ham and biscuits and pie? We'd be much obliged if you'd join us. The food's getting cold while y'all are playing around out here."

Their mouths fell open, and one of them gave a snort of

amusement. Then, to my surprise, they lowered Dorian and removed the noose.

Laney hurried into the house and returned outside with steaming plates. None of the ladies could eat, but Dorian sat with his tormentors, shoveling food into his mouth, joining in their loud, bragging talk, and occasionally laughing. He amazed me.

The thieves left soon after. They didn't have the cows or Star, thank goodness, but they took away Gus-the-mule; Dorian's nervous Grindill, who stamped, plunged, and tried to knock into the horsenapper with his great, bony head; a bag of squawking chickens; and just one goose dangling by a rope from a belt. I had heard the geese hissing and honking, so perhaps they'd made too much trouble to be worth catching, or maybe even bushwhackers didn't want to take everything we had.

"They'll be sorry they stole Grindill," Dorian said, glaring after them with a hard set to his mouth. "They'll soon find no bummer can ride him."

"They didn't get all the money," Miss Elsa said. "I stuffed the gold pieces into my stockings; they're weighing me down. But I had to give them all the paper bills in order to be believable."

We congratulated her on her quick, clever, out-of-character thinking.

"Why, you're acting like a real grown-up mother," Sunny said.

Miss Elsa gave a tremulous smile, fluttered her hands, and then dashed away from us, probably anxious for her medicine.

As we went into the house, Dorian put his arm about my waist in what I hoped Sunny realized was a cousinly manner. "Good thinking on your part, coz. How could you guess half-starved men would take home-cooked food over a hanging?"

"I couldn't," I whispered, and tears suddenly blurred my sight and I began to shiver.

Dorian squeezed my waist while Sunny watched with narrowed eyes.

"I'm just thankful they were only starving," she said coolly. "There are other things to lose besides animals and money."

Dorian gave me a swift wink and deserted me for Sunny's side. "And there are things worth protecting and fighting for, beautiful Sunny."

She thawed visibly and edged closer to him. "It was so terrible when I thought they were going to murder you, Dorian. If they had, I would've—I would've—just screamed and screamed and never stopped."

Michael and King came wandering up, and Laney filled them in on what had happened while they were out digging ditches. King's face was a study of alarm.

"Where's Master Seeley?" he asked frantically. His voice seemed to echo around deep in his chest before it found its way out.

I caught King's sleeve. "He wasn't with you?"

He wagged his head.

"Then where can he be?" I started to head toward the woods but Dorian stopped me.

"He's probably up a tree somewhere. Probably been watching the whole thing. I'll go look for him after we survey the damage."

Tiredly we moved through the house. The bushwhackers had knocked apart furniture right and left. The destruction was dreadful, but I hardly cared. It could have been so much worse. All of my muscles unclenched when I saw that my harp and dulcimer were untouched.

"They ruined things for no reason," Sunny said. "How could they possibly think we had money stashed in a wooden chair?"

Stuffing was pulled from the sofa and armchairs, and bricks had been knocked loose from about the fireplaces. The bittern stared up accusingly with one beady eye, its belly slashed open. The bookcase was smashed and volumes strewn and torn. I began frantically gathering scattered pages but stopped myself. Soon enough I would mend each one.

When I discovered the empty stalls of the barn, with Star and the cows missing, I knew where Seeley was. I lifted my skirts, ran across the field, and plunged into the woods, briars tearing at my legs, until I reached our hideaway. Before I pulled up the trapdoor, I called loudly, "Seeley! It's me!" so he wouldn't be frightened.

"Violet?" squeaked a small voice out of the blackness. A soft lowing sounded from one of the cows down in the hole.

"Oh, my dear," I said, descending the ramp, "you've been squatting down here in the dark and the standing water all this time."

"I didn't dare light the candle," he said, stretching up now so that the late-afternoon brightness could reach his face, "in case the bummers could see it through the cracks."

I hugged him. "And you saved Star and Lily and June. You're amazing!"

Together we led the animals up the ramp and back to the barn. As we walked, he told me what had happened.

He had been playing in the pasture when he caught sight of the ragged strangers approaching far down the road. He quickly drove the cows and led the mare by her bridle to the hole in the ground. "I wasn't scared of Star, but I didn't dare try to save Grindill, and there was no time to get the mule or warn y'all."

"I'd say it's good riddance to Grindill."

Seeley's thin cheeks were flushed and bright. "They didn't take the chickens, did they? I've been worrying about Rowena and all the others."

"They took some."

His face fell. "I should've saved them."

I gave him a little shove. "Goose. You couldn't rescue everything. You're a hero. You saved one horse and all our milk and cheese and butter."

As we approached the house, the thunder of hooves sounded. Grindill came galloping up the lane with a ragged bit of rope dangling from his sweat-lathered neck and, though it seemed impossible, a smug expression on his long face. He had broken free to return to his owner. When Dorian saw the horse, he slapped his thigh and laughed. "I knew they couldn't hold on to Grindill."

That evening, after everyone else had gone upstairs, I sat alone in the sitting room, too unsettled after the events of the day to sleep, and began to knit a gray soldier's stocking. The lamp smoked, so that my eyes streamed. I sniffed and sopped up tears with a wad of snipped yarn.

I could feel someone watching, and when I glanced up, Dorian immediately came to my side. "Who's been making you cry, Violet?" he demanded fiercely. "Was it Sunny? If it is, I'll—"

I stopped him. "It's only the smoky lamp. The last oil we've got is terrible."

He looked as if he didn't believe me. I sensed a confusion in him, as if this protective emotion he was experiencing was unexpected and unaccustomed. He nodded slowly, then, as the fumes reached his own eyes. "You tell me, though. You tell me if anyone ever makes you unhappy and I'll fix them."

I could only wonder—if it had been Sunny making me weep, what would he have done?

CHAPTER 14

THE ROBBERS' LAIR

"Laney Lou!"

Laney frowned and glanced up from the cornmeal mush she was stirring. "You haven't called me that in years, and I didn't like it back then."

"Sorry, Laney Lou." I put my arm around her waist. "Guess what I was thinking of when I woke up in the middle of the night?"

"I bet I know." She waggled her eyebrows. "You were fondly remembering what's-his-name—that Pratt fellow."

I snatched off her head wrap. "Don't say that even in jest. Guess for real."

"Stop it," Laney said, grabbing back the kerchief. "I can't guess."

"The Lodge! Remember our old robbers' lair!"

A light kindled in Laney's eyes. "Oh," she breathed. "We loved that place, didn't we? Why'd we stop going there?"

I shrugged. "We got too old and they kept making us do responsible things. Finally we forgot about it. But when I awoke with it in my head, I could hardly hold myself back from jumping up and paddling downriver right then."

"You've got to take Seeley—I mean, Master Seeley—there," Laney said. "Be sure to rub on Aunty's lemongrass and basil salve, though. You know how bad the mosquitoes are."

"You don't have to call him master. Not an eight-year-old."

"I sure do." Laney's voice was quiet and firm. "Sometimes you don't understand the world we live in, *Miss* Vi."

I dismissed this with a flick of my hand. "Scuppernong isn't the world."

"It is with Mr. Dorian and Miss Sunny here."

I sighed but didn't press the issue. "Well, thank goodness Dorian's gone till day after tomorrow. The whole house seems more relaxed with him away, doesn't it?"

"Even though Miss Sunny's moping loud enough," Laney said. "Where'd he go? He took King, didn't he?"

"Yes." I dipped out a spoonful of mush and dribbled honey over it. "He's visiting friends in Holly Springs. Anyway, I already woke up Seeley and told him to get ready to go in the canoe. I didn't tell him where, though. How about you and Cubby come along? The work can wait for once. We've gotten most of the bummers' damage patched up."

"Uh-uh. I'm not taking any baby of mine out on any river. Y'all have fun. I'll pack a picnic. Remember how we always toted one?"

"Because we stayed gone all day. And that's what I aim to do with Seeley." I sucked the spoon clean and left the kitchen with a spring in my step at the prospect of this outing.

Seeley and I set off as soon as the lunch was ready. His thin arms strained with the paddle in front. He wore his red satin cape—from which I had removed the lace ruffle—and appeared mystical and elf-like, with the morning fog rising up from the river in wispy patches like white steam from a kettle.

"You're doing fine for your first time," I assured him. "Try to slice through rather than slapping, though. I'm a terrible smacker myself, but I bet you'll get better than me at quiet paddling. Laney and Rush were both good at it, while I spoiled the atmosphere. I hate it when I spoil atmospheres."

Our paddles sloshed and splashed through the sleek river—shiny and shimmery like green-black watered silk. Because we were inexperienced paddlers, we hugged the bank.

The air smelled of moss and wet earth, pine straw and honeysuckle. Varying hues in the wall of leaves beside us blended into one thick summer green. The woods were busy and vibrant, everything always moving. Trunks swayed ever so slightly, leaves quivered almost imperceptibly, insects darted, squirrels and birds left branches quaking in their wake.

Soon the fog burned off the river, and stinging flies and mosquitoes buzzed close. They didn't land because we had slathered Anarchy's insect repellent all over us. I pushed up my sleeves and adjusted my bonnet, as already the day was heating up. Seeley's hat would have to stay on—our brilliant Mississippi sun could do quick damage to noses and foreheads when reflected off water.

After we had canoed for twenty or so minutes, the bank rose and turned rocky. We paddled beside a great bluff, where trickles of water seeped out of the stone, staining it with minerals. It reminded me of Moses striking the rock to make water gush forth for the Children of Israel.

"We're almost there," I said.

"Almost where?" Seeley asked. "You haven't told me where we're going."

"I'll tell you in a minute."

A rivulet cut through the bluff, and we steered the canoe into the gap. We took it as far as it could go, to a pool where the water gurgled against sheer cliffs on two sides and lapped softly on a narrow, sandy beach on a third.

"Can we stay here?" Seeley begged. "I want to swim."

"Later," I said, pulling off my boots and stockings. "First I need to show you the best robbers' lair in all the world. If it's still standing. And safe to go inside. As Heath Blackstock, you have to see it. Who knows what villains lurk there, needing to be banished?"

"Who does the lair belong to? Really."

"Some rich man from New Orleans had it built for his hunting lodge. He named it Carter Hall, but Rush and Laney and I always called it the Lodge. The owner didn't use it long, and it had already been abandoned for years when we found it. Many a happy day we spent there. We were careful to never mention it around grown-ups for fear they'd order us not to go inside again. It really wasn't the safest spot to play, but we didn't care a pin for that." I hitched up my skirt and stepped into the pool to drag the canoe ashore. Seeley took off his own boots and jumped out. Bathtub-warm water caressed our calves and ankles.

We replaced our boots and climbed up out of the little gulch, using fern-sprouted stone ledges that almost seemed planned for such a purpose. Something grew on them that released a wild, wet, heady scent when we crushed its leaves beneath us.

For just a moment, at the top, with the forest so tangled and overgrown even this early in the summer, I worried that I wouldn't remember the route. But when I stopped thinking and thrust through the dense undergrowth, somehow the right way beckoned. Perhaps there remained a nearly invisible thread of path that I unconsciously recognized.

"Sorry," I said after I accidentally let a plumy pine branch whip back into Seeley's face. "It makes you admire the first settlers, doesn't it? If they left the rivers behind, everywhere they went was like this. When we used to come here, Rush always carried a scythe to cut through at the beginning of the season."

"Let's bring one next time and I'll use it." Seeley chopped at some vines with the side of his hand.

He trotted ahead now, jumping over clumps and darting here and there. I was glad his red cape was easy to follow from a distance. I could only hope we weren't wallowing in poison ivy and picking up ticks.

"Wait!" I called when he got too far ahead. "You don't know where to go."

He paused impatiently, his cheeks flushed and his body tense with eagerness. Suddenly the way was easier and I stopped in my tracks. We had stumbled on a clearing, with wild grasses trampled down all around and with only one great tree left standing near the middle. It had grayish bark, a twisted, gnarled trunk, and very prominent aboveground roots. Nearby, a wide ring of stones circled the blackened remains of a huge bonfire.

An eerie sensation crept over me. This evidence that people, not long ago, had lingered on this spot made me uneasy. On our many trips here in the past, we had never met another soul. Bushwhackers, deserters, and other dangerous flotsam and jetsam of war all came to mind.

"Who could have been way out here?" I whispered. "And lit such a gigantic fire?"

Seeley's eyes grew large, and I realized my voice had taken on a spooky tone. I hastened to reassure him. "Probably hunters. Hunters tromp around everywhere." Except why would hunters need such a big cooking fire?

And then the words of Miss Ruby Jewel echoed—"They dance around a bonfire at dead of night in the middle of the woods." The VanZeldts. Even though Shadowlawn was over a mile away, it was still the closest habitation. This might even be Shadowlawn property since the doctor now owned many acres stretching along the river.

My disquiet mounted as we approached the Lodge. The route was too effortless to lead to a building abandoned for years; a path had been cut through. Had someone taken up residence?

The structure still stood two stories tall, although the roof had caved partially in. A sapling grew where the roof was missing, and vines shrouded the windows. I blew out my breath in a little sigh of satisfaction. No one could be living in this ruin. Clearly the place was as empty as it had been on that long-ago day when we first discovered it.

It looked much more derelict than I remembered, and every bit as romantic. There was something both frightening and beautiful in the decay. Built of half-timbered plaster and bark-covered logs, these walls had been erected in no typical local style. Instead, the

Lodge reminded me of some haunted, fairy-tale manor house. Its eaves were low-pitched and its windows (amazingly, mostly intact) were diamond-paned.

A bird flapped up out of the dark hole gaping where the chimney had tumbled down and broke the spell. Seeley shuffled his feet and tugged at my sleeve. "Look!" he cried, pointing. "Ears!"

Grub-white, half-circle lichens clustered in the rotting center of a log in the wall. They did indeed resemble a garden of grotesque ears feeding on the old wood.

He plucked two and held them up against his hair. "I've got ears in the back of my head."

"That's supposed to be 'eyes,' " I said, wincing at the sight. " '*Eyes* in the back of your head.' You look . . . disgusting."

He grinned and offered me a set. When I shrank away from the misshapen things, he chased me with them. I ducked and ran into the trees, slowed from the burden of the picnic basket, my flapping black skirt, and my ill-fitting boots. We were snagged by briars and smacked and scraped by branches as we dashed. My bonnet fell back on its ribbons and bounced against my shoulders. The snood beneath was ripped from my hair by a twig. I stuffed it in my pocket, letting my wispy locks fall loose. Finally we ended up, breathless, back in front of the Lodge.

"It's perfect!" Seeley yelled. "A perfect robbers' lair."

I put my finger to my lips. "You'd better hush if you want to surprise the villains," I said, and then added, "Mr. Heath Blackstock, sir."

"Aw, villains are always so stupid they wouldn't even notice *you* clomping around."

I pretended to thump him on the head, and we stifled giggles.

Mingled with the creepers clambering up the walls were yellow climbing roses. The air was sweet with their perfume and murmurous with bees. I wondered if they were *my* bees. Seeley plucked a bloom and presented it to me. I thanked him and tucked it behind my ear.

In spite of the general decay, the Lodge's walls still stood straight. I assured myself there'd be no danger for us to enter. The plank door had fallen from the hinges. It leaned over the entrance now. I lifted it out of the way and cautiously poked my head inside.

A clear, dim green light filled the front room. It was as it had been seven years earlier—empty except for rubble on the sagging floor, clinging dirt daubers' nests, and a pale, ghostly rag of a curtain dangling over one window. It had made us sad that every last stick of furniture had been removed from the place. The staircase had collapsed, which was just as well since I didn't want Seeley trying to go upstairs into that dark, precarious space. We picked our way through the debris to the doorway opposite. Our movements echoed.

A few sunbeams filtered in through veiled windows in the next room. Yes, there still stood the stumps we had rolled in for chairs, and there—I caught in my breath sharply—

A body lay against the wall.

CHAPTER 15

THE SOLDIER

It was a man, head tipped back and lips slightly parted, with jutting cheekbones and closed, sunken eyes. A scanty blanket covered him to his waist.

"Violet, you're blocking the way. Let me see." Seeley squeezed under my arm. "Gosh—is he dead?" he whispered.

Before I knew what my cousin was doing, he had snatched up a broken stair spindle and crossed the few feet to poke the body in the protruding ribs.

"Seeley!" I cried, but watched, frozen, as the man jerked and groaned and his eyes slowly fluttered open. A pulse beat visibly in his throat. Alive, then.

"Who's here?" he murmured.

I grabbed Seeley's hand and stumbled backward and would have run out but my feet wouldn't take me. All I could do was stare.

The man lay on a pallet of pine boughs. Their scent hung in the air, along with a pungent, sharp herbal aroma I didn't recognize.

He raised himself up on his elbows. His arms were skeletal.

"Are—" His voice sounded hoarse, as if from disuse. He cleared his throat. "Tell me you're real."

I could see his face better now, and for a fraction of a second was caught by it. Even so emaciated, with skin like yellowish wax and with a messy growth of dark beard and greasy hair falling every which way, this was a handsome man. The lips were firm, the nose straight, the jaw square. And not old—probably in his mid-twenties.

My mouth had been hanging open. Now I closed it, swallowed, and said, "We're real, all right. I beg your pardon. We didn't know anyone would be at this place, and, well, you're a bit of a shock. We'll go now." I tugged at Seeley's hand. "Sorry to have disturbed you," I said over my shoulder.

"No. Please, miss," the man said, "don't go yet. I haven't seen another person except—I haven't seen anyone in so long."

I turned slowly back around. His expression was strained, but eager.

"Look, Violet!" Seeley cried. He had left my side and trotted across the room to nudge his boot against a mound of ragged clothing stuffed in the blackened hole of the crumbling fireplace. A tattered, filthy blue coat with brass buttons was visible. "That's a Yankee uniform. He's a Yankee. Maybe a deserter."

I should have noticed immediately that the man's accent was all wrong. "Seeley, come away now," I said, starting for the door once more.

In a note of desperation the man said harshly, "Don't leave!" His voice softened. "Please don't leave. I won't hurt you. I'm wounded. Can't even walk. I would never harm you. Please, please don't go yet."

I hadn't realized he was injured; I had thought he was only resting.

Now I saw that the stains on the uniform in the fireplace were stiff, clotted blood. Also, a sickroom smell—an odor I recognized from my work at the hospital—lurked under the other scents of the place.

He was the enemy, but an enemy helpless and hurt is entirely different from an enemy in health and power. I set down the basket.

Even if I didn't know what to do next, Seeley did. The Christian thing. "My name is Seeley Rushton," he said, and knelt at the man's side. "And I own Panola Plantation. That's near Richmond."

"I was"—a slight tremor passed over the soldier's features—"yes, I was in Virginia last summer. Beautiful country."

I stiffened. Was he remembering the men he had killed and the homes he had ransacked in the beautiful country?

He raised a hand for Seeley to shake. "I'm Thomas Lynd. Lieutenant Thomas Lynd of the Fifth Connecticut." He turned to me. "And you are Miss Violet?"

How did he know? Oh yes. Seeley had said my name a moment ago. I nodded slightly. "Violet Dancey from Scuppernong Farm, just upriver."

"Pleased to meet you, Miss Dancey." Lieutenant Lynd looked back at Seeley and said seriously, "Seeley Rushton is a good name, but I was expecting you to say Heath Blackstock, because of that daring cape of yours."

Seeley flushed with pleasure. "You know the Heath Blackstock books? I made my mother buy me every new one that came out." His eyes grew larger and his jaw dropped. "Wait! Your name . . . You said your name is Thomas Lynd. Did you . . . ? You wrote them! You wrote my books?"

The soldier answered, "Yes, I suppose I did."

"I can't believe it," Seeley said with an expression of wonder. "I can't believe you're right here."

"You only 'suppose' you wrote them?" I asked, puzzled.

"It seems so many ages ago, it's hard to believe it really was me," Lieutenant Lynd said.

"Will you write more?" Seeley asked, wriggling with delight. Evidently this man was his hero.

"Maybe. I don't know."

I hadn't been aware the character came from a book. How . . . *interesting* that a real, published author was here in the Lodge.

"Can I see your gun and your sword?" Seeley asked enthusiastically.

"I'm afraid I don't have them anymore. Actually I don't have anything anymore but what you see here. I didn't even know my uniform was over there. It's unwearable, isn't it?"

"Completely," I said. "Someone's taking care of you, aren't they?" A tin water pail with dipper, a small covered cast-iron kettle, and a bucket (probably serving as the chamber pot) clustered beside him. I didn't wait for his answer. "Where were you injured?"

" 'Where' as in geographical location or 'where' as in part of my body?" Lieutenant Lynd gave a wince that might have started as a smile. "Probably both, eh? It's hard to collect myself. To rightly recall." His voice was deep and quiet. He drew his hand down his face, making it appear even more haggard. "It happened after the battle near Shiloh Church. Up in Tennessee. Perhaps you've heard about it. Terrible, terrible losses on both sides. So ironic that *shiloh* means 'peace' in Hebrew. Anyway, I made it through that nightmare, but three of us rode a little ways south afterward to—to look things over."

"To spy!" I cried sharply, holding back the tremor in my voice.

"No, miss. Forgive me for contradicting, but if we'd been spying, we wouldn't have worn uniforms. We went just to look things over, trying to stay out of everyone's way. We weren't far from some northern Mississippi town—didn't even know the name. We'd gotten off our horses to drink at a sweet little spring. Next thing we knew, a popping noise sounded and a bullet whined past my ear like a giant mosquito." At first he spoke slowly, with pauses between phrases, but gradually the words poured out faster and faster. "Never saw who did the shooting. Something knocked me flat, and when the gunfire stopped and it was silent for a while, I dared look around. They'd left us all for dead. Wheeler's face was in the spring, with the back of his head missing and red spreading out in the water. He died just like that. Never raised up at all. I remember thinking, *Dash it! Now we can't get a drink.* Imagine that—thinking such a thing with my good friend not ten minutes gone."

"You were in shock," I said. "People's thoughts are distorted at such a time, I expect."

He made no response to my words—just gazed at nothing as if he hadn't heard. "Jorgenson was lying nearby, all covered with blood but with his chest still rising. I didn't even realize I was hurt until I couldn't move. And then when I glanced down, I kept staring. It's a weird and fascinating thing to see your hip clean blown away, both joint and socket. Couldn't believe it was really me. My body. I got my coat off and pressed it against the wound, but that was all

I could do. There was no real pain—then. When I saw the state I was in, I figured the end had come for Jorgenson and me, as well as Wheeler. All we could do was wait till we bled out."

"Were you afraid?" I asked.

"Excuse me?" the soldier said, seemingly startled at the sound of my voice.

"Were you scared when you thought you were dying?" I held my breath, waiting for his answer. It was important. Isaac Lafarge at the hospital had said he was not afraid of death, and perhaps if this man had not been either, it would mean that Rush might not have been frightened. I was still haunted by the possibility of my twin's terror in his last minutes of life.

Lieutenant Lynd looked thoughtfully at me and said gently, "There was no fear."

"What did you think about then?" Seeley asked. "My parents died. . . ."

"I thought about home and how I'd never look upon everyone I loved again in this life."

"Horrible," I said.

"You would think so," he said, "but rather I felt a deep calm. I knew everything would be all right with them. And I was curious to see where I was going."

Isaac Lafarge had also said he was curious. Both soldiers seemed to have considered the moment before death as if they were beginning a curious adventure. No fear.

The lieutenant continued, "I supposed I'd go to heaven since I've always tried to be a decent human being. I started to pray and then everything went dark. Must have fainted."

I guessed it was possible for a few Yankees to slip through the pearly gates.

"When I regained consciousness, I was being lifted onto a sort of litter," Lieutenant Lynd went on.

"By whom?" I asked.

"Didn't know for a while because I fainted again. This time when I came to, I was lying here in this place, and Jorgenson was stretched out across from me. Such a relief to see him there. To know he was still alive and I wasn't alone. And—"

He hesitated, and Seeley and I, in the same breath, said, "And what?"

Lieutenant Lynd shook himself as if to awaken further. "Please." He motioned to the tree stumps. "I'm forgetting my manners. Forgive me. It's just so good to talk to people. Won't you take a seat? I would offer you some refreshment, but all I have is water."

This wounded soldier, none too clean, lying in a derelict ruin in the middle of nowhere, was a gentleman. Unexpected in a Yankee. It was clear the soldier was not being given enough to eat, and his plight tugged at me. I lifted the picnic basket and jiggled it slightly. "We have food—enough for three, if you'd join us."

Seeley awkwardly dragged a couple of stumps closer. I pulled out a cloth to spread on the floor beside the man and laid out plates for the fried chicken and corn bread spread with strawberry preserves.

Perched on the edge of my stump, I smoothed down my skirts, waiting impatiently for the next part of the story but expecting the poor fellow to commence tearing into the chicken first.

His eyes started a little at the sight of the meal. However, he made no move to reach for it. "I think perhaps I can sit up. I haven't dared try before, but . . ." The muscles in his face and neck stood out as he strained to raise himself.

"Seeley," I said, "help him."

The boy rushed forward and, with an impressive gentleness, assisted the soldier in scooting backward to lean against the cracked plaster wall.

Lieutenant Lynd still didn't touch the food. Instead he carried on with his story as if he needed to keep on relating it now that he had begun. "Our rescuers were so peculiar. Unlike any people I've ever seen before. They looked peculiar and they walked peculiar, sort of melting or flowing—no, *seeping*—and they were utterly silent. They're handsome people; I call them the Shadows."

The Shadows. They could only be the VanZeldts. I had thought of them that way when I had seen them with the doctor in town.

"Then," the lieutenant continued, "the old woman put a cloth soaked in ashes and lye into my wound. She did it again and again. Each time mashed flesh and splinters of bone came away with the cloth until the wound became pale as raw chicken flesh."

I glanced down at the still-untouched fried chicken and suppressed a shudder.

"She laid a poultice on it," he went on, "and gave me something to drink. I slept for a long time after that. When I awoke, Jorgenson was gone." His mouth worked a little. "He must have died as I slept, without us ever exchanging another word. I tried to use motions to ask the Shadows about it, but they gave no response. Every evening since then, one or two of the younger ones come. I haven't seen the old one again. They bring water and food, and they change the poultice. A sort of flexible gristle seems to have filled in the hole in my hip. It doesn't hurt anymore; in a week or two maybe I'll try standing. If it's possible." He opened and shut his hands, stretching the fingers. "I hate to think how weak all my muscles have grown from disuse. Including my brain, I'm afraid."

"You think you're not as smart anymore?" Seeley asked. I was glad Seeley was there to ask the silly questions I was thinking.

Lieutenant Lynd's smile ended almost before it started. "My memories of the past weeks come and go. I'm never sure what's real and what's not. For instance, I think that once, early on, they brought a snake. They held its head forward and its tongue flicked in and out as they carried it right up to my face. At least that's how I remember it. Maybe I was delirious from the pain, or maybe it was a dream. I've had loads of dreams lying here."

A snake . . . My mouth was dry and every one of my senses was on edge. A Yankee . . . the VanZeldts . . . serpents . . . this whole situation was too uncanny. My very softening toward him put me on my guard again. Carefully I licked my lips. Should I take Seeley away right now? He couldn't stop us.

I must have had an odd expression on my face because Lieutenant Lynd said hastily, "Of course it sounds as if I've lost my senses. Maybe I have." He rubbed his forehead. "The solitude for so long. And I shouldn't have related such grisly details. This whole setting is unfit for a lady. I'm so sorry."

My days of being sheltered from grisly details had ended when I began working at the hospital. I might have told him that, but I did not—it was nice for a young man to expect me to be sheltered.

He continued, "It's been a long time since I've communicated with a gently bred lady. Especially one with a rose in her tresses."

The warmth rushed to my cheeks, and I reached up to snatch out the flower but lowered my hand when Seeley said proudly, "I gave it to her."

So I left the blossom but tried to smooth my hair now that I remembered it hung down every which way. "I'm afraid my appearance isn't at all that of a lady. I must look a mess. We had a wild time coming through the woods."

"And you've got dirt all over your face, Violet," Seeley commented smugly.

I frantically tried to rub away the grime with my fingers.

"Still there," Seeley said.

The soldier smiled then, slowly, the first real smile he had shown. "Here," he said, "allow me." He groped for a rag and dipped it into his water pail. "This is clean. They brought it just last night."

I hesitated a second and then moved closer. He wiped my cheeks as softly as if I were Cubby's age.

"Thank you," I whispered, thinking how ridiculous that had just been. And then, looking down at my lap with confusion, I said, "So, you can't talk to your rescuers?" Was that the right term for the VanZeldts?

He shook his head. "I speak to them. I thank them and that sort of thing, but they don't respond. Of course, much of the time I'm asleep when they come." His yearning eyes strayed to our picnic.

I caught the glance and pushed the food toward him. "Please, sir, eat."

"I will, but won't you have some too?"

The starving gentleman was waiting politely for me to partake first. A lump grew in my throat.

I handed him a plate. "We're not very hungry," I said. "We had a big breakfast."

"We did no—" Seeley started to say, but I kicked his leg and he stopped.

Lieutenant Lynd saw the kick and smiled at me with his eyes. "Forgive my slowness," he said, breaking off a bit of corn bread. His hand shook so that he could scarcely raise it to his mouth. "I mustn't—eat—too quickly. Or too much at first."

"You're right. It might make you ill. They do feed you, though, don't they?" I asked. "I saw the kettle there." I was trying not to stare at the soldier's bare chest (although, believe me, there was nothing sensual about protruding washboard ribs).

"One of them comes every night bringing stew and changing the dressing and emptying—"

He ceased talking and I knew he meant the slop bucket. I quickly lowered my eyes.

We were silent now in order to let him eat. The only sound was his quiet, careful chewing.

I was sitting in a cabin in the woods with an unkempt, bare-chested Yankee soldier. Oddly my heart pounded as if I were afraid, but at some point I had stopped being afraid.

After a while I spoke. "The town you were near when you were shot is probably Chicataw, and I believe the spring you were drinking from is Freshwater Springs. They found a dead Federal soldier there several weeks back." I didn't mention how upset the locals were that the water had been polluted. "Your 'Shadows' sound like the VanZeldts—they're the servants of a man who lives nearby. I didn't know there was an old one. I've only seen the three others."

"Do they move peculiarly?"

"Very. I might use the word 'slither.' "

Lieutenant Lynd choked as if he had started to laugh but it wouldn't quite come out.

"I want to see the VanZeldts," Seeley said. "I want to see people who slither. Do they look like snakes?"

"No, but they're certainly unusual," Lieutenant Lynd said. "However, they've saved my life. Perhaps are still saving it. Using some sort of native herbal knowledge. Whatever it is, it works. How long has it been? How long since Shiloh? I have no idea how much time has passed."

"That was the beginning of April, and now"—I paused, trying to remember the date—"it's May twenty-ninth."

He sighed. "So many weeks alone. Except for birds flitting in, and sometimes a squirrel. They were completely unafraid and I spoke to them. I told myself they understood."

I nodded, thinking of my bees.

"Once in the darkness," he added, "something walked right across my legs. Maybe an opossum. Normally I would have been startled, but at the time it seemed as if I were just part of the earth."

As I reached down to place more corn bread on Lieutenant Lynd's plate, he clutched my wrist. I was so startled I could only gape at him.

"Hold still," he whispered. "Both of you. Don't move."

I warily followed his eyes to the doorway. A shadow flickered. Then—

A black-and-white animal waddled in, followed by her fluffy babies. Three of them. Slowly the lieutenant released me.

"Skunks." Seeley barely moved his lips.

We sat frozen in silence while the little family leisurely explored. They poked about in corners and nudged the kettle with their noses. One of them sniffed Seeley's boots. Seeley was shaking— whether from fear of setting them off or hilarity at the situation, I could not tell. I myself had to choke back the laughter bubbling up in my throat.

After what seemed ages, the skunks calmly left the room.

Seeley crept to the door and reported back that they had gone outside.

Then we did laugh, all of us. Lieutenant Lynd had a very nice laugh—a very present and aware one—and I was happy to hear it.

"Whew." The lieutenant wiped his brow.

"I thought skunks came out at night," Seeley said.

"I thought so too," Lieutenant Lynd said. "They've never come in here before."

"Well, Lieutenant," I said, "you wouldn't have felt you were simply part of the earth anymore if they had sprayed you." And then I worried that he would think I was making fun of him. However, he didn't seem offended. I thought of all those dark nights he had lain there. "So you have no light at all?"

"Only the moon," he said. "There's a gap in the vines on that window. Lying here, I could watch the sky through it. The daylight would fade to gray, and I'd stare out there at the one bright star in the same place every night."

"It's probably not a star," Seeley said, visibly proud of his knowl-edge. "It's probably a planet. They're bigger and brighter."

"Probably so." Lieutenant Lynd's hands lay still in his lap. Once again he was gazing into nothing. Sometimes the man slipped into a remoteness that reminded me of Miss Elsa, as if he had forgotten we were present even while he was speaking.

I glanced about the nearly empty room. "You've had a great deal of time to spend thinking. However did you pass the time? The lying here in silence and lonesomeness and idleness?"

He bent his head. "I saw portents in everything." He indicated a vine that had worked its way through the plaster. "See this?"

A long tendril ending in a tight yellow bud waved right next to the soldier's pallet. I nodded.

He touched it lightly. "I told myself that when and if it blos-somed, someone would find me. And you two have come, haven't you? And now I can hear someone—two someones—breathing besides myself and I don't feel the trees whispering and pressing close anymore. Which, I would have to say, is much more normal."

He was looking at me now with an unexpectedly sharp, clear glance that made me nervous. I bent over hurriedly and began to pack away the empty plates. "You say one of the VanZeldts comes daily? At what time?"

"Right around dusk."

It could only have been early afternoon, but suddenly I was anx-ious to go. "We'd better leave."

He didn't urge us to remain. "Thank you," he said. "For every-thing."

Something in his tone made me look at him closer and consider how he must feel, alone and wounded and vulnerable. I turned and scurried about, trying to replace everything we had moved to exactly as it had been when we arrived, kicking rubble and dust over our footprints. I didn't want the VanZeldts to know we'd been there.

Although he didn't ask if we'd come again, Seeley told him anyway. "We'll be back. We'll bring more food."

I didn't confirm this. Instead I stepped carefully over the debris and hurried outside. Once Seeley was out, I carefully leaned the door over the entrance.

We didn't run but made our way swiftly back to the canoe. Seeley didn't veer off exploring as he had earlier, and I was in no mood to allow it if he had. However, when we reached the pool, he began shedding his shoes, stockings, and shirt.

I had promised him a swim. A few more minutes out couldn't hurt. I perched on the rocky ledge and pondered the chance that laid up the author of Seeley's favorite books so close to Scuppernong. I was struck by the many improbable situations brought about by the war, the many dissimilar lives drawn together.

And what quirk had caused the VanZeldts to care for a Union soldier? Out of the kindness of their hearts? Although Dr. Van-Zeldt and Amenze had approached me with friendship, they were odd, detached people. But why wouldn't Amenze talk to Lieutenant Lynd when she could speak English?

Everything was twisted and troubling.

Maybe Dr. VanZeldt was a Northern sympathizer and therefore ordered his servants to attend to the lieutenant. Yankee partisans certainly existed down here. Or perhaps Lieutenant Lynd had had the same effect on all of the VanZeldts that he had on me—it's a much easier task to hate faceless foes in blue uniforms than it is to hate a helpless man in dire need. They must have stumbled across him and could not leave him lying there. They wouldn't dare take him to Shadowlawn in case it was discovered they were harboring a Yankee.

Seeley crawled up toward me through the water, dragging himself by his hands like an alligator. "You're not going to turn the lieutenant in, are you, Violet? You wouldn't do that, would you?"

I picked up a handful of gravel and threw it hard against the cliff face across the pool. "I should. He's the enemy. If he lives, in a few months he might be the one shooting at my father. And also for his own good, I should turn him in. Our soldiers would take him to one of our hospitals, where he'd have the advantages of modern medicine." We were civilized. The doctors would try to heal Lieutenant Lynd before he got locked away in a prison camp.

Seeley scrambled onto his bottom and let wet sand dribble through his fingers. "He doesn't seem like an enemy. He made up Heath Blackstock, so he has to be a good fellow. Heath is always nice to everyone he rescues. You should read *Castle Sliverbone*. It's somewhere in my room."

"With that captivating title, I certainly will."

"If you turned in Lieutenant Lynd, they'd probably saw his whole leg off clear up to the top, wouldn't they? Since it's his hip that's hurt. Isn't that what they usually do?"

And he'd probably die shortly afterward, just as Isaac Lafarge and so many others in our hospital had died, with our fine modern medicine. I didn't answer Seeley.

"Please don't turn him in," he begged. "Promise you won't."

I sighed and tried not to look down into his beseeching eyes. I fingered the lump of my amulet beneath my bodice. As always, it felt reassuring, as if the energy it held were on my side.

Seeley would not stop nagging until I finally answered. "All right. I won't."

"And we'll bring him food every day. And other things. He needs pen and ink and paper so he can write books. Think how awful it was for him to lose his horse and his clothes and all his belongings."

Like the owner of Star. Star, who had wandered magically into our pasture in early April. Or perhaps not so magically. I gave a little gasp, remembering that Star's owner was a Union soldier named Thomas.

It wasn't so great a coincidence. I would have connected them immediately if I had been thinking clearly. So the saddlebags were Lieutenant Lynd's. The letters and photograph. The interesting mind that had created such fanciful carved figures.

"What, Violet?" Seeley was tugging at my skirt. "What did you just think of?"

I hardly dared tell him. "Well . . . I'm not sure, but . . . You'll never guess what else we might be bringing the lieutenant."

"What?"

"His own saddlebags full of his own things."

"How—"

"Star is probably his horse. Scuppernong is only a few miles from Freshwater Springs, where the lieutenant was shot. And Star was carrying saddlebags."

Seeley's eyes shone. "That's perfect! How did such a perfect thing happen?"

I lifted my hands. I couldn't begin to grasp all these twists of fate.

Seeley was tugging at my skirt once more. "And can we go see him sometime at night? I want to show him the constellations."

"I don't know, Squiddy. Maybe. Come on. Into the canoe with you."

As I lay wakeful in the dark that night, I saw the face of the man in the Lodge. There was a tranquillity in his good looks, an unselfconsciousness. Of course, part of that, I told myself dryly, could be that he hadn't bathed or shaved in a couple of months—just how attractive could he be feeling? No. That wasn't it; the lieutenant's manner came from something more than skin-deep. He was the kind of man Rush and I would have called a friend.

CHAPTER 16

AN ACCIDENT

The next morning, I was stitching up slashes in the armchair that the bushwhackers had ripped when Seeley sidled up to me.

"Can we take the stuff to the lieutenant now?" he whispered.

"Tomorrow. We mustn't draw attention by going there two days in a row. He'll be all right till then."

Seeley nodded and left the room. A moment later, he popped back in and plunked down eagerly on the arm of the chair. "There's a fox slinking around the henhouse. In broad daylight. He's littler than you'd think a fox would be from all the stories. Not much bigger than Goblin, but I bet he's mean. I bet he wants to eat up the only chickens we got left."

"Probably so," I murmured, stitching away. "Bad old fox."

"He might get Rowena. I'm going to stop him."

"Please do."

I had settled back to my stitching when a boom sounded from outside that rattled the windows and made me drop my needle. I ran out the back door while everyone else dashed from wherever they were. A flash of red, black, and white zoomed across the lawn and into the woods.

Seeley was sprawled facedown in the barnyard. A few feet away from him lay the old rifle from the barn, bits of its stock scattered, shattered, and blackened upon the ground. For one heart-stopping moment, horror clenched my whole body.

Then Seeley moved. He was scrambling to sit up even as I was at his side, kneeling in the dust. His hair was sticking up all over, his cheeks were smudged, and skin was scraped from his nose and forehead where he had fallen face-first. Other than that, he appeared unharmed. Except that his eyes were scared. His mouth drooped. "I—I was trying to shoot the fox and fell over something. The rifle jumped out of my hands and it—I guess it blew up."

I hugged him tightly. "You're all right, Squiddy. It's all right." I must have repeated that several times.

"I *know* it's all right, Violet," Seeley finally said, pulling away. He was shaking all over and tears weren't far off. He was perfectly aware of what could have happened. Strange that this time it was his clumsiness that had *saved* him.

"How'd you get that rifle?" Michael demanded, picking up one of the pieces. "You get it down from the rafters yourself? Mr. William, he left it up there till he could have it fixed because the firing mechanism was broke—he thought it might would jam and explode."

"It was leaning against Star's stall this morning," Seeley said. "I figured it was just an old gun nobody cared about, so I could use it. I always wanted a gun."

Michael and I looked at each other. Someone had been very irresponsible to take the rifle down and leave it lying around. My guess was that it was King, but I wasn't going to say so right now.

"Don't ever, ever touch a firearm again until Michael teaches you to use them," I said. "Anyway, I didn't mean for you to shoot the fox; I meant to chase it away."

A furrow showed between Michael's brows. "However it got down, we wouldn't never have left no ammunition in it."

I shook my head. There was no answer to any of this. I scanned the yard around Seeley and saw nothing he could have tripped over. His guardian angels must have had a hand (or foot) in it.

Seeley was tense all day because of the rifle incident. It required the enticing candy jars at Maloney's Mercantile later that afternoon to take his mind off it. The store was better stocked than it had been in a long while. A small shipment of supplies had made it in, including flour, at twenty dollars a barrel, and some sweets—horehound drops, rock candy, lemon drops, and taffy. After several minutes of contemplation Seeley finally chose lemon drops that looked like fat yellow bees. He brightened as he sucked them on our way home.

"You know I may not eat supper now," he said complacently. "Mammy never let me have candy before supper."

"Mammy was right," I said, wishing that sugary treats could make me recover as quickly.

"You don't know much about raising children, do you, Violet?"

"How could I? Will you be sad not to gobble your share of suppertime ham hocks?" I asked this just as I heard my name called, and there was old Jubal, waving us down from the edge of Miss Ruby Jewel's property.

"Would you kindly come have a word with my mistress?" he said. "She sent me to watch for you. Said it's important."

Reluctantly I left the road with Seeley. "You may want to stay outside," I whispered. "It's kind of horrible in Miss Ruby Jewel's house. She's got way too many cats."

"I want to see way too many cats."

"Then take a big breath of fresh air before you go in."

Seeley followed as Jubal showed us into the parlor and across to another doorway. "In here, please. Miss Ruby Jewel has taken to her bed." He put his head inside. "Miss Violet Dancey, ma'am."

I saw why Jubal didn't enter the space himself—there was no room. A narrow path wound through towering crates and boxes and barrels on either side. Cats leaped from one height to another or watched us from above, unblinking. At the end of the trail was Miss Ruby Jewel's bedstead. The old lady huddled inside it, covered with cats. Her mouth was gaping and her eyes were closed. They flickered open at Jubal's voice. The familiar, quick, cunning light seeped slowly into them.

"Sorry to wake you, ma'am," I said.

"Good night a-living! I wasn't asleep," she said. "Just checking for holes in my eyelids."

Seeley stared closer at that. A spotted tom pawed a gingersnap off a plate on a candlestand beside the bed and jumped down to nibble.

The old woman shifted. "Help me set up, you, girl."

I tried to plump the limp pillows behind her, without much success, and gingerly lifted her up against them. The tabby on her stomach barely budged. I had never touched such an old person before. Beneath her grimy nightgown her arms felt like bones with crepey skin slipping and stretching over them. I was afraid I would break her.

"You're unwell, ma'am?" I said.

"Feeling right puny. Don't I look it?"

She did. I would not have thought it possible for Miss Ruby Jewel to appear any more shrunken or frail, but evidently it was. Her flesh had taken on a gray tinge.

"What does Dr. Hale say?"

"That fusspot wouldn't tell me nothing 'cept to leave off the gingersnaps and tobaccy. I ain't about to give up the two things— besides my kitties—that make me happy—I'd as soon croak and be done with it—so I thought to get a second opinion."

"And you did?"

"I did and that's why I done told Jubal I needed to talk to you. But first, who's this young whistle britches hiding back there? Ile your beau?"

Seeley had been watching the cats with interest. At Miss Ruby Jewel's words he flushed, and she grinned her wicked, black-gummed grin.

"This is Seeley Rushton, my cousin," I said, and shoved the boy forward.

I was proud of him as he took off his hat and bravely held out his palm. "Pleased to meet you, ma'am."

She pulled her arm out from beneath cats and shook his hand. "So you're the gentleman owns Panola, are you?"

"Yes, ma'am."

"Think you're mighty highfalutin to have your own plantation, eh?" She looked up at me. "Well, girl, you done good for yourself to have snagged a fancy planter sweetheart."

"I'm not—she's not—" Seeley stuttered.

Miss Ruby Jewel cackled.

"It's all right, Seeley," I said. "She's teasing."

"Oh," he said. He dug in his pocket, drew forth a lemon drop, and held it out to the old lady. "Would you care for some candy, ma'am? It's fresh."

"Why, thank you, young feller," Miss Ruby Jewel said, taking the drop and popping it in the corner of her mouth. "You're a good boy to give an old lady sweeties. And now why don't you go find Jubal and get him to fetch you some lemonade. I got private business with your cousin and can't no one else listen in."

Seeley went out the door. Something that I had taken for part of the old lady wriggled beneath the quilt to the edge of the bed and dropped down to follow him out. A kitten.

"Now," Miss Ruby Jewel said in a lowered voice, and her black eyes darted about like water bugs, as if she feared someone else might have stolen in when Seeley went out, "I done sent Jubal for that Dr. VanZeldt scoundrel. Thought maybe with all his foreign quackery he might know something that could fix me. He come with that young buck slinking in behind—the one so skinny there'd have to be two of him to cast a shadow."

I pictured the young man looking disdainfully down his nose at Miss Ruby Jewel, at the cats, at everything in the place but Jubal—no one could despise Jubal. "And did he help you?"

"I swanny, he done told me same as old worryguts Hale. No more sweeties and no more tobaccy. And I ain't about to give them up. So I'm a goner and I know it. Only a matter of time." She sucked at the candy for a moment. "But that's not what I got to tell you. Come closer, girl." Something about her lowered tone made me look at her sharply. Her eyes bulged and her mouth trembled. Miss Ruby Jewel was frightened.

I knelt beside her bed. She snatched at my hand when I laid it on her quilt.

"My kitties didn't like the doctor. Hissed. And he"—she grimaced—"he was asking about you." She began plucking at the skin of my hand. The lemon drop slid from her lips and plinked to the floor and neither of us paid it any heed.

"About me?" My voice was unusually high. It wasn't the old lady's words so much as her distress that sent shivers down my spine. "Why would he ask about me?"

"Don't know. Prodding and poking about your family and friends and did you have a lover. Used that word—'lover'— slow and slippery-like. Licked his lips. Seemed pleased that your father was away."

"I know he wanted me to be friends with the girl, but from what you say . . ."

"Ain't no telling," Miss Ruby Jewel said, "only he's up to no good. You don't suppose he's fixing to court you hisself?"

I recoiled in horror. "*No*. He couldn't."

She didn't respond. Instead she seemed to sink deeper into her bed. Her grip slipped from my hand and her eyelids fluttered shut. "There," she murmured, "I done told you and it's off my chest. Now go away, girl. I'm tired."

I lightly kissed her sunken cheek and left the room, pondering.

Surely it meant nothing. The doctor was merely making conversation. Still, I couldn't melt the ice that edged my bones.

That night Sunny and I hunched over our handiwork after both Miss Elsa and Seeley had gone early to bed. My stepsister punctuated her stitching with loud sighs.

"This braiding is so hard to poke the needle through," she said.

I lifted the hem of her project. "Do you really think Pa—or any soldier—wants his underclothes trimmed with itchy gold braid?"

"Why not?" she asked. "A gentleman should be distinguished both inside and out. Just as a lady's underpinnings ought always to be as elegant as her outerwear."

I contrasted the gorgeous lemon-yellow satin chemise I had glimpsed Sunny wearing that morning with the plain, black-dyed cambric underclothes I wore and gave a little sigh of my own.

The sound of the front door opening reached us just then, along with the thud of a carpetbag dropping to the hall floor.

"Dorian's back!" Sunny cried. The sparkle returned to her eyes as she hastily tugged down the lace on her neckline.

He entered and surveyed the room.

She rushed to his side and clung to his arm. "Did you have a nice time?" she asked, leading him to a seat.

Dorian made a careless gesture. "Boring, really."

"Tell us everything you did while you deserted us for two whole long days, Dorian Rushton," Sunny demanded.

My cousin shook her off and moved back to the doorway. He glanced up the stairs, then back at us, as if he were having trouble focusing. "I'm not sure that's any of your business, Anna Bess

Sluder." He spoke a little too loudly and was unusually flushed; I wondered if he was slightly tipsy. He seemed to remember himself and smiled. "I'll answer anyway. Not much. The Baxters held a party in my honor, and a young relative, Maria something or other, hogged all my time. Wouldn't hardly let anyone else near. She was pretty, but not pretty enough." He winked.

"Mmm," I said.

"'Mmm,' is it?" Dorian exclaimed. He strode to my chair and snatched my yarn away. "Is that any sort of response to my story?"

"Did I say 'mmm'?"

"Quite distinctly, coz dear."

"Mmm . . ."

"Maria deserves to be slapped," Sunny said crossly.

"Yes," Dorian said. "That's a better reaction to Maria." He tossed back my yarn and fiddled with the folds of his paisley silk cravat. "I guess you heard New Orleans has fallen? Yanks will circle us soon. We'll feel the squeeze." He idly picked up the garment Sunny had been sewing and pretended to inspect it. However, I doubted he was really seeing it since he made no comment about the braiding. He dropped it abruptly. "No more talk of my doings or the war—do I assume nothing interesting happened while I was gone? Tell me what you ladies have been up to. I missed you."

"Prove it," Sunny said boldly, tipping her head to one side.

"Pardon?" Dorian said.

"Prove you missed me."

His eyes narrowed and he advanced toward her. "Be careful what you ask for, my girl."

She giggled and I ducked out quickly as his hand slid low around her waist.

Upstairs, a half hour later, I wrote in my journal, although there was little I dared put down on paper. A noise made me pause in mid-stroke. It was a soft, regular sound—stealthy footsteps crossing the upstairs landing. And then the faintest scraping of Sunny's bedroom door opening, a giggle, breathy whispers, a shushing, the creak of the bed. I closed my ears.

I had been asleep for a while when the patter of rain on the roof awoke me. Usually I loved to lie there listening, but now I worried. The Lodge was bound to leak. Lieutenant Lynd was alone in the pitch dark, unable to move away from dripping water. The aloneness was the worst part. If only his fellow soldier hadn't died.

I went rigid because another picture came to mind—that of the redheaded corpse lying in the courthouse yard with a gash across his throat. The memory sickened me as always, but now it had a new meaning: there had been a mojo bag about the neck, connecting the corpse with the VanZeldts. Did the lieutenant's friend Jorgenson, who disappeared as Lieutenant Lynd slept, have red hair?

I was swiftly certain that the body was Jorgenson's. The VanZeldts had killed the poor man after rescuing him. Why? I sat bolt upright and had to stop myself from leaping out of bed and dashing off to warn Lieutenant Lynd.

How easy it would be to slit the throat of a sleeping cripple in the night.

CHAPTER 17

THE COURSE
OF TRUE LOVE

I told myself that until two days ago I hadn't even known Lieutenant Lynd existed. Nothing was any more likely to happen to him this morning than at any other time. However, the early chores had never seemed to take so long.

As I swept the kitchen, my thoughts about the soldier were confusing, changing from moment to moment. Was I anxious to see him to warn him? To bring him more food? To show off the fact that I was not the disheveled hoyden I had appeared the day we met? Was I a traitor to the Cause because of all of these things?

"King's out in the barn," Laney mentioned. "You better say something to him about that gun. It's him got it down, don't you reckon?"

"Probably," I said, making her move her feet so I could sweep beneath them. "I hate to accuse anyone, though, when we don't know it for a fact. And even if he did leave it there, he would be devastated if he thought he almost hurt Seeley. He loves that boy."

"Don't go accusing. Just warn him to be more careful."

When I went to the barn for the milking, King was indeed there. His lower lip hung down in concentration as he hunched on top of a barrel, painstakingly polishing his master's silver spurs and bridle buckles. His shirt gaped open where buttons were missing, showing a massive belly.

I spoke his name.

The big man looked up sluggishly, as if it were an effort to switch his attention.

"Did you hear that Seeley got hold of an old, broken rifle in here yesterday and it exploded when it fired?"

King sat up straighter and his eyes bulged. "Master Seeley all right?"

"Yes, he is," I hastened to reassure him. "But he might have been killed. Someone had taken the gun from the rafters and left it down low."

He gave a shake of his bald head. "No, Miss Violet. Didn't never hear 'bout that. That's bad. Shouldn't never leave them things lying around. No, sir."

Evidently he wasn't going to admit that it was he who had taken down the gun. "Big people have to watch out for young ones."

His small eyes squinted as if in pain. "I always tries to look out for Master Seeley. He's my little friend."

The spurs King was working on glinted in the morning light.

"Don't you think those are shiny enough now?" I said.

There was a stubborn set to his lips. "No, Miss Violet. I gots to do it perfect. Master Dorian, he told me to make them perfect, and won't do to get him mad. Won't do at all."

I stood watching the poor man. Dorian, for all his laughter and winning ways, was persnickety and must be an exacting master. "Do you have another shirt? A second one?"

"Yes'm."

"Will you go change into it now, while I'm milking the cows, and bring this one to me so I can sew new buttons on it?"

He started to rise, heavy with reluctance, then sank back down. "Sorry to disoblige you, Miss Violet, ma'am, but can't do that. Not till I finish this work. Master Dorian told me to polish them right quick. Can't get him mad. No, ma'am."

"Is Master Dorian so very bad-tempered with you?"

King made no response.

I sighed. "Then bring me this shirt tomorrow, all right?"

"All right, Miss Violet. I'll do that. Thank you, ma'am."

Star nickered softly, and I gave her a pat.

After finishing the milking, while Seeley drove the cows to pasture, I scurried upstairs to my bedroom and removed the figurines and packet of letters from their hiding place. I unwrapped the carvings to look upon them once more. Their eyes seemed to be upon me as well. Beautiful, fascinating, and somewhat disturbing. I would miss them.

The string tying the packet was loose. Some of the letters had slipped out, and I caught another glimpse of the spritely Addie's rounded handwriting. Hastily I stuffed them back in, retied the packet, and slipped everything into my pocket. Now that the owner was no longer a stranger, I was ashamed of reading the letter from his sweetheart. But I was glad I knew about her. It was the sort of thing a girl needed to know about a man.

I still took extra pains with my grooming, combing my hair until it was silky smooth and adding a pale blue ribbon around my snood and dainty opal earrings to my ears.

As I passed the sitting room on my way to the kitchen, Miss Elsa called out. She beckoned with one thin white hand so that the trailing sleeve of her gauzy gray dressing gown flapped. It was unusual for my stepmother to be awake so early; she must have come down expressly to catch me.

"Violet, darling, could you speak to Michael about my poppies? They simply aren't growing quickly enough. I only have two remaining bottles. . . ."

"I'll talk to him," I said, entering the room, "even though I'm sure he's doing whatever can be done. The buds are forming now. At what stage should you harvest them? Do you know?"

She sighed. "Yes, I know. I've studied the article I clipped from the *Ladies' Monthly Home Companion* most carefully. I must wait until the petals drop off naturally, and then the capsules ripen for two weeks after that. But oh, it has been raining, and the instructions say particularly that the plants must be kept dry during blooming time. Michael must do something. . . ."

Sunny had been standing by the window, the curtain pulled back in her hand as she gazed out. She glanced over her shoulder. "Mama," she snapped, "Michael can't control the weather. You'd better ask Violet to speak to God instead."

Dorian stepped in then, still in his shirtsleeves and fumbling with the cuffs of his white linen shirt. "Morning, y'all."

"Good morning, kind sir," Sunny said, sweeping up to him. "Here, let me do that."

He held out his wrists and she fastened one mother-of-pearl cuff link. She had begun on the other when, with a provocative look from under her eyelashes, she whisked the stud behind her back and scurried to the opposite side of the room.

"What will you give me for it?" she asked, wide-eyed.

"The devil!" Dorian rolled his eyes. "Not in the mood, Sunny. I'm in a hurry. I've business in Tennessee this afternoon. Be a good girl and hand it here."

She pouted. "You just got back. You're smuggling from behind the lines, aren't you? You promised you'd take me next time."

"And I *will* next time. But not this time. I'm meeting a friend and he doesn't believe in mixing ladies with business."

"Does it matter to you what he believes?" she asked with scorn.

"Yes," Dorian answered.

"How silly. I shouldn't care a pin for it."

"I daresay not, since you haven't a clue what you're talking about."

"You said ladies make good smugglers because of their hoops to hide things under."

"So they do," Dorian said with carefully controlled patience. "But not—this—time."

Seeley had entered during the confrontation and watched its course with wide eyes as he raised and lowered his bandalore. Up and down, up and down.

Two spots of crimson showed on Sunny's cheeks as she fixed Dorian with a fiery green glare. "You certainly don't seem to mind me forgetting conventions when it suits you, Dorian Rushton. Well, I want to go and I shall go and you shan't have your cuff link back until you say you'll take me!"

Dorian's mouth thinned and hardened as his eyes glittered

dangerously. No wonder King feared his master's anger; I should have been terrified had I been its target.

"Give it over, Sunny," he said as he thrust forth his open palm.

She looked daggers at him for a moment, but his expression, combined with the tone of his voice, was too much for her. She stalked across the carpet and slapped the cuff link down into his hand.

"Here! Take the horrid thing!" she flashed. "You—you horrid thing! Nothing matters to you but yourself. Now *go away!*"

Dorian strode out.

Sunny's eyes darted about the room searching for something to hurl after him. She lit upon poor little Seeley. No, she did not hurl Seeley, although she looked as if she wanted to. Instead she ripped the bandalore out of his hand and flung it hard at Dorian's receding back. "And I told you this child would drive everyone daft with that thing," she screamed.

Dorian flinched at the blow but kept walking.

My stepsister turned now to glower at me. "It's true! He cares for no one and nothing but himself!"

I had no response. Most of the time I liked my older cousin, but as I had come to know him better, it was plain he was indeed self-centered. He was kind now to Seeley, and could be sympathetic to others in an offhand, casual sort of way, if it suited him. He had no burning interests except frivolity. There was nothing noble about his blockade-running—he did it for the excitement and for the money. Still, he couldn't be called completely shallow; he cared *deeply* about himself and his things.

Sunny flounced from the room and burst into stormy tears half-way up the stairs.

Seeley looked after her. "She better watch out," he said softly.

Throughout the whole exchange, Miss Elsa had been gazing off into nothing as if she hardly noticed it. "They'll be all right," she said now with complacence. "They're falling in love with each other, and with such passionate personalities, as William Shakespeare said, the course of true love never . . . Oh, how does it go?"

"Runs smooth," I said. "Come, Seeley, pick up your bandalore and then let's go pack our picnic lunch."

I had grown fond of Miss Elsa and Sunny and Dorian, but today I couldn't bear to hear another word out of any of them.

Luckily Laney was nowhere in sight, so we were free to prepare anything we wished in the kitchen without being questioned. We made egg sandwiches and gathered an entire sweet potato pie and leftover-from-breakfast corn dodgers.

"You're sure a good cook," Seeley said.

I smiled. He knew I hadn't made the dodgers or pie. He was being kind. Or was he teasing me? I tweaked his ear.

I took two candles out of the candle box and wrapped them up with several matches. Now Lieutenant Lynd could have some light. My hands shook a little as I tucked the bundle into the basket. Soon we would be with him, and I felt almost light-headed at the prospect.

Napkins in hand, I paused. What exactly was I doing? Rather than anticipating seeing this Union soldier again, for whatever reason, I should be marching straight to the authorities. But if I did, it would all come to an end—for everyone. Our secret would be laid open, the Lodge would be abandoned, and the lieutenant would be sent off to some unknown but probably terrible fate. We would never see him again.

Carefully I wrapped the napkins around a small brown crock of calf's-foot jelly, which was supposed to be good for invalids. I would continue as planned—first Lieutenant Lynd must be warned of what I suspected about the VanZeldts and then he must be helped to grow strong enough to walk again. What would happen after that—to him, to me, to the South—was a mystery.

"The lieutenant—" Seeley started to say.

I brought my finger to my lips and whispered, "Later." Dorian and Sunny were passing by the kitchen doorway, arms about each other's waists and heads close together. Clearly they had made up. She looked up at him meltingly. "So you see why—" from him. "I didn't mean—" from her. The front door slammed shut.

Seeley and I made our way toward the little dock. A pair of raucous blue jays squawked and pecked at each other in a sweet gum tree, sounding just as my cousin and stepsister had sounded earlier.

We ran across the happy couple again as we passed the scuppernong arbor. Dorian sat on the bench beneath it, and Sunny was balanced on his lap.

He leaned around her in order to call out in a jovial voice, "Off for a picnic, are you? I've always found nature uncomfortable myself. So few soft seats and so many insects flying into people's mouths."

Sunny giggled. "Y'all can see what a soft seat *I've* found."

Dorian grinned and tickled her waist, making her giggle louder.

They were so annoying.

"You're not canoeing again?" Dorian said. "With the thunder-heads piling up?" He pointed upward and Sunny nearly fell off his lap.

Seeley nodded solemnly.

Dorian shook his head. "Oh, well. What might deter some mariners evidently doesn't sway you brave folks. For you, the dangers of lightning on water are vastly exaggerated. So what's in the packs?"

Seeley had been so impressed with the saddlebag discovery that he had insisted on carrying them both. He hugged them close now, his big eyes wary.

"Equipment for collecting samples," I said lightly. "The sorts of things we lovers of nature can't do without. Good luck in Tennessee."

"And good luck to you with your nature loving—or whatever it is you're doing."

CHAPTER 18

BEING DIFFERENT

"Are they exaggerated?" Seeley asked after we had taken our leave of Sunny and Dorian. "The water and lightning dangers?"

"No," I said, "they're not. That's why, at the first distant rumble, we'll climb up on the bank."

"But then we'd be under trees in a thunderstorm. Isn't that bad too?"

Impatience rose in me. "Do you want to stay home today, Squid? You don't need to come if you're worried."

"Uh-uh," he said quickly. "Maybe the dangers of standing under trees during lightning are overrated."

We paddled our canoe with a sort of nervous hastiness. Either Seeley was anxious on his own or he had caught my apprehension. Lieutenant Lynd was lying there, waiting for us to come or not to come. Unless the VanZeldts had done away with him in the night. I paddled faster and clenched my teeth to keep them from chattering.

Part of the tension in the air came from ashen clouds pressing down, turning the river drab and steely. The rain held off as we canoed, with humidity swathing us like a clammy quilt.

There was no talk of swimming when we beached our craft and no playfulness as we made our way through the forest. Seeley was weighed down by the saddlebags, and I by the basket. It was a relief when a light, misty rain finally fell. At first we were protected by the thick canopy of leaves. Soon, however, water seeped through and trickled beneath to penetrate our clothing and even my bonnet, making my hair cling drearily to my head. Sodden leaves and mud stuck to our boots. Seeley resembled a drowned puppy, and I knew I must look the same, only larger and less appealing. So much for a more refined appearance on our second trip.

We approached the Lodge cautiously. All seemed peaceful except for the patter of rain. I lifted the door from the entrance and wrung out my skirt as we crossed the front room.

My heart gave a leap of joy when I entered the next doorway because he was all right, sitting up, leaning against the wall with his hands lying quiet in his lap. He sat so motionless that his stillness filled the room. He seemed to take no notice of the drip, drip, dripping that happened right beside—though thankfully not actually on—his pallet. His expression was thoughtful, and rather austere, but when he saw us, the gaunt lines softened.

"You came," he said simply.

I took an involuntary step forward and then stopped myself. I didn't wish to voice my fears concerning the VanZeldts immediately. For one thing, I would have to get Seeley out of the way before I discussed such matters. And now, looking at the lieutenant,

I suddenly thought it unlikely that the VanZeldts would harm the soldier when they had cared for him all these weeks. "I could hardly wait to see you again," Seeley said. "I was afraid you wouldn't still be here. Oh, and I made Violet promise she wouldn't turn you in." He plopped the saddlebags down just inside the doorway and then plopped himself down as close as he could to the lieutenant, narrowly missing the puddle. "We brought you food and stuff and"— his expression turned shy—"I brought paper and ink so you can begin writing another Heath Blackstock book. I've been thinking— maybe Heath could meet some snake people with forked tongues and scales and everything."

"First the food, Squiddy," I said. "The lieutenant needs a meal before anything else." I was anxious for Lieutenant Lynd to eat. He needed to put meat on his bones. So he wouldn't look so tenuous. It seemed a long way to cross the floor with Lieutenant Lynd watching. I had started to spread out the food within his reach when I noticed something I hadn't the other day. A red flannel mojo bag hung around Lieutenant Lynd's neck.

I pointed. "The VanZeldts tied that thing on you."

"They did," he said, "right after they brought me here."

"You weren't wearing it when we came before."

"Sometimes I take it off. The smell is pungent. But I always put it back on, because whatever the Shadows are doing, it seems to be working." He picked up a corn dodger and leaned conspiratorially closer to Seeley. "In the army we had special names for the rations we were given." The lieutenant was whispering, but I could hear. He caught my eye with his own smiling eyes so that I knew he knew I could hear. "We called the desiccated vegetables 'bales of hay.' If a fellow made the mistake of eating too much dry hay, he would swell up until he exploded."

Seeley laughed with delight. "Really?"

"Well, I never saw it actually happen, but that was the rumor. And guess what we called 'worm castles'?"

Seeley drew his brows together. "Nasty old Swiss cheese?"

"Good guess, but no. Our bread. Because by the time we got to Fort Donelson, the hard kind we had in our rations was full of maggots."

I sucked in my breath. The room seemed to have darkened.

"Ugh." Seeley shuddered. "Earthworms are nice, but . . . maggots. Ugh."

"You were—" My throat had closed up, so it was hard to make the words come out. "You were at Fort Donelson?"

"Yes. Under General Grant. Before we crossed the Tennessee and headed south."

"Excuse me." Abruptly I deserted Seeley and Lieutenant Lynd.

Outside the Lodge, I strode across the clearing through the rain. I ducked beneath the spreading boughs of a great pine tree and sank to the ground, slumped against the trunk.

He was at Fort Donelson. He might be the soldier who killed my brother.

I banged my head against the bark until I scared myself and stopped.

Lieutenant Lynd was the enemy.

I stayed beneath the tree until I could regain control. Eventually I had to go back inside.

Seeley and the lieutenant were still munching away when I entered. Lieutenant Lynd looked up inquiringly. I turned away and set my jaw as I seated myself on a stump as far from him as I could get. It wasn't far enough. The room was small.

"The lieutenant was saying how hard it was for the Yankees to cross the Tennessee," Seeley told me. "They had to build a pontoon bridge. It was nearly washed away."

"Too bad they weren't all swept off with it," I said, low and fierce.

Seeley stared. Lieutenant Lynd put down the sandwich he was holding. I had effectively stopped the conversation.

"Thank you for everything, Miss Dancey," the lieutenant said finally, hesitantly. "You're very good to me, and I know it's difficult for you as a Southern lady. It's hardest on the women when we've taken occupation of their towns. It seems they hate us more than the men do."

"I loathe all Yankees," I said. "You kill our brothers, fathers, husbands, and destroy our homes and way of life. Why shouldn't we hate you?"

He drew back slightly at my words. "The ladies in Nashville averted their eyes and crossed the road to get farther away from us. They twitched their skirts out of the way as if we were the most disgusting, filthy creatures they'd ever encountered. Believe it or not, that was more painful than a bullet."

How ridiculous that an enemy should be hurt because, naturally, the conquered despised him. I turned from his gaze. However, there was no place in particular to look, so I could only watch the rhythmic spatter falling into the puddle beside Seeley as Lieutenant Lynd continued.

"The Southern men don't act that way. Probably because soldiers shooting at each other sense how alike we really are under the uniforms. I could look in the haunted eyes of the other army and see my own ghost. We were alike in the mud, the bullets, the noise, the smoke, the question of what we were doing there. Some pickets even got friendly as they patrolled and exchanged tobacco and stories."

"And then went back to killing each other the next day." I shook my head. Idiotic men.

"Yes," he said, "they went back to doing their duty."

"So, how many Confederates have you killed?" Seeley asked.

"Oh, I'm a terrible marksman. Probably as many of them as they killed of me."

"How can you possibly know the number of men you've struck down?" I was clutching my black-edged handkerchief so tightly that my nails cut into my palm.

"You have a point," the lieutenant said slowly. "I guess I really have no idea. The smoke is so thick once the firing starts that all you can do is shoot into the haze."

For a moment no one spoke. Seeley began flicking droplets from the puddle my way.

I ignored him. "Go on, though, Lieutenant. I'm curious about your opinion as to why the ladies react differently from the men?"

He didn't answer for a moment. He finished his sandwich before speaking again and I found myself watching his mouth as he chewed. He wiped it with a napkin. "The ladies don't get to take action. They have to stay home, to worry, to suffer, to do without. They picture the enemy as alien beasts come to take everything from them. So naturally they hate us—who could blame them?"

I broke away from the study of his mouth and busied myself with brushing away crumbs. I spoke very fast as I did so. "All we asked was to be allowed to leave with what was ours. All that talk, talk, talk, and we don't understand each other at all. I don't believe we even speak the same language. You Northerners march down here and expect to change everything we know and to make us cold and rough like yourselves and you burn our harvest and steal our stock and waste our country and you kill—you kill our loved ones." I dashed away hot tears with the back of my hand.

"You're wearing mourning," Lieutenant Lynd said gently. "Who . . . ?"

I swallowed. "My twin brother, Rush. Fort Donelson."

"Oh." His voice was flat. He nodded slightly and looked down at his hands. "What a horrible thing war is. There's nothing I can say to let you know how sorry I am."

We sat in brooding silence for several minutes.

Seeley twitched, shifted, and finally asked, "Shall I bring him the other things now?"

Lieutenant Lynd shook himself and sat up straighter. "Let me finish this sweet potato pie first. Once I see everything you brought, I may forget to eat, and eating is important." He gave a weak grin. "Did you hear that?"

"Hear what?" Seeley asked.

"How I said 'sweet potato pie'? With a drawl like a Southerner. It's impossible to say those words without putting on a rebel twang. See, I do speak the same language."

"Try 'Alabama,'" Seeley said. "That's a hard one to say Yankee."

"Alabama," Lieutenant Lynd said. "You're right. I sound just like—"

He was making fun of me. "And what," I interrupted, "makes you think you're so enlightened that you can tell us our way of life is wrong? What gives you the right to come down here and take away our property?"

"Because, Miss Dancey, your 'property' is men, women, and children." For the first time the lieutenant's tone was impatient. "Our pastor brought an old black man to a church meeting and had him remove his shirt. His back was so crisscrossed with scars from whipping that it was scarcely recognizable as skin."

"Of course it's wrong to treat a servant so. Almost everyone I know would agree it's wrong. No one in my family has ever laid a hand on any of our people." Except for Sunny.

Lieutenant Lynd shook his head. "I had to do more than spout that it's 'wrong.' I had to put on a uniform and do something about it. People must take responsibility and stand up for innocents who have been so ill treated and oppressed they can't stand up for themselves. The sin would be upon our heads if we continued to do nothing when we have the means to right things."

Seeley was playing in the puddle again, staring at it so fixedly that I knew he was upset.

"There are slaves in the Bible," I muttered. "Abraham had slaves."

"Thousands of years ago. No civilized, advanced society should allow such injustice." He took a deep breath. "Let's not talk about the war anymore. I don't want to quarrel with you when you're my benefactor, and when you've had such a terrible loss, but if we talk about it, we'll quarrel."

I bit the inside of my cheek but couldn't make myself hush. Red-hot anger shot through me. Now I knew how Sunny had felt only a few hours earlier when she couldn't be quiet no matter how Dorian reacted. "If you Northerners ruin the economy of the South, you'll ruin your own. You just better hope we win or you'll be in trouble."

His brow furrowed with something like pity, and that only made me angrier. He opened his mouth to say something, then closed it.

"What?" I cried. "What were you about to say?"

His head bent.

"Tell me," I demanded.

He sighed. "Only that it's unlikely to happen."

"What's unlikely to happen?"

"The Confederates don't have a chance."

"Violet," Seeley said, touching my shoulder, "please stop talking. The lieutenant doesn't want to argue. I hope I can free my own slaves when I'm big enough, especially Mammy, even if the South wins, so be mad at me if you want to be mad."

"Oh, Seeley, you know I'm never mad at you. But"—I returned to Lieutenant Lynd—"what do you mean, we don't have a chance? We've got cotton. Europe will step in and help us. They need Southern cotton."

"Europe doesn't care that much," he said carefully. Reasonably. "They'll manage without it. They can get cotton from other sources. The North has all the country's manufacturing, and their numbers far outweigh yours. They haven't even started to tap into their resources."

He might have said "our" but instead said "their" when referring to the North. He might have pointed out that it was South Carolina that fired the first shot, but he did not. He was a fair fighter, and some tiny, hidden piece of me was relieved that he seemed much sharper and more aware than he had two days ago. More present. But that didn't mean I could let him get away with anything.

"One rebel can whip five Yankees." I stated what I had heard our boys say so often.

Lieutenant Lynd ignored the stupid boast. I was glad. "I only hope the end won't be too long coming," he said. "And when it does, we'll have lots of mending to do so we can be one nation again as we're meant to be."

My face was set. I made no further response.

He began consuming corn dodgers one by one with determination, as if he were not enjoying them but knew he needed the nourishment.

"Be sure to eat all the calf's-foot jelly," I said shortly. "It's good for healing."

We continued in uncomfortable silence until Lieutenant Lynd dropped a dodger and said suddenly, "Why can't the three of us be different from everyone else?"

"Different how?" I asked.

"Why can't we be friends? Here, in this place so far away from the battlefront?"

"Of course we can," Seeley said.

I bit my lip and was turning away when a slight movement from the wavy-glass window caught my eye.

"Oh, my land," I breathed.

CHAPTER 19

SPARROW

"Sparrow!" I cried. The lieutenant looked startled as I jumped up.
Seeley followed me outside.

The girl was darting, deerlike on her skinny legs, into the dripping, misty trees. She would have disappeared if I hadn't called out
once more. "It's me. Miss Violet. Your cousin Laney's friend. Don't
run off."

The girls at school had been frightened of Anarchy, Sparrow's
grandmother, and considered her a witch. On the rare times she was
seen, they were also nervous of Sparrow, who was an odd, elusive
child. I, however, had visited Anarchy's little cottage now and again
and was delighted by them both.

Sparrow halted. Slowly she turned and came toward us through
the drizzle, her great brown eyes wide. "I seen them," she said. Her
voice was so soft I had to lean in to hear.

"Seen who?" I asked.

"The People Things. I seen them a little bit ago, yonder by the
big house."

She was obviously disturbed. I put my arm around her shoulders and she flinched slightly. "We won't let anything hurt you, honey. You're safe with us. This is Seeley. You're about the same age, I think."

Seeley held out his hand. Sparrow simply stared at it.

"What have you got there?" Seeley asked, pointing to the sling she wore across her middle.

"Coon Baby." Sparrow pulled the cloth back a little. A pointy nose poked out, along with bright, curious eyes set in a black mask.

Seeley grinned. "Can I pet him?"

Sparrow nodded.

"Come inside where it's dry—or rather dryish," I said. "There's a nice man there. Come tell us about what you saw." It was the simple truth that the lieutenant was a nice man.

The girl let me lead her to the Lodge. Seeley continued awkwardly petting Coon Baby as Sparrow picked her way with dainty, muddy bare feet through the debris in the front room and on to Lieutenant Lynd's chamber.

She halted just inside the doorway, twisting her hands together and acting as if she might turn and run any second.

"Look who we found," Seeley announced to the lieutenant with pride.

"Lieutenant Lynd," I said, "this is Sparrow. She lives a long ways off with her grandmother in the forest."

"I'm pleased to meet you," the lieutenant said, smiling. "I couldn't wait to see who Sparrow was."

"What on earth are you doing so far from home?" I asked the girl.

It took a moment for her to answer. When she did, she spoke

carefully and solemnly. "I been seeking a good place to leave Coon Baby. I tended him 'cause some critter ate his ma, but Memaw says 'tis time he be going to stay with his own kin."

"Why can't you keep him?" Seeley asked.

"Memaw says it ain't right to hold tight to a wild critter. I hate it, though, 'cause I raised him by hand."

Seeley couldn't seem to stop looking at Sparrow. It wasn't just her possession of Coon Baby that was fascinating. With her slight body, wild cloud of black hair, triangular face, and enormous, eyes, she made an enchanting figure. "I like your dress," Seeley said.

She glanced downward but did not smile. Her gown was of green-striped gingham, drenched from the rain, and much too short for her.

"Come and sit down over here," I said. "There's still some pie left, if you'd like some."

She lowered herself tentatively to the edge of the stump while Seeley sat down beside her. I handed her a slice of pie, but she did not eat it. Instead, Coon Baby stuck his nose out and bit. Lieutenant Lynd gave a short, surprised laugh at the sight.

"Now," I said, "tell us who it was that scared you."

Sparrow shuddered. "Don't know as I should talk about them," she whispered. "Might be they're listening."

We all glanced toward the dusky window.

"I'll go look around outside. To make sure no one's near." I made myself speak firmly, although I was by no means feeling as confident as I sounded.

Outside, the drizzle had stopped and a breeze had picked up, swirling a rising mist. I walked to the edge of the clearing and peered as far as I could. Trunks swayed and leaves rippled, but I could see no person. When I returned, the lieutenant was talking quietly to Sparrow. She seemed less jumpy. The man had a calming way about him.

"No one's there," I said.

Sparrow beckoned to me to come closer. When we were all huddled together, she whispered, " 'Twas the People Things I saw."

Lieutenant Lynd leaned forward. "Who are they?"

"They look like folks, and walk on two legs like folks, but they ain't folks."

Her words sent trembling bits of ice through my veins.

"Does she mean the VanZeldts?" Seeley asked. "How come I never get to see them?"

"Perhaps you saw the servants of a man who lives near here," Lieutenant Lynd said quietly. "They're odd, but they *are* people."

Sparrow shook her head gravely. "No, they sure 'nough ain't. They only playacting they're folks like us. I seen them before, but this time they had got big wooden heads on their necks."

For a moment no one spoke.

"Masks?" Lieutenant Lynd asked finally. "Were they wearing masks?"

"All carved to look like monsters. At first I thought they *was* real monsters. I like to died."

"It would be a terrible shock," I said. "Right here in our woods. I've heard that the VanZeldts dance outdoors at night. Maybe the masks are part of their dancing."

"I want to see it," Seeley said.

"No," I said. "We're staying as far away from them as we can. Where were they when you saw them, Sparrow? Close by?"

"Yonder. A right far piece, near a big house. They wasn't dancing, though. I don't know what they was doing. I ran fast to get away, and it took me a while to come to this place. In all my born days, I ain't never come across this place before."

A smile quirked the lieutenant's lips. "I'm glad you found us—after all your born days."

"The VanZeldts won't be here till the evening," I said. "I guess we'll stay a bit longer. There's things we need to talk about. Seeley, will you grab Lieutenant Lynd's bags?"

Since Coon Baby had made a mess of Sparrow's pie before falling asleep, I passed the girl another slice. She nibbled it as Seeley trotted over to the saddlebags. He heaved them up and dropped them beside Lieutenant Lynd. "Aren't you surprised?"

The lieutenant stared as if he couldn't believe his eyes. "Why, those are mine. I never thought I'd see them again. How—where did you find them?"

"They showed up with Star in our pasture a while back," Seeley said.

"You have my horse? She's at your place?"

"Sure is," Seeley said. "We're taking care of her."

"But how did you know Star and these bags were mine?" Lieutenant Lynd touched the leather with wonder.

I was glad he was so surprised he didn't ask how we knew his horse's name. I could never let him know I'd read his letter. Would he believe the horse had told me? "We didn't *know*," I said. "We brought them because we thought they *might* be yours. We don't have that many riderless Union horses around here—yet."

He began pulling out item after item. "My toothbrush! And soap! Unheard-of luxury!" When he drew out the shirt, the carvings fell from it. He was wriggling into his sleeves when Seeley reached for the figures.

"Can I see these?" He took them up before the lieutenant could answer and rubbed his palm along the woman's flowing gown.

"This is so much better," Lieutenant Lynd said as he fastened his buttons. "One feels vulnerable without clothing."

I was more comfortable with him in a shirt as well.

He nodded toward the carvings. "I never did get those polished as smooth as I wanted them."

"You thought these up and made them yourself?" Seeley asked.

"I did."

"With just a pocketknife?"

The lieutenant nodded.

"Would you teach me how?" Seeley reverently traced the man's curling beard with his finger. "I've got a pocketknife too."

"I can show you how I do it, anyway," Lieutenant Lynd said. "I sort of taught myself. It was as if the figures just grew naturally out of the wood."

"Are they elves?" I asked.

"Don't know," Lieutenant Lynd said. "I don't know what they are. I didn't really think as I shaped them."

Sparrow had been watching with interest. Now she spoke. "They be People Things."

I started to laugh but couldn't because it wasn't funny; it was true.

"We'll bring you wood," Seeley said, handing the figures to the lieutenant.

Lieutenant Lynd rubbed his bearded chin. He held out the carvings to me. "Would you like these? I really don't know what to do with them."

It had caused me a pang to turn the figures over to him, and now I could keep them. He removed the sapphire velvet case, opened it, studied it a moment, and held it out to us. "My sister, Addie."

His sister. Oh.

"She's pretty," I said.

Next came the packet of letters. He unfolded one and smoothed out the paper. "You're already doing so much for me, but is there any way you could get a note across the lines to my family? They've got to be worried sick."

"I can try," I said. "Our older cousin is staying with us and he does some smuggling now and then, so maybe he can get it sent."

"Smuggling, eh? Sounds awfully adventurous."

"Yes, indeed. Dorian is most definitely an adventurer. I can't even tell you how many times he's run the blockade—he's a Southern patriot. I guess I'll pretend your letter is from me. I'll make up some story."

"Isn't it funny?" Lieutenant Lynd retied the string around the packet, and for the first time I noticed a ring on his pinkie finger—a carnelian stone set within a scrolled gold frame. "The rest of the world seemed so unreal until you came the other day. If I strained to clearly remember people and places, they eluded me, as if I were trying to recall a dream, but now everything has come rushing back. I wonder . . ."

"You wonder what?" Seeley asked.

"Oh, nothing." The lieutenant glanced out the door. "Look, Seeley. There's a toad hopping right there. Could you and Sparrow catch that one and find some more, do you think? We could have a toad race."

The two children jumped up and ran outside.

I waited until they were out of earshot. "Now, what did you want to say without them around?"

His face was grave. "Do you mind if I confide in you and ask your advice?"

"Of course not."

"Even though I'm a Yankee?"

"I suppose the whole war isn't entirely your fault." I examined my nails as if it really mattered that they were stubby and chipped. "I think—I think you would have liked Rush if you had ever met him. And he would have liked you."

"I'm sure that would have been the case. I wish we had known each other. I—there's nothing I can say except, once again, how sorry I am."

I gave a slight nod, accepting his words. "I guess I'll have to admit here and now that I've had some doubts about things myself. Slavery and—everything."

"I knew it! You're too smart not to have questioned it."

Should I be insulted or flattered? "You must know," I said slowly, "even if Mississippians want to free their slaves, the law makes it almost impossible. You can't just do it because of a change of heart.

You have to get permission from the state legislature, and it's rarely given."

Lieutenant Lynd nodded. "I understand."

"Now," I said, "there's things I need to tell you too, so we better talk fast. For instance, do you know what that bag is that you're wearing around your neck? That mojo bag?"

"Hmm. 'Mojo,' it's called? There's dried leaves and flowers and some little pebbles in it."

For a moment I toyed with the notion of showing him my amulet, then dismissed it. Right now I was too unsure of everything, and Amenze's gift was too personal to display to anyone else. "Their magic is called 'hoodoo.' You may have heard it called 'voodoo'— that's when it's practiced as a religion. Some of the slaves brought it with them from Africa. On some plantations it's a common practice, even though preachers preach against it and masters try to stop it. I've always thought of hoodoo as something frightening, but the VanZeldts are healing you, so maybe it evokes good as well." I lifted my chin. "I believe it really can have some power."

"So do I. Now. But *why* are they healing me? That's one of the questions I need answered. They don't seem to actually care about me. They're saving my leg and keeping me alive, but I feel no compassion coming from them. They bring me food and change the dressing with almost a—a contempt."

"And the fact that they don't speak to you and leave you no light, with only that skimpy blanket as a cover . . . All that is cruel. I've thought they could be acting under orders from their master, Dr. VanZeldt. Maybe he's a Northern sympathizer. Has he ever come here?"

"Not that I know of. But I've slept an abnormal amount during these weeks, and when I've been awake, my brain has been foggy; he may have come when I wasn't quite present. Could I have been drugged? That's what I was about to say before the children left. They bring an odd-tasting drink every night with the stew. There's a bitter taste to it, disguised with molasses. I've been drinking it because I supposed I needed all the nourishment I could get. Last night, though, I poured it out after they were gone. For the first time since I came here, I woke with the dawn and my mind has worked clearly."

"Perhaps they gave it to you in order to ease the pain."

He stretched out his arms and shoulders. "Well, no more. I don't like being unaware of reality and having no control of my thinking."

"When we were little, we used to play around pretending we could cast spells because we'd heard a few things about hoodoo from Anarchy. That's Sparrow's grandmother. She's oh, I'll tell you about her later. Anyway, Aunt Permilla—she was a servant, but acted as a mother to me—she caught us doing it once and said"—I deepened my voice to mimic Aunt Permilla's—"'Hoodoo sounds like foolishment when you're setting in your cozy house, but when you seen what I seen when I was a child and a conjure man stayed right there on the same plantation, you don't laugh no more.'" I shivered. Aunt Permilla's normally snug manner had prickled as if her every sense were on edge.

"Did she tell you what it was she had seen?"

"When we prodded, the only thing she ever said was, 'Door-nail dead one minute, then walking around live as you or me the next.' She pursed up her lips after that and wouldn't explain or say anything more about it. Her silence made it all the scarier. Ever after, we took spell casting seriously. And that's why I need to tell you something else."

He waited.

It was hard to know how to voice it out loud. I licked my dry lips. "Back at the beginning of April, right around when you were wounded, I was working at the hospital in town."

"Commendable."

"No. I was not a good nurse. I tried, but there really wasn't much I could do but bring food and water and write letters for the poor men."

"And that's a great deal."

I waved my hands through the air as if waving his words away. "Afterward the bodies were laid outside waiting to be taken off for burial. One of them had red hair."

He frowned, questioning.

"What color was your friend Jorgenson's hair?"

"Oh. Red."

"This corpse also had a mojo bag like yours. And—and his throat was slashed above it."

Lieutenant Lynd drew in a sharp breath. "They killed him."

"That's what I thought. It wasn't the sort of injury that would happen in battle."

"Jorgenson's wound was to his stomach." The lieutenant put his head in his hands.

I waited a moment to let everything sink in before going on. "That's why I may not be able to keep the promise I made to Seeley.

I said I wouldn't turn you in. But if your life truly is in danger from the VanZeldts, I'll go to the marshal in a flash in order to save you."

"I understand," he said as he raised his head. "And I trust you to do what's best. In fact, I'll ask you myself to turn me in if I think they're about to harm me. Somehow I believe I'll be able to detect a change in their manner in time to be warned. At least now, for whatever reason, they're keeping me alive and they're saving my leg." He paused and studied his hands. "You don't—you don't know how mutilated I was and what a miracle it is that I'm healing. If I leave here anytime soon, a surgeon would still amputate, and with the wound so high on my hip . . ." He looked up at me earnestly. "But if I keep progressing as I am now, I think I could be walking in a few weeks, even though I'm almost scared to say so out loud."

The children returned. Seeley held some moving things folded up in his shirttail. "It took so long because we wanted three to race. You two each get one, and I'm sharing mine with Sparrow." He set the toads down in a line against the far wall. They squatted unmoving and unblinking.

"How do we know which is whose?" I asked.

"The smaller, faster-looking one is mine and Sparrow's," Seeley said, "and the biggest is Lieutenant Lynd's. The other is Violet's."

"The prettiest," Lieutenant Lynd said.

"Where is it pretty?" I demanded.

"Oh, you know . . . for toads. . . ." Lieutenant Lynd was watching me closely. "By the way, the blue of your ribbon exactly matches your eyes."

I looked quickly back at the toads. "How do we make them move?"

"Tickle their feet, Seeley," Lieutenant Lynd said. "That's how I always did it."

Seeley complied, and soon it was a real race across the floor. We were all—even Sparrow—cheering on our favorite and laughing noisily.

"Them toads are sure 'nough having a good time too," Sparrow said.

Seeley studied me. "Violet, you never laugh that loud."

My face grew hot, but I laughed again. "They look so funny galumphing like that. Maybe Lieutenant Lynd should write about toad people instead of snake people. Because villains with legs would be more threatening."

Seeley's eyes danced. "Ooh. I think they'd be more creepy slithering around with their tongues poking out. You know—like this." He narrowed his eyes to slivers and his tongue flashed in and out.

Sparrow gave a little shuddering cry.

"Stop it, Seeley," I said.

"I'll try it both ways," Lieutenant Lynd said. "We'll see which works best."

Suddenly, with a roar, the rain came down again as if the bottom had let loose from the sky. I jumped. "We need to go."

Lieutenant Lynd shook his head. "You can't leave in weather like this."

"We've got to." I stood. "It's getting late and we need to be long gone before the VanZeldts come. Sparrow, will you be all right? Won't you come with us to Scuppernong and stay till the storm stops?"

She looked scornful. "The warm rain feels good on my skin."

"Do you know your way home?" I had to ask.

"Course. I go everywhere all the time. Sometimes I even sleep all night out in the trees. Memaw don't never fuss about me."

"Oh," Seeley said, "I just thought of something. Don't tell your memaw about Lieutenant Lynd. He's a secret."

I had been wondering how to ask Sparrow to keep quiet.

She gave a sober nod. "When I find nests and things, I don't tell nobody. 'Tis best."

Without another word, before we knew it, she was gone.

"We'll see her again," I told Seeley. "We'll visit her at Anarchy's." I picked up the saddlebags Lieutenant Lynd had repacked. "Do you think we should hide these?"

"Yes," he said. "Even if their motives are entirely innocent, from the way the VanZeldts act, it's obvious I'm their secret. Let me remove the shirt. Then you better take everything away with you."

"We can hide them here," Seeley said. "Look, there's a little shelf a ways up the chimney that no one can see unless they stand right in here like I'm doing."

His shoulders and head were out of sight.

"Well, it's unlikely the VanZeldts will do that," I said, and handed Seeley the bags. "What about keeping out candles, Lieutenant? You saw we brought some."

He seemed torn. "I would love a candle, but I don't dare risk it shining through the windows. Someone might see. Thank you, though, for bringing me light."

I bustled about, once again scattering dust over our footprints. "Seeley, say farewell to the toads and toss them out."

When we were about to leave, I stood in the doorway, looking at Lieutenant Lynd, wondering about everything. A smile flickered at his mouth but didn't reach his eyes.

"We *will* come back," I said. "We can't come every day, though."

He nodded, but he looked abandoned.

Seeley and I rushed out into the deluge, the drops striking our faces like pellets. Sparrow was long gone. I grabbed the boy's hand because it would be too easy to lose him in this downpour.

We put our heads low and surged on, slipping and squelching. The droplets that blinked in my eyelashes, along with interlaced light and shadows, played tricks with my vision. Out of the corner of my eye I kept thinking I saw dark figures slipping between tree trunks.

Even though it meant a longer hike, we avoided the clearing with the fire pit. We weren't far from it, though, when, blending in with the pounding of rain came another, deeper sound.

The beating of drums.

A throbbing rose up and swelled around us, as if it emanated from everywhere and nowhere. The very earth beneath my feet pulsated. All I could do was clutch Seeley's hand tighter and pray we wouldn't run into People Things banging on drums in the middle of a rainstorm in the middle of the forest.

CHAPTER 20

CIRCLE
OF ENCHANTMENT

There we were in our enchanted circle in a green-lit, vine-shrouded ruin. It lay in the middle of a dense forest inhabited by dark, threatening fairies. Day after day, in this charmed sphere, we were safe and secure and each of us shone in a way that I, at least, never did in the real world.

Or perhaps the glow was from the sweat on our faces. The Lodge was sweltering in June.

"You're looking awfully robust," I told Thomas one day. He was filling out and able to move more easily now, to sit up and shift himself on his pallet. His body was finely and strongly built. His face was still lean but had a returning vitality. And he was more handsome than ever in spite of the beard and general dishevelment. I had never trusted handsome men, but I trusted Thomas. I had despised Yankees, but not Thomas. "I'm surprised the VanZeldts haven't noticed." A wave of fear swept over me, and my smile fled. "You don't think they have, do you?"

"No. I suck in my cheeks and close my eyes and lie limp when they're around."

"Like the fairy tale of Hansel and Gretel."

"The gingerbread house."

"Yes. The part where Hansel's in a cage being fattened for eating. He has a chicken bone he pokes out so when the blind old witch touches it to see how plump he's gotten, she feels the bone instead of Hansel's finger. Too bad the VanZeldts aren't blind, because here's a perfectly skinny chicken bone."

"I hated that story."

"Me too."

"When I was eight years old, our teacher, Mr. Meaty, threw chalk at us if we displeased him." Thomas shook his head at the memory. "Yes, his name really was Meaty."

"There's a new French novel I'm going to bring to read with you next time. It's called *Les Misérables*. My cousin Dorian lent it to me. You'll have to excuse me, though, because I can't help weeping openly over Fantine and Cosette and Jean Valjean."

"I'll look forward to hearing it. And weeping openly."

We called him Thomas now, and he called me Violet. Seeley and I had come to the Lodge several times in the past couple of weeks. I would hurry through my work, and if the rest of the day was free, we spent honey-gold, honey-sweet hours there. The time was deep and full of meaning, but very narrow—never enough.

Nobody at Scuppernong noticed how often we were gone or acted curious about where we went so long as we did our chores and I kept Seeley out from underfoot. Laney and Michael had their family and their own work, Miss Elsa inhabited her dreamland, and Dorian and Sunny were absorbed in each other, continually laughing without telling anyone else what was funny, squabbling and making up, snuggling. This would have been irritating normally, but it was convenient now. Both Seeley and I hugged our clandestine world to ourselves. Sometimes we would catch each other's eye and grin over our sweet secret.

Of course, many days were not free, and if a while went by between visits, Thomas never asked why. He never tried to keep us longer when it was time to go. But when we entered the room, a brightness came over him.

The conversations between Thomas and me were spiced and enlivened by the feeling of mind leaping to meet mind, by the keen awareness of the other's every movement and word and look. I could open up to Thomas as I never had to anyone else. Maybe not even to Rush and Laney.

We had rambled on about the war, literature, religion—nearly everything except the details of our everyday lives. Somehow I was afraid of bringing up the real, current world—as if it would break the spell of this place—and perhaps Thomas felt the same. He told us he had been a teacher and that he wrote the Heath Blackstock books while still in college. Other than that, I knew little about his life before he joined the army. However, from our hours together, I understood him in more important ways. Usually he was calm and clear-sighted, but he could suddenly turn awkward and hesitating. I believed this change was due to the vulnerability of his position. What never changed were his clear insights, his intelligence, his creativity, and how good he was to Seeley.

Patiently he was teaching my little cousin simultaneously to whittle and to play chess. During the hours when they carved the rough chessmen from ivy root, Thomas explained moves and strategies. I liked the smell of the wood shavings, but the slice-slice-slice of the knives made me anxious. I had to avert my eyes.

We brought a checkerboard from home, and they'd begun playing, even though some of the irregular pieces were barely recognizable. They would set up the board on a stump between them and lay out the chessmen. The tip of Seeley's tongue would poke out of the corner of his mouth, as it did whenever he was in deep concentration, and he always took ages to make each move. Thomas studied his own strategy as well, as deeply absorbed as if Seeley were a formidable opponent.

One mid-June day, I brought along my dulcimer.

"What is this?" Thomas asked as I unwrapped it from its shawl.

"A dulcimer," I said. "I thought you might like some music."

"I made her bring it," Seeley said. "Because when I told you Violet played the harp, you were sad that you couldn't hear her."

"I've never seen such an instrument," Thomas said. "This will be exciting—to listen to songs other than the birds'."

I settled myself on the stump near his pallet and started out with "Oft in the Stilly Night." As I plucked the beautiful, thin, haunting melody, I peeked up at Thomas. His head was cocked to one side and a smile lingered about his lips. My heartstrings strummed along.

Next I moved on to foot-stamping, hand-clapping tunes of my own creation, as well as popular favorites. I played "Camptown Races" and "Blue Tail Fly." Thomas and Seeley both sang at the top of their voices. The Lodge's walls reverberated with sound. As always, I soon lost myself in the music. We were enthusiastically singing "Listen to the Mockingbird" when a clear, high little voice joined in from outside. Seeley leaped up and shouted, "Sparrow!"

She entered, smiling and shining-eyed. She sidled up close to me, and we finished the song together.

"How are you?" I said. "I'm so glad you came again."

"Is Coon Baby gone to his own kin now?" Seeley asked.

Sparrow nodded and blinked, then snatched my sleeve. "Play it again. I need to sing it again."

I did as she asked.

"Do you know 'Cotton-Eyed Joe'?" she said when I finished. "Memaw sings that tune and I dance to it, round and round."

"Hum it," I said, "and I'll follow along."

Once I got the chords down, Sparrow jumped up and grabbed Seeley's hands. They promenaded wildly around the room. I played faster and faster until Seeley was practically flinging wispy Sparrow about. They fell down laughing. For a moment my eyes blurred, and it was Rush and Laney there on the floor.

"Will you play 'The Minstrel Boy'?" Seeley asked after he'd recovered. "I like how it makes my stomach feel."

I nodded. "It's beautiful. I don't know if I'll be able to get through

it, though. It's so . . . timely. The way it tells of falling in war . . .
and of . . . slavery."

"We'll help," Thomas said.

I managed the first verse but choked up too much on the second.
Thomas and Seeley continued alone.

> *"The Minstrel fell! But the foeman's chain*
> *Could not bring his proud soul under;*
> *The harp he lov'd ne'er spoke again,*
> *For he tore its chords asunder;*
> *And said, 'No chains shall sully thee,*
> *Thou soul of love and bravery!*
> *Thy songs were made for the pure and free,*
> *They shall never sound in slavery!' "*

I thought of Rush. I thought of Michael, Laney, and even little
Sparrow, who had been bought out of bondage by her grandmother.
The verse exposed so many facets of pain and guilt in me that I laid
down the instrument. "Excuse me," I said, and went outside until
my tears would stop.

Seeley came out a few minutes later. "Thomas told me to check
on you. Are you all right?"

I sniffed and gave my eyes and cheeks a final swipe with my
handkerchief. "Yes. Let's go back in."

He grabbed my hand and held it tightly as he led me inside.

Thomas looked up, full of compassion. I gave him a wobbly smile.

Sparrow was reverently holding the dulcimer. She strummed it
gently. I showed her how to grasp it properly and where to place her

fingers on the fret board in order to play some chords. She listened intently. Then, amazingly, she played a few bars of "Cotton-Eyed Joe."

"Someday, if you wish, I'll teach you to really play it," I told her, wondering where on earth I could come by another instrument for her. From her expression, it was something she needed to have.

"I wish," she said. "When?"

"During the winter, when there's less work to be done, come to Scuppernong and I'll show you how."

My heart swelled at the sight of her glowing face. Sometimes my awareness of the terrible, troubled world outside the Lodge only intensified the beauty of the things that happened inside it.

"Hey," Seeley said, "do you want to go outside and do something, Sparrow?"

She nodded and the two of them left Thomas and me alone.

"How did you learn to play your music?" Thomas asked.

"This belonged to my mother," I said as I carefully wrapped the dulcimer in the shawl. "So did the harp, but I never remember her playing either of them. I never dared touch them when I was little, even though I longed to. My mother had been dying slowly ever since I could remember, and we were taught to tiptoe around and never disturb her; that's why we children spent so much time outside." I glanced at Thomas on his pine straw pallet and pictured my mother—huddled bones beneath a sheet. "One day, though, she got my father to pull the harp up close to the sofa. She had me sit in front of her. She wrapped her arms around me and showed me where to place my fingers and how to pluck. She only helped a little, and I taught myself the rest, but that one time is the only memory I have of her doing something with me. It makes me think now that maybe, rather than being unaware of us, she had actually been our angel silently keeping watch. When I'm playing my music, I believe she's still watching."

"Of course she is" was all Thomas said. His response was simple, but it was nice to hear my hope stated as a conviction in his deep voice.

My eyes were welling once again. Thomas reached out his hand. I took it for a moment, and his warmth spread to me. I released it, suddenly shy. "What do you think Seeley and Sparrow are doing?"

"Maybe we should go and see," Thomas said, stretching. "The fact that my legs were itching to dance when those two were prancing around must mean something. How about this is the day I try to get up and go outside?"

The idea of Thomas walking left me excited for him, but also a bit dismayed. It would mean that he must leave soon. "Are you sure? Hadn't you better wait a while longer?"

"I don't think so. It's time. Suddenly I don't know if I can stand another hour without the sun on my face."

"Very well," I said, standing. "If we're going to get you outside before I have to go, we'd better do it now. Seeley and I've got to leave early; I have a bazaar to attend later on."

"A bazaar! How bizarre. What kind?"

"The kind that raises money for the war. The local ladies have been creating all sorts of handiwork for it. I made pen wipers to sell that no one could possibly want."

"If I were there, I'd buy every one. One can never have too many pen wipers. So is that all it is? A sale?"

"No, it's also a dance for the Texas brigade that's passing through."

"And you like dancing?"

"I do indeed. I may even come out of mourning so I can join in. Most people agree that young folks don't have to wear black now for more than a few months."

"Will your cousin be there?"

"My cousin?" I looked up from the stump I was rolling back in place.

"Yes. The one you said was so heroic with his blockade-running."

"Probably. I expect he enjoys dancing."

"Has he mailed my letters yet?"

"Next time he crosses the lines, I'll ask him to do it."

"So tonight you'll be whirling around the room with him and all those other Secesh boys."

"I will—and don't call them 'Secesh.' It's an awful word."

"I'm sorry." He gave a slight bow. "I meant with all the Southern gentlemen. They do say ladies admire men in uniform."

"You've got a uniform."

"Oh yes, I'd forgotten. Pity it's ragged and bloody and needs to be burned. I expect ladies also admire gentlemen who don't have giant chunks blown out of them."

This was a new mood for Thomas. Till now he had never sounded bitter or the least bit self-pitying. "Well, I'm sure you looked splendid in your uniform before. . . ."

"Thank you, Violet," he said dryly.

"And you'll look splendid in it again," I said quickly.

He compressed his lips and turned away so I couldn't see his expression. "Have a wonderful time. You deserve it. I forget you have a whole busy life I know nothing about. It's amazing you've been able to steal away as often as you have."

I started for the door. "I'm going to go find you some walking sticks."

He stopped me. "First could you bring me my trousers out of the bag? So I can come out from under the blanket."

"Oh, my goodness, yes." The foolish blood rushed to my cheeks and I was thankful to hurry outside after I did what he asked.

The children dashed off when I sent them to find two straight sticks. Meanwhile, I cleared a path through the rubble of the front room. By the time we joined Thomas, he was fully clothed, sweating from the exertion of struggling into his trousers. Seeley and I helped lift under his arms while Sparrow stood close. Shaking a little, he stood. He was even taller than I had thought. The muscles in his face and neck strained as though they would burst through as he grasped the sticks, but slowly, determinedly, with a swinging gait, he made his way from the room where he had lain for more than two months.

My hands dropped to my sides. I followed, tense. All my skin tingled from touching him. So interesting. He stumbled slightly and every one of us leaped forward, but he righted himself before we could reach him.

Outside was hot and bright and bees hummed in the riotous yellow roses that climbed nearly to the roof of the Lodge. Thomas picked one blossom and awkwardly tucked it behind my ear.

He and I both lifted our faces into the full brilliance of the sun.

CHAPTER 21

A BETROTHAL

When Seeley and I returned home soon afterward, we walked in on Dorian and Sunny huddled together on the sofa.

Dorian's eyes were holding hers steadily. "You know what you must do," he was saying, "what would speed things up."

She started to speak, but he put a finger over her lips. "Don't say anything out loud. Just think of our future."

He noticed Seeley and me then, and turned on a smile, showing all his very white teeth. There was something in the curve of his mouth that didn't match the expression in his eyes. I shrugged inwardly; I had no desire to know what plots those two were hatching.

"Y'all are going to the Summer Bazaar, aren't you?" I asked.

"So bizarre," Dorian murmured, and I was unfairly annoyed because he had used Thomas's joke. He picked an infinitesimal bit of lint off the sleeve of his blue broadcloth coat. The hue made his eyes bluer than ever and his hair a brighter gold. "Are you going?"

"Yes, I am. In fact, I'm heading up into the attic to see if there's anything I can wear."

"Tossing out the black?" Dorian said. "About time."

I expected Sunny to comment as well, since it was a subject on which she had strong opinions, but she said nothing.

"Am I going?" Seeley asked.

"No," I said. "It's not a children's thing. Run wash your hands, Squid. Goodness, we get dirty these days."

Seeley trotted off obediently.

"It's all your nature loving 'these days,'" Dorian said. "What've y'all been doing lately out in the wilds?"

"Oh," I said vaguely, "you know . . . exploring, hide-and-seek—that sort of thing."

"Better you than me," Dorian said. "Anyway"—he flexed his fingers—"I don't believe Sunny and I will be attending this particular grand social occasion. I've got to meet someone here this evening, so I'm unavailable for keeping an eye on Seeley, but Sunny'll do it."

My stepsister's head had been drooping in un-Sunny-like fashion. At Dorian's words she jerked it up. "No, not tonight. Actually I *am* going to the bazaar. I've got to take the tea cozies I've been sewing my fingers to the bone over."

Dorian rolled his eyes. "Is that what those creatures are? I've been wondering. Violet can take them, if tea cozies are so vital to the Cause. She deserves an evening away since she's with the boy every day. You ought to stay with him this time, Sunny."

"No," she said flatly. "Not tonight. I'm going."

I laughed inwardly. Poor Sunny, having to desert Dorian just so she wouldn't have to attend to Seeley. "That's fine. Laney won't mind staying to tuck Seeley in bed and bring him his honey milk."

"Sunny, my beauty," Dorian said, reaching for her arm, "you're going to be too tired for our foray if you go gamboling about till all hours. I'm taking her on her first smuggling adventure tomorrow," he explained to me. "You wouldn't believe the things ladies can fit under their hoops. In fact, my meeting here is with Colonel Riding of the Texas Fifth to get commissions from him."

I remembered that I also had a commission. "I've got some letters I'd like you to mail, actually, if you wouldn't mind. A couple that will stay in the South, but also a letter to some friends in Connecticut. I'll give them to you as soon as they're ready."

"Of course we'll take them," Dorian said.

Normally Sunny would have pried into who I knew in Connecticut, and I had a lie all ready, but she wasn't acting like herself today. She returned to the subject of the bazaar. "I'm going whether you want me to or not, Dorian. I want to dance."

Let them fight it out.

Dorian frowned and leaned down to whisper in her ear. I wasn't sure because I was already headed out the door, but I thought his fingers dug hard into the white flesh of her upper arm. When I was halfway up the stairs, I heard noises that made me freeze. A squeal, a short scuffle, and then—a resounding blow.

He hit her. Surely I must be mistaken—no gentleman would do that. But no, he had hit her. What was I to do? I started to whirl around to go back in and confront Dorian, but the sitting room door flew open. I jumped and bolted up to my bedroom like a startled rabbit.

Sunny's door slammed.

One minute, then I would go to her. I perched on the edge of my bed, trying to catch my breath.

From under the floorboard I took the correspondence Thomas had given me to mail. It was a temptation to snoop and read it, but I resisted, although I did catch a glimpse of "Dearest sister Addie" scrawled on one of the pages. He had very bad handwriting. It occurred to me that I had been vaguely jealous of the sweetheart-Addie-of-my-imagination who had written so familiarly to the Thomas-of-my-imagination even before I had met Thomas himself. And she had been his sister all along. A little smile curved my lips as I placed the letters in an envelope and wrote the address. I also gathered up a letter to Aunt Lovina and another to a school acquaintance I had scrawled a few days earlier. Mixed among other envelopes, the one to the Lynds would be less noticeable.

I went across the hall and knocked softly on Sunny's door.

"Come in," she said. "Just in time to tighten my stays."

The candy-pink gown she had worn lay puddled on the floor. I picked it up and shook it out. One dainty puffed sleeve was dangling, nearly ripped off.

I stared at her.

She shrugged. "See why I have to change?"

"Did Dorian do this?"

"Yes."

"He—he hit you?"

"No," she said coolly. "He tore my dress grabbing at me when I left, but actually it was *me* who slapped *him*. Hard. He deserved it, with his pestering and plaguing."

"What is he plaguing you about?"

She suddenly looked tired and pinched. "Oh . . . nothing important."

I started to tug at her corset laces but stopped short. Five reddish finger-shaped bruises were forming on Sunny's upper arm, and a large, splotchy, older bruise, purplish, discolored the back of her neck.

Words clogged in my throat. When I could finally speak, I said, "Sunny, the way you two act is not normal."

Over her shoulder she flashed a brilliant smile with a ghastly edge to it. "Maybe not, but it's exciting. I should detest a mealymouthed little man who says, 'Yes, darling,' and 'No, darling.' And"—she dropped down on her bed—"you'll never guess. Last night Dorian asked me to marry him."

I sank down beside her. She gripped my hand and squeezed it, giving a delighted shiver.

"Are you sure this is what you want?" was all I could say.

"Of course. I totally adore him. And you wouldn't believe the delicious promises he's been making. The gowns and jewels I'm to have and the trips we're to take and my precious sweetheart to boot!" She tugged playfully at my hair. "Why, I'm the luckiest girl in the world!"

Dorian must have done much better with his blockade-running than I would have suspected.

"When is the wedding to be?"

"Not sure. We're to keep it secret for a bit, but of course I have to tell you and Mama. It all depends on—oh, boring things like finances and the progress of the war and all that nonsense."

So, Sunny, as so often happened with her, had gotten exactly what she wanted. Wasn't it odd that getting exactly what one wanted often didn't make for happiness? I couldn't believe Dorian had asked her to marry him. Why? Much of the time my stepsister seemed to annoy rather than captivate my cousin—adequate only for a dalliance when he had nothing better available. But I must be mistaken; he had stayed here a good deal longer than he had planned and the reason had to be Sunny. He *must* love her. They must have the sort of affection where sparks of all kinds flew. I would hate such a relationship, but perhaps the two of them loved each other all the better for it.

"Now," Sunny said, "after you help me with the buttons on my dress—drat, it'd better be the cinnamon-striped since I suppose I'll have to cover up with sleeves and my hair down over my neck—we're going to go up into the attic to find you the most perfect gown. Then we'll fix you up prettily so you'll catch the eye of five or six—no, *ten!*—gallant Texans. You shall be my pet. And don't you dare say no."

I didn't.

In the attic we pawed through trunks until Sunny pulled out a china-blue silk taffeta edged with tiny ivory embroidered rosebuds. "It's so darling it makes my knees go weak. Also, blue is a good color to follow mourning. You're quick with your needle, unlike frivolous, useless me, so you can raise the waist in no time." She paused and studied my face. "Aren't you excited?"

"I am and that's what surprises me. I never thought I'd be excited over fashions again."

"Silly goose. As if dead people would want you to go about looking like a drab for the rest of your life when you're only seventeen."

Downstairs I sought out Laney in the kitchen to ask her to do the evening milking and to watch out for Seeley while we were gone. I displayed the gown I was about to make over.

"It'll look good on you," Laney said.

"If you get yourself some dresses from Mama's trunks, I'll help you fix them up. Aren't we lucky she brought so many pretty things from Panola? There's a dark red cambric would suit you perfectly."

"Thank you. I will." She glanced toward the door. "Did you hear—" She stopped and her lips tightened.

"Hear what?"

She shook her head.

"Laney, tell me."

"Did you hear that fight going on between those two?"

"Between Sunny and Dorian? Yes, I did."

"Well, you couldn't have heard much of it because they've been at it all the livelong day. I couldn't hear well enough to tell what they were caterwauling about, but it's something bad."

I sighed. "However they quarrel, Sunny still adores him. In fact, she's—" I stopped myself before I told Laney about the engagement. Not my secret to share. "Sunny could have almost any man she wants, but it's Dorian she chooses."

"Ain't no telling with some folks," Laney said.

I agreed. No telling. I left Laney and settled myself in the sitting room with my sewing basket and the dress. Seeley wandered in soon after and dropped down to lean against my knee and read his book.

"You're not worried about me being gone tonight, are you?" I asked, since he didn't normally position himself quite so close.

"No," he said. "But you'll come and see me when you get back, won't you? Even if it's past midnight?"

"Yes, but you'll probably be asleep by then. I mean, past midnight is awfully late."

Miss Elsa and Sunny entered, with my stepmother looking bliss-ful and Sunny cross, as she was so often with her mother. Miss Elsa patted my shoulder and whispered, "Isn't it lovely news about Dorian and Anna Bess? I told you they were falling in love, didn't I? I'm going to start on her wedding gown right away." She turned to Sunny and said more loudly, "Buy some ivory satin when you're in Tennessee with your smuggling or whatever it is you and Dorian are doing there, won't you? I must work out the yardage before you go."

Sunny grimaced and hissed, "Mama, don't start that sort of thing when we don't even know when the wedding will be." She wrinkled her nose. "Oh, drat! I didn't finish that last ghastly tea cozy, and if I don't do the full amount, all the silly old biddies will spread it around that I didn't donate my share." She swept up her needle and thread. "Serves them right that they're hideous."

She snatched up the maligned tea cozy and dropped into a chair, but she never began stitching. Instead her hands lay clenched in her lap for several minutes. She had such an odd expression on her face that I followed her gaze. Her eyes were fixed on Seeley's head, bent over his book. When he made a sudden move to look up and say something to me, she started.

"Are you all right, Sunny?" I asked.

"Of course. Why shouldn't I be? It's just this stupid—stupid sewing. I'm sick of it."

She was acting so strangely, but I couldn't make my stepsister tell me anything she didn't want to. And that was what was so worrisome—*why* didn't she want to? Sunny always before had tended to dramatic gushings, reveling in being comforted and pet-ted. In spite of what she claimed, was she unsure about the whole betrothal business? Her mood had to be Dorian-related, since every thought in Sunny's head these days was connected to him.

As soon as I finished taking up the dress and pressing it in the kitchen, Sunny led me up to her bedroom. There she helped me into my gown, lacing it so tightly that I gasped and fastening all seventy-five mother-of-pearl buttons in the back.

"Let me fetch my ruche," I said when I glanced downward and could almost see right down my bosom to my stomach. Evidently my mother had been more daring than I.

"Bless your heart, honey," Sunny called as I raced across the landing to my bedroom, "how can you be a dashing belle who attracts scores of Texans if you aren't at least a little improper?"

I ignored her and carefully tucked the lace ruffle along my bosom. Back in her bedroom she pushed me into a chair, curled my hair with hot tongs, dusted my neck and arms with scented powder, smeared on a touch of rouge, dabbed my lips with coralline salve, and fastened her own Venetian bead necklet about my throat.

"What is this?" she asked, tugging on the leather thong of my amulet.

"Oh, just a silly thing I always wear for good luck," I said quickly.

"How queer. Put it in your pocket or something, then, because you can't wear it with this dress."

I did as she instructed.

She surveyed me critically. "Shoes." She pulled open her wardrobe door and squatted down to riffle through the mound of shoes piled on the bottom. Finally, with a ladylike grunt, she drew out a pair of high-heeled, dove-gray silk slippers. "These will do nicely, although I expect they'll be too small for you."

Such satisfaction when they were actually too big, but wearable if I curled my toes; I was unfortunately used to shoes that didn't fit. I tucked Thomas's rose back into my hair.

"Now," Sunny said, placing me in front of her bureau and tilting the mirror up and down so I could view my entire body, "behold my work of art. I'm much more talented at this sort of thing than sewing."

If only Thomas could see me like this.

She pursed her lips. "Must you keep that bedraggled thing in your hair?"

I reached up to lightly touch the blossom. "Yes. And before you say anything more, no, you can't talk me out of wearing it."

"How funny. You're an odd girl, Violet, but I like you anyway. So much more than I did before we were sisters."

I could have said the same about Sunny. We smiled at each other.

Before we left, I sought Dorian out to give him the letters for posting. I found him beneath the scuppernong arbor, hunched on the bench, hands clasped beneath his chin, evidently deep in thought.

He gave a long, low whistle and stood when he saw me. "Why, coz, I'm going to have to give you three cheers and a tiger! I've never seen your arms before—or at least not so much of them. I approve. You're a dashing young lady who will attract scores of Texans with or without impropriety."

I drew in my breath. "Oh, my land, you overheard Sunny!"

He laughed. "Naturally. That minx has a voice that carries. Well, I'm jealous of all those gentlemen who'll be vying for a dance."

"It's Sunny you should be jealous over. She looks ravishing this afternoon. Be sure to tell her. In order to make up for—for—"

"Clearly I'm not the only one to overhear things," he said coolly.

He gave me a second to blush and feel uncomfortable before he continued. "Yes, we had a spat; your stepsister can be infuriating." He dug in his pocket. "Here, do you have one of those splendid— what were they?—pen wipers you were making? Let me buy one."

"They're in the house. Thank you. I'll leave the very finest one on the table, but be sure to get a tea cozy from Sunny too."

"Tea cozy, shmea cozy. Who would want a tea cozy if he can have a"—he edged closer—"pen wiper."

He was flirting with me again and he was engaged to my step-sister. I thrust the little packet of letters at him. "Here. You said you'd take these."

"So I did. Let's see. . . . Aunt Lovy, Miss Lucy Taylor, and who are these Yankees you're so anxious to correspond with? Hmm . . . Mr. and Mrs. Josiah Lynd."

"They're old friends of my mother's. I'd like to reassure them that we're doing all right down here."

He continued to study the address.

"Dorian, must you be so nosy?" I said, grinning to soften the words. "Now I've got to go. Sunny's waiting."

I scuttled away, praying he'd take no further notice of the letter.

CHAPTER 22

HOW BIZARRE

Sashes, scallops, ruffles, and curls flapped in the wind as we bowled along in the buggy toward Chicataw and the Summer Bazaar.

Miss Elsa had pulled herself together enough to join us. "So tiresome having to venture out without my beloved husband, but I cannot send you off unchaperoned. And after all, one must support our gallant gentlemen." Her eyes shone at the prospect of an outing. She wore a grass-green day dress with a wide silk fringe and a straw bonnet with streaming green ribbons. The summer sun was still bright this late in the day. She squinted at the unaccustomed brilliance, and the breeze whipped pallid rose into her pearly skin. She should be encouraged to leave the house more often.

"Miss Dancey!" I heard my name called above the rumbling wheels.

Old Jubal stood once again under the arbor of Miss Ruby Jewel's house, waving his arms to catch our attention.

Sunny gritted her teeth. "No! Not now. Pretend you don't see him."

"I can't. Let me down and y'all go on ahead. I'll see what he wants and walk the rest of the way."

"No, no, no," Sunny sighed. "And ruin my handiwork with you getting all dusty and sweaty? We'll wait, but be quick."

Michael reined in Star and I hopped down.

"I wasn't sure, Miss Dancey," Jubal said as I approached, "if you had heard about Miss Ruby Jewel."

"Why, no. What is there to hear?"

"She's—she's dying. You always were kind to her—never ran when she asked for you, as some did." A little fire blazed at the back of his dark eyes. "I got so angry at those folks who ran; she only asked for a few minutes of their time. You always came, so I wanted you to know."

Guilt tickled the back of my neck. I might never have run, but I certainly walked quickly past this house. And she had tried to help me that last time—to warn me. I had almost forgotten it with all else that had gone on. "I'm so sorry," I said. "Is there anything I can do?"

"Dr. Hale says nothing can be done but wait. Maybe you would be so good as to pray for her."

"I will. She's a lucky lady to have such a loyal friend in you. I'm sure she's known all these years how blessed she was." I would have headed back to the buggy, but something in Jubal's expression made me hesitate. Coming from him was a sense of strength and sorrow and a bewildered loneliness. To whom else could Jubal confide his grieving? "Let's go into the shade so you can tell me more about what's going on." I waved to the buggy, trying to signal them to drive ahead, but I didn't wait to see if they did.

On the porch, Jubal removed one of his mistress's wide lace collars from the chair where evidently he had been sitting to mend it. I took the seat and gestured for him to take the other chair.

He lowered himself rustily and dragged one long, gnarled hand down his sagging cheeks. "She doesn't hardly talk and doesn't want visitors. Can you imagine that? Poor little thing. Poor little mistress."

I shook my head. It couldn't even be Miss Ruby Jewel anymore if she didn't want company.

He gave an almost sob and raised his hands in a gesture of frustration. "'Twas those blamed gingersnaps. So many times I'd say, 'Please, please, Miss Ruby Jewel, don't make me bake any more of those things.' I begged her and begged her, but she never would listen. 'Twas the devil in her. Just couldn't get enough of them. Dr. Hale said she'd die of gingersnaps, and looks as if he was right. She always has loved sweeties, even after she got the disease that makes them death to her."

"And yet it's the way she wants to go. She said so once." I touched his sleeve. "Why did you stay here so long, Jubal? In all these years why did you never try to run away? She couldn't have stopped you."

He smiled a slow, sad smile. "Used to think about it in the early days. Sometimes I'd plan how I'd bolt all the way to Canada. Or sometimes I dreamed about returning to the Farridays—those were the folks I worked for back in Virginny and who my mammy and pappy worked for before I was born. I'd picture the smile lighting up master's face when I came home to him." He smoothed out the collar across his knees. "But Miss Ruby Jewel, she was so small and so pitiful and alone I just couldn't leave her. She can talk big and mean, yet I've seen her frightened and weeping like a child. She never did have anyone but me. Her husband was worthless. Then the years went by and, if you believe it, we became friends. We really did."

"I believe it."

"Whoever gets this place will think I come with it, but I don't expect I'll stick around. Too old to get used to someone else. Of course, my folks are all dead back in Virginny, but I might . . . The gingersnap misery's eating away on mistress's innards, and when it finally eats clean through"—he swallowed with obvious pain—"I have a little put by and I reckon I'll slip off and mosey on up there finally. To talk to master as one man to another, if he's still lingering in this vale of tears. And even if he's not, I'll go there just to see the place again. 'Twas called Rosedown and the garden had a hundred kinds of roses." He brought out a big red handkerchief and wiped his forehead.

From inside, Miss Ruby Jewel shrieked out. I pictured her lying on her bed as I had seen her last—short, stiff, and bony, covered with cats.

Jubal grimaced. "Poor little girl. Poor little mistress. Most of the time I sit by her, but I come out here when I can't stand it anymore. Dr. Hale gave me a powder to mix in her drink to help her sleep, and she screams without waking." A slinky black tomcat came up and wound himself around Jubal's legs. "What's worrisome to me is, if I go, what will become of the cats?"

My mouth wanted to say I would care for them, but I closed my lips tightly until the temptation passed. No matter how sorry I felt, I would not offer to take those repulsive beasts. I rose. "Let someone else figure that out. Don't take on that problem."

He held up the collar and then let his hand drop again as if it were heavy as lead. "I was trying to fix this rip. I'm afraid this one is beyond me, even though I've gotten right handy with a needle through the years. It's her favorite collar too." A slow tear trickled down a seam in his cheek.

"Let me do it," I said. "I can fix it good as new."

He started to hand me the collar, but hesitated. "It needs to be done quickly. So she can wear it in her—her final rest."

"I'll bring it back to you soon. Promise. And I'll bring a book you can read to her too as you sit beside her. A boys' adventure book. It's called *Castle Sliverbone*."

"Thank you kindly. I'm sure going to miss her."

"I know you will."

I left him sitting there on the porch, his head bowed and his big hands hanging between his knees. I shook my head slightly in wonder. He actually loved Miss Ruby Jewel. And my feeling was that Miss Ruby Jewel had loved him too, all these years.

To my surprise the buggy was still there. "Took you long enough" was all Sunny said. She was flapping her skirts, hoping to waft in a little breeze. Her powder was beginning to cake in the creases of her skin. I rubbed at my powder to smooth it out. It was far too hot for dancing.

Sunny was subdued all the way to the church hall, and so was I, clutching Miss Ruby Jewel's collar. Neither of us was in the mood for such a gala affair as this was planned to be.

On the church lawn, soldiers and civilians were involved in sack races. Inside, the hall was decked out in braided ribbon streamers. A

Stars and Bars flag hung from the rafters, while banks of billowing flowers were strategically placed to cover anything unsightly. Planks balanced on barrels against the walls held the handicrafts for sale. The supper, consisting mainly of brown beans, bread, and watermelon, was set up on tables in the center.

Miss Elsa pulled open the drawstring of her reticule and pulled out her little red morocco coin purse. With the air of someone bestowing bounty, she presented Sunny and me each with a few coins. "Enjoy yourselves, my darlings," she said before drifting over to a group of middle-aged women. Half of them wore widow's veils, and their grim smiles glimmered eerily from beneath the crepe.

Sunny sniffed. "Mama acts as if we're seven years old and will be ecstatic over a few pennies." She paused and then poured her handful into mine. "Here. Get something for what's-his-name."

I laughed. "Do you mean Seeley or Dorian?"

"Whoever you think would like a pinwheel the most."

The handicrafts were impressive—running the gamut of all the foolish little things modern women make to keep their hands busy. Any cloth that might be embroidered was embroidered, any surface that might be painted was painted, and anything that might be covered was glued with anything that might cover it. We tucked our poor little offerings under some rag rugs.

Treats also were for sale. I wondered where people had gotten the sugar for them; perhaps it was like the biblical loaves and fishes that appeared out of nowhere when there was need. Ladies had scraped together the sweetening for popcorn balls, caramels, meringue kisses, and gingersnaps.

I will never eat gingersnaps again.

I bought a Jacob's ladder and an assortment of treats in a paper cone for Seeley and gave them to Miss Elsa for safekeeping.

The musicians began tuning up. A banjo and a couple of fiddles commenced playing a rollicking "Dixie's Land," and the dancing commenced.

The evening progressed strangely. I couldn't decide: Was it reassuring that life went on—young folks dallied, ladies gossiped—while not far away men they loved and strangers they hated struggled and died violent deaths? Or did the mingling take on a grotesque, nightmarish quality?

Because there were more men than available females, thanks to the Texas brigade, all the girls danced every set. However, I felt like an outsider, as if I were merely pretending to be a young lady socializing. My partners, mopping their faces, said the same things: "What is your name?" "Are you enjoying the dance?" "What do you think of the progress of the war?" I would make appropriate answers, but inside I would think such things as, *If you were Thomas, I would point out the rabbits' candles in the window, but since you're not Thomas, it's not worth the bother.*

Everyone but Sunny and I seemed to be having a grand time. The place was loud with stomping boots and laughter, nearly drowning out the music. I kept expecting Sunny to find her stride and gather a throng of admirers about, but something in her was askew, her eyes gazing into emptiness beyond her partners' shoulders.

When the band struck up "Darling Nelly Gray," I fell to brooding, although my feet continued to trip along as though I were an automaton. The verses told of a slave in Kentucky who mourned the loss of his beloved, who had been sold south to Georgia: "Oh, my darling Nelly Gray, they have taken you away. I'll never see my darling anymore." I began thinking of Jubal and Miss Ruby Jewel and it was all I could do to keep from sobbing on my partner's shoulder. And then I smiled to think how horrified the poor young sergeant would be if I did so. He thought I was smiling encouragingly at him and squeezed me significantly about the waist. I turned away in confusion.

So much lately was making me look squarely at something I had shoved to the back of my mind—the institution of slavery. It had always seemed a necessary part of our life around here. The color of their skin had nothing to do with my love for Permilla and Laney. Yet . . . guilt weighed on me heavily. Was the South's noble Cause indefensible?

Sunny sought me out after I left the dance floor. "I miss Dorian," she said. "Let's go."

I nodded. We gathered up Miss Elsa and my purchases, woke Michael, who was outside snoozing in the buggy, and headed homeward.

Cubby was asleep in the cradle in the kitchen, and Laney was nodding away in the rocking chair beside him, with the lamp lit low in the center of the table.

"Laney," I whispered, and softly shook her shoulder as I knelt beside her.

She started awake.

"Did Seeley do all right?" I asked.

"Just fine. He played with Cubby some and hung around the front porch. I guess hoping you'd be home early. Anyway, he went to bed a while ago, and I brought him his honey milk."

"Thank you."

She yawned and began to rise. I stopped her.

"No, stay just a minute. There's something on my mind." I clutched at her sleeve, not looking into her face. When I realized what I was doing, I made myself lower my hands.

She studied me closely. "What's wrong?"

I drew in my breath and plunged in. "Laney, you know I love you like a sister, but this—our life—is what's wrong. I've told myself you were happy and well, but still, by law, we've owned you, and that couldn't ever be right. And I'm so sorry for all these wrong years."

Laney turned to give Cubby's cradle a push and kept her eyes downcast. "You've been worrying about this a right smart time, haven't you, honey? It's true. Slavery is a great evil. Michael and I have been talking about it. If the North wins the war, they'll free us all. And we sure want to be free. But the fact is, we hope we can stay here and go on working, with pay to give us dignity, if your pa has any money himself. This is our home and you're our people. Neither of us has anyone else."

Joy flooded through me. "I'm so glad you would stay" was all I could say for a moment. But I knew I had to say something else. "Of course, if the South wins—if it would be best for you . . ." I stopped, unable to continue.

"I know." She sighed and stood up. "If we need to, we'll leave. No matter what, though, you and I will always be close, won't we?"

We looked into each other's eyes then, and in that look was all

our past—our listening together to Aunt Permilla's tales, our playing house in the Lodge and running through the woods with Rush.
Laney held out her arms and we hugged each other. A lightness
lifted me as we did so. A freedom from something that had chained
me for a long time.

Upstairs I left my candle on the landing and quietly pushed open
Seeley's door. I would put his presents by his bedside to surprise
him in the morning. Moonlight streamed in through the small,
high window, casting shadow bars across the floorboards and outlining all in pale light. Amazing that darkness could be so vivid.

I smiled to see the mess the bed was in, the covers all wadded
up. Seeley must have done some tossing and turning before finally
sleeping. I set his gifts on the floor beside the bed, but when I stood
and looked down, the crumpled bedclothes were not Seeley-shaped.
I sighed in exasperation. He must have taken to sleeping in unusual
places again.

The wardrobe. I softly opened the cupboard doors in Rush's
room so as not to awaken him if he was inside. No Seeley. He was
not in Rush's bed either. Or in any nook or cranny in either room.
More and more I panicked and threw open chests and cabinets and
squatted to inspect under beds.

He had been anxious for my return; could he be waiting in my
bedroom for me to come home? In the split second it took to cross
the hall and fling open my door, I pictured the little boy in some
corner, sound asleep, or else sitting up, grinning in anticipation of
my surprise.

No little boy awaited, grinning or otherwise.

CHAPTER 23

FIRELIGHT

I rubbed my fingers across my lips. Should I stir up everyone and begin a full-scale search? Dorian would be angry, though, and blow everything out of proportion when surely Seeley was simply carrying out some thoughtless little-boy caper. Maybe he had gone outside to wait for my return and fallen asleep on the porch or in the grass along the drive. I peered out the window.

A spark of white light bobbed down near the dock, erratic as a will-o'-the-wisp. It couldn't be. Surely not.

It's him.

Down the stairs I flew, out the door, and across moon-shadowed fields to the top of the bank. There stood my little cousin, holding a lantern aloft with one hand and gingerly touching the edge of the canoe with the other.

"Seeley!" I cried. "What are you doing?"

His giant, frightened eyes looked up. He set down the lantern, scrambled up the bank, and threw his arms around my waist. "Thank you for coming home. I waited and waited. Finally I was going to go by myself, but I was scared I couldn't paddle without you."

"Because you can't. Go where? To Thomas?"

He nodded into my side.

"Why? What's so important you couldn't wait?"

He pulled away. "Dorian was talking to an army officer. I couldn't get close enough to hear what they were saying 'cause they were whispering too low, but Dorian looked guilty, like he was revealing a big secret. So I knew he'd found out about Thomas and was telling on him. We've got to warn Thomas. We need to get him away."

"Seeley," I said. "Squiddy. That wasn't what Dorian was talking about. Dorian doesn't know anything about Thomas; we've been too sneaky. He was arranging some smuggling for the army. He and Sunny are crossing the lines tomorrow. That's what they were discussing."

For a moment Seeley looked as if he didn't believe me, but then understanding seeped in. "Oh. I did hear the word 'boots.' I didn't know why he'd be talking about boots while he was turning Thomas in."

"Right." I took him by the shoulders and faced him toward the house. "Now go to bed, and never, never try to do such a thing again."

With a stubborn set to his jaw, he jerked out of my hands and stood gazing over the river, where moonbeams floated and rippled. "I don't want to go in yet."

"You don't have to want to; you just need to do it. Besides, I've brought you surprises from the bazaar. I'll even let you eat a popcorn ball in bed."

"Please."

"Without brushing your teeth afterward."

"Please."

"It's late. Past your bedtime. Feel the official dead-of-night air."

"Can't we still go see Thomas? He would be so surprised and I can show him the constellations. Remember, I asked if I could do that sometime and you said yes."

"I said maybe." I hesitated. Actually, I didn't know what time it was, although we had left the bazaar after ten o'clock. His eager little face looked up into mine. How could I refuse? Especially when I longed to be with Thomas myself.

"All right," I said. "Let's do it. Blow out the lantern. It's bright enough we can see without it."

Our paddles sliced through the water as the full bone-white moon watched. Frogs sang and crickets and cicadas shrilled; the night was not silent, but our paddles were. Our canoeing skills were better now because we worked hard not to disturb the mystic atmosphere. An owl hooted once from the forest and then came gliding low over the river, its pale, luminous wings spreading three feet across.

Quiet canoeing was also slow canoeing, and it seemed a long trip to the inlet. At last we climbed the bluff and made our way through interwoven light and shade. Noises stirred the forest, similar to daytime noises, but more disquieting because of the dark. Sometimes the glint of low, golden eyes shone.

My skirt caught on a bramble and it took me a moment to loose myself. It was then that I felt the pulsating of the earth. The rhythm spread up from my feet and through my limbs and on until it mingled with the beating of my heart.

"What's that?" Seeley whispered.

"Drums."

Almost without knowing what I did, I took his hand, and this time we did not run from the sound. This time we were pulled toward it. As we drew closer to the clearing, the illumination from the great bonfire became coarser and more brilliant than the soft moonlight. It bathed the tree trunks with flickering vividness. The thrumming and throbbing of the drums combined with the crackling of the fire and with a woman's voice singing, low and rich.

We stopped just outside the glow and peeked around a trunk.

Beneath the great gray-barked central tree, on tall-backed thrones woven of straw, sat Dr. VanZeldt, beaming benevolently, his white suit glowing. Beside him was a very old woman. Somehow I knew she was ancient, even though there were few of the outward signs associated with age. She sat ramrod straight, her cheekbones chiseled and her eyes deep set and hollow. A headdress of leaves looped down over her forehead, and she wore a long skirt of golden cloth. If she had on a blouse, I could not see it because of layers of violent-colored beads that began high on her neck and continued down to her waist. Her bare, bony arms gestured to the music in undulating, serpentine motions. It was she who sang in some mysterious language and whose voice mingled with the drumming to rouse my primal Violet.

The bearded VanZeldt servant sat on a stump, hunched over two hourglass-shaped drums, his long, supple hands beating faster and faster. Round and round the fire whirled the other, younger man, clothed in a bright-colored loincloth, with bands of feathers about his calves that swirled as he moved. His perfectly honed muscles undulated and rippled. His stomach contracted and released. He performed wheeling kicks and low crouches. He stamped and made jerky, whiplashed movements with his elongated neck, tossing the feathers on his headdress.

My blood ran quicker as I watched.

The fire was so dazzling that all beyond it loomed black. If I looked off yonder, the radiance still burned in my eyes. Inside the hissing blaze, wavering dancers of flame darted and twisted, seeming to echo the man's movements. Herbs must have been thrown into the fire because the clearing exuded a heady, pungent aroma that mingled with the smell of smoke and burning sap. I swayed a little on my feet as I breathed it in.

The dancer snatched up a clay pot and dashed some dark liquid against the silvery trunk of the central tree. At that moment, out of the darkness on the other side, Amenze materialized. She wore a headdress of beads and feathers, a short grass skirt, a band of cloth over her breasts, and rattles of shells about her wrists, ankles, and neck. Her dancing began slow and seductive, but quickened to a feverish pitch when she joined the man, leaping and turning in amazing, explosive physical feats.

Seeley shivered. His face lifted to mine, rapt. I nodded faintly. The sounds and the moonlight, starlight, and firelight made the air hotter and more intense and more stirring to our souls until it seemed we could hardly contain it. These movements were wild, alien, pagan, and so full of joy that they tugged at me nearly irresistibly. A silent whisper slid through the sticky, sparkling air: "Come, join, dance." I gripped the tree trunk so hard my nails dug into the bark.

From the shadows beside us, a small figure emerged. Green stripes on a skirt writhed in the flickering light. Sparrow.

As the little girl tensed, ready to spring out into the clearing, Seeley and I both gasped. I reached for her, but Seeley was faster. His arm shot out and grabbed Sparrow's arm. She jerked backward. I wrapped my arms around them both and held tight.

Sparrow hardly seemed to notice us, in spite of the fact that we were pressed close. As she watched Amenze spin like a top, she threw back her head and laughed. Her eyes and teeth flashed white within the cloud of black hair.

The drumming ceased suddenly and the two dancers dropped to the ground, seeming to melt into it.

I was left limp and exhausted. Sparrow's breath was heaving.

The men and Amenze rose and with that familiar smooth, boneless VanZeldt stride made their way up to the thrones. The old woman held a carved cup, which she handed first to one, then to another, and each took a sip. They laughed and drank more.

No one doused the fire. Dr. VanZeldt and the old woman stood, and the menservants hefted the straw chairs. I waited while they all disappeared from view.

As soon as they were gone, I pulled Seeley and Sparrow deeper into the trees. I sank to my knees and put my hands on Sparrow's shoulders. "What are you doing out so late?"

She did not answer me.

"Is she all right?" Seeley whispered.

Sparrow's head drooped. Tears shone on her cheeks. "So beautiful," she breathed.

"They were the People Things," Seeley said. "They *were* beautiful, but you shouldn't ought to have tried to dance with them."

"People Things," she said. "Why was I a-scared of them before?"

I spoke with difficulty. "We don't know what they are. They may be very, very bad. You mustn't ever go near them again, you hear?"

The moon was reflected in her eyes as she arose. "If them drums call, I got to answer. I got to."

I clutched her hands tightly as I looked her in the face. "You *don't* have to. We're going to walk you partway home now, Sparrow."

After a bit she nodded. I took both the children's hands and we made our way through the trees. At first Sparrow dragged, still bewitched. Gradually, though, her steps lightened, and soon she was leading us, tugging at my hand.

I asked my question once more. "What were you doing out so late?"

"'Twas the moonlight," she said. "It seemed almost daytime. And then I could feel the drums even before I could hear them, so I went further than I meant to."

I was glad she didn't ask what we were doing out in the night. I didn't want to explain that Seeley and I were about to go to the Lodge without her.

"Will you go straight home if we leave you now?" I asked.

"Yes'm."

The moment I dropped her hand, she was off twining through the trees so swiftly that she probably didn't hear Seeley say softly, "Good night, Sparrow."

We hurried to the Lodge, not even considering that, because of the lateness of the hour, we should have headed home. More than ever, the Lodge resembled a fairy-tale cottage as it stood bathed in moonlight. We stumbled through the front room. I paused inside the doorway to Thomas's chamber.

There he lay asleep, a bar of moonlight from the window shining across his face. He looked younger and more vulnerable, somehow *softer* than when he was awake.

Seeley gave me a little push.

"Thomas," I whispered.

He scrambled to sit up. "Violet?"

"Yes," I said, "it's us. Don't worry. There's no emergency. I don't really know why we're here, but we are."

He laughed a sleepy laugh. "Welcome."

"We saw the VanZeldts dance," Seeley said.

"You what?"

"Just now," Seeley said, "in the clearing with the fire. We hid behind trees while the VanZeldts jumped around to the drums. Sparrow was there too."

"Sparrow?" Thomas said sharply.

"Yes," I said. "She must have been wandering close enough that the music drew her there. I don't know what to do about it. What if she begins to seek them out?"

"You must warn her grandmother," Thomas said.

His calm, quiet tone eased my jangled nerves. "You're right. I'll visit Anarchy tomorrow."

He yawned and stretched. "I must have sensed the rhythm in my sleep. Dreamed I was dancing." He leaned forward. "Will you help me get up? All I can make out is your silhouettes. Let's go outside, where I can see you better."

I gripped his arm and heaved to help him rise. He was nearly standing when his legs gave way; he fell back on his bed, and I tumbled on top of him. I would have scrambled off, but his arms held me tightly.

"Are you all right?" I cried. "Did I hurt you?"

"I'm very all right. How about you?"

Seeley snorted. "You're both fine. Here, let me help this time."

I rolled off and we moved awkwardly out of the Lodge, arms entwined. Through the distant trees the bonfire still winked.

"Let's go back over there," Seeley said. "I want Thomas to sit by the fire."

"I don't guess they'll be coming again tonight," I said doubtfully. "And they couldn't see the fire from Shadowlawn." I looked at Thomas and then quickly away because his face was so very close, with his dark hair curled around his ears in an especially enticing manner. "Can you make it that far?"

"Where are my sticks?"

Seeley hurried to fetch them.

And so, beneath the sharp sparkle of stars, we made our way to the clearing, where the blaze had died down to low flames licking black logs. The great tree loomed above us, its trunk and leaves pale and unearthly, outlined with moon silver. Seeley dashed in and out of the edge of the trees, gathering brushwood to toss in and build up the fire. I, meanwhile, helped Thomas lower himself to the ground with his back against a trunk a ways from the ring of stones, where we wouldn't be too hot. I settled down beside him, trying to arrange my frilled petticoat and hoop and skirt to one side. I had forgotten I was still wearing the blue taffeta, which was hopelessly splattered and snagged by now.

"Hoopskirts," I said, "are not made for sitting on the ground."

"They look nice, though," Thomas said. "And you look especially pretty in that dress. Your cousin and all the Sece—soldiers at the dance must have thought so too."

I smiled toward the darkness. "Well, I did dance all the dances. But then, there were a lot more men than women, so that's not saying much."

"No. Admit it—they were vying for your attention. I'm just glad I wasn't there to have to share you."

"We left early, actually, and it was a good thing because Seeley was fixing to come here all by himself. I caught him just as he was about to climb in the canoe."

"Well, I'm sorry your fun was cut short, but I'm glad you came."

I gave a happy little sigh. "This is exactly where I want to be."

Thomas's fingers lay close to mine on the ground and I was acutely aware of them. My hand felt twitchy, drawn to his. I fought it.

"You should've seen the VanZeldts dance," I said. "The picture of pagan and free and glorious. Compared with them, our finicky, stodgy motions at the bazaar seem absurd. There needs to be another word for what they did, if reels and waltzes are called 'dancing.'"

"If I hear the drums again, maybe I'll sneak near enough to watch."

"Too risky. We shouldn't have done it."

Once the fire was going well, Seeley settled himself down cross-legged beside us. "Tell us a campfire story, Thomas."

"The night does call for it, doesn't it?" Thomas seemed to consider. "Do you want to hear how one time Heath Blackstock was nearly the main dish of the fat dragon Nebo? Or how long ago I stole a fairy princess from the cave of a demon king and lived to tell the tale?"

Seeley laughed. "How did you do that when you were busy grading lessons at school?"

"During recess, of course. But you're right. I'm remembering it wrong—it was actually the princess who rescued *me*; it wasn't a cave, it was a lodge; and it wasn't all that long ago."

Seeley jumped up again. "The dragon one, but not yet. The fire's not big enough. I want it as high as the VanZeldts had it."

"How far is Shadowlawn from here?" Thomas asked.

"About a mile," I answered. "No one there would be able to see it. Especially with the forest between."

Seeley scurried off into the shadows and soon returned with an armful of branches. Spurts of red-gold shot upward as he tossed them in. He took a long pole that was leaning against a tree and poked at the coals. There was something primitive and otherworldly about Seeley there, with his pointed chin and tense, sharp-edged body in the wriggling firelight.

I leaned forward. "Look at him. He could be an elf or a godlet stirring a cauldron, couldn't he?"

Thomas didn't answer. I glanced back. His eyes followed my cousin, but the expression on his face showed that his thoughts were elsewhere. I wanted to know what he was thinking, but I didn't dare ask.

He felt my gaze and turned. His eyes shone darkly. He shifted and his hand touched mine. Neither of us pulled away. I scarcely breathed. He slid his fingers through mine.

We sat in silence. Maybe the air still held fumes from the Van-Zeldt herbs. Maybe that lent to the magic. The night was full of an eerie beauty as the great darkness closed around. When I tore my eyes from the fire, I could look up, up, up into the incredible vastness of the universe. It made me dizzy, and my head swam so that I swayed. Next thing I knew, Thomas had drawn me close and his arms were so tight I could feel his heart pounding. He kissed me, hesitantly at first, but then long and sweet and soft. Just a little salty. It felt as if I were soaring upward with the sparks, a part of the vastness. I wanted to memorize this moment, this first time.

We finally drew slightly apart. He brushed my hair back from my ear so he could whisper, "You know I love you."

"I hoped so," I said softly. "I didn't know, but I hoped so."

He stroked my back, and that place tingled warm. I was no "ice maiden" now. I raised my face so he could kiss me again, and he did.

After a while I managed to pull away enough to murmur, "I love you too."

The next time we parted for breath, I whispered, "I have never said those words to another person and I have never kissed another man."

"I'm glad."

I wondered how many girls he had embraced.

"You're probably wondering," he said, "so I'll tell you the truth—it was my first kiss too. Which is surprising, old as I am. I never had much time for romance before. I wanted to be in love for it, so I waited until I was in love."

"Good." Sunny had desired an experienced man. I was the opposite. I wanted Thomas to learn right along with me. I wanted him just as he was. And our first-time kiss had been flawless.

"Is the beard unpleasant to you?"

"Everything about you is perfect."

"Well, hopefully you'll like me just as well when I'm not so bushy," he said. "And this is awfully unromantic, but I'm glad there was a toothbrush and tooth powder with the other things you brought me."

I giggled. "Me too."

"Part of the reason I haven't wanted to leave this place, that I haven't been anxious to heal completely, is that I don't ever want to be far from you. I don't want this time to end."

"Nor do I, but I know it can't last forever. I'm both happy and sad that you're doing so well. Another few weeks and it'll be time for you to go, even though I don't like to think of it."

"As soon as I can, I'll come back for you."

This was serious. For just a moment I was frightened by the grown-up thing he was saying, but then the fear ceased and only joy remained. I traced the line of his jaw with my finger and was amazed at my own boldness. "There's so much we don't know about each other. You don't even know my favorite color."

He bent his head to kiss the center of my palm. "Blue."

"You're just guessing that because of this dress, but yes, it is. The shade like shot silk, where the color looks blue in one light or lavender or silver when the silk ripples in another light. And I bet yours is blue too."

"How did you know?"

"Only because anytime I've ever known a gentleman's favorite color, it's always been blue."

"I don't need to know every single detail about you, Violet, because I know *you*. Your soul shines through. I'm the luckiest fellow in the world, my shining girl."

"And I'm the luckiest girl." I snuggled up against him. "So tell me, what was your favorite plaything when you were little?"

We murmured back and forth. He bent his neck so that our foreheads rested against each other, and I nestled within the circle of his arms. When Seeley finally noticed, from across the fire, he grinned with satisfaction, as if our coming together was an enchantment he'd cast.

CHAPTER 24

TOO MANY SECRETS

He loves me.

A sweetness swept through me the moment I awoke the next morning. My mouth couldn't stop curving upward. I couldn't run off to Thomas until I had paid a visit to Anarchy, but the minute that was accomplished . . .

Before going downstairs, I quickly scrawled an entry in my journal so I would remember the date. I didn't dare even mention Thomas's name in case someone somehow found it; I wrote only of my delight in my lovely secret.

Laney noticed my general glow at breakfast. "Those must have been some mighty fine dreams you had last night."

"The best." I touched my lips and then slathered molasses over a biscuit. Why did I feel ravenous when people in love were supposed to shun food? Maybe that was those poor, unfortunate girls in *unrequited* love. "In fact, I'm so cheerful you may have to begin calling me Sunny Junior or Sunny the Second or something like that." I took a big bite.

As if on cue, Sunny Senior breezed in, decked out in a smart, plum-colored traveling ensemble. "I declare," she said, pulling on her gloves, "I'm itching so bad to get out of this war-weary-dreary place and over to somewhere civilized I can't even tell you. Maybe I won't come back. Take care of Mama if you never see me again." She tweaked my hair.

"You do realize that the civilized territory you're entering is Yankee-occupied?" I asked.

"Yes, I know, I know." Sunny waved her hand dismissively. "But can't you at least allow me to enjoy buying some fun things we haven't been able to get for ages? Don't worry, Vi-let. I was jesting; I will return, and I'll bring back all sorts of boring Confederate boots dangling from my hoops, so I *am* doing my itty-bitty part for the Cause."

"Come on, Sunny," Dorian called from the hall. "We need to get going if we're to make it back before midnight. And it's best to catch the pickets early."

Sunny's eyes twinkled. "Oh, the danger of it all. Wish me luck." She pranced off before I could wish it.

Laney and I shook our heads.

"Bless her heart," Laney said.

"Bless her heart." As I finished a second biscuit, I tried to decide how much to tell Laney. I had to let her know about meeting Sparrow because she'd probably learn of it sooner or later. However, I didn't want to make too much of it, or more mysteries might get revealed. There were getting to be more and more secrets between Laney and me, which was distressing, but I couldn't share them. "By the way, I'm fixing to go over to Anarchy's. Seeley and I have run into Sparrow a couple times recently and I'm a little worried; Anarchy doesn't keep her close enough. Not with the VanZeldts and the war dangers all around."

Laney wrinkled her nose. "That wild child won't come to any harm. She's more at home in the woods than in her own bed. Aunty would never cage her up. Go talk to her if you want, but it won't do any good."

"You don't want to come, do you?" I hoped she wouldn't. More explanations might be required.

Laney hesitated. "Nope," she said finally. "Cubby's a mite puny today. I'd best keep him inside. Tell her hello from me and that I'll come see her soon."

I found Anarchy in the middle of her herb garden, stooped over mint plants, cutting sprigs and dropping them in a bag. The clearing seemed full of light, with the sun overhead now. The air was heavy with scent and buzzing with fat, happy bees.

Winding grass paths led to Anarchy, edged by rosemary bushes, lavender, and marigolds. She straightened with a discernible crack from her back and gave a delighted cackle when she saw me. "That you, li'l Miss Violet?"

"It is. How are you, Anarchy?"

"I feels right pert. You come for herbs or just a little visit?"

"I need to talk to you about something." I glanced around. "Is Sparrow here?"

Anarchy wagged her head. "That baby gal ain't never here. No, sir. She come in late last night and runned off early this morning. She be magic with the wild animals. Gots an old, wise, healing spirit to her. I don't never know what she's going to bring home next. Foxes, possums . . ." Anarchy's wiry frame stiffened with pride. "Finds hurt critters and fixes them. Knows all the cures. Even some I don't know. You got any squirrels needs fixing?"

"No, ma'am. But if our Goblin gets torn up in another fight, I'll be sure to bring her to Sparrow."

"Here"—she indicated a rough wooden bench against the wall of her little house—"set yourself down. Don't mind me keeping on snipping—got to labor while the sun shines—but you go on and talk. No, don't try to help. I got my own way of doing things. You want a little mint to chew? Cleans the teeth. That be why I still got my own." She grimaced to show crooked yellow teeth.

I smiled and accepted a pinch of the green leaves. Anarchy was the sort of person you had to smile at, with her clear, bright bird eyes and sticklike limbs, her iron-colored corkscrews of hair bobbing beneath a scarlet silk turban, and her giant, brightly flowered calico apron that seemed to have swallowed her whole. Once, when I asked her how old she was, she had made some quick calculations with her twisted fingers and said, "I be over ninety, but don't know exactly how far over. Don't matter none, anyhow; I reckon the good Lord done forgot I is still here and He's going to leave me forever."

I rolled the mint between my fingers. "I hope Sparrow didn't run back to where she was last night."

"What you mean, 'where she was last night'?" Anarchy gave me a sharp look. "How'd you know where she was at?"

Without explaining why Seeley and I had been roaming the woods so late, I told about the VanZeldts and her granddaughter joining in their dancing. "Sparrow used to be afraid of them, but she's not anymore. They aren't the sort of people she ought to trust. They've been kind to me, but . . . I can't trust them. I was thinking maybe you could keep her close to home for a while."

Anarchy left her weeding and came to sink down on the bench beside me. "Uh-uh-uh. That Sparrow do love tunes. Might as well try to pin down one of Lord Jesus's own sparrows. I heard of them Van-whosits, but ain't never set eyes on one. Probably ain't no harm in them. I'm just a root woman, so I don't know all things about hoodoo, but I does know it gets used for good same as bad. Still, ain't no reason for my baby gal to mosey around no conjure folks." She rubbed her chin. "You say she ain't a-scared of them no more? Well, then I reckon I just better make her a-scared again. I'll tell her tales of the bocor—that's a conjure priest who dabbles in dark magic—who stayed at my plantation when I was a child. It'll put the fear in her right quick, bless God."

"Aunt Permilla's stories about hoodoo sure made Laney and me careful of it."

I stayed a few more minutes before I took my leave, hoping I could still make it out to the Lodge.

As it turned out, I couldn't go to Thomas that day. One task after another kept me at Scuppernong. After supper Miss Elsa demanded that I distract her.

"I haven't been able to paint," she said, her voice plaintive. "My muse eludes. I'm so nervous and at loose ends with Anna Bess and Dorian gone."

And so I spent the whole long evening trying to divert Miss

Elsa. All the chatting was my responsibility, as she was absorbed in painstakingly sorting her mountains of embroidery silks into shades, while Seeley was kept busy with his horses. In spite of her plea for company, my stepmother didn't actually seem to hear a word I said or notice my presence. However, when I started to rise, she said tremulously, "No, don't go. I can't bear to be alone tonight."

Eventually I began to mend Miss Ruby Jewel's collar. After tying off the last thread, I escaped long enough to put Seeley to bed, and had barely returned to the sitting room when Sunny flung open the door and announced, "Home at last."

Miss Elsa leaped to her feet and threw her arms around her daughter, weeping. "Oh, you're safe! Thank the Lord!"

Sunny pushed her away with an "Oh, Mama." She dropped down on the sofa, skirts spread wide. "We had a highly successful smuggling venture. Dorian says I took to it like a duck to water. But you would not believe how tired I am." She giggled. "Or how much fun we had!"

I blinked as she held up a particularly pretty new reticule, black velvet with delicate, opalescent blossoms. "Isn't this delicious? Fish scales—that's what the design is made with; can you believe it? The second I saw it, I had to have it, so my darling Dorian got it for me. No one else around here has ever imagined such a thing, and Mary Clare will be green with envy. She'll probably try to make one herself. Can't you just picture—and smell—her huddled amid a pile of trout, scraping off scales?"

Miss Elsa fluttered over her daughter. "It's charming. And you've a delightful new hat." She tilted her head in admiration.

Only then did I notice that Sunny's head was adorned by a beguiling wide-brimmed confection with a plume that dipped down to tickle her cheek.

"Isn't it, though?" she said. "Dorian bought it too. And everything I admired in those stores—real stores, not what we've got down here—he said he'd buy once we're married." She gave a sigh. "Why, a girl can hardly stand the anticipation of such spoiling."

"So," I said, yawning, "you bought a hat, risked your life, and didn't get shot even once."

"Oh, my poor sister, were *you* worrying about me too? Well, you needn't have. The pickets were impudent, but amusing. One of them told me they never even consider shooting 'purty little Secesh gals,' just the old ugly ones. Wasn't that a shocking thing to say? And probably every one of them with an adoring sweetheart left behind—soldiers just can't help being fickle, being so far from home and all."

"Shocking. And you know you loved it."

"Of course. After that he asked if all the Mississippi 'gals' were as brave and pretty as me, and I didn't know how to respond to that, I was so flustered. I feared Dorian would be seething with jealousy, but he seemed in a dandy mood. Didn't mind in the least. Which made me angry at first, but then he was so adorable afterward that I forgave him. He can seem heartless at times, but when he's being sweet, it's obvious he doesn't intend it. I'm so wild about him I can't begin to think clearly." She slumped against the back of the sofa and absently stroked the plume of her hat. "Why, I believe I'd do anything he asked me to do and it wouldn't be my fault; I absolutely couldn't help it."

She bolted straight up. "Oh! And we bought everyone surprises. Run outside, Vi-let, and ask Dorian for yours. I warn you, he's a little tipsy—honestly, you should've seen how fast he drove home. I declare, my heart was in my mouth. But don't mind him. I can't wait another minute for you to see your gift."

Why not? I stood. "So exciting," I said. "It's been forever since I got a present. And, Sunny—I really am glad you made it back all right."

Dorian stood between porch and wagon in an island of lantern light, stretching his arms above him. If last night Seeley had resembled an elf, tonight Dorian, with his bronze skin shining golden, also appeared otherworldly—like some confident, dangerous young god. Then he raised his face, and the quirk of his mouth and the gleam in his eye showed him more satyr-esque than godlike.

As I descended, the smell of whiskey rose up the steps. Dorian looked me up and down and his smile was too intimate. He stumbled slightly approaching me. He was downright drunk.

"Cousin Violet," he cried, reaching up to capture both my hands, "coming to welcome the wanderer home."

"I came out," I said, "because Sunny says y'all brought me a present and she's eager for me to see it. I'm eager to see it too, actually."

"And I thought you were simply anxious for my safe return." His speech was slurred.

"Oh, I wasn't worried. You'll always emerge from any scrape unscathed."

He burst out laughing. "You know me well. Survival is one of my talents." He looked at me in a way that made me nervous. "Another is that I don't rest till I get what I want."

I searched for a distraction. His brocade waistcoat caught my eye. "That's new, isn't it?" I withdrew my hands and pointed. "What color would you call it?"

"You noticed. Yup, straight from Paris. Bought it just today. The shade's called magenta, after a town in Italy. When I first saw it, I had to have it because it's the same color as the crape myrtles that line Panola's drive. Actually made me go misty-eyed." I thought he was jesting, but from his expression, he did indeed feel sentimental. He shook himself. "Anyway, this is one of the new aniline dyes. You want to touch it, don't you? Go ahead. Stroke me."

"No thank you," I said, backing away.

He threw his head back and laughed again. "Oh, all right. Here." He pulled a pasteboard box from the rear of the wagon and tossed it my way.

I riffled through a cloud of silver paper and drew in my breath.

Shoes! Not even boots. Shoes! The most beautiful shoes I had ever seen. They were bronzed kid, with black velvet tops, black silk ribbons, and embroidered butterflies in shining pink. The satin-covered heels were more than the fashionable inch high. And since anything higher than an inch was considered too fast for a young lady, I, Violet Dancey, would be considered fast. How exhilarating!

"Dorian," I said, "they're so beautiful I may weep."

"Poor little coz, to have been deprived of pretties for so long that new shoes make you cry." He squeezed my shoulder. "Here, sit down on the step and let me help you put them on."

He knelt in front of me like the prince with Cinderella. I lifted my skirts high enough for him to unlace and remove my boots.

With a look of disgust he dropped those ugly things. He slipped the new shoes on my feet and tied their bows with a flourish.

"Perfect fit," I said. "Thank you so much. I'll show them off at church this Sunday."

I waited for him to rise, but he did not. Instead he put his hand on the back of my calf and crept upward.

"D-Dorian!" I sputtered, pushing him away as I dropped my skirts. "Stop that!"

He stood awkwardly. "Why? Why should I stop? I've been resisting you for weeks, and I'm tired of the chore. Just try me. You'll like me." Before I knew what he was doing, he bent over and lifted my chin. To my horror he leaned in and would have kissed me, but my wits returned. I ducked away and scrambled to my feet.

"You're drunk," I said.

"Yes," he said. "I must be. That would explain why it's so hard to walk straight."

"And you're forgetting Sunny. Remember—the girl you're in love with. The girl you're going to marry." I backed away as I spoke.

He snorted with disgust. "So she told, did she? The girl can't keep a secret, which is a concern."

"It's true, isn't it? You did ask her to marry you?"

"Yes, it's true. I asked her for reasons I can't go into, but I assure you, coz, I wish it were you. The fact is, my Sunnys come cheap, but my Cousin Violets are rare." The more I withdrew, the more he edged closer. "You're smart, you're brave, and—you saved me from hanging. Let me repay you in the best way I know how." His arms shot out to grab me, but I darted away.

"Don't, Dorian! And don't you ever, ever speak to me this way again." I would have scooted into the house, but I needed something from him, some reassurance. I lifted my hands, pleading. "Don't you love Sunny at all?"

"Oh, that." He gave a careless shrug. "I'm not the sort of fellow who loves people. I can like girls well enough, though, and be enormously attracted to some. Isn't that enough for you and me tonight?"

My mouth fell open in disbelief. "You just better treat Sunny well, or I'll—I'll—"

"I'll treat her well enough. Got to. So no kiss, eh? I did so hope to be the first to touch your virgin lips. Oh, well, if you don't want to play, then be off with you."

With my scorned boots clutched tightly to my chest as though they were suddenly precious, I resisted the temptation to tell him that the virginity of my lips had gone to a much better man.

"One more thing." He caught my arm and I jerked it away. "You won't—uh—say anything to Sunny about this, will you, dear, sweet, yet feisty Violet? You can't blame a fellow for trying."

"I can blame you."

Just as I reached for the doorknob to flee into the house, I glanced back at him standing at the bottom of the steps, and his expression drew me up short. He wore a dark look, angry brows drawn together, lips compressed in a thin line, so different from any look I had seen from him before. Then he caught my eye and grinned. The mask had slipped back in place.

CHAPTER 25

AWAKENING

Scoundrel, cad, villain, blackguard . . . Dorian, with his ready smile and easy, worthless affection. The question was, should I tell Sunny? I would certainly want to know if my sweetheart was not constant. It had been horrid when I saw Ben Phillips with Mary Clare, but it would have been worse if he had been sneaking around behind my back. Of course, Sunny was so infatuated with Dorian that she probably wouldn't believe it anyway.

I had lifted out the floorboard to remove my journal, hoping that writing about it would help clear my mind, when something caught my eye. A folded paper that had slipped into the darkness beneath the boards. I drew forth the sheet, smoothed it out, and recognized Thomas's sister Addie's handwriting. It must have slipped from the packet. A fragment of a last paragraph was all it contained.

no idea about you and Delia! Of course, I did know you were rather smitten with her. I do not blame you a bit, as she's ever so pretty and stylish, but I did not realize it was anything serious. Last night, right in the middle of the love scene of opera Lily of Killarney, *Delia leaned over and confided that you two are secretly betrothed and will marry when the war ends. Shame on you, Thomas, for keeping this from me! How could you? I never would have told the Parents. I'm sorry I wrote to you that I did not really like her. Truly, she's not so bad; it was simply schoolgirl jealousy between us. From now on I will love her dearly and will invite her over more often since she is to be my sister. Also, for your sake, I will do my best to keep her from flirting with other gentlemen. (Lily of Killarney was splendid, by the way, and the new opera house is simply too gorgeous.)*

Continue to stay out of the Seceshes' clutches, even though you do keep secrets from—

Your loving sister,
Addie

My hands shook. I read it through once more.

Thomas was betrothed to another girl.

He told me he hadn't had time for romance in the past. And that I was the first girl he had kissed.

It felt as if someone had hit me in the stomach.

An icy little knot twisted about my heart as Seeley and I made our way through the woods the next morning, even though the world was drenched with summer sun. I should never have given in to my feelings. Why had I let myself tell Thomas all those things—those *lovery* things? It had been the intimate setting. But now I understood fully the phrase "cold light of day." The fact that Thomas was promised to another was only one of the reasons he and I could never be.

We passed through the bonfire clearing, and all that was left in the pit was ashes and charred bits. The flames that had burned so dazzlingly had done their job well; everything was devoured and destroyed.

Thomas's eyes were bright with love (or whatever his feeling for me was) when we entered the Lodge. The knot squeezed upward into my throat.

He struggled to rise and reached for my hand. I gave him the basket instead. I watched as he and Seeley poked through the contents and began eating.

Thomas glanced my way. "Won't you have some?"

"I'm not hungry."

My tone made him look at me more closely. "Something wrong, Violet?"

"Just tired."

"Yes, you do look tired."

How nice to know my appearance was saggy and baggy. "Thank you."

"As well as pretty." He paused. "As pretty as usual, I mean."

It was painful to watch him try to turn his comment into a compliment. I slumped down against the wall and ringed my arms around my knees.

For a while Thomas and Seeley tucked into the lunch and ignored me. Contradictorily I longed for Thomas to look at me again with that special warmth. He was laughing with Seeley now. He simply didn't care how I was feeling.

Seeley was telling Thomas about Panola and how, when he

returned there after the war, he wouldn't let anyone keep him from exploring his estate whenever he wanted to. "I'll go everywhere—they can't stop me."

"From the time I was small," Thomas said, "my father wanted me to know every last inch of our factory—all about the business. I couldn't have cared less at the time. Lately I've wondered why I was like that."

"Because it was boring?" Seeley suggested.

Thomas smiled. "No. It's not boring. Part of the problem, I think, was that I was ashamed of our family's fortune. It seemed so common, so ordinary, to have grown rich from making thread. Of course, it didn't bother me to use the money for clothes and horses and making the grand tour, but other than that I scorned it."

"What's the grand tour?" Seeley asked.

"The traditional European trip taken by young men who can afford it. Everyone I knew was going, so I went too. When I remember how I acted now, I cringe at my self-righteousness, thinking I was so much better than my parents, who worked hard for all they have. After the war, God willing, I'll go back to finally listen and learn." He was speaking to Seeley, but his eyes were on me now, as if it were me he was really telling this to.

"You're rich?" Seeley asked.

"My family is, and I suppose Addie and I will inherit."

I squeezed my eyes tight shut. Now I'd learned that Thomas was an heir to a fortune as well. A man born to such circumstances could never care for me in a lasting way. He belonged in the world of gorgeous opera houses and his fiancée, Delia.

Seeley tossed a peach up and down and considered Thomas's

words. He stopped and held the peach. "Violet, am I rich? Owning Panola and all?"

I pulled myself from my distraction. "You might be," I said cautiously, "but who knows what anything is worth with the war going on."

"You mean if the Yankees steal everything or burn it up or something?"

I nodded. That was indeed what I had meant, but I hadn't known such possibilities had occurred to Seeley.

His eyes grew wary. "Why would they set Panola on fire? There's no soldiers there. When we were coming to Mississippi, we saw places the Yankees burned, but I thought those had soldiers inside. Not houses with regular people in them."

"They won't touch Panola."

"No one knows that. What about Mammy and Aunt Lovy?" His voice took on an edge of panic. "What if they do burn it and Mammy and Aunt Lovy are inside?"

"The Union soldiers wouldn't be that cruel," Thomas said. "So far in the war they rarely torch civilian houses, and if something must be destroyed, they make sure everyone's out."

I could almost watch Seeley's brain working rapidly. "It's made of brick, so if they burn the house, it won't all go up. And I'll build it again." His brows were fiercely knitted, and his whole small body was tense. "But where will Aunt Lovy and Mammy and all our other people go if there's no plantation left?"

Sudden tears pricked my eyes. *Oh, my Seeley.* "We're just talking and imagining. Your people will be fine. The Yankees aren't monsters."

Thomas reached over and put his hand on my cousin's shoulder. Seeley blinked and took a bite of the peach.

"What do you think about what I was just saying, Violet?" Thomas asked, turning to me.

"About what?"

"About my going into business with my father. I was so determined to steer clear of it and make my own way, and that's how I became a teacher. But now . . ."

"How should I know?" My tone was sharper than I intended. "It's up to you. Do whatever seems right."

He looked a bit bewildered, but pressed on. "I'd like your opinion. I wouldn't want to make any future decisions you wouldn't agree with."

"It has nothing whatsoever to do with me."

Thomas studied me for a moment. "Seeley," he said abruptly, "would you go out by the bonfire and make sure we left no signs we were there? It was too dark to check the other night."

Seeley readily accepted this and trotted off.

"Now," Thomas said once the boy was safely away, "tell me what's wrong. And don't say you're just tired."

I took a deep breath. "Well, then, I won't say that. But I'm not sure what to say instead."

"How about the truth? Do you regret what you told me by the fire?"

I swallowed. "Yes, I do."

"Ah. Will you please tell me why?"

With clammy fingers I feverishly began pleating my skirt into folds. "Because you're betrothed to another girl." There. I had stated it.

He stared. "What on earth are you talking about?"

"Someone named Delia. Do you deny it?"

"Where did you hear this?"

"I read a piece of a letter from your sister last night—it had fallen out of the packet."

Thomas gave a long, low whistle. "Delia lied," he said carefully. "I can't imagine why. I wrote to Addie and told her that."

I bowed my head, miserable.

"Do you believe me?" he asked.

When I was with him, everything about Thomas spoke of sincerity and integrity. He never would have betrayed that girl. Of course he spoke the truth. "Yes, I do, but it doesn't change anything. I thought about it all night. It still could never work out between us."

"I've told you I'm not engaged," he said. "If you believe me about that, then what else is the problem?" He hesitated, then asked haltingly, "Is it your cousin? When you told me about him, I got the impression that he was—that you found him attractive. Did you realize it was him you care for instead of me? Please tell me. It would hurt worse for you to lie."

I shook my head in disbelief at what he was asking. "This has nothing to do with Dorian."

"Then what has changed?"

"Shall I list everything? You're a Northerner. You're handsome. You're rich. And you're wounded, weak, and alone, so your judgment is clouded. If it wasn't, you'd recognize the impossibility of all this without me telling you."

I forced myself to meet his gaze, although the hurt in his eyes made me want to cower. But just when I could stand it no longer and was about to turn away, it was he who turned away. His mouth worked for a moment as if it were hard to make words come out. Without looking at me, he at last said quietly, "Of course some of what you say is true. It's true I was wounded. I suppose I am still physically weak. I realize I cut a pitiful figure, especially when I'm trying to walk." He was twisting his ring round and round on his finger. "I can't help where I come from, and even if I were handsome, I can't help how I look. We'll forget the money if you don't like it, and I'll go back to teaching." He faced me now. "None of that signifies. It's not as if we're a different species; we're alike in the things that matter."

I had never felt more wretched. I rubbed my forehead. "We're enjoying this season here, pretending your feelings could last, but they can't. We both know the time is soon coming when you'll leave this place and join your people in the real world. When you do, you'll wake up and grasp only too well what I am—a plain *Secesh* farm girl from the wrong side of the war. You'll ride off on Star and go back to being a soldier and start shooting at my—"

"I never—" He tried to interrupt, but I wouldn't let him.

"—family and friends and after the war you'll be wearing white gloves and dancing in ballrooms with Delia-like girls in—in imported magenta French taffeta, and you'll be ashamed you once thought of me fondly. You'll wince at the memory." A slow tear trickled down my cheek. I couldn't bear for him to wince over me.

Thomas reached out his arms. "Come over here. You're too far away."

I shook my head.

"Then I'll come to you."

Now it was me wincing to see how painfully he pulled himself up with his sticks; it was hard not to jump up and help. He hobbled over to my side and dropped awkwardly down.

"Look at me, Violet."

I wanted to refuse, but I tightened my lips and lifted my head.

His expression was taut with earnestness. "Under the circumstances, I can't court you in the traditional way. We can't let the world know we belong to each other—yet. I can't bring you hothouse flowers or chocolates or books of verse—yet. But I'm not so stupid—my judgment isn't so 'clouded'—that I don't know that what I feel for you is as deep and genuine as the ground beneath us. Although I do have to rejoin the army since I still believe in what they're fighting for, for your sake I'll try to get a clerical position. I promise I'm coming back, even though I can't tell you precisely how long it will take."

"You won't."

"Don't tell me what you don't know!" For the first time his voice was harsh. He struggled to regain patience. "How can I prove myself?"

I didn't answer.

He bowed his head so that his dark hair fell over his face. I could still see that his lips were taut and that his knuckles were white from clutching his walking sticks too tightly.

The silence between us lengthened.

Finally he carefully laid down the sticks and raised his head. "What you say might make sense for some people, but not for us." His expression as he looked at me held such mingled love and frustration that I had to hold back from throwing myself into his arms. So softly that it was almost a breath, he repeated, "Not for us."

Seeley returned at that moment.

"Come on," I said, springing up and grabbing his hand. "Time to go."

"We just barely got here."

"We're going." I pulled him along as he waved goodbye to Thomas.

The tears were so blurring my eyes as we scurried from the Lodge that I nearly knocked over Amenze, who stood in our path.

CHAPTER 26

JITTERS

Dim and dancing forest light played over Amenze's exquisite features. "Violet Dancey, what are you doing here?" I had forgotten how musical her accent was.

"I'm—um—" What could I say?

"You have been to visit our soldier. I knew something had happened. These last few weeks there has been a new quiver in the air around him." She held up her fingers and rippled them in front of her as if in water. "Even as he sleeps. It told me he has not been as alone as he once was. This makes me happy. I had wanted to talk to him, but I was not allowed. I spoke to my grandmother about what I sensed, but she said it could not be so. She believed her juju had guarded our soldier too well. However, the juju allowed you through because you are no threat. And I see you have already become close to the young man."

I had not met Amenze since the day she offered to raise Rush from the dead, and everything I had learned of the VanZeldts since then made the hair rise on my arms. In spite of Amenze's friendliness, I know I must be on my guard with her. Her people murdered Jorgenson, and something mysterious was going on with them and Thomas. I opened my mouth and closed it again, then pushed out the words, "We must go."

Seeley stared at Amenze as he clutched at me. I pulled him along behind, edging past the girl. It was better to be rude than to further betray Thomas. She moved into step beside us, tall and graceful. I thought of Thomas's comment about he and I being of the same species. The VanZeldts belonged to a different one. They were People Things.

Amenze gave a delicate sliver of a smile. "You need not fear. Now that I know it is you, I will not tell my grandmother. But it would not matter if I did. She would not mind you knowing our secret. What harm is there in you? In one young girl?" She reached down and stroked Seeley's hair with a slender hand. He winced. "The little boy—he is your brother?"

"No," I said. "He's my cousin."

"Ah, just a little there is a likeness between you. How nice to meet again this way. Since the first time, I had hoped somehow we might be friends, even if you would not let me help you with your brother—you are so pleasant, so sweet. But I did not know how to make it happen."

"I'm sorry," I said. "I can't stay and talk; I need to get my cousin back home. So you'll—you won't tell Dr. VanZeldt or the others that you saw us here?"

"I will not, although as I said—it does not matter. Father Van-Zeldt is a good man. He likes you very much. The other people here, both white and black, are not kind to us. They do not welcome us because we are different. They think it is bad to be—oh, is there a saying?—birds of different feathers."

Dumbly I nodded, and as I did so, my coldness toward her began to thaw. I hated to be classed among the unkind people, and I could not believe this girl would willingly hurt Thomas.

"It was the same in our old land," Amenze said. "They would only come to us for help when they were desperate. Many and many a year ago, my family was as these others, save more learned in ways of healing and cursing. Then our grandfather's grandfather received greater truths from the stars." She gestured to the heavens.

"Because my family's beliefs became different from those of their neighbors, who they did not understand it and feared us—hated us—our grandfather's grandfather hid us away in the mountains. It was a wild and dangerous place. Most children did not live to grow up in spite of our good medicine. When I was very little, my grandfather—our last high priest and our link to Raphtah— died. There were only the five Children of Raphtah left—I, my cousin, Ekon, my brothers, Uwa and Ahigbe, and our grandmother, Cyrah. Cyrah was very ill when Father VanZeldt stumbled upon us in his search for further knowledge. She was dying. Father healed her. This made us believe he himself was Raphtah, come again in disguise from the sky." She laughed as though this were a hilarious assumption. Her laugh was deep and melodious. "Even when we knew he was not that person, that he had simply used white man's medicine, we loved him. He is a wise man. Once he learned of our beliefs, he became enthralled by them. He became the high priest of Raphtah, accomplished in all juju, second only to Cyrah in understanding. After Ekon—died"—she appeared to swallow painfully—"Father knew what we must do. We left the mountains and crossed the ocean."

"Then you aren't the doctor's slaves?"

She laughed again. "Oh, no, no. You have been thinking that? How amusing! We are not like these poor people here. We are as kinsmen with Father VanZeldt. It is a small family, though, so soon we must find mates so that we may multiply."

Of course it was illegal for free Negroes to enter Mississippi nowadays, but Dr. VanZeldt had sneaked them in somehow. I'd never thought Amenze could talk so much, and I wondered if she spoke so to her family or if it was the pleasure of speaking to another girl that made her almost prattle. "Why did he choose to bring you to Mississippi, of all places?"

She shrugged. "We had always wanted to live in a new country and we hoped the Americans of the South would not notice us because there are others from Africa here."

I smiled. "You and your family could never really blend in."

She made one of the fascinating, fluid motions with her hands. "My grandmother does not want us to be friends, exactly, with people in town, but she did hope—" She paused, struggling to articulate what she wanted to say.

"She hoped you would be treated with consideration and not too much curiosity—from a distance," I suggested.

"Yes," she said. "Yes. That is it. Father VanZeldt also thought perhaps he could help others here with his healing skills and then they would value us."

"But not many will let him. Seeley!" My cousin had grown bored with the conversation and surged on ahead. At my call, he reluctantly slowed to let us catch up.

"No," Amenze said. "He tried to teach us all the English so we could talk to people in the town, but only I could learn. We speak it back and forth together, he and I. He also thought no one would notice us here because they would be too busy fighting the big war among themselves. It is odd. You people call some of our ways 'evil'—very, very bad—if we cause one necessary death of one little person. Clearly we do not view evil as you do. To me your war is this thing—this very, very bad." She shook her head. "Your people are so clever; you can do great things. And yet you take your cleverness and you use it to make thousands of men die all at once and proclaim it good. So peculiar."

Was Jorgenson "one little person"? And why was his death "necessary"? I did not dare ask. In spite of my wanting to be sympathetic to her, she still frightened me—every word she said was alien and fearsome. "War is not a good thing, but we're told it's a necessary thing. I'm no longer sure."

She had subtly steered us toward the bonfire clearing, even though I had intended to avoid it. We broke into it now.

"You have been here before," she said, making a statement. "You have wondered about this place. It is where we dance." She clasped her hands. "Oh, wonderful. Maybe someday you will join us."

"I can picture it," I said softly. "Your dancing would be wonderful indeed."

"And do you see this?" She laid a reverent palm against the trunk of the great tree under which the straw thrones had stood.

"Yes."

"It is the silk cotton tree. Normally it does not grow so far north. Father VanZeldt has wondered if perhaps some slave smuggled the seedling here from Africa long ago. Perhaps beneath his clothing. It is a sacred tree whose roots contain the spirits of our ancient ancestors, those who first met Raphtah when he came down to them. When we saw it that first time, we rejoiced because it showed we had come to the right place. We knew we must stay here to protect the tree. It would be a terrible thing if anyone were to lay an ax to it."

An eerie, indefinable something in her voice as she spoke of these things made my flesh crawl. I nodded because some response seemed required, even though my brain couldn't catch up to anything she was saying about her peculiar beliefs.

"We would like to have you as our guest one day soon," she continued. "Will you come to visit us?"

"Someday," I said. "Right now, though, Seeley and I have got to get home." Impulsively I touched her shoulder. "Thank you so much for my amulet. It was a wonderful gift. Goodbye—my friend."

I had thought she would smile, but a shadow passed over her face. She reached up as though to grasp at my hand, then stopped herself. "You will come soon enough, my friend."

Long after we parted, I was aware that she remained standing straight and silent beneath the silk cotton tree. My fingers sought the amber amulet beneath my dress; it was not there.

I searched for the amulet in all my drawers, beneath the bed, in my jewelry box, and under sofa cushions. Nowhere. Considering how lightly I had at first taken this gift from Amenze, I was now filled with anxiety at its loss. Suddenly it seemed of great importance.

Somehow I made it through the rest of the day. As the light finally grew gray, Dorian, Sunny, and I sat out on the porch, watching fireflies wink. Tears kept pricking at my eyelids. I longed to go upstairs to my room for a good cry over Thomas but had to wait until Seeley returned from wherever he had wandered.

Sunny was jittery, twisting her bracelets about her wrists and then jumping up to peer over the porch railing. "Where's Seeley?" she asked.

"Out looking for Goblin," I said.

"Oh." She sat again, still twitchy.

Dorian had been uncharacteristically quiet, but he broke the silence suddenly. "You know, Scuppernong is a nice, cozy house and naturally you're fond of it, but you should see Panola." His voice took on a dreamy note. "It looks like a Grecian temple on top of the hill, with soaring columns and a portico all around and acres of green spreading out behind. Uncle Roger had it painted gleaming white every five years. It was due for painting last year. If this ridiculous conflict will ever end, I'll take care of it immediately."

"No," said a small voice from the bottom of the porch steps. Seeley had come around the corner of the house, clutching Goblin to his chest. "I will. It's my house. When I go back, I'll be older and I'll take care of Panola. You won't need to anymore." He spoke with a solemn dignity.

"Then God help Panola." Dorian's sneer twisted his features. He stood abruptly. "I'm going into town. I'll stay the night, as I've business there in the morning." He stalked out to the barn.

"God will! It's my house and it's my land too!" Seeley called after him.

"Seeley!" I said sharply after Dorian thundered away on his horse. "Everyone knows it's your place, but you don't have to act like that. It's ungentlemanly."

The boy turned pale. "Dorian thinks—he thinks it's his, but it's not. It's mine." His chin trembled and he darted back around the house.

"Go on up to bed!" I called out. "I'll come to tuck you in soon!" I sighed and turned to Sunny. "What on earth is wrong with those two?"

"Oh," she said, "Panola's about the only thing in the whole wide world Dorian takes seriously. You wouldn't know, of course, but to me he'll go on and on describing every last shutter and outbuilding and field. It drives him crazy that it might fall into Yankee hands or that Seeley might ruin it someday." Now it was her turn to stand abruptly. "It's not right. None of it is right." Her lips trembled and she fled into the house.

I sought solace from everyone's vexing behavior in the kitchen. Laney was there, her arms plunged in dishwater.

"Let me do them," I said. "It helps me to think when I'm washing dishes."

"Suit yourself," she said, wiping her hands on the dish towel. "I'll dry. And while we're both alone here, how about you tell me what's going on? Something's happening. Y'all are jumpy as a cat in a room full of rocking chairs."

I heard Seeley's feet clattering up the stairs to bed as I drooped over the gray dishwater, arms submerged, without making a movement.

Finally I spoke. "This has been such an unusual summer. A lot has happened, and some things I can't tell you."

"Huh."

"I'm sorry—I just can't. Some things aren't my secrets to tell. And then, some things I don't know."

"Well, what about the things you *can* tell?"

Before I could answer, my stepsister's penetrating voice preceded her into the kitchen. "Vi-let? Vi-let!" She entered. "Oh, there you are. How about you let me make Seeley's bedtime honey milk? I'll take it to him too. Since you're up to your elbows in dishwater and all." Her tone was light, and her eyes were wide and innocent but a trifle over bright.

She saw my surprise and said, "With Dorian gone, I'm restless. I need something to do."

Laney and I raised our eyebrows at each other. Sunny offering to help? Such an unusual proposal could not be refused. I nodded.

Sunny puttered around, dipping the milk from the pail, pouring it into a kettle on the hearth for warming, reaching the crock of honey down from the shelf, dribbling it in, and stirring.

"Are you making enough for me?" I asked my stepsister.

She was pouring the warm milk into a mug. "No. No, only enough for Seeley. Sorry." Her hand shook. Some of the liquid sloshed out and her face crumpled as she gave a little cry, but she was out the door before I could do more than wonder at her nerves or say, cleverly, "No use crying over spilled milk."

"What is wrong with her?" I whispered after I heard the floorboards of the upstairs landing creak.

"It's got to be something to do with Mr. Dorian." Laney

sopped up the milk with a rag. "He sneaks into her room at night, doesn't he?"

"Yes, he does. But that's not what's causing the friction between those two. Although . . . what do I know? Anyway, Dorian is nagging at Sunny about something. She's always told every last thought in her head to anybody who'd listen. Until now. Now she won't breathe a word about whatever it is. They still laugh a lot together, but I don't like the sound of Sunny's laughter. There's a—a *wildness* to it." I wiped the last dish and took up the broom to sweep. "And then there's Dorian and Seeley. I had thought they were doing so well. Dorian doesn't pay much attention to Seeley—he's been too busy with Sunny—but whenever he does, Seeley drinks it up. Seeley was positively radiant the other day when Dorian took him out hunting arrowheads. Just now, though, out on the porch, they were bristling up at each other like they did when they first came here. It's baffling."

Laney scooped up Cubby to take him home for the night. "All I know is—" Her mouth tightened as if to hold the words in.

"What?"

"I shouldn't say." She started for the door.

I jumped in front of her. "You can't start to say something and then stop like that. You know you can tell me anything."

"Which is more than you tell me."

"I told you, I can't—"

"I'm teasing. What I was fixing to say is that Mr. Dorian is always playacting around y'all."

"How do you mean?"

"I mean, Michael and I see a side of him y'all don't. When y'all aren't watching, he's got the look of a fellow whose innards are all twisted and gnawed."

I remembered the moment it had seemed to me that Dorian's mask had slipped, and goose bumps rose on my arms.

Laney and her baby headed out into the darkness and I started up the stairs, candle in hand.

CHAPTER 27

DARK DEEDS

I had already brushed out and braided my hair, undressed, and climbed into bed when an appalling retching sound burst from Seeley's room. I dashed to his bedside. He sat hunched over in bed, white as a sheet, with his covers soaked and splattered with bile.

"Sorry," he gasped, and vomited again.

"I'll fetch a basin," I said quickly, somewhat queasy myself. I had thought after my experiences in the hospital I would be immune to retching.

I was stopped short on the landing by Sunny, standing there in her trailing white night shift, twisting her hands together like Lady Macbeth. She looked nearly as ill as Seeley, phantom pale, and with a ghastly expression in her eyes.

"Is he—is he very ill?" Her voice was barely a breath.

"Right now he is," I said, skirting her. "It's probably one of those stomach flu things that always seem to happen in the night. He'll be over it by morning."

From behind me she said, "Yes, yes, he will, won't he? But what if he isn't? Oh, Vi-let, I'm so afraid. I've done a terrible thing."

I whirled around. "What do you mean?"

She opened her mouth and shut it. Her hands raised jerkily to her chest, then to her hair, and then to her cheeks as if she had no control over their movements. She shook her head and dragged the skirt of her nightgown up to cover her face and began sobbing great, wrenching sobs.

I touched her arm. "Go in your room and wait while I get Seeley a basin and fresh bedclothes."

After I cleaned him up, Seeley lay curled on his side, very small beneath the covers. I left him briefly for Sunny.

She huddled on the floor in a corner of her bedchamber, knees drawn up to her chest and head in her arms, shoulders shaking. She raised a twisted, tear-streaked face. In the flickering light from the one candle, she—who was always so perfectly groomed, so pretty—appeared grotesque. "Dorian's not back yet, is he?" she asked frantically.

"No," I said. "He said he wouldn't return until tomorrow."

"Right. Of course. He said he needed to stay away till then, but I was worried. . . ." A spasm flicked across her features.

I squatted down beside her. "Sunny, tell me right now what's going on. I need to get back to Seeley. What's wrong? Does it have something to do with Dorian?"

"Yes. Yes. Dorian and Seeley."

"What about Dorian and Seeley?" I asked harshly.

"Dorian's been after me and after me. He won't let up. He said if

I didn't do it, we could never marry. It's not my fault. I could hardly think anymore, he plagued me so. I withstood him for as long as I could, but finally—" She gave a gulping sigh.

"Finally what?"

Her voice came in a whisper. "I said I'd do it and I did. I didn't put as much powder in as he told me to. That way I could tell him I had done as he asked, but probably nothing would happen. Hopefully Seeley threw it all up," she finished in a rush.

"What kind of powder?"

"Some sort of poison," she said simply, her eyes blank.

Sunny's words stabbed like a splinter of glass in my heart.

I gave a short, strangled cry and jumped up to run into Seeley's room. He appeared to be sleeping deeply, drawing ragged breaths. I shook him. He made no response. I dashed back to Sunny.

She scrabbled at my hand. "He said Seeley'd only be sick—so sick he'd never recover completely and Dorian would have control of Panola. But what if he dies? If he dies, you won't tell anyone, will you? You won't let me be hanged?"

I shook her free. "I've got to send Michael for Dr. Hale."

"He's out of town," Sunny said. "Dorian made sure I did it when he knew the doctor was gone so no one—no one could help."

For some reason, in that moment, my brain composed itself and my mind worked coldly, clearly. I knew immediately what I must do, even though the thought of going to Dr. VanZeldt, of begging for his help, terrified me. Yet there was no other choice. I must do it. Michael did not know the way to Shadowlawn and it would be tricky going in the dark. I would fetch Michael to sit with Seeley while I went myself.

"You stay here in your room while I'm gone," I told Sunny. "Promise you won't go near Seeley, or I'll lock you in."

"I promise. But isn't—isn't there something I can do to help?" she asked piteously.

I couldn't even answer her. I threw on a dress and raced downstairs. As I passed her room, Miss Elsa called, "My dear, why are you still up? Is something wrong?"

"Seeley's ill," I said shortly.

"Oh no. I'm useless in a sickroom, but if you need me . . ."

"No, ma'am, there's nothing you can do. Stay in bed."

Cubby awoke and wailed when I banged on Michael and Laney's cabin door. Michael answered, with a quilt covering his nightshirt. Laney stared wide-eyed over his shoulder. They quickly took in at least part of the situation when I explained that Seeley was severely ill and that I must fetch Dr. VanZeldt.

"I'd best stay here with the baby," Laney said. "He doesn't need to be in a sickroom. Michael, you go up to sit with Seeley." She looked at me closely. "You all right, honey?"

I shook my head wordlessly. She reached out and squeezed my hand.

As Michael went into the back to pull on his clothes, I called out, "And whatever you do, don't leave Sunny alone with Seeley."

Then I was off. I rode Star because that would be quicker than going by water. The journey to Shadowlawn remains vague in my memory. The night was overcast and ink black; not a pinprick of light pierced the glowering clouds. I leaned forward, clutching a lantern and digging my heels into the poor mare to urge her to go faster, ever faster. All the while my breath came in little sobs as I

prayed without ceasing for Seeley. This seemed to be some nightmare where I would ride and ride without end.

At last, miraculously, I reached the dirt road to Shadowlawn. It
was much overgrown, with saplings sprouting and forest boughs
reaching out to snag, slap, and slow. I ducked my head so that my
cheek rested against Star's sweaty neck. Some measure of comfort
and calmness spread from her to me.

I had been to Shadowlawn only once before, when I was young
and my father had taken me to pay a call on the former owners. My
impression had been of a graceful brick mansion in the French style
with curlicue, wrought-iron balconies and sweeping double stair-
cases up to the first floor. It wasn't a plantation, so no fields surrounded it, but there had been a green lawn, a rose garden, and an
alley lined with magnolia trees leading all the way down to the river.

Even with only my dim moving circle of lantern light it was obvious how unkempt the place now was. Encroaching wild forest crawled
ever closer to the buildings. The stables and sheds were misshapen
blobs of creeper, while vines hung in dense curtains from the iron
balconies and slithered up the house's walls like long, spindly fingers.

Star stood still as I slid to the ground and tossed her reins over
a hitching post. If only I could speak to Amenze first, but that was
unlikely. My distrust of the VanZeldts, which had been driven out
by the urgency of my mission, now cramped in my stomach as I
climbed the front steps. *This is for Seeley.* I could do anything to save
Seeley.

I firmly grasped the iron door knocker shaped like a pair of
intertwined serpents and banged on the peeling front door. A patter of paint chips showered down onto the floorboards.

Please make him come.

Crickets chirped; the cicadas' song swelled and ebbed. From somewhere nearby came the soft, sleepy clucking and cooing of chickens and doves. I banged again. From deep within the recesses of the house I heard footsteps approach.

The door creaked open. There stood Dr. VanZeldt holding a lamp. He was dapper even at this time of night in his white suit minus the straw hat. He had beautiful, wavy silvery-white hair, and he cocked his head to one side and fixed me with a long stare through his thick glasses. A slow smile spread across his face.

"Miss Violet Dancey," he said. "What an agreeable surprise. What brings you all the way out here? And so late at night."

"We're in desperate need of a doctor," I blurted out. "My eight-year-old cousin has been poisoned. Please, will you come?"

His expression did not change as he tutted, "Terrible, terrible. Do you know the nature of the poison?"

I realized I hadn't a clue as to that important fact and I shook my head helplessly.

"No matter. My methods will work for anything toxic to the body. Let me gather a few things. Did you come by—no, I see your horse. I will have Ahigbe and Uwa take me to your place by boat. I will get there ahead of you. Have I your permission to enter the house?"

"Yes, yes, of course. Our place is—"

"I know where you live. Scuppernong Farm. Run along, then, my dear, and don't worry. The boy will survive."

He closed the door in my face. Feeling almost anticlimactic and suddenly so weary that my legs turned liquid, I sank down onto the steps. For just a moment I let the heavy lids drop over my eyes, then opened them. Nothing was over. I couldn't let go yet. Still, I slumped frozen, unable to order my body to move.

Dr. VanZeldt had stirred the household. Lights began to shine. Beams shone from a nearby window onto the porch floor. From around the corner came the glow of a lantern, and out strode the bearded man—I later learned he was Ahigbe—hastening to one of the nearby outbuildings. He pushed open the door and I watched in fascination as something inside moved, writhed, undulated. I gasped. It wasn't just one thing—it was a glass case of living snakes, many-colored and -patterned. The man entered the shed and kicked something roundish and pale out of the way as if it were a ball. It clattered in a dry, hard, brittle way. It couldn't be. It couldn't be what it had seemed. A human skull.

Stomach, stop convulsing. Body, stop quivering.

The doctor was going to save Seeley. He would. Nothing else mattered now.

I squared my shoulders, rose, clambered onto Star's back, and galloped down the drive.

When I reached the farmhouse, several windows were alight. I met Sunny in the downstairs hall, carrying a glass of wine. She had donned a dark dress, and her chestnut locks hung long and loose down her back. Dark purplish shadows splotched below her eyes, but her green irises sparkled with a nervous intensity.

She squeezed my hand as she passed. "Oh, Vi-let, Seeley's going to be all right. The doctor says so. He needs warm wine, so I raided

Dorian's store and heated some up." She gave a high-pitched giggle, tinged with hysteria, while tears streamed down her cheeks. "I don't know why I'm laughing. Why am I laughing? I guess because I'm so relieved."

I moved swiftly past her up the stairs.

They had transferred Seeley into Rush's bigger room. Dr. Van-Zeldt hunched over the bureau, grinding leaves with a mortar and pestle. Seeley lay on the bed with his mouth open, panting, his eyes rolled back in his head. Michael had pulled a chair up beside him, but he relinquished it to me now. I took my cousin's limp, hot hand.

"Ah, there you are, my dear," the doctor said without turning. "I'm just making a concoction of mimosa leaves for the warm wine. The other girl is bringing—yes, there it is."

A faint motion caught my eye. Uwa and Ahigbe stood near the window, in the shadows outside the candles' glow, watching silently, impassive, like carved figures.

Dr. VanZeldt stirred mashed leaves into the wine. "Now, my boy," he said, laying one arm under Seeley's neck and raising him, "you must take this slowly. Slowly, but it is vital that you drink it down to the dregs. There is medicine in it that will cure what ails you, and you must swallow it down with the wine."

Seeley was so weak that his head lolled back on the doctor's arm and he made no motion to hold the glass. The doctor tipped it to his lips and the boy's throat swelled sluggishly, painfully, as he swallowed.

When the last had been drunk, Dr. VanZeldt held out his hand toward Uwa and Ahigbe and said something in another language.

"I do wish they'd just speak English," Sunny whispered from behind me. "They were jabbering on and on like that before you got here."

The younger man knelt beside a covered basket I hadn't noticed before.

"Now," Dr. VanZeldt addressed Sunny and me, "I must warn you, since young ladies often have decided opinions against reptiles, that in that basket lies a serpent. It is a black mamba—highly venomous, but my two sons are impervious to the poison. Uwa will hold its head toward the boy and then carry it to every corner of the room. The snake will suck the toxin from the boy's body and free his spirit. It is necessary for his recovery. You may leave the room if it bothers you unduly."

Uwa opened the lid and pulled forth coil after coil of a sleek, olive-skinned serpent, which he wrapped around his arm. With his other hand he held it just behind its narrow head.

"Eww," Sunny gasped, and fled out the door.

I remained firmly in my seat, grasping Seeley's hand. My own hands were ice-cold. I could feel the blood throb in my fingertips.

The young man brought the serpent's head to within a few inches of Seeley's face. The snake's mouth opened wide and it was pitch-black inside. Its forked tongue flicked out. I held back from thrusting myself between my cousin and the serpent, biting the inside of my mouth till it bled.

Uwa began a steady murmur in his strange, sibilant language as he passed the snake in a cross pattern over Seeley. An eerie ambience settled in the room. I squeezed Seeley's hand tighter.

As the serpent was carried to the corners, Seeley began to shake harder and harder until he was convulsing from the top of his head down to his toes and the headboard of the bed beat a violent staccato against the wall. He kicked the sheet from his body and his skinny legs thrashed. I stood and tried to wrap my arms around him to hold him down. I flashed a look back at the doctor. "Is this what he's supposed—"

"Absolutely right, my dear. I could not ask for better. See, he is beginning to sweat it out."

A flush spread over Seeley until he was bright red all over and the sweat beaded up and trickled. I would have dabbed him with a cool, damp cloth, but Dr. VanZeldt stopped me.

"No. Leave him."

Tears streamed down my face from helplessness and worry. I began to softly sing Aunt Permilla's lullaby. After I sang, "We'll stop up the cracks and sew up the seams," I broke off. It hurt too much that I hadn't stopped up the cracks for Seeley. I had let in this awful thing.

Dr. VanZeldt sat in a chair on the other side of the bed while Uwa and Ahigbe stood in their dark corner. I was acutely conscious of their presence in spite of their silence and stillness. Uwa especially. Occasionally I would glance away from Seeley and find him watching me with an intent, probing gaze. Once he smiled, slowly, showing lots of long white teeth. I looked away quickly. When eventually the two left the room, taking their basket with them, I let out a low sigh of relief.

After what seemed hours the doctor touched my arm. "There is nothing more anyone can do. He will be resting peacefully by morning. I will sit with him. He will be perfectly safe. You go to your bed. Try to sleep."

I shook my head but found myself rising and crossing to the door. I had to do as Dr. VanZeldt ordered.

As I lay on my bed in my own room, fully dressed, rigid beneath the sheets, I heard the doctor's voice as if in a dream.

"And Raphtah came down from the stars, from the constellation the Greeks called Draco, in the form of a man. He found the Family among all the world, and they were beautiful to look upon, as precious gems among drab pebbles. They fell upon their knees and worshiped him, and they were called Children of Raphtah. He taught them his ways so that if they had wished, they might have been rulers among men, but they did not wish. They desired only to be left alone. He taught them the sacred dances—those of joy and those of mourning. Those of worship. He taught them the use of herbs. Herbs that heal and herbs that harm. Potions of forgetfulness and tinctures of remembrance. Others knew these same secrets, but only the outer edges, not the fullness. He taught them to drink the venom of serpents, that they might dream dreams and see visions and be impervious to the sword. He showed them his true self, his glorious self, his scales gleaming like gold, like rubies. Then he told them, 'I must leave, but if the time is right, if there is great need, you may call me back. You must dance the sacred dance and sing the Words. You must make the sacrifices, not out of cruelty, but necessity. . . .'"

What sort of tale was he telling my cousin? I dragged myself down the hall to Seeley's bedside. "I can't sleep," I said to Dr. Van-Zeldt. "Please try to get some rest yourself. I'll stay with him."

"As you wish," the doctor said, cleaning his glasses. I was surprised to see that without the lenses his eyes were actually small and squinting. "I shan't leave the house yet. I will be just outside if you need me." He went out and shut the door.

I owed him Seeley's life, yet I couldn't trust that man. The business with the snake was so disturbing, and his story had been so peculiar. I couldn't rid myself of the idea that I had made a deal with the devil, that there was a bond between us now that I did not want.

The room was turning gray with dawn when Seeley gave a sigh and his eyes fluttered open. The sweating had ceased.

"Violet," he whispered.

I jerked forward. "Yes, my squidlet."

"My stomach hurts."

"I know. It'll get better."

"It was poison, wasn't it?"

"Why do you think so?" I licked my lips carefully.

"I heard that man—that man with the pink face—talking about it." There was no point in lying. "Yes, it was."

"Was it Dorian?" His face had no expression.

"I can't—Seeley, I don't—"

"It's all right, Violet. It was him, wasn't it? Back before we came here, after my parents died, I could tell he wanted to hurt me. Because he wants Panola." Although he made the statement flatly, his forehead puckered in bewilderment. "How could he hate me so much? He must always have hated me." After a long pause he said wistfully, "I wish I had a real brother."

I flinched at the pain in my heart. At that moment I could have strangled Dorian with my bare hands. Or, better yet, fed him poison, drop by measured, burning drop.

"Seeley, my darling, Dorian is—there's something terribly wrong inside him, something missing. But he'll never be allowed near you again. I'll make sure of that. You mustn't be afraid. The world is actually full of good people. I know it doesn't seem that way when you're surrounded by war and death and you had the bad luck to have Dorian Rushton as a cousin, but such cruelty, such evil, and such selfishness are rare. And for the rest of my life I want to show you what fine people there really are and how loved and precious you are."

"Was it in my honey milk? I thought it tasted funny."

"Yes. If it tasted funny, why did you drink it?"

"Because I thought it tasted funny since *she* made it, and I didn't want to hurt her feelings. So did she want to kill me too?" His mouth was tightly drawn and gave his face an old look. Tears welled in his eyes.

"No, no," I said quickly. "Sunny didn't know anything about it. She didn't know what she was giving you." I lied. I had to lie. "Now close your eyes again and I'm going to tell you the story of the amazing adventure that came about when Heath Blackstock threw up all over his hideout."

Seeley gave a feeble grin. "I'll tell Thomas on you."

"Thomas has been through enough with battles and wounds that he knows even heroes vomit sometimes."

I had just begun the story when I paused mid-sentence. A soft click sounded from out in the hall. I sensed a watchfulness, a listening, coming from behind the closed door.

CHAPTER 28

CONVALESCENCE

Tumbles from trees and accidents with rifles—the events of the past weeks with Seeley took on a new, sinister quality as I replayed them in my mind. Dorian had been so cunning, playing the frivolous, heedless young man, making a show of his kindness to Seeley, while all the while plotting and calculating. How had I been so dense? He had troubled me, but I had thought it was only because of his falseness to Sunny.

With daylight, now that my younger cousin was out of danger and the VanZeldts were gone, came the realization that I must address my older cousin's villainy. As I sat beside sleeping Seeley, so innocent, so vulnerable, my reflections were chaotic. Bewilderment, horror, and outrage were all compounded with exhaustion. How could anyone be so evil as to try to harm this child? If Sunny had not told me what she'd done, we would probably be washing Seeley for burial right now. I shuddered.

Sunny. *What about Sunny?*

When Laney poked her head inside to check on us, I asked her to stay with Seeley so I could talk to my stepsister. I found Sunny huddled in one of the rockers on the front porch, her face pinched and white, her hands limp in her lap.

"Are you watching for Dorian?" I asked.

She didn't answer. Instead she said, "Is Seeley still all right?" in a voice that sounded dead.

"Yes." I dropped into another rocker beside her. "It was all Dorian's scheme, I know, but, Sunny, how could you?"

She gave a boneless shrug. "Dorian is so persuasive and I wanted him so badly. Somehow it was as if I were watching someone else do what I did. Someone else pouring in the powder. I didn't want it to happen. I never really believed anything *would* happen. Could happen. Dorian said he'd only be ill."

I didn't speak for a moment because of the hot red rage that clogged my throat. It wasn't directed at Sunny. It was at Dorian. Those weeks of whispering into Sunny's ears, niggling into her mind, pressing and pushing until her weaker nature gave in. It was surprising she'd held out as long as she had. My voice shook when I finally spoke. "Dorian is a liar. He does have a powerful personality. I understand that. But you're not five years old, Sunny. You know what an *awful* thing it was! You did make a choice and you're going to have to accept what you almost brought about."

Her trembling hands covered her face. In a shivering rush of breath, she cried, "I know I will! I know it! How could I ever forget?"

I patted her shoulder. "Thank goodness Seeley's going to be all right. And you'll be punished enough without the law knowing about you. Dorian is another story. Michael needs to go for the marshal."

Sunny's arms dropped. "No!" she cried so violently that I started. "You're not turning him in. You can't do that to us. To your own family. He—Dorian's not a bad person. It was just wanting Panola so desperately and wishing to be able to marry me soon that drove him to it."

"You can't expect me to do nothing about this."

"Seeley's alive and Dorian will never try again now that you know everything. We'll go away together, he and I. You owe me that much. Don't look at me like that, Vi-let! Seeley would be dead now if I hadn't told you what was going on. If you try to get Dorian hanged, I'll—I'll swear Seeley was just ill and the rest is all your sick imagination."

She would do it. I could see from her face that she would do it. I wanted to scream at her, pummel sense into her; I shook from the effort of holding myself rigidly in check. After a few seconds she looked away and slumped down again in the rocker, facing the wall. Without Sunny's support there was nothing I could do. I had no concrete proof. So far it had seemed best to tell no one else, not even Laney and Michael, what had really happened. Dr. VanZeldt believed it was poison only because I had said it was.

"All right," I said slowly, evenly, although I was gripping my hands so tightly they began to tingle. "We'll let Dorian move on if he swears to never come near Seeley again, since it's between family." I shook my hands out to make the blood flow. "But you can't really still want to marry him after what he tried to do."

"Of course I do," she said quietly, as if there were no question. "I love him. Especially after all this he needs me."

"But won't he be furious because you told me and spoiled things?"

"Not if he never knows I did. Tell him—I know—tell him you saw the sludge left from the powder in the bottom of the cup and guessed Seeley'd been poisoned. And then you knew it was us. We'll tell him that."

I shook my head and sighed.

The sound of hooves coming down the lane reached us. I sat up straighter in my chair.

Dorian came riding up, hair and teeth glinting in the sun. He dismounted Grindill and slipped the reins over the newel post. He looked from Sunny's face to mine as he climbed the steps. "What is it?" he asked. "What's happened?"

"Not what you think," I said coldly. "Seeley's fine."

I could see his brain working as he quickly took in the situation. His blue eyes went wild around the edges, like a trapped animal's, but only for a moment. Then they settled into their usual cheerful, casually cunning expression as he leaned against the porch post. "Why? Is there a reason he shouldn't be?"

I glared. "You know good and well that you tried to kill your own cousin. You did it through Sunny and poison this time. And the rifle last time. And I bet you partially sawed through that limb when it broke beneath Seeley right after you got here."

There was an ugly little pause as Dorian's eyes widened. "So, Sunny tried to poison Seeley?" He turned on her. "You poor, silly girl! I knew you were despairing for money so we could marry, but this. . . ."

Sunny sat straight up, staring.

"Sounds like there's no harm done," he continued, turning back to me. "She's a fool, but I doubt she'll be a danger to anyone again.

And blood's thicker than water, so we'll stand by her and not make it a matter for the law. Oh, wait, she isn't actually your sister. Oh. Well, I hope you're not bent on revenge against Sunny, coz. Could be tricky and unpleasant."

My stepsister sputtered and so did I.

"You—you—cold-blooded, fiendish—*Dorian!*" Aunt Permilla had raised me too well to know names bad enough. "You can't brazen your way out of this. You tried to murder Seeley. I know it's you. All you, Dorian, and you can't kill me and Sunny and everyone else who knows." Of course, the others had no idea about the truth, but my cousin couldn't know that. "If it were up to me, the marshal would have been waiting for you here. However, Sunny convinced me and I can convince the others not to turn you over to the law if you'll swear to never come near Seeley again. Because if you do, if you do come within—within a hundred miles of him or Panola or Scuppernong, I promise I'll see you hanged." I ended on a high, shrill note.

"Well, well, coz! I knew there was passion buried in you just waiting to surface. So, is it the soldier—Thomas, isn't that his name?—who's brought it out?" He spoke in a slow, insolent drawl.

My face went numb. My lips felt so thick I was surprised I could form words. "You know about—how do you know about Thomas?"

"Oh, that letter you had me mail to his family. Of course I read it. At first I didn't think much except to admire you for your slyness, but afterward it told me why you've been immune to my advances. And lately—in fact, just now—it occurs I have something to hold over your head. Remember that—I'll go away and keep quiet about your soldier if you keep quiet about me. Even though really I've done nothing. Nothing's happened."

"Your 'advances'?" Sunny squeaked as if she'd heard nothing else. "You tried to seduce Violet?"

"Oh, ho hum." Dorian yawned. "Why not tell you now that it's all blown up in our faces? Yes, of course I tried with Violet, but she'd have none of it."

Sunny gave a terrible cry and leaped up to cling to him. "I love you! I did everything for you."

He extricated himself none too gently. His eyes narrowed and his expression of mild mockery changed to one of undisguised malevolence. "That's why it was so easy, sweetheart. I did worry you'd make a mess of things, as indeed you did, but I had to work with what I had."

Sunny dropped into her rocker, swinging her head back and forth as if in pain. "You don't mean it. He doesn't mean it."

Dorian snorted and clapped. "Well, there, it feels good to let that out. And, Sunny, in case you haven't gathered, our delightful betrothal is at an end. I leave you a free woman. I'd best be going now. Let me fetch King, and do you mind if I just grab my things out of the spare room? I won't go upstairs at all."

I staggered to my feet, amazed at his breezy recovery. It was all too fast. Everything was too fast. I didn't know if I myself would ever recover from the knowledge of what my cousin Dorian was capable of. Of his cheery, smiling soullessness.

"No, no, no," he said, and gently pushed me back into my seat. "No need to disturb yourself on my account." He started for the door and then turned around. "Oh, and thank you, coz, for saving me from hanging—twice."

Sunny was crying, a high, brittle, terrible sound. I touched her hand to comfort her. She snatched it back as if I were poison.

An awful few days followed. Seeley had little appetite and was weak and listless. Dr. VanZeldt had warned it would take the boy some time to heal from the ravages worked on his innards and that nothing would speed up the process. Even if there had been something the doctor could do, I didn't know if I could have borne approaching him again.

Everyone was miserable. Miss Elsa agonized over Dorian's departure and the end of Sunny's betrothal. We told her simply that Dorian had turned out to be a rascal and had broken off the engagement. She was as heartsick as if it were she who had been jilted. She worried Sunny with her fussing, and when the daughter spoke sharply in response, the mother hid in her room, snuggling her last remaining drops of laudanum.

Laney watched us all with worried eyes, but said little. A new wedge was forced between us from the secrets I could not share.

Sunny never asked me about Thomas. Probably she had been in such a state she hadn't even heard Dorian allude to him. My stepsister fluctuated between trying to avoid Seeley and begging to do things for the boy—bring him treats or play cards. I watched her warily. I was prepared to forgive, but couldn't forget, and for Seeley's sake I had to be cautious. Sunny seemed aware of my holding back. Sometimes I would find her eyes on me, pleading. I couldn't yet give her what she wanted.

The first time she offered my cousin a cool drink, he smiled, took it, and said, "Thank you. I'm not scared of it hurting me. I know you didn't mean to the other time."

Her face scrunched, and she burst into tears and fled the room. I followed her to her bedroom, where she punched her pillow with a fist, crying, "I hate him!"

And she didn't mean Seeley.

Another time I caught her staring strangely at the face carved on the back of the sofa. She gave a thin, humorless laugh. "Look at that. It's got a smirk like Dorian's." She popped her hand over her mouth. "Oh, I meant never to say his name again." Suddenly she was beating the old sitting room armchair with a cushion, crying, "He should not have done that to me! He had no right!"

Anger was probably a good sign.

I, meanwhile, was at a loss over Thomas. . . . Dorian would not trouble him as long as I kept the law ignorant of his treachery, but there were still the VanZeldts. Despite the fact that they had cured Seeley, I couldn't trust them. As Thomas recovered further, their healing might turn to something more threatening. He still needed me, even though I had painfully broken off the romance.

And about that—whenever I had a spare moment to think of anything other than the current mess we were in, I had begun to question my reasoning. I had thought I was being so grown-up, so wise, facing facts; was I actually a fool?

However, I told myself firmly, at this moment it didn't matter. I couldn't leave Seeley right now, no matter what, since he fretted if I left his side for more than a few minutes. Food must be taken to the Lodge. . . . I made a decision. I must confide in Michael—and, of course, in Laney, since he would have no secrets from her. Three mornings after Dorian left, I related to them what Seeley and I had been doing for the past weeks.

Laney snorted. "So that's what you've been up to. I knew something was going on." She tweaked my shoulder with one finger. "And you looking so innocent when I mentioned food missing. I thought it was Miss Sunny."

I gave a sigh of relief. "I'm so glad you're you, Laney."

"What do you mean?"

"Because you don't hold it against me that I couldn't tell you about all this till now."

"Of course you couldn't. And I'm not even surprised that you helped a Yankee after all your going on about hating them. Everything's different when you really get to know folks. The man trusted you with his life. I would've done the same as you."

"Thank you anyway, for being you. All these years you've been my example of good sense and—and *stability*. You're absolutely wonderful, my friend."

Laney laughed and shoved me, but I could tell my words pleased her.

Michael carried a basket to Thomas and returned with a report that he seemed all right. I breathed a sigh of relief and longed for details, but didn't want to make my concern too obvious. Instead I only thanked Michael and asked him to run into town to return Miss Ruby Jewel's mended collar.

He wasn't gone long, and I was on the front porch shelling peas when he came back with two pieces of news.

The first was that Pratt Wilcox had died of pneumonia somewhere in Maryland.

My hand flew up to cover my mouth. Pratt! And so far from home. Would the deaths never end? How could we bear for more men to be gone?

As Michael related his next news, at first I scarcely heard him, but slowly his words sank in. Miss Ruby Jewel had passed away two days before and had left her house and all she possessed to Jubal. I nodded slowly. There were usually bad feelings about Negroes owning property, but probably in Jubal's case no one would bother him. The whole county sympathized with the old man.

I blinked back tears. Pratt and Miss Ruby Jewel, each so awful in their own way, were lent a certain dignity by their deaths.

"Jubal, he said to tell you the gingersnaps finally done their dirty work and thank you kindly for the collar," Michael told me. "The funeral's on Tuesday, and she'll be laid out with it then. Jubal said don't bother sending the book you offered, as he's going to sell everything and quietly mosey away. He may head up to Virginny to see his old home, but then on to freedom. He just don't know what to do with them dang cats."

"Next time you see him, tell him we'll take a couple," I said.

Michael gave a grimace, and I managed a smile. "Yes, they're dang cats, but it's the least we can do for Jubal."

As he started to turn away, Michael hesitated.

"Miss Violet, didn't you say Mr. Dorian's gone for good?"

"Yes. He's not welcome here anymore. We shall never see him again."

"Well, could be my eyes was fooling me, but I thought I seen that big old roan horse of his at the stables in town. Maybe not, though."

I grasped Michael's arm. "He's still around?"

He started at my grip and scratched his head. "Does it matter? He ain't out here at Scuppernong."

I dumped the peas from my lap and moved swiftly to the porch rail, where I peered out over the yard to the shadowy woods. Dorian could be out there right now, watching. "It does matter." I turned back to Michael. "You don't know the whole story of Seeley's illness. He wasn't sick in the normal manner. He had been—he had been poisoned. By Dorian."

Michael drew in his breath. "He tried to kill the boy?"

"Yes. To gain Seeley's plantation for his own."

"Ooo-eee." Michael's lips tightened. Slowly he began to nod. "Can't say I'm too surprised. Mr. Dorian, he sure put on a good show, but there was something about him didn't set right with Laney and me."

Laney had said the same thing the night Seeley was poisoned. She and Michael had never mattered enough to my cousin for him to bother charming them.

"Thank goodness we stopped it," I said, "but what if he tries again? What if he's skulking around, waiting for his chance? He swore he'd go far away if I didn't inform the marshal, and there are reasons I don't want to go to the law. He's family and he knows about Thomas. He said he'd turn him in if I didn't let him go unhindered. But if his horse is still in town . . ."

"I might not have seen right. Or maybe he sold it to make the trip out. King said his master ain't all that plump in the pocket, for all his fine clothes."

"Yes. Yes, you're probably right. All the same, Michael, carry the pistol with you. And let's get that old rifle from the barn fixed and buy some bullets. We'll keep that in the house."

After Michael left, I continued gazing out into the dark trees. I slumped a bit, as if the burden of all these twisted, terrible worries were literally weighing down my shoulders. I needed . . .

Thomas. He was still there. He needed me and I needed him. I needed his quiet good sense and quick wit. I needed his peaceful face. I needed him with an ache that was nearly unbearable. I needed to warn him about Dorian and tell him everything that had happened and feel his arms around me. I would head out to the Lodge first thing tomorrow.

That evening I couldn't shake the feeling that someone was watching from outside in the dark. A restless wind was blowing, making the walls shudder and the treetops sound like the sea. I drew the curtains in the sitting room. It was late and had been a long day.

Seeley lay on the sofa and I sat across a little table from him. We played chess and he criticized my moves. A commotion sounded from the kitchen yard—the frantic honking and squawking of geese.

My heart skipped a beat. *Dorian.*

I made a quick reckoning. Michael and the pistol were at his and Laney's cabin, over by the edge of the woods. If there was an intruder, the culprit was out back with the geese. I could sneak through the front door and make my way to Michael and the gun.

"What's wrong with those birds?" Sunny asked.

"Probably a fox," I said. "I'll go look." I had thought it best not to tell her about Dorian's horse being seen in town.

The door opened with the tiniest of squeaks, which didn't bother me; I could have stomped across the porch and the tumult of the geese would have kept anyone out back from hearing. I slipped down the steps. Light streamed from the cabin to guide me as I crept silently from bush to bush. The wind sent silver clouds sailing across the moon, alternating darkness and light. I was opposite the kitchen yard when a break came in the sky.

A cloaked and hooded figure was pushing its way through the fowls, struggling to get to the gate. It was eerily silent—no grunts or cries. Only the ruckus of the geese.

I waited, watching to see where it would eventually go.

When the figure finally got out the gate, it stood straight and briefly faced my direction. The hood had fallen back. Not Dorian.

"Amenze!" I cried, and stepped out of the shadows.

She made no sign she heard or saw me. Moonbeams outlined the delicate, sharply defined bones of her face. Its expression, or rather the lack thereof, was frightening. There was a curious blankness and a total absence of recognition in her eyes. Not only no recognition of me as an individual but no recognition even of my existence.

"What is it?" I asked sharply. "Why are you here?"

She slid swiftly off into the night with that slick, silky VanZeldt motion. By the time I tried to follow, there was no sign of her.

CHAPTER 29

FIGHTING FIRE

The next day Michael rode off on Star, carrying the pieces of the old rifle. He warned us not to expect him back early. He would have to travel far to find ammunition and a gunsmith. He left the pistol in my keeping. It scared me, sagging so heavy in my pocket. And could I really use it on a person?

Yes, I could if that person was menacing someone I loved.

The day was dim and sultry from dark clouds that hung low. They refused to let down rain but continued to threaten, with ominous thunder rumbling in the distance.

With Michael absent I didn't dare leave Scuppernong, which was a shame—although where I would have gone, I did not know. It seemed as if some important task were calling urgently, but no matter how I tried, I couldn't think what it was.

Laney suggested that maybe I was restless from missing traipsing through the woods with Seeley. I supposed that could be it. I went about my chores, frequently checking in with my young cousin on the sofa. I was sweeping the sitting room right beside him when the pistol tore out the bottom of my pocket and landed on the floor with a thunk.

Seeley's eyes widened. "You're carrying a gun in your pocket?"

"I *was* carrying a gun in my pocket, but obviously not anymore." I picked up the pistol, put it on the mantel, and continued sweeping.

"Because Dorian might come back? Is that why you have it?"

"No, Seeley. He's not coming back. I've just been worrying about . . . intruders." I left off sweeping and sank down on the sofa beside the boy.

His face had a pinched look. "How do you know he's not coming back?"

I wiped the sweat from my brow. "Because he's aware I'll have him jailed if he comes near you. He's long gone."

Seeley's eyes flicked toward the open windows. "Will you shut those, please?"

"It's too hot."

"Please!"

I closed the windows and picked up the broom to take it to the kitchen.

"And stay in here with me."

"Let me put this away, then I'll come back."

He bit his lip. "All right," he said grudgingly, "but don't be long."

As I crossed the hall, voices sounded from outside. Miss Elsa had been out under the big magnolia, painting, and Sunny must be with her. I needed to consult with them about what food we should take for Miss Ruby Jewel's funeral luncheon. I hurried out.

I could hear only the hum of Miss Elsa's animated prattle as I went toward the tree. She sounded so lively that it almost, but not quite, gave me pause.

The other person answered, and at the very moment I heard him, he broke into view. If the voice hadn't been unmistakable, it would have been hard to recognize him in such shabby, ill-fitting clothing.

"I don't know, Miss Elsa," Dorian said. "Your picture looks about perfect. I wouldn't add another—why, look who's joined us. Good to see you, coz."

"Violet!" Miss Elsa cried. "Dorian's come back! I knew he would! Run and get Sunny." She looked blissfully up at my cousin. "She'll be so happy you've returned. She's been miserable since you left."

I had stood frozen; now I tensed to turn and run to Seeley but stopped when Dorian grabbed Miss Elsa's arm and whipped a gun from its holster in one lightning-quick movement.

My stepmother gasped. We had made a fatal mistake not confiding in her about Dorian's villainy. Now she knew.

"What do you want?" I forced my dry mouth to say.

"Money," he said. "Among other things. I left too quickly, without proper preparation. Miss Elsa, darling, give me your purse right now, and then we're going to walk together into the house to get the gold. All of it. I know how much you have, so no holding back."

"Dorian." She gave a little sob, drawing her purse from her pocket and thrusting it at him. "I don't understand. You can't take it all."

"Yes. I can and I will." He pulled her to a standing position and shoved her toward the door. "You first, coz."

Our awkward little procession entered the front hall. I staggered forward, shock making my legs feeble.

I promised Seeley that Dorian was gone. Seeley knew better.

"Call the others to come here," Dorian ordered.

"Please," I begged. "You don't want to bring them in on this. Michael has a pistol and—"

Dorian snorted. "Unworthy, coz. Generally you're an unusually proficient liar for such a nice girl. Michael's away. I watched him leave and heard him say he'd be gone a long while."

"Just take all the money and go. We'll give you everything."

He gave an ugly little laugh. "Everything. These last few days I've realized what I have to do in order to get . . . everything." He poked the gun harder into Miss Elsa's side and she whimpered. "Go on, call them. Sunny and Laney and Seeley."

If I could dart into the sitting room and snatch the pistol off the mantel—

I didn't dare try when he had that thing held on Miss Elsa. I did as he commanded. What else could I do? I called, watching dispassionately and feeling almost as if it were not me standing there, as they came, one by one. First Seeley dragged in, terror blanching his face when he saw Dorian. I reached out and pulled him close to my side.

Then Laney, from the kitchen. "What do you need, Miss Vi? I just got Cubby to slee—" She broke off and backed against the wall.

Seeley was shaking violently. I roused from my stupor. Could I jump at Dorian? Grab the gun? I tried to loosen Seeley's grip on my skirt, but even as I did so, I knew it wouldn't work. An image of us all, full of holes, sprawled bent and contorted on a blood-puddled floor, flashed into my head. That's what Michael would come home to find if we didn't play our parts carefully. We needed to obey Dorian for now and watch for our chance. Maybe he didn't intend . . .

Last came Sunny. She stood stock-still. Her eyes popped. Then she stamped her foot. "Dorian Rushton, you've got a lot of nerve coming back here after what you did. And those clothes! Have you turned bummer? Leave! Leave at once! We have nothing to say—"

"Shut up, Sunny," Dorian said.

Her mouth hung open. "Oh, my stars. Is that a gun?"

"Shut up, Sunny. Y'all go on up the stairs to Seeley's room and no one will get hurt. The key's there in the lock as usual, isn't it? Everyone in front of me. That's right. You're doing just fine."

We filed up the stairs and crowded into Seeley's room, clutching each other.

"Not you, Miss Elsa," Dorian said. "You go fetch that gold."

He shut the door and turned the key on the rest of us. None of us moved, except Laney, who crumpled to the bed. "Cubby's down there in the cradle. What'll he do to my baby?"

"Nothing," I said. "He wouldn't hurt Cubby and he won't hurt us if we do as he says. As soon as he's gone, we'll break out of here." I seemed always to be giving firm reassurances with nothing to back them. Soon no one would ever believe me again.

A moment later the key turned once more, the door opened, and my stepmother was stuffed inside.

"Been a pleasure, y'all," Dorian said as he relocked the door. The sound of his footsteps hurtling down the stairs reached us.

Miss Elsa sank to the bed and put her arms around Sunny. Laney immediately shoved at the door. Seeley and I joined her, and Sunny after a second, but it was thick oak, strong and unyielding. Next my stepsister stood on a stool to push open the tiny, high-up window. Much too tiny for even Seeley to climb out.

"Seeley," Sunny said, squatting, "get on my shoulders and squeeze through."

He scrambled onto her but couldn't poke more than his head out the opening, however he twisted and wriggled.

Miss Elsa was deathly pale. "I don't understand. Why is Dorian doing this?"

"Because he's a fiend. I'll explain later. Ouch," Sunny said, dropping Seeley and then helping him up. "It's no use. Even if we could get you out, we couldn't risk your life with the drop down. Y'all think we can break through the wall?"

"Hush," Laney whispered. "Listen."

We all paused, wide-eyed. From outside came thudding sounds, as of objects being thrown against the house, and then voices—King's rumbling tones and Dorian's higher ones.

"What's going on?" Sunny cried. "Seeley, get on me again and look."

The boy clambered onto Sunny and stretched his neck to see out the window. "King's dumping brush and logs in a pile against the house."

"What on earth?" Miss Elsa jumped to her feet. "No, they wouldn't!" she cried as realization set in.

"Uh-oh," Seeley said. He shouted now and waved his hands out the window. "King! King! Don't do it! We can't get out!"

The smell of smoke wafted up.

"He's torching the house!" screeched Sunny, dumping Seeley and shoving against the door once more. "He'll burn us alive! We've got to get out of here!"

"Dorian!" I screamed toward the window. "We'll give you anything. Seeley will give you Panola. Don't do this!"

By turns, we shouted, prayed out loud, beat at the door, whacked at the plaster, sobbed. I don't know which things I did. Maybe all of them.

"Let me see out again," Seeley said. This time it was me who lifted him. "King's arguing with Dorian. Dorian's holding the gun on him. King won't let—the kitchen's caught fire—"

Laney gave a shriek and clawed at the door. I dropped Seeley down. "Enough—don't look anymore." Cubby's faint, faraway howling reached us. The rest of us joined Laney to heave, push, and work at the hinges, but the door might have been a mountain for all we could move it.

One by one, we sank to the floor. The noise of flames whipping, snapping, and crackling grew louder till it almost drowned out our screams and moaning.

A sharp bang rang out. A shot. And then a second one. Poor King.

No hope. Smoke hung heavy in the room and we crouched under it. Sunny and Miss Elsa clung together. Laney, Seeley, and I wrapped our arms around each other and rocked a little. Tears poured down Laney's cheeks, but I was tearless now, sick and numb, waiting for the end. I had told Dorian he couldn't kill everyone who knew of his treachery. I had been wrong. Certainly he would lie in wait for Michael as well.

But something . . . Another sound . . . It took a moment for my brain to register what it was—feet pounding up the stairs.

"I'm coming, Master Seeley!" King's voice boomed. I loved King's voice. So deep. So reassuring. "Y'all stand back," he hollered. "I got to bust this open."

At last our stunned minds could grasp the fact that we were

being rescued. We scurried to a corner as the door came flying inward with a crash and the screech of hinges torn from the frame.

King bounded to Seeley's side, squatted, and put his big hands on the boy's shoulders. "You all right? I couldn't let Master Dorian burn you up. No, sir." He picked Seeley up in his arms, thick as tree trunks. "Y'all come on out. We got to put out the fire."

Coughing and sputtering, we all dashed downstairs and toward the blazing, smoke-filled kitchen. Laney reached it first. Gasping, she backed out of the doorway and into the hall, her eyes huge. "The cradle's gone." She swayed on her feet.

"Don't you worry none," King called back as he headed out onto the front porch. "Cubby's safe—hear him caterwauling outside? I got him out first."

Laney raced down the steps and around to the barn, where Cubby yowled reassuringly. The rest of us stumbled outside and immediately formed a line to pass buckets of water from the well and douse the kitchen. Thanks to the recent damp weather, it was still the only portion of the house that had caught. King took an ax and hacked away the burning parts. Bucket after heavy bucket, we began to turn the tide, and then, miraculously, the weighty clouds finally let loose, and rain poured down to finish the job. It was over—the kitchen destroyed, everything blackened and smoke-damaged, but the rest of the house safe.

We dropped to the front porch floor, out of the weather, exhausted, dripping, and relieved. A goose wandered past the steps; the kitchen yard fence was down. I didn't even think of corralling it. I wasn't going to do anything ever again. Except—I started up in a panic.

Dorian.

I said it out loud now. "Where's Dorian?"

We looked at each other blankly—Seeley, Laney, Sunny, Miss Elsa, and I. King was nowhere to be seen. I jumped up. "Let me fetch the pistol," I said, and hurriedly grabbed it from the mantel. Outside again, I led the way around the house.

King was kneeling in the grass beside Dorian's body. It sprawled stiff and contorted with a dark bullet hole in the chest. Rain diluted the blood to a pale rose. Blood and water on the shirt, blood and water puddled beneath.

The big man looked up, his eyes black as chasms and his mouth distorted. "I done it. I shot him. Couldn't let him burn y'all up." His homely face seemed to dissolve. Great, wrenching sobs racked his body.

"It's all right, King," Miss Elsa said, patting his shoulder.

He raised his head. "'All right, ma'am? It ain't all right. I done killed a man."

"You had to do it," I said, "to save our lives. You're a hero."

For a long moment Sunny, stunned, stared down at Dorian. with his bright hair spread in the grass. She turned slowly and went out of sight around the barn.

Miss Elsa stood. "I'm going to get bandages to bind your wound, King. It looks like you got grazed."

Only now I saw that King's upper sleeve was torn and showed ragged, bleeding flesh.

"He tried to kill you as well," I said. "The law would have hung him if he wasn't dead already. Leave him, King. Come out of the rain."

King trudged after the rest of us onto the front porch. He

slumped down against the rail, his head in his hands. Gently Miss Elsa bandaged him.

Michael came home. Laney fell into his arms. After finally untangling all our scrambled explanations, he said, "So what are we going to do with the body?"

No one seemed to have an answer.

At last Miss Elsa spoke firmly. "If we fetch the marshal, there'll be too many questions. So, Michael, would you please bury it out in the woods somewhere? Then, as soon as dear, wonderful King feels up to eating, we're going to give him the best meal he's ever had and send him off to the Yankee lines. They're near Corinth, aren't they? King, we've got a map somewhere that we'll give you. Can you sneak through the woods without letting anyone see you until you reach the bluecoats? When you get to them, you'll be free."

King nodded slowly.

Miss Elsa paused before turning again to Michael. "And, it's awful to ask, but can you find our money on the body? We'll need to send some with King." Her shoulders sagged suddenly. "I think I'll go in now. First I'll open all the windows to air out the smoke. And then . . ." Her voice trailed off.

I couldn't blame her for seeking laudanum tonight.

It all played out as Miss Elsa had said. We prepared to rebuild our lives. And the kitchen.

During the following days, we scrubbed the house until everything smelled only a little of smoke, and a few charitable men from church began coming out daily to rebuild the kitchen.

With Dorian's final and forever departure, we should all have felt more peaceful and secure. Somehow, though, peace eluded us. Four days later Seeley didn't seem to have recovered at all. I didn't know if it was still the original poison or the nightmare Dorian had put us through. Whatever it was, Seeley did nothing but lie on the sofa, wan and languid, with a sheet covering his face. He whimpered if I left the room and would hardly speak. He wanted nothing to eat. He even pushed Goblin off every time she tried to lie on him.

My worry over Seeley tangled with that nagging sense that there was something I needed to be doing or somewhere I needed to be going. Someone . . .

I watched Seeley, pondering what I could do for him. "Shall I read to you?"

He barely shrugged. "I guess."

"What do you want me to read?"

"Maybe *Castle Sliverbone*."

"That's a book you brought from Panola, isn't it? Is it up in your room?"

He nodded.

Upstairs it took me a few minutes to find the book under Seeley's bed, mixed in with dust, peach pits, and dirty undergarments. As I held the volume in my hands and read the cover, an odd feeling came over me. The author's name—Thomas Lynd—seemed so familiar. I shook myself. Seeley must have mentioned it before or else I had caught a glimpse of the cover.

Downstairs, when I started to read *Castle Sliverbone* to Seeley, he stopped me. "I guess I don't really want it." He turned his face away.

I tapped my fingers on the book for a few minutes. Then I slammed it down and announced, "Time for you to go outside,

Squid. There's something I need to do and you're going to help me. Do you have any of those lemon drops left from the other day?"

Sluggishly he rose up on his elbows. I thought he was going to rebel, but instead he told me where to find the few remaining pieces of candy in a twist of paper. I got them.

Seeley's legs gave way when he stood. I started to lend him some support, but he pushed me away. "I'm not a baby."

However, when he almost keeled over on the porch steps, he let me assist him down. We made our way across the yard. As we went, I remembered. . . .

Rush is about to leave for the last time, although we don't know that's what it is. His gray uniform is too big across the back and his rifle is shiny new. Laney prepares his favorite meal, but no one really eats it. It's time for Rush to go, but still we scrabble to delay. I play the songs he loves on the harp.

Pa stands finally, stretches, and says, "Well . . ."

"Soon, Pa," Rush says. "Violet and I need to take a walk first."

He and I walk down to the river, and then along the edge of the woods.

He puts his arm across my shoulders. "It's been a long time since we visited the bees." We head toward the gums.

"Don't forget them," he says, halfway there. "There's something in the bees that's very wise, and if you're the right sort of person and you treat them with the right sort of respect, they'll be with you when you need them. And Violet"——he stopped in mid-stride and faced me——"if I don't come back, don't think it'll be betraying our secret to share this with someone else."

I shove him. "Don't even say that." He knows I mean the part about not coming back.

He gives a faint, sad smile, but says nothing.

He did know it was the last time.

"Now," I said to Seeley when we stood on the slope above the gums, "the hives are the city of the bees. They are wise far beyond what most folks believe. I'm going to teach you to do something that Rush taught me. No one else knows I can do it. You talk to the bees. You tell them all the news and give them little gifts. And if you're the right sort of person, you can also call the bees to you when you're in need. I think you can do it. It'll take some courage on your part, but you've shown how brave you can be through all this business. Now put the lemon drops on the ground by the gums."

He did as I told him. I taught him the rhyme and we repeated it together.

"My lady queen and noble bees," I said, "this is Seeley Rushton, whom you probably already know a little. Please care for him and let no harm come to him. All right," I told Seeley, "you'll have to hold very, very still."

I showed him how to lie down in the grass, hands flat against the ground, feeling the earth, imagining blossoms and honey-sweet smells.

"We summon thee. . . ."

They came.

Most landed on me, but several alighted on Seeley. I heard his sharp intake of breath at first and then his steady, soft breathing beneath the humming.

Afterward, on the way back to the house, Seeley shambled a bit but smiled and shook his head when I made a move to help him.

CHAPTER 30

FORGOTTEN
AND REMEMBERED

It continued to tug at me—that restless, fearful sense that there was something I was forgetting. Something important. Urgent even. I would try to pin my mind to whatever it was, but it always slipped away like an oily, elusive dream.

No one else had any idea as to what it could be or what commitment I might have made.

Well, there was plenty to keep me busy these days without borrowing some problem that didn't exist, and I tried to shake myself free of it. The cotton fields were growing cushiony and puffy. We were still putting things to rights in the new kitchen and canning the first harvest from the garden.

A large basket of withered poppies sat in Miss Elsa's room. First she pierced the capsules with a needle. Next she dropped them into a glazed crock near a small fire that she kept burning on her hearth, in spite of the heat, to allow the opium to sweat out. Afterward she mixed it with sugar and alcohol to make her medicine.

However, nothing enabled her to escape completely from the

aftereffects of Dorian. Finally she requested details about what had happened between him and Sunny. She listened, with pain lining her face. "It's all my fault," she said sadly.

"How is it your fault, Mama?" Sunny demanded. "You couldn't know what that vermin was up to."

"I spend so much of my time in a fog from my medicine. Maybe—maybe I would have seen something if I'd been lucid. I should never have left you to deal with him alone. And you didn't even think you could tell me anything. I'm a terrible mother."

"Don't you dare blame yourself!" Sunny cried, throwing her arms around Miss Elsa and squeezing hard. "I won't let you."

"You were quick-thinking when you knew what to do with King and Dorian," I said. I would never forget how my stepmother had acted in those moments when the rest of us were at a loss.

"I'll try harder. I really will," Miss Elsa said, sobbing. "I'll take less and less until I stop completely. This time I will do it."

Even Goblin was having a hard time. I had left Seeley with Laney in order to attend Miss Ruby Jewel's funeral and brought home two cats—the least moth-eaten-looking ones—whom Goblin did not take to at all. They were to stay out in the barn. "Now, my kitty," I had told Goblin, "you may not have wanted new cats around the place, but you may grow to love them. It happened to me."

I should have had no time to worry over anything. I worked in the house and in the barn, sewed a new shirt to send to my father, and finished a pair of stockings.

Maybe I had given someone a promise. Someone who needed my help. Perhaps that was what caused the prickling sensation that wavered at the back of my brain. *Who is it?* I was on edge and weepy.

The unsettled feeling was soon compounded by the weather and an unpleasant discovery I made because of it. For three days, a violent storm raged, toppling trees and bombarding Scuppernong with sheets of black rain and flotsam and jetsam torn from the woods. We huddled inside and worried that shortly the wind might form a funnel and blow us clean away.

When the deluge finally stopped, the cotton fields looked battered and beaten, mushrooms had sprouted all over the yard, and a gray fungus, which grew back nearly as soon as I scrubbed it away with carbolic soap, clouded the walls of the parlor.

The river had topped its banks and gushed foaming brown, littered with roiling, swirling, tangled muck. We had been hauling branches and trash to a fire for burning when I took a break to stand on the edge of the bank, watching the endless flow and listening. Just barely, if I strained my ears, the faint, faraway booming of cannon sounded. The war crept closer.

Something pale caught my eye, wedged in a massive clump floating my way. At first I thought it was a child's rubber ball, mud-spattered and trapped within the twisted debris. But as it approached, I realized with horror that what I had taken for muddy grass stuck to the ball was actually filthy hair and that a stiff hand reached through the sticks farther down. It bobbed closer and the face emerged, blanched, puffy, and swollen from a long time in water.

I screamed and screamed and screamed.

Michael came running and managed to snag the mass and pull it to shore. I fled to the house, sick and shaking, while Michael fetched help from town.

Somehow a part of me had feared the body was Dorian's, come

back to torment us, but it turned out to be that of a stranger with a bullet hole in his belly. It was probably a soldier, but whether Southern or Northern could not be determined since his clothing had been torn away.

The sense grew that something terrible and unknown was brewing, waiting just around the corner. A vague and shapeless doom.

One morning I pulled my journal from its hiding place. Perhaps some clue might lie there as to what was nagging just below my consciousness. My most recent entry read:

June 18, 1862

I'm going to tell him I'm his if he still wants me. I don't care. I don't care if he loves me only for a month or a week or a day. I need to love him and let him love me as long as he can. If only I haven't spoiled everything.

I riffled back through my other entries, and each was familiar, although some were a little puzzling. I wrote of secrets, but I could not imagine what I meant. And *this* entry . . .

It was my handwriting. I had written it ten days ago, just before Dorian and the fire, yet I had no idea who "he" was. I must have been imagining some pathetic daydream. Similar to practicing writing my name as "Violet Phillips" when Ben had been interested in me. How embarrassing. But why couldn't I recall doing it? A new, nasty anxiety attached itself to my growing collection—that something was wrong with my mind. Crazy people lived in dreamworlds and had melancholic humors and experienced memory lapses. My nerves were taut as harp strings.

The weight of a terrible loss fell on me, so that I sank to the bed. Maybe it was myself that was misplaced. Here I was in my own well-loved, familiar home, and I was hopelessly lost. I pulled at my hair as if I could yank the forgotten thing from my foggy brain. A physical pain exploded in my head.

I lay, moaning, until the agony subsided. Slowly I rose, dabbed my drawn face with water from the basin, and threw on one of my black gowns. I had begun wearing mourning again. These dreary days demanded it.

A sewing circle was being held in town today and I planned to attend. Seeley had done all right with Laney when I'd gone to the funeral, and I hadn't been to the circle in ages. Other people, the latest gossip, and war news might help take me out of myself. I had urged Sunny and Miss Elsa to come as well.

My stepsister troubled me. She had lost her sparkle. Today she came downstairs in a faded cambric gown much too large for her. Her hair was stuffed into a snood, and even her green eyes seemed dull, as if a dusty film coated them.

"No, Sunny," I said. "You can't go out in public wearing that."

She rallied enough to flash back, "You should talk. Look at what you've got on."

"I'll change if you will."

She shrugged and trudged upstairs. I followed.

In my room I took the china-blue taffeta off its hook. It hadn't been worn since the bazaar. I shook out the folds and saw how the skirt had been snagged and how much dirt and how many burs and bits of grass clung to it. Had I rolled in a field of weeds? I didn't deserve nice things. I spread it out on the bed and brushed my hands over the fabric. As I did so, I bumped a hard bulge in the pocket. Puzzled, I reached in and drew out an amulet. My amulet of raw amber.

That was where it had got to. I remembered now—Sunny wouldn't let me wear the thing since it showed above the gown's neckline, so I had stuffed it in the pocket. I held it up by the leather thong. The honey gold spun and glowed translucent in the light pouring in from the window. I squeezed my other hand around the stone and dropped it immediately to the floor with a cry.

Thomas!

The amber had burned my skin as if it were a living coal. Before it had left my fingers, his name flamed through my mind. And everything about him, every detail, flooded over me like lava— the warm, steady look in his gray eyes, the way his shirt set on his still-bony shoulders, his expressive hands, and his smile just for me. *He* was what had been flickering in the back of my brain. It was him. Of all the people in all the world whom I might have forgotten, how could it have been him? I staggered against the wall.

The words Laney had once said when we were speaking of hoodoo came back to me: "There are ways you can make folks forget things you don't want them to remember."

They had done this to me.

I gave a little hiccoughing half sob, threw the amulet over my head, not caring if it still burned, and dashed down the stairs. In the kitchen I hastily wrapped a bandage around my scorched fingers, snatched up a burlap sack, and stuffed in corn bread and ham.

I stammered excuses to Sunny and Miss Elsa. They stared after me in amazement as I tore away, frantic and wild-eyed, down the river and through sticky, shifting, stirring greenness to the Lodge.

He might have asked where I had been with his food for the past two weeks. He might have asked, "How could you have left me so long to the untender mercies of the VanZeldts?" He might have said, "You needn't have bothered to return after what you said last time." He could have said any number of well-deserved and terrible things, but he did not.

Instead he swept his long, dark hair back from his face and gazed as if he couldn't believe his eyes. Then he held out his arms. I cried into his chest and told him almost all that had happened. He drew in his breath with horror at our close escape. He held me and told me I was valiant and strong and clever to have handled such challenges as I had. His voice was rough with emotion when he called me his "sweet girl."

A burden lifted off my shoulders because he was all right and because he had not only forgiven me but understood exactly why I had done all that I had done. He assured me that, under the circumstances, I had been right not to call in the marshal with Dorian. He listened for a good long while. I did not tell him I had forgotten him. I couldn't bear him to know this.

After I had talked myself out, he kissed me—a gentle, tender embrace. It was nothing like our passionate kisses by the bonfire, but still it made me glow clear through, partly because it showed that all was mended between us.

The two weeks had left him noticeably thinner. His eyes were shadowed and his cheeks hollow. His every movement was slower, as if each took an effort. I pushed the sack toward him. "Please eat now. I should have given you the food first thing."

After he ate, he demonstrated that he could walk without his sticks. He had to swing one leg out a bit, but not much.

"This last week," he said, "when I began to think you might not return, I figured I'd better speed up my departure. I've worked at the walking every day. Are you suitably impressed?"

I nodded, but my mouth went dry. "This means you must leave soon."

"Are you so eager for me to run off?"

"You know I'm not. It will break my heart. But it's time. The sooner you're away from the VanZeldts, the better. I'm grateful to the doctor for healing Seeley, and I really do like Amenze—the girl—but they scare me. That last time I was here, Amenze caught Seeley and me leaving the Lodge. She said she wouldn't tell the doctor, but . . . Very soon I'll bring Seeley so he can say goodbye, and I'll have some of my brother's clothes for you. That last time, we won't come by river. We'll bring Star and a map so you can ride to the nearest Federal camp."

"You're right," Thomas said soberly. "Even though I don't want to leave, it's best I go soon. They've caught me awake a few times lately and it seems as if their attitude has changed. They used to be completely detached, but now the girl looks at me with pity and the young man sneers. At least they don't know I can walk, thank goodness, so my escape will be a surprise."

"They have powers we can't comprehend," I said, shivering. "You should have seen their place: there was a human skull on the floor of the shed."

"You don't suppose they're vampires, do you?" Thomas gave a mischievous smile.

I couldn't make light of such a thing. "I wouldn't be surprised if they were. I've also wondered if they're fairies—not tinkly, floaty ones but dark, deadly ones. For sure, though, they're practitioners of some strange religion that worships a snake god all mixed together with hoodoo."

Thomas squeezed my hand. "Good old down-home hoodoo—wish I knew more about it. Skull aside, though, maybe there's nothing so bad about what the VanZeldts believe. Maybe it's just dissimilar from what our Western culture understands. Our scientific knowledge covers only a fraction of the forces at play in the universe. You know, a few hundred years ago the electric telegraph would have been considered witchcraft. Why can't we take the good that comes from different sources and leave the bad? Why do we accept the miracles of our Christianity but deny other cultures' beliefs?"

I didn't remind him of the evil of the VanZeldts' magic where Jorgenson had been concerned. Instead I reached out and brushed the hair from his eyes as if I had all the right in the world to touch him whenever I wanted to. An amazing assumption. "Do you believe people can communicate with creatures in—in odd ways?"

"I think I experienced it sometimes during those first weeks I lay here. Those animals that poked around inside."

"Well, I have a funny sort of talent. If people only knew, I expect they would be shocked. Maybe even scared."

"Really? What is it?"

Within the triangle of his legs, I leaned back against his chest, encircled by his arms. "My gift involves bees. . . ."

And so we spent an enjoyable hour informing each other of things we should have divulged before and never had.

It was time to go, but I couldn't bear it.

"Thomas," I said urgently.

"Yes?"

"Oh . . . nothing."

"Just 'Thomas.' "

"Yes."

He smiled, but in a wistful sort of way, and I knew he understood. He pulled the carnelian signet ring from his pinkie and slipped it onto my ring finger. "When I'm gone, this will reassure you that I'm coming back. It came to me from my grandfather and is my most precious possession."

I shook my head. "No. You don't need to make promises like that. Neither of us knows what the next months will bring. You don't—"

He put his fingers lightly over my lips. "I am promising."

CHAPTER 31

THE LAST LODGE VISIT

"May I go to the woods with you?" Seeley begged the next day as he watched me start out the door for my visit to the Lodge. "It's been ages since I've been anywhere."

"No, Squid. Soon. Hopefully this Saturday. Right now you aren't quite strong enough."

He frowned but didn't protest, as he would have a few weeks ago. His terrible experiences had left him too solemn and pliable. I missed the old Seeley.

Neither he nor Laney remembered Thomas. When I had returned the night before, I had tested them both, and they had acted only bewildered by my hints. Evidently my memory had returned because of the amulet, but the spell still held over the others. I couldn't let Seeley touch the amber, lest he be burned. In a few days I would take him to the Lodge, and maybe the sight of Thomas would restore his memory—or else he could grow new ones.

But not today. The fact was, I didn't want Seeley along today. I selfishly yearned for one more visit with Thomas alone. It was so delightful to say what we wanted to say and kiss when we wanted to kiss without an audience. No wonder our society never allowed young ladies to go about unchaperoned—being isolated with the opposite sex was dangerously freeing.

I wore a new dress I had brought down from the attic and stayed up late altering the night before. It was of apple-green muslin with thin brown satin ribbons lacing up the front of the bodice to a low, circular neckline. Because of the neckline, I carried the amulet in my pocket. This time I wouldn't forget where I had put it. Throughout the trip to the Lodge, I moved carefully so as not to spoil my pretty dress.

Thomas lay with his head resting on his hands and his long limbs extended. When I entered, he smiled a slow, lazy smile, sat up partially, and stretched his arms out to me in a graceful, fluid motion. I squatted down beside him and started to take his hand. Instead he clenched my wrist and pulled me down to lie pressed full length against him.

I gave a little laugh. "You're eager."

He answered with a low wordless murmur. He drew my face to his and kissed me, deep and passionate. I responded, with every cell of my body tingling and reaching for him. Our legs twisted around each other, tangled in my skirt. His hands passed over me, stroking. His tongue flicked out over my neck and bosom, teasing and tantalizing.

"Thomas," I breathed, "we shouldn't—"

He stopped my words with his mouth, then leaned back and looked at me with burning, hungry, narrow eyes, absolutely unlike the Thomas I knew, but intriguing. He took one finger and outlined the neckline of my gown and then dipped lower inside. I caught my breath. He fumbled with the lacing of my bodice. My hands flew to my chest. He chuckled deeply and grasped my skirt now, edging it upward.

Our hearts banged together, pushed tight against each other. The heat from his body wrapped around me, curling like tendrils of vine around my limbs, and I melted into him, closer, closer. It was too hard to deny him. I hadn't the strength. Besides, I was hungry too. This was Thomas, with whom I was absolutely head over heels in love. A slippery, delicious desire swelled inside to give in, to finally learn all about this thing I had heard of in late-night whispers at school. And it was with my darling Thomas, who would return to marry me. I reached behind him and pulled up his shirt to caress his back. So smooth and warm and velvety. I wanted to feel my skin against his.

And then I paused, stiffened, and withdrew my arms. *What am I doing?* It didn't matter that we were in love. I had been taught better, and could not feel right about this. There was an order to such things.

"No," I said. "We need to stop."

He ignored my words and only grasped tighter as I attempted to pull away. Annoyance gave strength to my objections. How dare even Thomas try to force his will, as if I had no say in what we did, how far we went? As I pushed upon his chest, I looked into his countenance. There was a feral curl to his lips, and the craving in his eyes was sly and slick. Something wasn't right. These were Thomas's features—the lean face and firm chin, the gray irises and dark hair curling behind his ears—but the expression was all wrong. These were Thomas's long fingers and lanky limbs, but their movements were sinuously smooth, which should have been pleasing, but wasn't. Instead they were menacing. Something else . . . he smelled wrong. Not unpleasant, but musky, different. This was Thomas—wasn't it?

"What's happened to you?" I whispered.

I made myself relax so that his arms would loosen and he'd begin groping again instead of imprisoning. I reached down into my pocket and closed my fingers over the amber stone—and gasped.

With all my strength I shoved against the man's chest so he fell away. I leaped up before he could collect himself and ran, ran, ran faster than I could possibly run, not looking back, listening for the pounding of feet behind me, expecting any second to be wrenched backward.

I was nearly halfway to the canoe when my too-big boots finally did what they had been waiting to do ever since I bought them: they sent me sprawling face-first. I scrabbled in the mud and roots and loam, fighting with my skirts to right myself. I rose up on my hands and knees, looked up, and froze. There he came, sauntering, because speed wasn't necessary. I could not flee. I could not fight. I could not move a finger. All I could do was wait. His gaze held me, as if I were a bird hypnotized by a snake. This was it. He smiled.

From the corner of my eye I could see something rising from the trees and coming toward me. A wavering cloud. A cloud of . . . bees. They swarmed about and lit upon me, covering me from head to toe. Their wings whirred. They hummed reassuringly. I huddled there in my armor of insects ready to sting, still watching him.

The smile fled from his face as he came close enough to see clearly.

He stared and a stifled sound rose from his throat. He turned on his heels and loped away.

"Thank you," I whispered when I was sure he was long gone.

The bees lifted now, hovered about for a moment, and swarmed away once more.

Able to move again, I pulled myself together and made my way to the canoe. When I was at last safe in the middle of the current and thought of what had happened, I wanted to scream. I wanted to vomit. I wanted to scrub myself until there was no skin left.

When I'd touched the amber, Thomas's features had blurred and another face slid over—Uwa's. Thomas's skin had been stripped away and there had lain Uwa's flesh in its place. In the end, only the bees had kept him from doing what he wanted with me.

What have they done with Thomas?

My confusion and shame gave way to terror. I didn't understand how the VanZeldts did what they did, but I believed in their powers now with a biting, painful certainty. I had thought I'd seen the limit of it with the forgetfulness that had plagued me. But this—if they could do this, could make me see so clearly what was not there, how could I possibly fight such a force? They must somehow have realized their spell had been broken, that I had visited Thomas again. So they had hidden him away somewhere till they could complete their plans. Or worse. Could it be they *had* finished carrying out their plot? That he was already gone?

No! I would not think that way. *I will find him. I will rescue him.*

"But I don't know what to do," I whispered aloud. "Please tell me what to do."

I needed help.

CHAPTER 32

FIGHTING FIRE WITH FIRE

I told them everything, as simply as I could relate it. I had to. I needed every one of them—Michael's strength, Laney's good judgment, Sunny's survival instincts, Miss Elsa's calm and creativity, and Seeley's sense of adventure and love for our soldier. I had learned to my sorrow what could happen when people were kept in the dark about important things.

When I first told of our visits with Thomas, Sunny murmured, "Sly minx," and Seeley made an odd squeaking sound since I was relating events he had forgotten completely. Other than that, everyone was silent until I came to the part about forgetting Thomas and finding the amulet, and then the bit about Uwa (suitably censored). These elements caused some sharply indrawn breaths. "Thomas is missing," I said in the end, "and I'm so scared; please help me save him."

Michael, Laney, and Seeley all looked bewildered, struggling to believe me as they came to terms with their failed memories.

Michael gave a low whistle and rumpled Seeley's hair. "This puppy sure kept the secret good."

Seeley grinned and looked down, rubbing nervous fingers over one of his little horses. "It must have been easy to keep *that* secret. Especially once I forgot everything." He squinted a little, and I wondered if his head hurt, as mine had, with all the forgetting and straining to remember.

Laney had been rocking with Cubby in her arms, her head cocked to one side as she listened. She rocked faster and faster as the story unfolded. Now she said, "Why do you guess Dr. VanZeldt helped with Seeley when he's up to these terrible tricks? What's his reason?"

I shrugged. "I'm not sure, but I think he really did want to make Seeley better. He genuinely does like to heal people. Amenze—the girl—said they don't think of evil as we do. To them, if their purposes are considered good things for their people, then they're justified in whatever they do. Other than that, I guess you could call the doctor a kind, considerate person. Amenze thinks he's wonderful."

"No one is all good or all bad," Miss Elsa murmured.

"I can't believe you didn't tell me," Sunny said. "All this time sneaking off, having a secret life."

"You were busy with Dorian, and anyway, it's not as it seems," I hastened to say. "It started as just an adventure—like in one of Thomas's books—but as it got more serious, we couldn't take any chances. Seeley and I were all Thomas had. For one thing, I didn't know exactly what your feelings would be toward a Union soldier and I didn't want to put any of you in the position of breaking the law. Then, as I began to distrust Dorian, more than ever I didn't dare breathe a word—who knows what he might have done?"

There were some nods when I mentioned Dorian, and Sunny sniffed. "Oh, pooh. As if we'd have let that cad betray the poor soldier." No one was cruel enough to remind her how deep she had been in the cad's pocket. The red flash from Thomas's ring caught her eye. "I declare, Violet Dancey, what do we have there?"

I blushed as I held it out. "Thomas gave it to me yesterday. As a token of his—his constancy."

A light had begun to slowly seep into Seeley's eyes. Suddenly he cried, "I remember! I remember now. He kissed her too." He sounded smug and they all grinned. "You didn't think I saw, but I did. I see and hear everything."

Sunny giggled. "No wonder you're so eager to rescue him."

"'Constancy'!" Miss Elsa looked concerned. "Oh, my dear, are you sure? A Northerner . . ."

I nodded. "I'm sure. But there's no time to waste. Thomas—and possibly all of us—is in grave danger. We must act quickly. What do we do? Should we go to the marshal? Or to the nearest Federal officer since he's one of their own? Or is it something a minister like Mr. Stone is better equipped to deal with?"

"We go to my aunty," Laney stated flatly. "These folks practice hoodoo and there's nothing regular folks can do to stop them, even a man of God like Mr. Stone. Aunty will know."

We discussed it briefly, but we all knew she was right. Anarchy was our best and only choice, and it was decided that Laney would accompany me.

Sunny reached for Cubby. "Come to Aunt Sunny, honey. They

don't need to tote a baby along." She bounced him in her arms—too heartily, but Cubby was a forgiving infant.

Laney hesitated for just a moment, then sent Michael a speaking look. He would make sure Cubby came to no harm with "Aunt Sunny."

Sunny caught my eye and mouthed, "Am I forgiven?"

I nodded. She blinked and buried her face in Cubby's neck. Taking care of a baby was so out of character for Sunny that it nearly brought a tear to my eye to realize the sacrifice she was making. How awkwardly but determinedly she held the baby. And I think for the first time she considered us—all of us—family.

As we made our way through the forest to Anarchy's house, I caught a glimpse of Sparrow flitting along ahead, under cover of the trees.

I called to her, but she gave no sign that she heard.

She was standing beside Anarchy in the herb garden by the time we arrived there. "My baby gals," Anarchy said. "Sparrow told me you was on your way. I been waiting on you."

"Aunty," Laney said, "we didn't come just to visit. Miss Vi's got a big problem. She's been messing with those VanZeldts—those hoodoo folks. She needs your help."

"Laws a-mercy, child," Anarchy said. "Don't I know it? Of course I do. I been worrying over you, li'l Miss Violet. The last few days them bees been warning me for your sake. Why'd you go and mess with them folks?"

"I didn't mean to. It's them who are messing with me," I said. "So you know about the bees?"

Laney looked at me questioningly; I'd explain later.

Anarchy grinned. "Sure 'nough. And they know about me. You

best come inside and set a spell. Tell old Anarchy all about it. Bees can't explain all the details, even when they buzz to high heaven. Just *bzzz* this and *bzzz* that—right hard to decipher."

Anarchy's house was clean, cozy, sweet-smelling, and full of color. Yellow-sprigged curtains hung at the windows and a scarlet-sprigged cloth covered the table. In the center of the table sat a ribbed yellowware bowl that reminded me of an upside-down bee skep. It held peaches, pears, and weirdly shaped roots. Herbs hung from the ceiling.

Laney and I pulled out chairs. Sparrow retired to a dim corner so I could not see her well, but I knew she was watching solemnly and listening.

Anarchy brought us each a cup of chamomile tea. "Now," she said, "tell me."

I glanced significantly toward Sparrow.

Anarchy bobbed her head. "It don't matter that my Sparrow will hear. Sometimes I thinks she understands these odd things better than I does. Her spirit be old."

For the second time that day, I told my story, this time adding the details Dr. VanZeldt had related of the snake god, Raphtah-from-the-stars.

Sparrow spoke only once from the shadows. "The People Things," she whispered, early on.

Dusk deepened as I spoke, and Laney and I exchanged uneasy glances while Anarchy drew the curtains and lit a candle. In its flickering light the tight-stretched skin over Anarchy's cheekbones made her face appear skull-like. Her expression was grim and her tone hushed. "That creature might've been half snake, but it wasn't no god. Whatever it was, though, it ain't up to no good in this here world. I ain't a conjure woman—I is only a root woman, and a Christian one at that—but I got to know a little black magic in order to fight it. This is bigger doings than any hoodoo I ever heard tell of, but it's got bits of the same. Them mojo bags and all."

"Have you ever heard of a grigri?" I asked, and pulled my amulet from my pocket.

"Uh, uh, uh," Anarchy said, holding the stone carefully. "Who give you this?"

"Amenze. One of the VanZeldts. She isn't a bad person. She meant to help me with this. It's how the forgetting and illusion spells were broken."

"No one ain't ever all good or all bad."

This was the second time in the day that someone had said this. Dorian flashed through my mind. Perhaps even he had once or twice genuinely cared about us—a little.

"'Cept Cletus," Anarchy added a disclaimer. "He was the bocor back at Oakhill Plantation, where me and Permilla was borned. He was all bad. Killed babies just to use their tiny pieces for bone reading. Hold on to your grigri. It ain't real strong, but it do got power for good. Now, this forgetting spell—you look on the tops of your outside windows and doors. Also dig round your steps, and I bet you find a little packet of nasty trash—lizard heads and bloody chicken feathers. That'd be what caused your forgetting."

"I caught Amenze in our kitchen yard a while back. I think . . . it's foggy still, but I think that was right before I forgot Lieutenant Lynd. She acted so strangely. She didn't speak and her eyes didn't focus."

"Drugged," Anarchy said. "Drugged so she seemed like walking dead. I seen it at Oakhill. The bocor slave had a slave hisself. I used to feel so sorry for poor Floyd. One day he up and died. We buried him, but next thing we knows, there he come back again, shuffling about, not looking at no one and doing Cletus's chores. Later I learned how Cletus done it. Dosed Floyd with some powder so's he couldn't move a limb and his heart almost didn't beat and we buried him. Then Cletus dug Floyd up, waked him a bit, and give him jimsonweed tea to keep him in a trance. So much of hoodoo be drugs and tricksiness and creepy trappings. Like that Uwa fellow this morning. He didn't really turn his flesh and bones into your soldier's flesh and bones. He just fooled your eyes. You know what I'm saying—it ain't like in the old tales where a fox really do turn into a possum."

"Aunty," Laney said, "we need to hurry. They're fixing to hurt Miss Vi's soldier. How do we fight them?"

Anarchy sighed and suddenly looked haggard. "Ain't a lot I can tell you. You got your grigri. 'Twill help some with illusions. I reckon they're fixing to sacrifice the poor feller, sure 'nough, but they'll wait for some sign—some uncommon cloud or some shooting star or some unusual animal happening by. Be best if you sneak to their place and find him before the sign comes. Probably there'll be patterns of cornmeal dribbled around for a guard where he's hid away. Brush away them patterns while you pray. Then if you got any of them folks' spit or hair or toenail clippings—"

"Oh, Aunty," Laney groaned, "how'd Miss Vi come by those things?"

"Or that woman's blood from her female time . . ."

Laney snorted and Anarchy shot a look up to the ceiling. "Forgive this child for she knows not what she do, mocking her elders. I'm just telling you young'uns—if you had them things, we could make dolls to embody the Van-whoevers' spirits and 'twould cause such pain they'd do whatever you made them do. That's why bocors are so careful about them things. Why, Cletus, he used to hide out in the trees to pee and buried—"

"Aunty!" Laney said sharply.

"Miss Vi," Sparrow said.

We all looked at her. We had nearly forgotten she was there.

"You got the wooden dolls. The ones that favor them People Things."

I nodded slowly. "You're right. I have"—I hesitated, then made up my mind and continued firmly—"I have two carved figures that look just like Amenze and Ahigbe. Would those work?"

Anarchy's old eyes lit up. "Might would, might would, even without the spit. What you got to do is, you gonna take them dolls and you rub them with this oil I gives you and you write their names on them. Then pass the dolls over a burning candle. Utter the names and concentrate on the flame. Don't burn them all up—you don't want to out-and-out kill them, I guess, but just force them to let your feller go."

I twisted my hands together. "I hate to use such methods." I especially didn't want to hurt Amenze.

"Got to fight fire with fire. No decent, God-fearing folks wants to mess with ugly things, but 'twas them Van—them fools started the messing. Sparrow, run and get Miss Vi a flask of root oil."

Sparrow returned shortly to hand me a tiny bottle. As we stood to leave, Anarchy took my cold hands in her own warm, gnarled ones. "Honey child, it be true these folks can command some spirits—loa, they is called—to do their bidding, but them loa are puny earth-trapped beings, not like God's holy angels or the good Lord hisself. Say your prayers and remember what the prophet Elisha said. He said, 'Fear not: for they that be with us are more than they that be with them.' And 'tis so for you." She squeezed my hands. "You bring your young man here to meet old Anarchy when all this be over and done."

"I will if I can, but he's a Union soldier and I don't—"

"By 'all this' I meant *all* this. When them crazy, powerful men be done busting the United States wide open and have set themselves down to mend it. Then your young man'll scoot back to you and you bring him here. That be what I meant." She gave us each a hard, bony hug.

I think Laney and I both wished we could stay there in the safety of Anarchy's wings, in the candlelight, but we turned and walked out into the darkness. We were all Thomas had.

CHAPTER 33

HOLDING ON

The air was still and foggy when I left before dawn the next morning. Mist blanketed everything in a hush that was menacing in its quiet.

I made my way alone to Shadowlawn. I had wanted to run off to find Thomas as soon as we returned from Anarchy's, but Laney convinced me that such headlong action would come back to hurt me in the end. Instead I had stayed up all night, first with the others, debating how to proceed, next searching for Amenze's unpleasant hoodoo objects and then burning them. One revolting-smelling little bundle of blackened, shriveled animal bits, bound by twine, was found buried near the steps in the kitchen yard; another was above the door of Laney's cabin. I spent the final minutes by myself in my room, upon my knees, praying for help.

Against argument, I had insisted I go alone. In this case, physical numbers and strength would not help. If I failed, it would do no good for anyone else to be caught in the VanZeldts' web. In the end our only strategy was that I find Thomas undetected, release him, and bring him back to Scuppernong. If I was discovered, I would use the wooden figures as a threat. If I had not returned by the next morning, Michael would begin slowly burning the carvings. If I still did not return by the afternoon, he would inform the marshal of all that had taken place. Even if civilized man's law could not stop the evil, at least it could bring trouble to the VanZeldts. That was all. My only weapons were the figures, my only armor the amulet. I felt naked.

The pearly air turned the landscape into a faded dream with no boundaries between field, river, and wood. I must be extra watchful, extra wary in such a world. I paddled past the inlet where I left the canoe for Lodge visits and on a ways farther to the Shadowlawn dock. Just beyond the VanZeldts' boat, I hid the canoe behind a bushy outcrop. Heat dragged at my boots and at my bones, and my clothing hung heavy. I had donned a pair of Rush's old trousers to enable me to move quickly, unencumbered by billowing skirts. It had taken me a moment to put them on; it took courage to wear men's clothing. I found them less comfortable—hotter and more binding—than ladies' things. Still, they made for swifter travel.

The closer I crept to Shadowlawn, the more afraid I was of the forest. A pair of malevolent-looking squirrels glared down through the fog and scolded me. The normal stirrings of the trees made me recoil. Faint breezes curled vapor into swirls that confused direction.

Somehow I reached my destination. The house at Shadowlawn slept, floating on its cloud of mist like Sleeping Beauty's enchanted castle. For several minutes I lingered behind a trunk, searching for signs of life. None appeared. No one came out. No shapes moved behind dark windows.

A soft humming broke the stillness. Five bees flew in from the forest. They hovered around my head and then moved slowly to the left. I followed them as they darted from tree to tree and behind clumps of bushes. They led me to a shed where, just as Anarchy had said, someone had dribbled cornmeal before the doorway in a pattern of intertwined squiggles, arrows, and death's-heads. It was the shack where I had glimpsed the skull and snakes.

I attacked the designs with my boots, dashing away every last line. The bees floated off as I stormed the door, expecting to find it locked. If it was, I would beat it open. It swung inward easily, with only one short, agonized squeak.

Thomas rested in the shadows.

Wearing only his breeches, he lay on his side, knees drawn up to his chest. His bare skin was streaked with dried blood. He had been beaten. As I drew closer and my sight grew accustomed to the dusky interior, I could see that one part of his face was covered with purplish bruises, one eye was blackened, and his lips were swollen and misshapen. I hardly recognized him, and it seemed he did not recognize me.

"Thomas," I whispered.

He made no motion.

"Thomas," I said, louder.

Nothing. The slight rising and falling of his chest was the only indication that he lived. Was he unconscious? Yet his eyes were open, staring straight ahead. I squatted beside him and shook him, first lightly, and then harder.

He lifted his head a little. Slowly, ponderously, he rolled to a sitting position. His head hung low between his shoulders.

"Please, Thomas," I whispered, "we have to get you out of here."

Still, his eyes did not focus. I pulled at his arm, but it was heavy and unmoving as lead. It was the drugs, just as Anarchy had described—the drugs that made a man appear to be walking dead. Only Thomas would not walk. I hated how he looked—Thomas and yet almost as un-Thomas as the Uwa creature.

Frantically I pulled off my amulet and held it against his chest. It gave a feeble glow but brought no change to his condition. Perhaps it only held power for me.

The shed stank of dead things. I glanced desperately about, seeking help from somewhere, anywhere. Next to Thomas was the glass case of snakes. The serpents were motionless, all wound about each other, with varying sizes, colors, and patterns. Their only movements were the wink of a cold eye or flicker of a forked tongue. There, on the floor in a cobwebby corner, lay the skull. A wall of shelves held other empty-eyed skulls of various creatures, grinning down, along with a scattering of bones. There were also heads still covered with fur or desiccated flesh, including one that appeared to be human and capped with silky black hair, but that was too tiny to have ever belonged to a person. There were slimy things in bottles—some with obvious tentacles, some with eyes, and some with teeth—as well as what appeared to be empty jars labeled with writing in an unknown script. There were bundles of feathers and roots and pungent herbs, carved and painted chalices and bowls.

No help could be had from these unclean objects.

The snakes began to awaken. One uncoiled itself and others followed suit. The glass case roiled and seethed with slithering motion.

I gulped a deep, shuddering breath and tried to concentrate on Thomas. His hand lay stiff and unmoving when I took it in mine. His breathing was forced and raspy, as if whatever dulled the rest of him also affected his vital functions. If only I could talk to him, say something that would catch hold of some glimmer in his brain. And so I made the attempt. Beginning with what I knew of Thomas's family and his life before the war, I went on into the time we had spent together, things we had said to one another, moments we had enjoyed.

All the while I remained fiercely aware of the situation we were in. At any moment the VanZeldts might enter. I licked my lips and now resorted to tales of my own childhood and the years after my mother's death. I voiced memories I had never related to another soul, and as I did so, it seemed I was listening to someone else, gaining a new understanding, as if this eerie, deadly place made me see myself, my family, and events more clearly.

I had no idea what time it was, but my growling stomach told me it must be afternoon. "We can't just stay here talking," I said at last to the un-Thomas. "We have to take some action."

Thomas's sightless, bewitched gaze offered no response.

The door began to open. I scrabbled against the wall, making myself as small as possible.

Amenze entered, her head ducked under the low doorway, carrying a dark flask.

She showed no sign of surprise or any other emotion when she took in my presence, but neither was she in a trance, as she had been the last time I saw her. "Miss Violet Dancey. I thought you would come. You removed the guarding signs my grandmother drew outside, but as you've discovered, we don't actually need them to keep your soldier here."

"I've come to take him away."

"That is impossible. He is necessary. We have cared for him many weeks and we cannot let him go now, when it is so close to time for the ceremony. I am sorry."

"You're going to kill him." I nearly choked on the words.

She opened her lips to speak, then closed them. Her face looked taut, her eyes strained. "You do not understand our ways. It is a wonderful thing we would do. We would bring the god Raphtah down to live among us, as a man, our king. He is to be my husband and I will be a queen. But to call Raphtah it takes power, greater power than we have. So the power must be gleaned from life energy—which pours out with the life's blood of a healthy man. We tried here once before with another soldier, but he was too weak and wounded; it did not work. That is why we have labored so hard to restore this man."

"Someone has beaten him."

"That was Uwa. It happened before Father VanZeldt could stop him. My brother hates the soldier because—because of what happened between you and him."

"Your brother tried to trick me into lying with him."

"That was also necessary. You were chosen to be Uwa's mate. It is an honor to be the consort of one of the Children of Raphtah. You will learn it is an honor."

"I'm promised to Thomas—to Lieutenant Lynd, the soldier. I never, never will go with Uwa."

"You will have no choice. If you will not go freely, we will have to give you this." She shook the flask. "It is a brew we call *dakar*. It makes one docile and pliable."

"Why would I drink it?"

She looked at me with patience and pity. "Even I have been forced to drink the *dakar* at times." She sank down on the floor beside me. "You love the soldier, I know. You must understand—it is a hard thing, but it will bring such good. One man's death. Not like your thousands perishing in your war—more like your god, your Jesus, who died for the good of many. The ceremony would be difficult to watch if we were in our natural minds, but during the drinking and the dancing, the spirits of others from Raphtah's star come to possess us. They are not aware of human agony and human suffering. Even the sacrifice himself will feel no pain because he will have drunk the *dakar*, which removes all hurt and sorrow."

I could have added that it removed all agency, joy, and character as well, but arguing would not persuade her to help. Neither would threatening her with burning the carvings. I searched my mind for something to say, something that might touch her heart. It was touchable—I could tell from her expression. From somewhere, words shot into my mind, and then were on my tongue. "You had a cousin who died in your old country—Ekon. What happened to him?"

Her face fell as she turned away. "I do not wish to think of it."

"Please tell me. It's important. Was he your sweetheart?" Again I didn't know how I guessed this, but as soon as I did, I knew it to be true.

She blinked rapidly. "Yes. We—he—he offered himself as the

sacrifice. He was so good, you see, and knew it was right that I should be Raphtah's wife, even though he himself loved me. But the sacrifice did not work. My grandmother Cyrah said it had not been the right time. I—I miss Ekon still."

"Maybe Cyrah can't ever know the right time. You've offered two sacrifices and neither worked. Maybe it will never work and Thomas's death will be a waste as well. Not a regretted, necessary loss, but murder."

She seemed not to hear. "The last thing I remember is Ekon telling me not to weep, that what he was doing would make everything better. Then I drank and danced and knew nothing until the next day, when I saw his beloved body lying there, his blood all soaked into the dust. For nothing."

A tear slid down her nose. I took her hand.

"Amenze," I said gently, "we are friends. Please. Please don't let the same thing happen to Thomas and me."

She made a strangled sound in her throat and closed her eyes, her shoulders hunched and head bowed. I waited. There were no more words to say.

When she opened her eyes, a new spark of determination shone in them. She gripped my upper arm with sharp, tight fingers. "It shall not. I cannot help you take him away now, but I can tell you what you must do." She set down the flask beside the snake case. "I will not give this dose to the soldier, so the effects should fade in a few hours. Father VanZeldt believes the sign will come tonight, and that is when the ceremony will take place.

"Listen closely. Tonight, when Cyrah raises the knife, she will ask, '*Mesu yamga sil?*' In your tongue, this means 'Who claims this man?' Hide away in the bushes beside the clearing. When you hear those words, leap out and say, 'I claim him.' You must reach the soldier without anyone stopping you. I can do nothing to help. The spirit will be inside me, and that which is Amenze will not be present. Uwa and Ahigbe and my grandmother will be possessed also, so no one but Father VanZeldt will remember you exist and no one will be prepared for the interruption. Put your arms around the soldier and hold on tight. No matter what happens, do not drop your hold. That is the only way to break the binding. We will be forced to release you both then. It is a law. And no one in the family will ever be allowed to touch either of you again. Go now and watch for the sign. Then you will know to come to the clearing."

"I can't leave Thomas."

"You must. If they know you have been here, they will tie you up and lock you away so you cannot interfere in the ceremony. I could not stop them. I will not try to stop them." She paused for effect. "And they will give you to Uwa first." She gave me a shove toward the door. "Go!"

Tears streamed freely down her cheeks now. She covered her face with her hands and sobbed, "I have betrayed my family! Oh, I have betrayed them all."

I paused and tried to hug her.

"Go!" she whispered, soft but intense.

I took one last, fearful look at Thomas, peeked into the yard to be sure no one was there, then scuttled around the shed and into the forest.

The fog had disappeared and I could feel a waiting, an oppressive expectation in the muggy air, in the stillness of the close boughs, even rising from the hard, quiet earth. The day would not end without dire dealings. The ceremony would indeed be tonight.

At the clearing of the silk cotton tree, the two straw thrones, Ahigbe's drums, and an enormous pile of logs and brush already waited. I found a little, flower-soft dell a distance away, but still within earshot, and made myself a nest in the center. The wild blossoms were white, with veined petals like wings, and gave off a sweet fragrance as I settled myself upon them.

As the sun moved across the sky, my panic mounted. I rehearsed over and over the words Amenze had told me to recognize—the woman would say, *"Mesu yamga sil?"* My heart was pounding against my chest and I broke out in a sweat. I needed to *do* something. Perhaps I should race back to the farm and begin to torture the carvings. But one of them was Amenze. I could not hurt Amenze.

A few slanting sunbeams pierced the interlaced boughs above. Five bees, perhaps the same that had led me to Thomas, flew in from the trees. They hovered and revolved in the light, turning slowly around and around as if they were soaking themselves in the gold. They hummed low and soft. There in the pool of white blossoms, a peace grew in me. "Fear not: for they that be with us are more than they that be with them." The VanZeldts might have dreadful intentions, but opposing them was the strength and virtue of so many others, including all those I could no longer see. My mother. Rush. Amazingly, I slept.

Sharp white light awoke me. For a moment I didn't know where I was. It was a dream. It had to be, because above me, beyond the treetops, against a background of black night, stars fell like rain, streaks of dazzling white. Everywhere was nearly bright as day.

The brilliant light seemed to explode in pain in my head. I began to shake. This was the sign from the heavens the VanZeldts had awaited.

It lasted only a few moments, but it was as if the world came to life during that time. A breeze stirred and rustled the leaves. An owl swooped ghostly not far from where I huddled.

A fingernail sliver of moon now shone. I listened breathlessly until I heard the faint crackles, crunches, and swishes of people moving toward the clearing. Softly I slipped to a new hiding place behind a wide trunk opposite the silk cotton tree.

Uwa and Ahigbe led the way, each carrying a torch, which they threw on the pile of scrub and branches. The wood must have been soaked in some accelerant because it burst instantly into brilliant flames, soaring, sparkling, twisting white and gold and red-orange. Dr. VanZeldt and the old woman—Cyrah—seated themselves. Amenze led Thomas by the arm. He shuffled along, head bowed. She pushed down on his shoulders to make him kneel in front of the thrones, facing the bonfire.

The doctor wore his white suit, but all the others were naked save for loincloths. Even Thomas. With his swollen face, unkempt hair, and beard, he appeared brutish among the exquisite, exotic Van-Zeldts. The necklace of leaves he wore covered his torn and bloody chest. At first I thought the undulating, intricate lines of silver on their skin was the moonlight, but I soon realized their bodies were painted, the mottled glimmers running over them like rings of silver water—or perhaps scales.

Uwa threw a handful of leaves in the center of the fire. Almost immediately a sharp, acrid odor burned my eyes and nostrils and the air felt harsh in my throat. I swallowed with difficulty. My head swam.

Ahigbe drew the coils of a long yellow-and-black snake from a basket and held it looped before the old woman. She took a slender knife and made a slit—probably through some artery—to drain the serpent's blood into a carved wooden bowl. They passed it between them. Each took a sip. Uwa smacked his lips as though it were a most delicious drink.

Just then Thomas's blind, drugged gaze turned my way, and a greater fear than I had yet known washed over me. My feet seemed suddenly not to meet the ground, and the interwoven trees, the fire, the people all blurred and slid together. I caught at the tree trunk and clung to it.

The drumming began and the dancers burst again into vision. They had donned tall wooden masks that made them tower like giants, the faces of nightmares, with grimacing mouths and fierce, slanting eyes. They leaped, wheeled and stamped, crouched and sprang. Whereas the other dance I had witnessed seemed joyous, this was a scene from Dante's *Inferno*. The roaring conflagration before them and the flickering black shadows behind them wavered and reached.

The old woman joined them now, her movements slow, serpentine, lewd. She sang a low, hissing chant and wielded a wicked blade, which she flashed before Thomas. He did not flinch or blink.

Dr. VanZeldt stood. His body quivered with excitement. A trickle of crimson blood oozed from his nostrils.

The drums beat faster and faster and the dancing built in

intensity until the dancers tore off their masks. I gasped, for they were altered.

Golden eyes with black slits for pupils, flat gashes for noses, lipless, their skin glittering scales of ruby and gold.

I sank, tremulous, to the ground, huddled in a heap, no longer hidden by the tree. Luckily they were too involved in what they were doing to notice.

As I hunched there, somehow I became aware of a new movement, very slight but very important, coming from Thomas. He blinked when Uwa whirled close to him. His head drew back slightly. He was coming out of his trance.

The creature who was Cyrah stood behind him now. With one hand she held up his head by the hair; with the other she raised the knife. *"Mesu yamga sil?"*

The words.

I leaped up and dashed around the fire, moving as fast as I could, but still with nightmare slowness. I threw myself on Thomas, knocking him backward, flat to the ground. "I do!" I cried. "I claim him!"

His body beneath me changed, hardened, and suddenly was burning hot. My clothing smoked. He had turned into red-hot iron. I forced myself not to scream or jump away. I concentrated on sensing my amulet, and this time it felt cool against my chest. The searing pain in my hands was less acute. His body sank beneath me. I now lay in a pool of molten lead, but only momentarily. It swelled and solidified, and inches from my face were the sharp and snarling fangs of a lion. It blurred and changed even as it formed, and next came the rasping, dry, scaly feel of a great, golden snake. The muscles rippled and undulated beneath me, and its jaws opened wide. I did scream then, and closed my eyes tightly. But I held on, held on, held on.

A boom like crashing thunder sounded and the earth shook. From someone—I think it was the doctor—came a heartbroken cry.

The form shifted beneath me. I opened my eyes to see that I was holding my own Thomas once again. His breath cooled my cheeks. He stirred and blinked, confused.

"It's over," I whispered. "I think it's all over." I slid off him, still clutching with scorched, blistered hands.

He pulled me against him tightly. We clung together as if we would save each other from falling over the edge of a chasm. I buried my face in his chest, waiting for either another trick or more violence from the VanZeldts.

Neither came. Slowly, I drew away. Dr. VanZeldt had sunk to his throne, head in hands. All of the VanZeldts had reverted back to their normal features. The old woman seemed to have shrunk. She who had not looked ancient now looked ancient, her skin beneath the paint dull and ashen, lips puckered over toothless gums. Amenze, Uwa, and Ahigbe all watched, eerily impassive and motionless.

"Let's go," I whispered to Thomas. We rose. Thomas put his arm across my shoulders, and we awkwardly hobbled away, unhindered.

CHAPTER 34

EVER AFTER

Someone was watching me.

We were all cozily assembled in the sitting room four nights after Thomas and I had dragged ourselves, spent but triumphant, back to the farm. Thomas lingered here; he had taken this time to heal and to make the acquaintance of everyone at Scuppernong, although his presence was still hidden from the rest of the world. During the previous days, we had all talked and talked and laughed often together as people do after shared ordeals have ended happily. And Thomas and I had been memorizing each other so we would have something to hold close during the lonely days, months, years until the war ended.

Now, though, we were quietly busy with our separate diversions. I was perched on the stool before my harp. I could not play because my hands were mere knobs of bandages, pain still shooting through from the burns I had sustained that night, but I was composing a new song and it helped if I could look at the strings.

I was pulled out of my concentration by the feeling of eyes on me. I glanced quickly about.

Thomas was scratching away on his latest Heath Blackstock novel—the one about snake people. Seeley was playing with his horses and occasionally offering suggestions to Thomas. Sunny was ripping seams from an old dress, and Miss Elsa was nervously pacing. She was holding true to her vow to use less laudanum, and suffering for it. Michael had spent the day laboring out in the forest, doing I knew not what; he had returned after suppertime, the worse for wear. He, Laney, and Cubby had retired to their cabin early. None of them were watching me.

There was a gap between the curtains. Someone was out there in the blackness. I closed the gap and tried to disregard the tug that pulled me toward the door and out into the night. Finally I could ignore it no longer. I abruptly stood and left the room. I lit a lantern and held it before me so that it made a puddle of light out below the porch.

Just outside the glow loomed five shadows. One of them moved forward and into the brightness. It was him—Dr. VanZeldt. I would have turned on my heels and run back inside, but whatever had called me out kept me bound.

The doctor held his hat in his hands and made a little bow. "Miss Violet Dancey. So happy you were kind enough to listen to the summons to come out and hear our goodbyes."

"Goodbyes? You're leaving, then?" I kept my voice steady.

Some sort of spasm passed over his tight pink skin. "Today—I assume upon your orders—the silk cotton tree was hewn down. We cannot remain in a place so desecrated."

It must have been what Michael had been about earlier in the woods. In a flash I felt relieved, then slightly sorry, then relieved again. I said nothing.

Another of the shadows moved forward. The old woman. She looked shriveled and diminished, but there was nothing weak about the contempt glittering in her eyes as she spat out a stream of (probably) curses in her language. I flinched.

Dr. VanZeldt cleared his throat and said pleasantly, "Cyrah says that if she had known what you would do to us, she would have cut out the soldier's eyes at the first so he would never have beheld your face."

I started to turn, but my feet were stuck firmly to the floorboards.

"Oh," Dr. VanZeldt hastened to assure me, "you need not worry. It is over. We bear you no ill will. You battled fairly and you won. We have mattered a great deal to one another these last months—more than you realize, even now. I have grown fond of you, from afar. It may be hard for you to believe, but I was actually quite proud of you as you held on. True, I would have struck you down and let the earth close over you had I been allowed, but still I was proud. I see your hands are wounded." He snapped his fingers. "Ahigbe—the bag."

Ahigbe strode forward and held out a burlap sack. The doctor rummaged about and brought forth a little leather pouch. "Crush these leaves, my dear, mix them with lard, and spread it on the burns. Your skin will be healed in a matter of hours."

"Thank you," I said, taking the pouch and vowing to throw it on the fire. "May I—may I speak to Amenze? Privately?"

Dr. VanZeldt seemed to consider, then beckoned the girl forward. The others retired to a distance, where they could watch.

In spite of the lines of strain that showed around Amenze's mouth and eyes, there was something magnificent about her as she stood there, towering above me in a robe of black and bronze. Someday she might well be a queen of somewhere, someplace.

I felt shy of her as I spoke. "Amenze, you don't need to go with them. You could stay here. I know they could try to force you, but somehow we would fight them."

Her lips curved in a faint, knowing smile. "You cannot understand, can you?"

"Understand what?"

"That I love my people and choose to be with them. That I am a Child of Raphtah and I still believe, however I decided to help you. You have only seen the disturbing things; you have not seen the glorious."

I remembered the joyous dancing and thought that perhaps I *had* glimpsed it. "Very well. I wish you happiness in your choice." I paused. "Thomas—the soldier—is leaving tomorrow to return to the war."

"I am sorry to hear it," she said. "But you know he will come back to you."

"If that's what you sense, I do know it now," I said, and managed a smile. "Where will y'all go?"

"I do not know. Cyrah and Father VanZeldt know, but I do not."

I began to unpin the cameo brooch from my collar. "You gave me a wonderful gift in the amber amulet. Now may I give you something?"

She nodded, and I handed her the brooch. "It belonged to my

mother. Even though it has no magical powers, I hope it will remind you that you and I are true friends, no matter how far apart we are."

She reached out one long arm and rested a hand on my shoulder for a second, then dropped it.

They left, melting back into the shadows, and I never saw them again.

February 15, 1863

Dearest Thomas,

Imagine my surprise when the bedraggled, bewhiskered gentleman showed up at our door, bringing me such a treasure—a letter from my love. And he says he will wait while I scribble a reply, so Laney is feeding him in the kitchen.

I am sorry you're not as lithe and limber as you were before your injury, but I'm happy it's keeping you safely in the office. How wonderful that your father came to visit you and that all is well there. "For this my son was dead, and is alive again; was lost and is found."

Much has happened here since you left. My father remains alive and well, although always there are reports of fallen acquaintances.

I am a regular attendant at sewing circle. The girls know I am engaged to a soldier, as several of them are, but I fail to mention that you are a Union soldier. They will be mighty surprised someday. We share our worries and fears about our sweethearts and it is nice to speak of these things with others who understand.

I have become a teacher at Seeley's school. The things the children say are so funny! I struggle with discipline. Even Seeley is naughty at times. You do know he's ours forever, don't you? I have been assuming you assume it, although we never put it in words.

News reached us from Panola a few weeks ago. Aunt Lovina wrote to say that the Union soldiers had set fire to the house and scattered all the servants. Luckily the brick walls still stand. Aunt Lovina and Seeley's mammy are living together in a rude cabin on the place. Seeley frets sometimes but understands there is nothing he can do right now. Eventually we will have to help him put Panola to rights. It is so strange that I, who so worried that people would leave Scuppernong, will someday be the one who leaves.

I am happy to hear you have told your family about me. It will be lovely to have a second sister in Addie. Our Sunny is still Sunny, but an improved version. She is having a feeble little flirtation with an older man named Harper Grigg——he must be at least twice her age——who returned early from the army because his wife had died, leaving him with two small children. Right now it is feeble, but I have a feeling their romance may grow hale, hearty, and blooming. He really does think she's amazing. She loves the children; she's certainly grown since she first met Seeley.

Miss Elsa continues to paint her ugly pictures, free of the laudanum. She has awakened, and lives a much more active, vivid life than she once did.

Seeley has taken to following Michael everywhere when he's home from school, and often totes Cubby about, showing him bugs and, in Seeley's own words, "teaching him how to be a boy." Laney and I watch our fellows together and feel all glow-y inside.

So much that happened to us is hard to believe now. Sometimes I think of it and even I don't believe me. Yet it did happen. I thought of destroying my amber amulet because anything connected with that time makes me feel panicky, until I remember that that particular bit of VanZeldt-ness always seemed good and helped often. I no longer wear it. It's tucked safely away, wrapped in cotton, along with your beautiful carvings.

Since the VanZeldts left, Shadowlawn is for sale, and it's likely to remain so until it falls in a heap of rubble, as who in these times would buy such a place? I think of the VanZeldts when I look at the stars. Dr. VanZeldt said that we had mattered a great deal to one another, and I feel that. They still matter to me. I wish them well—but I hope never to see them again and I hope that, wherever they are, they will never again try to call down Raphtah-from-the-stars.

Darling Thomas, I'm afraid of so many things. I still cringe when I'm too close to fires. I'm afraid of snakes. I'm afraid my students will tie me up one day and run entirely amok. I'm afraid the time will come when at Scuppernong we will have nothing to eat but beetles, and then the beetles will run out. But I'm not afraid you won't come back to me. It may take a year . . . or two . . . but it will happen. The war will end, and we'll never again be apart.

And so, adieu, my love.

Your very own,
Violet Aurelia Dancey

ACKNOWLEDGMENTS

I am grateful to whoever first wrote the legendary Scottish *Ballad of Tam Lin* for providing me with a compelling story to re-create in a Southern setting.

My writing is not the sort that pops out perfect without much editing. I need many other people's discerning eyes and brains to help me know what must be done. I'd like to once again thank my tireless agent, Wendy Schmalz, and my patient editor, Allison Wortche, for their encouragement and the time they put into this book. I am also indebted to the many people who worked on it in the many stages.

Thanks and much love to Ellen, Carol, James, Emily, Bethany, Phillip, and Stella for their willingness to read and give me ideas. (It was Bethany who requested voodoo.)

And, as always, I am eternally grateful to my husband, Ted, who steps in and helps with all the things I can't seem to do myself.

ABOUT THE AUTHOR

For many years, Jane Nickerson and her family lived in a big old house in Aberdeen, Mississippi, where she was a children's librarian. She has always loved the South, "the olden days," gothic tales, houses, kids, writing, and interesting villains. Her first novel, *Strands of Bronze and Gold*, is a captivating retelling of the Bluebeard fairy tale. Jane and her husband recently moved back to Mississippi from Ontario, Canada. Please visit her on the Web at jane-nickerson.com.